THE FIREWORKS OF GOD

The crowd on the patio began to react to the meteor shower. Lise looked up as three scaldingly-bright white lines scribed across the meridian. The meteors emanated from a point well above the horizon and almost directly due east, and before she could look away there were more of them—two, then one, then a spectacular cluster of five.

She was reminded of a summer in Idaho when she had gone stargazing with her father—she couldn't have been more than ten years old. There had been meteors that night, dozens of them, the largest intercepted by the invisible barrier that protected the Earth from the swollen sun, the smallest incinerated in the atmosphere. She had watched them arc across the heavens with a speed and brilliance that left her breathless.

As now. The fireworks of God. "Wow," she said, lamely.

"It's just dust," Turk said, "or that's what the astronomers say. What's left of some old comet."

But something new had caught her attention. "So what about that?" she asked, pointing east, lower on the horizon, where the dark sky met the darker sea. It looked to Lise like something was actually falling out there—not meteors but bright dots that hung in the air like flares, or what she imagined flares would look like. The reflected light of them colored the ocean a streaky orange. She didn't remember anything like that from her previous time in Equatoria. "Is that part of it?"

Turk stood up. So did a few others among the crowd on the patio. A puzzled hush displaced the talk and laughter.

"No," Turk said. "That's not part of it."

By Robert Charles Wilson
from Tom Doherty Associates

AXIS

**Robert
Charles
Wilson**

TOR®

A TOM DOHERTY ASSOCIATES BOOK
NEW YORK

This is a work of fiction. All of the characters, organizations, and events portrayed in this novel are either products of the author's imagination or are used fictitiously.

AXIS

Copyright © 2007 by Robert Charles Wilson

All rights reserved.

Edited by Teresa Nielsen Hayden

A Tor Book
Published by Tom Doherty Associates, LLC
175 Fifth Avenue
New York, NY 10010

www.tor-forge.com

Tor® is a registered trademark of Tom Doherty Associates, LLC.

ISBN-13: 978-0-7653-4826-5
ISBN-10: 0-7653-4826-8

First Edition: September 2007
First Mass Market Edition: June 2008

Printed in the United States of America

0 9 8 7 6 5 4 3 2 1

*Dedicated to the memory of
Dr. Albert Goldhar and Ella
Beautone (Bootie) Goldhar,
and to the family they created
and into which they generously
accepted me.*

It is necessary that things should pass away into that from which they are born. For things must pay one another the penalty and compensation for their injustice according to the ordinance of time.

—Anaximander

PART ONE

THE
34TH OF
AUGUST

CHAPTER ONE

In the summer of his twelfth year—the summer the stars began to fall from the sky—the boy Isaac discovered that he could tell east from west with his eyes closed.

Isaac lived at the edge of the Great Inland Desert, on the continent of Equatoria, on the planet that had been appended to the Earth by the inscrutable beings called the Hypotheticals. People had given the planet a whole panoply of grandiose or mythological or coolly scientific names, but most simply called it the New World, in any of a hundred or more languages, or Equatoria, after its most widely settled continent. These were things Isaac had learned in what passed for school.

He lived in a compound of brick and adobe, far from the nearest town. He was the only child at the settlement. The adults with whom he lived preferred to keep a careful distance between themselves and the rest of the world. They were special, in ways they were reluctant to discuss. Isaac, too, was special. They had told him so, many times. But he wasn't sure he believed them. He didn't feel special. Often he felt much less than special.

Occasionally the adults, especially Dr. Dvali or Mrs. Rebka, asked Isaac whether he was lonely. He wasn't. He had books, he had the video library to fill his time. He was a student, and he learned at his own pace— steadily if not quickly. In this, Isaac suspected, he was a disappointment to his keepers. But the books and videos and lessons filled his time, and when they were unavailable there was the natural world around him, which had become a kind of mute, indifferent friend: the mountains, gray and green and brown, sloping down to this arid plain, the edge of the desert hinterland, a curdled landscape of rock and sand. Few things grew here, since the rain came only in the first months of spring and sparsely even then. In the dry washes there were lumpish plants with prosaic names: barrel cucumbers, leather vines. In the courtyard of the compound a native garden had been planted, cactus feathery with purple flowers, tall nevergreens with weblike blossoms that extracted moisture from the air. Sometimes a man named Raj irrigated the garden from a pump that ran deep into the earth, and on those mornings the air smelled of mineral-rich water: a steely scent that carried for kilometers. On watering day, rock shrews would burrow under the fence and tumble comically across the tiled courtyard.

Isaac's days passed in gentle sameness early in the summer of his twelfth year, as his days had always passed, but that sleepy peace came to an end the day the old woman arrived.

She came, remarkably, on foot.

Isaac had left the compound that afternoon and climbed a small distance up the foothills, to a granite shelf that jutted from the slope of a ridge like a ship's prow from a pebbly sea. The afternoon sun had warmed the rock to a fine, fierce heat. Isaac, with his wide-brimmed hat and white cotton shirt to protect him from the burning light, sat under the lip of the ridge where there was still shade, watching the horizon. The desert rippled in rising waves of furnace air. He was alone and motionless—afloat in heat, a castaway on a sere raft of stone—when the woman appeared. At first she was just a dot down the unpaved road that led from the distant towns where Isaac's keepers went to buy food and supplies. She moved slowly, or seemed to. Nearly an hour passed before he could identify her as a woman—then an old woman—then an old woman with a pack on her back, a bow-legged posture, and a dogged, determined stride. She wore a white robe and a white sun hat.

The road passed close to this rock, almost directly beneath it, and Isaac, who didn't want to be seen, though he could not say why, scooted behind a boulder and crouched there as she approached. He closed his eyes and imagined he felt the bulk and weight of the land beneath him, the old woman's two feet tickling the skin of the desert like a beetle on the body of a slumbering giant. (And he felt another presence, deep in that earth, a quiescent behemoth stirring in its long sleep far to the west. . . .)

The old woman paused beneath the shelf of rock as if she could see him in his hiding place. Isaac was aware of the break in the rhythm of her shuffling steps. Or maybe she had innocently paused to sip water from a canteen. She said nothing. Isaac held himself very still, something he was good at.

Then her steps resumed. She walked on, leaving the road where a trail bent toward the compound. Isaac lifted his head and looked after her. She was many meters away now, the long light of the afternoon drawing her shadow alongside her like a leggy caricature. As soon as he saw her she paused and turned back, and for a moment it seemed as if their eyes met, and Isaac hastily ducked away, uncertain whether he had been seen. He was startled by the accuracy of her gaze and he remained hidden for a long time, until the sunlight angled deep into the mountain passes. He hid even from himself, quiet as a fish in a pool of memory and thought.

The old woman reached the compound's gates and went inside and stayed there. Before the sky grew wholly dark, Isaac followed her. He wondered if he would be introduced to the woman, perhaps at dinner.

Very few outsiders came to the compound. Of those who came, most came to stay.

After Isaac had bathed and put on clean clothes he went to the dining room.

This was where the entire community, all thirty of the adults, gathered every evening. Morning and afternoon meals were impromptu, could be taken at any time as long as you were willing to do your own work in the kitchen, but dinner was a collective effort, always crowded, inevitably noisy.

Usually Isaac enjoyed hearing the adults talk among themselves, though he seldom understood what they said unless it was trivial: whose turn it was to go to town for provisions, how a roof might be repaired or a well improved. More often, since the adults were mainly scientists and theoreticians, their talk turned to abstract matters. Listening, Isaac had retained few of the details of their work but something of its general content. There was always talk of time and stars and the Hypotheticals, of technology and biology, of evolution and transformation. Although these conversations usually pivoted on words he couldn't understand, they had a fine and lofty sound about them. The debates—were the Hypotheticals properly called *beings,* conscious entities, or were they some vast and mindless *process?*— often grew heated, philosophies defended and attacked like military objectives. It was as if in some nearby but inaccessible room the universe itself was being taken apart and reassembled.

Tonight the murmur was subdued. There was a newcomer present: the old woman from the road. Isaac, bashfully taking a seat between Dr. Dvali and Mrs. Rebka, cast furtive glances at her. She did not return them; in fact she seemed indifferent to his presence at the table. When the opportunity arose, Isaac studied her face.

She was even older than he had guessed. Her skin was dark and skeined with wrinkles. Her eyes, bright and liquid, peered out from skully chambers. She held her knife and fork in long, fragile fingers. Her palms were pale. She had changed out of her desert garb into clothing more like what the other adults wore: jeans and a pale yellow cotton shirt. Her hair was thin and cut close to the scalp. She wore no rings or necklaces. In the crook of one elbow was a patch of cotton held down with surgical tape: Mrs. Rebka, the community physician, must already have taken a blood sample from her. But that happened to every newcomer. Isaac wondered if Mrs. Rebka had had a hard time finding a vein in that small sinewy arm. He wondered what the blood test had been meant to detect, and whether Mrs. Rebka had found what she was looking for.

No special attention was paid to the newcomer at dinner. She joined in conversation but the talk remained superficial, as if no one wanted to give away any secrets before the stranger was fully approved, absorbed, understood. It was not until the dishes had been cleared and several pots of coffee placed on the long table that Dr. Dvali introduced Isaac to her.

"Isaac," he began, and the boy gazed at the tabletop uncomfortably, "this is Sulean Moi—she's come a long way to meet you."

A long way? What did that mean? And—to meet *him*?

"Hello, Isaac," the newcomer said. Her voice was not the harsh croak he had expected. In fact her voice was mellifluous despite a certain grit . . . and, in some way he could not pin down, *familiar*.

"Hello," he said, still avoiding her eyes.

"Please call me Sulean," she said.

He nodded cautiously.

"I hope we'll be friends," she said.

He did not, of course, tell her immediately about his newfound ability to distinguish the points of the compass with his eyes closed. He hadn't told anyone about that, not even stern Dr. Dvali or the more sympathetic Mrs. Rebka. He was afraid of the scrutiny it would bring.

Sulean Moi, who moved into the compound, made a point of visiting him every morning after classes and before lunch. At first Isaac dreaded these visits. He was shy and not a little frightened of Sulean's great age and apparent frailty. But she was steadily, courteously friendly. She respected his silences, and the questions she asked were seldom awkward or intrusive.

"Do you like your room?" she asked one day.

Because he preferred to be alone he had been given this room to himself, a small but uncluttered chamber on the second story of the easternmost wing of the largest house. There was a window overlooking the desert, and Isaac had put his desk and chair in front of that window, his bed against the farther wall. He liked to keep the shutters open at night, to let the dry wind touch the bedsheets, his skin. He liked the smell of the desert.

"I grew up in a desert," Sulean told him. A slant of sunlight through the window illuminated her left side, one arm and the parchment of her cheek and ear. Her voice was almost a whisper.

"This desert?"

"No, not this one. But one not very different."

"Why did you leave?"

She smiled. "I had places to go. Or at least I thought I did."

"And this is where you came?"

"Ultimately. Yes."

Because he liked her, and because he could not help being aware of what was unspoken between them, Isaac said, "I don't have anything to give you."

"I don't expect anything," she said.

"The others do."

"Do they?"

"Dr. Dvali and the rest. They used to ask me a lot of questions—how I felt, and what ideas I had, and what things in books meant. But they didn't like my answers." Eventually they had stopped asking, just as they had stopped giving him blood tests, psychological tests, perception tests.

"I'm perfectly satisfied with you the way you are," the old woman said.

He wanted to believe her. But she was new, she had walked through the desert with the nonchalance of an insect on a sunny rock, her purposes were vague, and Isaac was still reluctant to share his most troublesome secrets.

All the adults were his teachers, though some were more patient or attentive than others. Mrs. Rebka taught him basic biology, Ms. Fischer taught him the geography of Earth and the New World, Mr. Nowotny told him about the sky and the stars and the relationship of suns and planets. Dr. Dvali taught him physics: inclined planes, the inverse square, electromagnetism. Isaac remembered his astonishment the first time he saw a magnet lift a spoon from a tabletop. An entire planet pulling downward, and what was this bit of stone in its power to reverse that universal flow? He had only begun to make sense of Dr. Dvali's answers.

Last year Dr. Dvali had shown him a compass. The planet, too, was a magnet, Dr. Dvali said. It had a rotating iron core, hence lines of force, a shield against charged particles arriving from the sun, a polarity that distinguished north from south. Isaac had asked to borrow the compass, a hefty military model made on Earth, and Dr. Dvali had generously allowed him to keep it.

Late in the evening, alone in his room, Isaac placed the compass on his desk so that the red point of the needle aligned with the letter *N*. Then he closed his eyes and spun himself around, stopped and waited for his dizziness to subside. Eyes still closed, he felt what the world told him, intuited his place in it, found the direction that eased some inner tension. Then he put out his right hand and opened his eyes to see which way he was pointing. He found out a lot of things, mostly irrelevant.

He performed the experiment on three successive nights. Each night he discovered himself aligned almost perfectly with the *W* on the face of the compass.

Then he did it again. And again. And again.

It was shortly before the annual meteor shower that he resolved at last to share this unsettling discovery with Sulean Moi.

The meteor shower came at the end of every August— this year, on the 34th. (Months in the New World were named after terrestrial months, though each one lasted a few days longer than its namesake.) On the eastern coast of Equatoria, August signaled the beginning of the end of the mild summer: boats left the rich northern fisheries with their last harvests in order to arrive back at Port Magellan before the autumn storms began. Here in the desert it signified little more than the steady, subtle cooling of the nights. Desert seasons were nocturnal, it seemed to Isaac: the days were mostly alike, but winter nights could be bitingly, painfully cold.

Slowly Isaac had allowed Sulean Moi to become his friend. It wasn't that they talked much or about anything especially important. Sulean seemed almost as wordless as Isaac often was. But she accompanied him on his walks through the hills, and she was more agile than seemed possible for her age: she was slow, but she could climb as well as Isaac, and she could sit motionless for an hour or more when Isaac did. She never gave him the impression that this was a duty or a strategy or anything more or less than her way of sharing certain pleasures he had always suspected were his alone.

Sulean must not have seen the annual meteor shower before, since she told Isaac she had arrived in Equatoria only months ago. Isaac was a fan of the event and declared that she ought to see it from a good vantage point. So—with the uneasy permission of Dr. Dvali, who didn't seem to entirely approve of Sulean Moi—on the evening of the 34th he escorted her to the flat rock in the hills, the rock from which he had first seen her appear on the sun-quivering horizon.

That had been daylight, but now it was dark. The New World's moon was smaller and faster than Earth's, and it had traversed the sky completely by the time Sulean and Isaac arrived at their destination. Both carried hand lanterns to light their way, and both wore high boots and thick leggings to protect them from the sandfish that often basked on these granite ledges while the stone was still breathing out the heat of the day. Isaac scanned the location carefully and found no wildlife present. He sat crosslegged on the stone. Sulean bent slowly but without complaint into the same posture. Her face was serene, calmly expectant. They turned off their lanterns and allowed the darkness to swallow them up. The desert was blacker than the sky, the sky was salted with stars. No one had officially named these stars, though astronomers had given them catalog numbers. The stars were as dense in the heavens as swarming insects. Each star was a sun, Isaac knew, and many of them cast their light on inaccessible, unknowable landscapes—perhaps on deserts like this one. Things lived among the stars, he knew. Things that lived vast slow cold lives, in which the passage of a century was no more than the blink of a distant eye.

"I know why you came here," Isaac said.

He couldn't see the old woman's face in this darkness, which made the conversation easier, eased the embarrassing clumsiness of words like bricks in his mouth.

"Do you?"

"To study me."

"No. Not to study you, Isaac. I'm more a student of the sky than I am of you in particular."

Like the others at the compound, she was interested in the Hypotheticals—the unseen beings who had rearranged the heavens and the earth.

"You came because of what I am."

She cocked her head and said, "Well, yes, that."

He began to tell her about his sense of direction. He spoke haltingly at first, and more confidently when she listened without questioning him. He tried to anticipate the questions she might want to ask. When had he first noticed this special talent? He couldn't remember; only that it had been this year, a few months ago, just a glimmering at first: for instance, he had liked to work in the compound's library because his desk there faced the same direction as the desk in his room, though there was no window to look through. In the dining room he always sat at the side of the table nearest the door, even when there was no one else present. He had moved his bed so that he could sleep more comfortably, aligned with—with, well, *what*?

But he couldn't say. Everywhere he went, always, when he stood still, there was a direction he preferred to face. This was not a compulsion, only a gentle urge, easily ignored. There was a good way to face, and a less good way to face.

"And are you facing the good way now?" Sulean asked.

In fact he was. He hadn't been aware of it before she asked, but he was comfortable on this rock looking away from the mountains into the lightless hinterland.

"West," Sulean said. "You like to face west."

"A little north of west."

There. The secret was out. There was nothing more to say, and he heard Sulean Moi adjust her posture in the silence, adapting to the pressure of the rock. He wondered if it was painful or uncomfortable to be so old and to sit on solid stone. If so, she gave no indication of it. She looked up at the sky.

"You were right about the falling stars," she said after a long time. "They're quite lovely."

The meteor shower had begun.

Isaac was fascinated by it. Dr. Dvali had told him about meteors, which were not really stars at all but burning fragments of rock or dust, the remains of ancient comets circling for millennia around the New World's sun. But that explanation had only added to Isaac's fascination. He sensed in these evanescent lights the enacting of ancient geometries, vectors set in motion long before the planet was formed (or before it had been constructed by the Hypotheticals), rhythms elaborated over a lifetime or several lifetimes or even the lifetime of a species. Sparks flew across the zenith, east to west, while Isaac listened inwardly to the murmurings of the night.

He was content that way, until Sulean suddenly stood and peered back toward the mountains and said, "Look— what's that? It looks like something falling."

Like luminous rainfall, as if a storm had come down through the high passes of the divide—as they sometimes did, but this glow wasn't lightning; it was diffuse, persistent. She said, "Is that normal?"

"No," Isaac said.

No. It wasn't normal at all.

"Then perhaps we ought to go back."

Isaac nodded uneasily. He wasn't afraid of the approaching—well, "storm," if that's what it was—but it carried a significance he couldn't explain to Sulean, a relationship to the silent presence that lived under the Rub al-Khali, the Empty Quarter of the far west, and to which his private compass was attuned. They walked back to the compound at a brisk pace, not quite running, because Isaac wasn't sure that someone as fragile-seeming as Sulean *could* run, while the mountain peaks to the east were first revealed and then obscured by fresh waves of this peculiar cloudy light. By the time they reached the gate the meteor shower was entirely hidden by this new phenomenon; a sort of dust had begun to fall from the sky, and Isaac's lantern carved out an increasingly smaller swath of visibility. Isaac thought this falling substance might be snow—he had seen snow in videos—but Sulean said no, it wasn't snow at all, it was more like ash. The smell of it was rank, sulfurous.

Like dead stars, Isaac thought, falling.

Mrs. Rebka was waiting at the compound's main door and she pulled Isaac inside with a grip so intense it was painful. He gave her a shocked, reproving look: Mrs. Rebka had never hurt him before; none of the adults had hurt him. She ignored his expression and held him possessively, told him she had been afraid he would be lost in this, this . . .

Words failed her.

In the common room, Dr. Dvali was listening to an audio feed from Port Magellan, the great city on the eastern coast of Equatoria. The signal was relayed across the mountains by aerostats and was intermittent,

Dr. Dvali told the gathered adults, but he had learned that the Port was experiencing the same phenomenon, a blanketing fall of something like ash, and that there was no immediate explanation. Some people in the city had begun to panic. Then the broadcast, or the aerostat relaying the signal, failed entirely.

Isaac, at Mrs. Rebka's urging, went to his room while the adults talked. He didn't sleep, couldn't imagine sleeping. Instead he sat at the window, where there was nothing to see but a tunneled grayness where the overhead light bled into the ashfall, and he listened to the sound of nothing at all—a silence that nevertheless seemed to speak to him, a silence steeped in meaning.

CHAPTER TWO

Lise Adams drove toward the little rural airstrip on the afternoon of the 34th of August feeling lost, feeling free.

It was a feeling she couldn't explain even to herself. Maybe the weather, she thought. Late August along the coast of Equatoria was inevitably warm, often unbearable, but today the breeze from the sea was gentle and the sky was that indigo blue she had come to associate with the New World, deeper and truer than the smudgy pastel skies of Earth. But the weather had been fine for weeks, nice but not all that remarkable. Free, she thought, yes, absolutely: a marriage behind her, the *decree nisi* freshly-issued, an unwise thing undone . . . and, ahead of her, the man who had been a factor in that undoing. But so much more than that. A future severed from her past, a painful question hovering on the brink of an answer.

And lost, almost literally: she had only come out this way a couple of times before. South of Port Magellan, where she had rented an apartment, the coast flattened into an alluvial plain that had been given over to farms and light industry. Much of it was still wild, a sort of rolling prairie grown over with feathery grasses, meadows that broke like waves against the peaks of the coastal range. Before long she began to see small aircraft coming and going from Arundji's Airfield, which was her destination. These were little prop planes, bush planes: the runways at Arundji's weren't long enough for anything big. The planes that alighted there were either rich men's hobbies or poor men's businesses. If you wanted to rent a hangar, join a tourist excursion into the glacial passes, or get to Bone Creek or Kubelick's Grave in a hurry, you came to Arundji's. And if you were smart you talked to Turk Findley, who flew discount charters for a living, before you did any of those things.

Lise had flown with Turk once before. But she wasn't here to hire a pilot. Turk's name had come up in connection with the photograph Lise carried in a brown envelope, currently tucked into the glove compartment of her car.

She parked in the gravel lot at Arundji's, climbed out of the car, and stood listening to the sound of insects buzzing in the afternoon heat. Then she walked through the door at the back of the cavernous tin-roofed shed—it looked like a converted cow barn—that served as Arundji's passenger terminal. Turk's charter business operated out of a corner of this building with the consent of Mike Arundji, the airfield's owner, who took a share of Turk's profits in return. Turk had told her this, back when they had had time to talk.

There was no security barrier to pass through. Turk Findley worked out of a three-sided cubicle tucked into the north end of the building, and she simply walked into it and cleared her throat in lieu of knocking. He was behind his desk filling out what looked like UN Provisional Government papers—she could see the blue logo at the top of the page. He inked his signature a final time and looked up. "Lise!"

His grin was genuine and disarming. No recrimination, no why-didn't-you-return-my-calls. She said, "Uh, are you busy?"

"Do I look busy?"

"Looks like you have work to do, anyhow." She was fairly certain he would be willing to put aside anything nonessential for a chance to see her: a chance she hadn't offered him in a long time. He came around the desk and hugged her, chastely but sincerely. She was briefly flustered by the smell of him in close proximity. Turk was thirty-five years old, eight years older than Lise, and a foot taller. She tried not to let that be intimidating. "Paperwork," he said. "Give me an excuse to ignore it. Please."

"Well," she said.

"At least tell me if it's business or pleasure."

"Business."

He nodded. "Okay. Sure. Name a destination."

"No, I mean—*my* business, not your business. There's something I'd like to talk to you about, if you're willing. Maybe over dinner? My treat?"

"I'd be happy to go to dinner, but it's on me. I can't imagine how I can help you write your book."

She was pleased that he remembered what she had told him about her book. Even though there was no book. An aircraft taxied up to a hangar some yards away and the noise came through the thin walls of Turk's office as if through an open door. Lise looked at the ceramic cup on Turk's desk and saw the oily surface of what must have been hours-old coffee break into concentric ripples. When the roar faded she said, "Actually you can help a lot, especially if we can go somewhere quieter. . . ."

"Sure thing. I'll leave my keys with Paul."

"Just like that?" She never ceased to marvel at the way people on the frontier did business. "You're not afraid of missing a customer?"

"Customer can leave a message. I'll get back sooner or later. Anyhow, it's been slow this week. You came at the right time. What do you say to Harley's?"

Harley's was one of the more upscale American-style restaurants in the Port. "You can't afford Harley's."

"Business expense. I have a question for *you,* come to think of it. Call it quid pro quo."

Whatever that meant. All she could say was, "Okay." Dinner at Harley's was both more and less than she had expected. She had driven out to Arundji's on the assumption that a personal appearance would be more meaningful than a phone call, after the time that had elapsed since their last conversation. A sort of unspoken apology. But if he resented the gap in their relationship (and it wasn't even a "relationship" anymore, perhaps not even a friendship), he showed no sign of it. She reminded herself to focus on the work. On the real reason she was here. The unexplained loss that had opened a chasm in her life twelve years ago.

Turk had a car of his own at the airfield, so they arranged to meet at the restaurant in three hours, about dusk.

Traffic permitting. Prosperity in Port Magellan had meant more cars, and not just the little South Asian utility vehicles or scooters everyone used to drive. Traffic was thick through the docklands—she was sandwiched between a pair of eighteen-wheelers much of the way— but she made it to the restaurant on time. The parking lot at Harley's was crowded, unusually for a Wednesday night. The food here was reasonably good, but what people paid a premium for was the view: the restaurant occupied a hilltop overlooking Port Magellan. The Port had been established for obvious reasons on what was the largest natural harbor on the coast, close to the Arch that joined this planet to Earth. But its easy lowlands had been overbuilt and the city had expanded up the terraced hillsides. Much of it had been constructed hastily, without reference to whatever building codes the Provisional Government was attempting to enforce. Harley's, all native wood and glass panels, was an exception.

She left her name and waited in the bar for half an hour until Turk's elderly car chugged into the lot. She watched through the window as he locked the vehicle and strode toward the entrance through a deepening dusk. He was clearly not as well-dressed as the average customer at Harley's, but the staff recognized and welcomed him: he often met clients here, Lise knew, and as soon as he joined her, the waiter escorted them to a U-shaped booth with a window view. All the other window tables were occupied. "Popular place," she said.

"Tonight, yeah," he said, and when Lise stared at him blankly he added, "The meteor shower."

Oh. Right. She had forgotten. Lise had been in Port Magellan less than eleven months local time, which meant she had missed last year's meteor shower. She knew it was a big deal, that a kind of informal Mardi Gras had evolved around the occasion, and she remembered the event from the part of her childhood she had spent here—a spectacular celestial display that happened with clockwork regularity, a perfect excuse for a party. But the shower didn't peak until the third night. Tonight was just the beginning.

"But we're at the right place to see it start," Turk said. "In a couple of hours, when it's full dark, they'll turn down the lights and open those big patio doors so everybody gets an unobstructed view."

The sky was a radiant indigo, clear as glacial water, no sign of meteors yet, and the city was arrayed below the restaurant in a gracefully concealing sunset glow. She could see the fires flaring from the refinery stacks in the industrial sector, the silhouettes of mosques and churches, the illuminated billboards along the Rue de Madagascar advertising Hindi movies, herbal toothpaste (in Farsi), and chain hotels. Cruise ships in the harbor began to light up for the night. It was, if you squinted and thought nice thoughts, pretty. She might once have said exotic, but it no longer struck her that way.

She asked Turk how his business was doing.

He shrugged. "I pay the rent. I fly. I meet people. There's not much more to it than that, Lise. I don't have a mission in life."

Unlike you, he seemed to imply. Which led directly to the reason she had gotten in touch with him. She was reaching for her bag when the waiter showed up with ice water. She had barely glanced at the menu, but she ordered paella made with local seafood and seasoned with imported saffron. Turk asked for a steak, medium-well. Until fifteen years ago the most common terrestrial animal on Equatoria had been the water buffalo. Now you could buy fresh beef.

The waiter sauntered away and Turk said, "You could have called, you know."

Since the last time they had been together—since her expedition into the mountains, and a few uneasy arranged meetings afterward—he had phoned her a few times. Lise had returned his calls eagerly at first, then perfunctorily; then, when the guilt set in, not at all. "I know, and I'm sorry, but the last couple of months have been busy for me—"

"I mean today. You didn't have to drive all the way out to Arundji's just to make a date for dinner. You could have called."

"I thought if I called it might be too, you know, impersonal." He said nothing. She added, more honestly, "I guess I wanted to see you first. Make sure things were still okay."

"Different rules out there in the wilderness. I know that, Lise. There are *home* things and there are *away* things. I figured we must have been . . ."

"An away thing?"

"Well, I figured that's how you wanted it."

"There's a difference between what you want and what's practical."

"Tell me about it." He smiled ruefully. "How are things with you and Brian?"

"Over."

"Really?"

"Officially. Finally."

"And that book you're working on?"

"It's the research that's slow, not the writing." She hadn't written a word, never would write a word.

"But it's why you decided to stay."

In the New World, he meant. She nodded.

"And what happens when you're done? You go back to the States?"

"Possibly."

"It's funny," he said. "People come to the Port for all kinds of reasons. Some of them find reasons to stay, some don't. I think people just cross a certain line. You get off the boat for the first time and you realize you're literally on another planet—the air smells different, the water tastes different, the moon's the wrong size and it rises too fast. The day's still divided into twelve hours but the hours run long. After a few weeks or a few months people get disoriented on some deep level. So they turn around and go home. Or else it snaps into place and starts to feel normal. That's when they have second thoughts about going back to the anthill cities and bad air and septic oceans and all that stuff they used to take for granted."

"Is that why you're here?"

"In part, I guess," he said. "Sure."

Their meals arrived, and they ate and talked about nothing in particular for a while. The sky darkened, the city glittered, the waiter came back to clear the table. Turk ordered coffee. Lise summoned her courage and said, "Will you look at a photograph for me? Before they dim the lights."

"Sure. What kind of photograph?"

"A picture of someone who might have chartered a flight with you. This would have been a few months ago."

"You've been looking at my passenger manifests?"

"No! I mean, not *me* . . . you file manifests with the PG, right?"

"What's this about, Lise?"

"There's a lot I can't explain right now. Will you look at the picture first?"

He was frowning. "Show me."

Lise took her bag into her lap and withdrew the envelope. "But you said you had a favor to ask, too—"

"You first."

She passed the envelope across the linen tablecloth. He pulled out the picture. His expression didn't change. Finally he said, "I assume there's a story goes with this?"

"It was taken by a security camera at the docks late last year. The image has been enlarged and enhanced."

"You have access to security camera downloads, too?"

"No, but—"

"So you got these from someone else. One of your friends at the consulate. Brian, or one of his buddies."

"I can't go into that."

"Can you at least tell me why you're curious about—" He gestured at the image. "An old lady?"

"You know I've been trying to interview people who were connected with my father. She's one of them. Ideally, I'd like to make contact with her."

"Any particular reason? I mean, why *this* woman?"

"Well . . . I can't go into that."

"The conclusion I'm drawing here is that all roads lead back to Brian. What's his interest in this woman?"

"Brian works for the Department of Genomic Security. I don't."

"But someone there is doing you favors."

"Turk, I—"

"No, never mind. Don't ask, don't tell, right? Obviously, somebody knows I flew with this person. Which means somebody besides yourself would like to find her."

"That's a reasonable inference. But I'm not asking you on behalf of anyone else. What you choose to say or not say to anyone at the consulate is your own business. What you say to me stays with me."

He looked at her as if he were evaluating this statement. But, Lise thought, why should he trust her? What had she ever done to instill trust in him, besides sleep with him during the course of one exceptional weekend?

"Yeah," he said finally, "I flew with her."

"Okay . . . can you tell me anything about her? Where she is, what she talked about?"

He sat back in his chair. True to his prediction, the lights in the restaurant began to dim. A couple of waiters rolled back the glass wall that separated the indoor dining room from the patio. The sky was starry and deep, slightly washed out by the lights of the Port but still crisper than any sky Lise had known back in California. Had the meteor shower begun? She saw what looked like a few bright flashes across the meridian.

Turk hadn't spared it a glance. "I'll have to think about this."

"I'm not asking you to violate any confidences. Just—"

"I know what you're asking. And it's probably not unreasonable. But I'd like to think it over, if that's okay with you."

"All right." She couldn't push it any farther. "But you mentioned a quid pro quo?"

"Just something I'm curious about—I thought you might have picked up a word or two from one of those sources you don't like to discuss. Arundji got a memo this morning from the air regs department of the Provisional Government. I filed a flight plan for the far west, and all else being equal I probably would have been in the air by the time you drove up this afternoon. But they disallowed the flight. So I called around to find out what's happening. Seems like nobody's being allowed to fly into the Rub al-Khali."

"How come?"

"They won't say."

"This flight ban, is it temporary?"

"Also a question I can't get an answer to."

"Who imposed it? Under what authorization?"

"Nobody at the PG will own up to anything. I've been shuffled between a dozen departments and so has every other pilot who's affected by this. I'm not saying there's anything sinister about it, but it's kinda surprising. Why turn the western half of the continent into a no-fly zone? There are still regular flights to and from the oil allotments, and past that there's nothing but rocks and sand. Hikers and wilderness types go there—that's who had my charter. I don't understand it."

Lise desperately wished she had a factoid or two to barter with, but this was the first she'd heard of the flight ban. It was true she had contacts at the U.S. Consulate, her ex-husband chief among them. But the Americans were only advisory members of the Provisional Government. And Brian wasn't even a diplomat, just a DGS functionary.

"All I can do is ask," she said.

"Appreciate it if you would. So. Business attended to? At least for now?"

"For now," she said reluctantly.

"Then what do you say we take our coffee out on the patio while we can still find a table?"

Three months ago she had hired Turk to fly her across the Mohindar Range to a pipeline outpost called Kubelick's Grave. Strictly a business arrangement. She had been trying to track down an old colleague of her father's, a man named Dvali, but she never reached Kubelick's Grave: a squall had forced the plane down in one of the high mountain passes. Turk had landed his aircraft on a nameless lake while clouds like cannon smoke billowed between granite peaks north and south of them. He had moored the plane on a pebbly beach and set up a surprisingly comfortable camp under a stand of trees that looked to Lise like bulbous, mutant pines. The wind had whistled down that pass for three days while visibility declined to nothing. Set foot outside the canvas tent and you'd be lost within a couple of meters. But Turk was a passable woodsman and had packed for emergencies, and even canned food was delicious when you were barricaded against nature and equipped with a camp stove and a hurricane lantern. Under other circumstances it might have been a three-day endurance contest, but Turk turned out to be good company. She had not meant to seduce him and she believed he had not set out to seduce her. The attraction had been sudden and mutual and utterly explicable.

They had exchanged stories and warmed each other when the wind turned cold. At the time it had seemed to Lise that she would be happy to wrap Turk Findley around herself like a blanket and shut out the rest of the world forever. And if you had asked her whether she was on the verge of something more meaningful than an unexpected tryst, she might have said *yes, maybe*.

She had meant to keep up the relationship when they arrived back in the Port. But the Port had a way of subverting your best intentions. Problems that had seemed featherweight from the inside of a tent in the Mohindar Range regained their customary mass and inertia. Her separation from Brian was an established fact by that time, at least in her mind, though Brian was still liable to spasms of let's-work-it-out, well meant, she supposed, but humiliating for both of them.

She had told him about Turk, and while that stonewalled Brian's attempts at reconciliation it introduced a whole new vector of guilt: she began to suspect herself of using Turk as a lever—a sort of emotional crowbar against Brian's attempts to rekindle a dead fire. So, after a few uneasy meetings, she had let the relationship lapse. Better not to complicate what was already a complicated situation.

But now there was a *decree nisi* in the glove compartment of her car: her future was a blank page, and she was tempted to write on it.

The crowd on the patio began to react to the meteor shower. She looked up as three scaldingly-bright white lines scribed across the meridian. The meteors emanated from a point well above the horizon and almost directly due east, and before she could look away there were more of them—two, then one, then a spectacular cluster of five.

She was reminded of a summer in Idaho when she had gone stargazing with her father—she couldn't have been more than ten years old. Her father had grown up before the Spin and he had talked to her about the stars "the way they used to be," before the Hypotheticals dragged the Earth a few billion years down the river of time. He missed the old constellations, he said, the old star names. But there had been meteors that night, dozens of them, the largest intercepted by the invisible barrier that protected the Earth from the swollen sun, the smallest incinerated in the atmosphere. She had watched them arc across the heavens with a speed and brilliance that left her breathless.

As now. The fireworks of God. "Wow," she said, lamely.

Turk pulled his chair around to her side of the table so they were both facing the sea. He didn't make any kind of an overt move and she guessed he probably wouldn't. Navigating the high mountain passes must have been simple compared to this. She didn't make any moves either, was careful not to, but she couldn't help feeling the heat of his body inches from hers. She sipped her coffee without tasting it. There was another flurry of falling stars. She wondered aloud whether any of them ever reached the ground.

"It's just dust," Turk said, "or that's what the astronomers say. What's left of some old comet."

But something new had caught her attention. "So what about that?" she asked, pointing east, lower on the horizon, where the dark sky met the darker sea. It looked to Lise like something was actually falling out there—not meteors but bright dots that hung in the air like flares, or what she imagined flares would look like. The reflected light of them colored the ocean a streaky orange. She didn't remember anything like that from her previous time in Equatoria. "Is that part of it?"

Turk stood up. So did a few others among the crowd on the patio. A puzzled hush displaced the talk and laughter. Here and there, phones began to buzz or chatter.

"No," Turk said. "That's not part of it."

CHAPTER THREE

It was like nothing Turk had seen during his ten years in the New World.

But, in a way, that was exactly typical. The New World had a habit of reminding you it wasn't Earth. Things happened differently here. *It ain't Kansas,* as people liked to say, and they probably said the same thing in a dozen different languages. *It ain't the Steppes. It ain't Kandahar. It ain't Mombassa.*

"Do you think it's dangerous?" Lise asked.

Some of the restaurant's clientele evidently thought so. They settled their bills with barely-disguised haste and made for their cars. Within a few minutes there were only a few stalwarts left on the broad wooden patio. "You want to leave?" Turk asked.

"Not if you don't."

"I guess we're as safe here as anywhere," Turk said. "And the view is better."

The phenomenon was still hanging out at sea, though it seemed to move steadily closer. What it looked like was luminous rain, a rolling gray cloud shot with light— the way a thunderstorm looked when you saw it from a long way off, except that the glow wasn't fitful, like lightning, but seemed to hang below the billowing darkness and illuminate it from beneath. Turk had seen storms roll in from sea often enough, and he estimated that this one was approaching at roughly the local wind speed. The brightness falling from it appeared to be composed of discrete luminous or burning particles, maybe as dense as snow, but he could be wrong about that—it didn't snow in this part of Equatoria and the last snow he had seen was off the coast of Maine many years back.

His first concern was fire. Port Magellan was a tinderbox, crowded with sub-code housing and shacks; the docklands housed countless storage and transport facilities and the bay was thick with oil and LNG tankers, funneling fuel to the insatiable Earth. What looked like a dense squall of lit matches was blowing in from the east, and he didn't want to think about the potential consequences of that.

He said nothing to Lise. He imagined she had drawn many of the same conclusions, but she didn't suggest running—was smart enough, he guessed, to know there was no logical place to run to, not at the speed this thing was coming. But she tensed up as the phenomenon visibly approached the point of land at the southern extremity of the bay.

"It's not bright all the way down," she said.

The staff at Harley's started dragging in tables from the patio, as if that was going to protect anything from anything, and urged the remaining diners to stay indoors until someone had some idea what was going on. But the waiters knew Turk well enough to let him alone. So he stayed out a while longer with Lise and they watched the light of the flares, or whatever they were, dancing on the distant sea.

Not bright all the way down. He saw what she meant. The shifting, glittering curtains tailed into darkness well before they reached the surface of the ocean. Burned out, maybe. That was a hopeful sign. Lise took out her phone and punched up a local news broadcast, relaying bits of it to Turk. They were talking about a "storm," she said, or what looked on radar like a storm, the fringes of it extending north and south for hundreds of miles, the heart of it more or less centered on the Port.

And now the bright rain fell over the headlands and the inner harbor, illuminating the decks and superstructures of cruise ships and cargo vessels at anchor. Then the silhouettes of the cargo cranes grew misty and obscure, the tall hotels in the city dimmed in the distance, the souks and markets vanished as the shining rain moved up the hillsides and seemed to grow taller as it came, a canyon wall of murky light. But nothing burst into flame. That was good, Turk thought. Then he thought: but it could be toxic. It could be any fucking thing. "About time to move indoors," he said.

Tyrell, the headwaiter at Harley's, was a guy Turk had briefly worked with on the pipelines out in the Rub al-Khali. They weren't big buddies or anything but they were friendly, and Tyrell looked relieved when Turk and Lise finally abandoned the patio. Tyrell slid the glass doors shut and said, "You got any idea—?"

"No," Turk said.

"I don't know whether to run or just enjoy the show. I called my wife. We live down in the Flats." A low-rent neighborhood some few miles along the coast. "She says it's happening there, too. She says there's stuff falling on the house, it looks like ash."

"But nothing's burning?"

"She said not."

"It could be volcanic ash," Lise said, and Turk had to admire how she was handling all this. She was tense but not visibly afraid, not too scared to venture a theory. "It would have to have been some kind of tectonic event way out over the horizon, something at sea . . ."

"Like a sea volcano," Tyrell said, nodding.

"But we would have felt something before the ash got to us if it was anywhere close—an earthquake, a tsunami."

"Been no report of any such thing," Turk said, "far as I know."

"Ash," Tyrell added. "Like, gray and powdery."

Turk asked Tyrell if there was any coffee back in the kitchen and Tyrell said yeah, not a bad idea, and went to check. There were still a few diners in the restaurant, people with nowhere better to go, though nobody was eating or celebrating. They sat at the innermost tables and talked nervously with the waitstaff.

The coffee came and it was good and dense, and Turk added cream to his cup just as if the sky weren't falling. Lise's phone buzzed repeatedly, and she fended off a couple of friendly calls before shunting everything to her voice mail. Turk didn't get any calls, though his phone was in his shirt pocket.

Now the ash began to fall on Harley's patio, and Turk and Lise moved closer to the window to watch.

Gray and powdery. Tyrell's description was on the money. Turk had never seen volcanic ash, but he imagined this was what it might look like. It sifted down over the wooden slats and boards of the patio and drifted against the window glass. It was like snow the color of an old wool suit, but here and there were flecks of something shiny, something still luminous, which dimmed as he watched.

Lise pressed up against his shoulder, wide-eyed. He thought again of their weekend up in the Mohindar Range, marooned by weather on that nameless lake. She had been just as self-possessed back then, just as balanced, braced for whatever the situation might throw at her. "At least," he said, "nothing's burning."

"No. But you can smell it."

He could, now that she mentioned it—a mineral smell, slightly acrid, a little sulfuric.

Tyrell said, "You think it's dangerous?"

"Nothing we can do about it if it is."

"Except stay indoors," Lise said. But Turk doubted that was practical. Even now, through the glittering ashfall, he could make out traffic on Rue de Madagascar, pedestrians scurrying down the sidewalks covering their heads with jackets or handkerchiefs or newspapers. "Unless—"

"Unless what?"

"Unless," she said, "this goes on too long. There's not a roof in Port Magellan built to bear much weight."

"And it isn't just dust," Tyrell said.

"What?"

"Well, *look*." He gestured at the window.

Absurdly, impossibly, something the shape of a starfish drifted past the glass. It was gray but speckled with light. It must have weighed nearly nothing because it floated in the weak breeze like a balloon, and when it reached the deck of the patio it crumbled into powder and a few larger fragments.

Turk gave Lise a glance. She shrugged, incredulous.

"Get me a tablecloth," Turk said.

Tyrell said, "What do you want with a tablecloth?"

"And one of those linen napkins."

"You don't want to mess with the linen," Tyrell said. "Management's very strict about that."

"Go get the manager, then."

"Mr. Darnell's off tonight. I guess that makes me the manager."

"Then get a tablecloth, Tyrell. I want to check this out."

"Don't mess up my place."

"I'll be careful."

Tyrell went to undress a table. Lise said, "You're going out there?"

"Just long enough to retrieve a little of whatever's coming down."

"What if it's toxic?"

"Then I guess we're all fucked." She flinched, and he added, "But we'd probably know by now if it was."

"Can't be good for your lungs, whatever it is."

"So help me tie that napkin over my face."

The remaining diners and waiters watched curiously but made no effort to help. Turk took the tablecloth to the nearest exit to the patio and gestured to Tyrell to slide open the glass door. The smell immediately intensified— it was something like wet, singed animal hair—and Turk hurriedly spread the tablecloth on the patio floor and backed inside.

"Now what?" Tyrell said.

"Now we let it sit a few minutes."

He rejoined Lise, and, bereft of conversation, they watched the dust come down for a quarter of an hour more. Lise asked him how he planned to get home. He shrugged. He lived in what was essentially a trailer a few miles downcoast from the airfield. There was already a good half inch of ash on the ground and traffic was crawling.

"I'm only a couple of blocks from here," she said. "The new building on Rue Abbas by the Territorial Authority compound? It ought to be fairly sturdy."

It was the first time she had invited him home. He nodded.

But he was still curious. He waved down Tyrell, who had been serving coffee to everyone still present, and Tyrell slid open the patio door one more time. Turk gripped the open tablecloth, now burdened with a layer of ash, and pulled it gently, trying not to disturb whatever fragile structures it might have captured. Tyrell closed the door promptly. "Phew! Stinks."

Turk brushed off the few flakes of gray ash that clung to his shirt and hair. Lise joined him as he squatted to examine the debris-covered tablecloth. A couple of curious diners pulled their chairs a little closer, though they wrinkled their noses at the smell.

Turk said, "You have a pen or a pencil on you?"

Lise rummaged in her purse and came up with a pen. Turk took it from her and used it to probe the layer of dust that had collected on the tablecloth.

"What's that?" Lise asked over his shoulder. "To your left. Looks like, I don't know, an *acorn* . . ."

Turk hadn't seen an acorn in years. Oaks didn't grow in Equatoria. The object in the ashfall was about the size of his thumb. It was saucer-shaped at one end and tapered to a blunt point at the other—an acorn, or maybe a tiny egg wearing a minuscule sombrero. It appeared to be made of the same stuff as the fallen ash, and when he touched it with the tip of the pen it dissolved as if it possessed no particular substance at all.

"And over there," Lise said, pointing. Another shaped object, this one resembling a gear out of an old mechanical clock. It, too, crumbled when he touched it.

Tyrell went to the staff room and came back with a flashlight. When he played the beam over the tablecloth at a raking angle it showed up a number of these objects, if you could call them "objects"—the faintly structured remains of things that appeared to have been manufactured. There was a tube about a centimeter long, perfectly smooth; another about the same size, but knobbed like a length of spine from some small animal, a mouse, say. There was a six-pronged thorn; there was a disk with miniature, crumbling spokes, like a bicycle wheel; there was a beveled ring. Some of these things glinted with a faint remnant light.

"All burned," Lise observed.

Burned or otherwise decomposed. But how could something so completely cremated remain even partially intact after falling from the sky? What had these things been made of?

Also present in the ashfall were a few luminous specks. Turk hovered his hand over one of them.

"Careful," Lise said.

"It's not hot. It's not even warm."

"Could be, I don't know, radioactive."

"Could be." If so, it was another doomsday scenario. Everyone outside was inhaling this stuff. Everyone inside soon would be. None of these buildings was airtight, none of them filtered its air.

"You learning anything from this?" Tyrell asked.

Turk stood up and brushed his hands. "Yeah. I'm learning that I know even less than I thought I did."

He accepted Lise's offer of temporary shelter. They borrowed spare kitchen clothing from Tyrell, chef's jackets to protect their clothes from the falling ash, and they shuffled as fast as they could across the gray dunes in the parking lot to Lise's car. The ash cloud had turned the sky dark, obscured the meteor shower, dimmed the streetlights.

Lise drove a Chinese car, smaller than Turk's vehicle but newer and probably more reliable. He shook himself off as he climbed into the shotgun seat.

She steered the vehicle out the back exit from the parking lot onto a narrow but less crowded avenue that connected Rue de Madagascar to Rue Abbas. She maneuvered the car with a kind of cautious grace, nursing it over the accumulations of dust, and Turk let her concentrate on her driving. But as the traffic slowed she said, "You think this is connected with the meteor shower?"

"It seems like more than a coincidence. But who knows."

"This is definitely not volcanic ash."

"Guess not."

"It could have come from outside the atmosphere."

"Could have, I guess."

"So it might be connected to the Hypotheticals."

During the Spin, people had speculated endlessly about the Hypotheticals, the still-mysterious entities that had bounced the Earth a few billion years into the galactic future and opened a gateway between the Indian Ocean and the New World. Without reaching any reliable conclusions, as far as Turk could tell. "Could be. But that doesn't explain anything."

"My father used to talk about the Hypotheticals a lot. One of the things he said was, we tend to forget how much *older* the universe is now than it was before the Spin. It might have changed in ways we don't understand. Any textbook you pick says comets and meteors are junk falling in from the far edge of the solar system—here, or on Earth, or anywhere in the galaxy. But that was never more than a local observation and it's four billion years out of date. There's a theory that the Hypotheticals aren't biological organisms and never were—"

He waited while she turned a corner, the car's tires fighting for traction. Lise's father had been a college professor. Before he disappeared.

"That they're a system of self-replicating machines living out in the cold parts of the galaxy, at the fringes of planetary systems, with this really slow metabolism that eats ice and generates information . . ."

"Like those replicators we sent out during the Spin."

"Right. Self-replicating machines. But with billions of years of evolution behind them."

Was this how college profs talked to their daughters? Or was she just talking to ward off panic? "So what are you saying?"

"Maybe whatever falls into the atmosphere this time every year isn't just comet dust. Maybe it's—"

She shrugged.

"Dead Hypotheticals," he finished.

"Well, it sounds inane when you put it that way."

"It's as good a theory as any. I don't mean to be skeptical. But we don't have any evidence that whatever's falling out of the sky is from space."

"Cogs and tubes made of ash? Where *would* it be from?"

"Look at it another way. People have only been on this planet for three decades. We tell ourselves it's all surveyed and reasonably well understood. But that's bullshit. It would be wrong to jump to a conclusion—*any* conclusion. Even if this is caused by the Hypotheticals, that doesn't really explain anything. We've had a meteor shower every summer for thirty years and never anything like this."

The wipers piled dust at the margins of the windshield. Turk saw people on the sidewalks, some of them running, others sheltering in doorways, faces peering anxiously from windows. A Provisional Government police car passed them with its lights and siren on.

"Might be something unusual's happening out where we can't see it."

"Might be the Celestial Dog shaking off fleas. Too soon to say, Lise."

She nodded unhappily and pulled into the parking garage of the building where she lived, a concrete tower that looked as if it had been transplanted from Dade County. In the underground parking shelter there was no evidence of what was going on outside, only a mote or two hanging in the motionless air.

Lise slid her security card through the elevator call slot. "We made it."

So far, Turk thought, yeah.

CHAPTER FOUR

Lise found Turk a robe big enough to decently fit him and told him to put his clothes in the washer, in case the dust clinging to them was in any way toxic. While he did that she took a turn in the shower. When she rinsed her hair, gray water pooled around the drain. An omen, she thought, a portent: maybe the ashfall wouldn't stop until Port Magellan was entombed like Pompeii. She stood under the shower until the water ran clear.

The lights flickered twice before she was done. The electrical grid in Port Magellan was still fairly crude; probably it wouldn't take much to put a local transformer out of commission. She tried to imagine what would happen if this storm (if you could call it that) went on for another day, or two, or more. A whole population trapped in the dark. UN relief ships arriving in the harbor. Soldiers evacuating the survivors. No, better *not* to imagine it.

She changed into fresh jeans and a cotton shirt, and the lights were still on when she joined Turk in the living room. In her old flannel robe he looked deeply embarrassed but dangerously sexy. Those ridiculously long legs, scarred in places by the life he had led before he started flying passengers over the mountains. He had told her he was a merchant seaman when he arrived here, that his first work in the New World had been on the Saudi-Aramco pipeline. Big blunt hands, well-used.

He gazed around in a way that made her conscious of her apartment, the wide east-facing window, the video panel and her small library of books and recordings. She wondered how it seemed to him. A little upscale, probably, compared to what he called "his trailer," a little too back-home, too obviously an imported fragment of North America, though it was still new to her, still slightly uninhabited—the place she had brought her stuff after she split from Brian.

Not that he showed any sign of such thoughts. He was watching the local news channel. There were three daily papers in Port Magellan but only one news channel, overseen by a bland and complexly multicultural board of advisors. It broadcast in fifteen languages and was, as a rule, interesting in none of them. But now there was something substantial to talk about. A camera crew had gone out in the ashfall to get views from street level, while two commentators read advisories from various departments of the Provisional Government.

"Turn it up," Lise said.

The big intersection at Portugal and Tenth was shut down, stranding a busful of tourists desperate to get back to their cruise ship. Radio transmission had been compromised by the gunk in the atmosphere and communication with vessels at sea was intermittent. A government lab was doing hasty chemical analysis of the fallen ash, but no results had been announced. Some respiratory problems had been reported but nothing to suggest that the ash was immediately harmful to human health. Loose talk suggested a link between the ashfall and the annual meteor shower, but that was impossible to confirm. Best advice from local authorities was to hunker down, keep doors and windows closed, wait it out.

Everything after that was more of the same. Lise didn't need a reporter to tell her the city was shutting down. The usual night noises had gone silent, apart from the periodic wail of emergency-vehicle sirens.

Turk muted the display and said, "My clothes are probably clean by now." He walked to the laundry alcove and took his T-shirt and jeans into the bathroom to dress. He had been more brazen out in the lake country. But then, so had she. Lise made up the sofa as a bed for him. Then she said, "How about a nightcap?"

He nodded.

In the kitchen she drained what was left of her last bottle of white wine into two glasses. When she came back to the living room Turk had opened the blinds and was peering out into the darkness. A deepening wind swept falling ash past the window. She could smell it, faintly. That sulfurous reek.

"Reminds me of diatoms," Turk said, accepting a glass.

"Excuse me?"

"You know. Out in the ocean there's plankton? Microscopic animals? They grow a shell. Then the plankton dies and the shells drift down through the sea and make a kind of silt, and if you dredge it up and look at it under a microscope you see all these plankton skeletons—diatoms, little stars and spikes and so forth."

Lise watched the ash drift and thought about Turk's analogy. The remains of things once living settling through the turbulent atmosphere. The shells of dead Hypotheticals.

It would not have surprised her father, she thought.

She was still contemplating that when her phone buzzed again. This time she picked up: she couldn't exclude the exterior world forever—she'd have to reassure friends that she was all right. She briefly and guiltily hoped that it wouldn't be Brian on the other end; but, of course, it was.

"Lise?" he said. "I was worried sick about you. Where are you?"

She walked to the kitchen as if to put some symbolic space between Brian and Turk. "I'm fine," she said. "I'm home."

"Well, good. Lot of people aren't."

"How about you?"

"I'm in the consulate compound. There's a lot of us here. We thought we'd stick it out, sleep on cots. The building has a generator if the power goes down. You have power?"

"At the moment."

"About half the Chinese district is in the dark. The city's having trouble getting repair crews out."

"Anybody there know what's going on?"

Brian's voice came through the phone with a stressed reediness, the way he sounded when he was nervous or upset. "No, not really . . ."

"Or when it's going to stop?"

"No. It can't go on forever, though."

That was a nice thought, but Lise doubted she could convince herself of the truth of it, at least not tonight. "Okay, Brian. Appreciate the call but I'm fine."

There was a pause. He wanted to say more. Which was what he always seemed to want these days. A conversation, if not a marriage.

"Let me know if you have a problem there."

She thanked him and cut the connection, left the phone on the kitchen counter and walked back into the living room.

"Was that your ex?" Turk asked.

Turk knew about her problems with Brian. In the mountains, by the side of a stormy lake, she had shared a number of difficult truths about herself and her life. She nodded.

"Am I creating a problem for you here?"

"No," she said. "No problem."

She sat up with Turk watching more sporadic news, but fatigue caught up with her around three in the morning and she finally staggered off to bed. Even so she was awake for a while in the dark, curled under a cotton sheet as if it could protect her from whatever was falling out of the sky. It isn't doomsday, she told herself. It's just something inconvenient and unexpected.

Diatoms, she thought: sea shells, ancient life, another reminder that the universe had shifted radically during and after the Spin, that the kind of world she had been born into was not the world her parents or her grandparents had ever expected to see. She remembered an old astronomy book of her grandfather's that had fascinated her as a child. The last chapter was called *Are We Alone?* and it had been full of what seemed like naive, silly speculation. Because that question had been answered. No, we are not alone. No, we can never again think of the universe as our private property. Life, or something *like* life, had been here long before the evolution of human beings. We're on *their* turf, Lise thought, and because we don't understand them we can't predict their behavior. Even today no one knew with any certainty why the Earth had been preserved down four billion years of galactic history like a tulip bulb wintering in a dark cellar, or why a seaway to this new planet had been installed in the Indian Ocean. What was falling outside the window was just more evidence of humanity's gross ignorance.

She slept longer than she meant to and woke with daylight in her eyes—not sunlight, exactly, but a welcome ambient brightness. By the time she dressed, Turk was already awake. She found him at the living room window, gazing out.

"Looks a little better," she said.

"At least, not as bad."

There was still a flat, glittery dust in the outside air. But it wasn't falling as thickly as it had last night and the sky was relatively clear.

"According to the news," Turk said, "the precipitation—that's what they're calling it—is tapering off. The ash cloud is still there but it's moving inland. What they can see on radar and satellite images suggests the whole thing might be finished late tonight, early tomorrow, at least as far as the coast is concerned."

"Good," Lise said.

"But that's not the end of the problem. The streets need to be cleared. There's still trouble with the electrical grid. A few roofs collapsed, mostly those flat-roofed tourist rentals down along the headland. Just cleaning up the docks is going to be a huge project. The Provisional Government contracted a bunch of earthmovers to clean the roads, and once some mobility is established they can start pumping seawater and sluice it all into the bay, assuming the storm sewers accommodate the runoff. All this is complicated by dust in motors, stalled cars and so forth."

"Any word on toxicity?"

"According to the news guys the ash is mostly carbon, sulfur, silicates, and metals, some of it arranged in unusual molecules, whatever that means, but breaking down pretty quick into simpler elements. Short-term it's not dangerous unless you've got asthma or emphysema. Long-term, who knows? They still want people to stay indoors, and they're advising a face mask if you really need to go out."

"Anybody making any guesses about where it all came from?"

"No. We're getting a lot of speculation, mostly bullshit,

but somebody at the Geophysical Survey had the same idea we did—that it's spaceborne material that's been modified by the Hypotheticals."

In other words, nobody really knew anything. "Did you sleep last night?"

"Not much."

"Had any breakfast?"

"Didn't want to mess up your kitchen."

"I'm not much of a cook, but I can do omelettes and coffee." When he offered to help she said, "You'd just be in the way. Give me twenty minutes."

There was a window in the kitchen, and Lise was able to survey the Port while butter sizzled in the frying pan—this big, polyglot, kaleidoscopically multicultural city that had grown so quickly on the edge of a new continent, now blanketed in ominous gray. The wind had stiffened overnight. The ash had duned in the empty streets and it shivered down from the crowns of the trees that had been planted along Rue Abbas.

She sprinkled fresh cheddar onto the omelette and folded it. For once it didn't break and spill off the spatula in a gooey lump. She put together two plates and carried them into the living room. She found Turk standing in the space she used for an office: a desk, her keyboard and file holders, a small library of paper books.

"This where you write?" he asked.

"Yes." No. She put the plates on the coffee table. Turk joined her on the sofa, folding his long legs and taking the plate onto his lap.

"Good," he said, sampling the omelette.

"Thank you."

"So that book you're working on," he said. "How's that going?"

She winced. The book, the notional book, her excuse for prolonging her stay in Equatoria, didn't exist. She told people she was writing a book because she was a journalism graduate and because it seemed a plausible thing for her to do in the aftermath of a failed marriage— a book about her father, who had vanished without explanation when the family lived here a dozen years ago, when she was fifteen. "Slowly," she said.

"No progress?"

"A few interviews, some good conversations with my father's old colleagues at the American University." All this was true. She had immersed herself in her family's fractured history. But she hadn't written more than notes to herself.

"I remember you said your father was interested in Fourths."

"He was interested in all kinds of things." Robert Adams had come to Equatoria as part of the Geophysical Survey's deal with the fledgling American University. The course he taught was New World Geology, and he had done fieldwork in the far west. The book *he* had been working on—a real book—had been called *Planet as Artifact,* a study of the New World as a place where geological history had been deeply influenced by the Hypotheticals.

And, yes, he had also been fascinated by the community of Fourths—privately, not professionally.

"The woman in the photograph you showed me," Turk said. "Is she a Fourth?"

"Maybe. Probably." How much of this did she really want to discuss?

"How can you tell?"

"Because I've seen her before," Lise said, putting down her fork and turning to face him. "Do you want the whole story?"

"If you want to tell it."

Lise had heard the word "disappeared" applied to her father for the first time three days after he failed to come home from the university, a month after her fifteenth birthday. The local police had come to discuss the case with Lise's mother while Lise listened from the corridor outside the kitchen. Her father had "disappeared"—that is, he had left work as usual, had driven away in the customary direction, and somewhere between the American University and their rented house in the hills above Port Magellan he had vanished. There was no obvious explanation, no pertinent evidence.

But the investigation went on. The issue of his fascination with Fourths had come up. Lise's mother was interviewed again, this time by men who wore business suits rather than uniforms: men from the Department of Genomic Security. Mr. Adams had expressed an interest in Fourths: was the interest personal? Had he, for instance, repeatedly mentioned the subject of longevity? Did he suffer from any degenerative disease that might have been reversed by the Martian longevity treatment? Was he unusually concerned with death? Unhappy at home?

No, Lise's mother had said. Actually, what she said most often was "No, goddammit." Lise remembered her mother at the kitchen table, interrogated, drinking endless cups of rust-brown roiboos tea and saying, "No, goddammit, no."

Nevertheless, a theory had emerged. A family man in the New World, often apart from his family, seduced by the anything-goes atmosphere of the frontier and by the idea of the Fourth Age, an extra thirty years or so tacked onto his expected span of life . . .

Lise had to admit there was a certain logic to it. He wouldn't have been the first man to be lured from his family by the promise of longevity. Three decades ago the Martian Wun Ngo Wen had brought to Earth a technique for extending human life—a treatment that changed behavior in other and subtler ways as well.

Proscribed by virtually every government on Earth, the treatment circulated in the underground community of Terrestrial Fourths.

Would Robert Adams have abandoned his career and family to join that community? Lise's instinctive answer was the same as her mother's: no. He wouldn't have done that to them, *no,* no matter how tempted he might have been.

But evidence had emerged to subvert that faith. He had been associating with strangers off-campus. People had been coming to the house, people not associated with the university, people he had not introduced to his family and whose purposes he had been reluctant to explain. And the Fourth cults held a special appeal in the academic community—the treatment had first been circulated by the scientist Jason Lawton, among friends he considered trustworthy, and it had spread primarily among intellectuals and scholars.

No, goddammit—but did Mrs. Adams have a better explanation?

Mrs. Adams did not. Nor did Lise.

The investigation remained inconclusive. After a year of this Lise's mother had booked passage to California for herself and her daughter, bent by the insult to her well-planned life but not, at least outwardly, broken. The disappearance—the New World in general—became a subject one didn't mention in her presence. Silence was better than speculation. Lise had learned that lesson well. Like her mother, Lise had secured her pain and curiosity in the dark internal attic where unthinkable thoughts were stored. At least until her marriage to Brian and his transfer to Port Magellan. Suddenly those memories were refreshed: the wound reopened as if it had never healed, and her curiosity, she discovered, had been distilled in its enclosure, had become an adult's curiosity rather than a child's.

So she had begun to ask questions of her father's colleagues and friends, the few still living in the city, and inevitably these questions had involved the community of Fourths in the New World.

Brian at first tried to be helpful. He hadn't much liked her *ad hoc* investigation into what he considered potentially dangerous matters—and Lise supposed it had been one more in a growing number of emotional disconnects between them—but he had tolerated it and even used his DGS credentials to follow up on some of her queries.

Like the woman in the photograph.

"Two photographs, actually," she told Turk. When she moved out of her mother's house, Lise had salvaged a number of items her mother was forever threatening to throw away, in this case a disk of photographs from her parents' Port Magellan years. A few of the pictures had been taken at faculty parties at the Adams house. Lise had selected a few of these photos and shown them to old family friends, hoping to track down those she didn't recognize. She managed to put names, at least, to most of them, but one stood out: a dark-skinned elderly woman in jeans, caught standing in the doorway beyond a crowd of far more expensively-dressed faculty members, as if she had arrived unexpectedly. She seemed disconcerted, nervous.

No one had been able to identify her. Brian had offered to run the picture through DGS image-recognition software and see if anything turned up. This had been the latest of what Lise had come to think of as Brian's "charity bombs"—acts of generosity he threw in front of her as if to divert her from the path to separation—and she had accepted the offer with a warning that it wouldn't change anything.

But the search had turned up a pertinent match. The same woman had passed through the docks at Port

Magellan just months ago. She had been listed on a passengership manifest as Sulean Moi.

The name turned up again in connection with Turk Findley, who had piloted the charter flight that carried Sulean Moi over the mountains to the desert town of Kubelick's Grave—the same town to which Lise had been attempting to fly a few months before, following a different lead.

Turk listened to all this patiently. Then he said, "She wasn't talkative. She paid cash. I put her down at the airstrip in Kubelick's Grave and that was that. She never said anything about her past or why she was flying west. You think she's a Fourth?"

"She hasn't changed much in fifteen years. That suggests she might be."

"So maybe the simplest explanation is true. Your father took the illegal treatment and started a new life under a new name."

"Maybe. But I don't want another hypothesis. I want to know what really happened."

"So you find out the truth, what then? Does that make your life better? Maybe you'll learn something you don't like. Maybe you have to start mourning all over again."

"At least," she said, "I'll know what I'm mourning for."

As often happened when she talked about her father, she dreamed of him that night.

More memory than dream at first: she was with him on the veranda of their house on the hill in Port Magellan, and he was talking to her about the Hypotheticals.

He talked to her on the veranda because Lise's mother didn't care for these conversations. This was the starkest contrast Lise could draw between her parents. Both were Spin survivors, but they had emerged from the crisis with polarized sensibilities. Her father had thrown himself headlong into the mystery, had fallen in love with the heightened strangeness of the universe. Her mother pretended that none of it had happened—that the garden fence and the back wall were barricades strong enough to repulse the tide of time.

Lise had not quite known where to place herself on that divide. She loved the sense of safety she felt in her mother's home. But she loved to hear her father talk.

In the dream he talked about the Hypotheticals. *The Hypotheticals aren't people, Lise, you must not make that mistake.* As the unnamed Equatorian stars turned in the slate-black sky. *They are a network of more or less mindless machines, we suspect, but is that network aware of itself? Does it have a mind, Lise, the way you and I do? If it does, every element of its thought must be propagated over hundreds or thousands of light-years. It would see time and space very differently than we do. It might not perceive us at all, except as a passing phenomenon, and if it manipulates us it might do so at an entirely unconscious level.*

Like God, Lise in her dream suggested.

A blind God, her father said, but he was wrong, because in the dream, while she was entranced in the grandeur of his vision and safe in the boundary of her mother's sensibility, the Hypotheticals had reached down from the sky, opened a steel fist that glittered in the starlight, and snatched him away before she could summon the courage to scream.

CHAPTER FIVE

The dust fell more sparsely for another few hours, yielded to a gray daylight, and stopped altogether by dark.

The city remained eerily quiet apart from the intermittent growl of earthmovers ceaselessly shifting the ash. Turk could tell where the earthmovers were working by the billows of fine dust that rose around and above them, gray pillars lofting over the corduroy of shops, shanties, office buildings, billboards, commingling with saltwater plumes where pump lines laid from the harbor to the hills had begun to sluice the streets. A wasteland. But even at this hour there were people in the street, masked or with bandannas tied over their faces, kicking through the drifts on their way somewhere or just assessing the damage, gazing around like bit players in a disaster drama. A man in a grimy dishdasha stood for half an hour outside the locked Arabic grocery across the street, smoking cigarettes and staring at the sky.

"You think it's over?" Lise asked.

Obviously a question he couldn't answer. But he

guessed she didn't want a real answer as much as she wanted reassurance. "For now, anyway."

They were both too wired to sleep. He switched on the video display and they settled back on the sofa, trawling for new information. A newsreader announced that the dust cloud had moved inland and no more "precipitation" was expected—there had been sporadic reports of ashfall from every community between Ayer's Point and Haixi on the coast, but Port Magellan seemed to have been hit harder than most. Which was in a way a good thing, Turk supposed, because while this dump of particulate matter had been troublesome for the city it might have been a catastrophe for the local ecosystem, smothering forests and killing crops and maybe even poisoning the soil, though the newscaster said there was nothing terribly toxic in it, "according to the latest analyses." The fossil- or machine-like structures in the ashfall had attracted attention, of course. Microphotographs of the dust revealed even more latent structure: degraded cogs and wheels, scalloped cones like tiny conch shells, inorganic molecules hooked together in complex and unnatural ways—as if some vast machine had eroded in orbit and only its finer elements had survived the fiery descent through the atmosphere.

They had spent the day in the apartment, Turk mostly sitting at the window, Lise making calls and sending messages to family back home, itemizing the food in the kitchen in case the city was shut down long-term, and in the process they had reestablished a kind of intimacy—the mountain-camp-in-a-thunderstorm intimacy they had shared before, brought down to the city—and when she put her head against his shoulder Turk raised his hand to stroke her hair, hesitated when he remembered the nature of their situation here.

"It's all right," she said.

Her hair smelled fresh and somehow golden, and it felt like silk under the palm of his hand.

"Turk," she said, "I'm sorry—"

"Nothing to apologize for."

"For thinking I needed an excuse to see you."

"Missed you too," he said.

"Just—it was confusing."

"I know."

"Do you want to go to bed?" She took his hand and rubbed her cheek against it. "I mean—"

He knew what she meant.

He spent that night with her and he spent another, not because he had to—the coast road had been mostly cleared by that time—but because he could.

But he couldn't stay forever. He lazed around one morning more, picking over breakfast while Lise made more calls. Amazing how many friends and acquaintances and home-folks she had. It made him feel a little unpopular. The only calls he made that morning were to customers whose flights would have to be rescheduled or canceled—cancellations he couldn't afford right now—and to a couple of buddies, mechanics from the airport, who might wonder why he wasn't around to go drinking with them. He didn't have much of a social life. He didn't even own a dog.

She recorded a long message to her mother back in the States. You couldn't make a direct call across the Arch, since the only things the Hypotheticals allowed to travel between this world and the one next door were manned ocean vessels. But there was a fleet of telecom-equipped commercial ships that shuttled back and forth to relay recorded data. You could watch video news from home that was only a few hours stale, and you could send voice or text the other direction. Lise's message, what he overheard of it, was a careful reassurance that the ashfall had done no lasting harm and looked like it would be cleared up before long, although it was a mystery why it had happened, very confusing—no shit, Turk thought.

Turk had family in Austin, Texas. But they hadn't heard from him lately and wouldn't expect to.

On the bookshelf by Lise's desk was a three-volume bound copy of the Martian Archives, sometimes called the Martian Encyclopedia, the compendium of history and science brought to Earth by Wun Ngo Wen thirty years ago. The blue dust jackets were tattered at their spine ends. He took down the first volume and leafed through it. When she finally put down the phone, he said, "Do you believe in this?"

"It's not a religion. It's not something you have to believe in it."

Back during the freakish years of the Spin, the technologically advanced nations of the Earth had assembled the necessary resources to terraform and colonize the planet Mars. The most useful resource had already been put in place by the Hypotheticals, and that was time. For every year on Earth under the Spin membrane, thousands of years had passed in the universe at large. The biological transformation of Mars—scientists called it "the ecopoiesis"—had been relatively easy to accomplish, given that generous temporal disconnect. The human colonization of the planet had been an altogether riskier venture.

Isolated from Earth for millennia, the Martian colonists had created a technology suited to their water-poor and nitrogen-starved environment. They were masters of biological manipulation but chronically wary of large-scale mechanical engineering. Sending a manned expedition to Earth had been a last, desperate strategy when the Hypotheticals appeared to be about to enclose Mars in a Spin membrane of its own.

Wun Ngo Wen, the so-called Martian ambassador—Turk found a photograph of him as he leafed through an appendix to the book: a small, wrinkled, dark-skinned man—had arrived during the last years of the Spin. He had been feted by Earthly governments, until it became clear that he possessed no magic solution to their problems. But Wun had advocated and helped set in motion the launch of Martian-designed quasi-biological probes into the outer solar system—self-replicating robotic devices that were supposed to broadcast back information that might shed useful light on the nature of the Hypotheticals, and in a way they had succeeded—the network of probes had been absorbed into a preexisting, previously unsuspected ecology of self-replicating devices living in deep space, which was the physical "body" of the Hypotheticals, or so some people believed. But Turk had no opinion about that.

The version of the Archives Lise possessed was an authorized redaction, published in the States. It had been vetted and organized by a panel of scientists and government officials and it was acknowledged to be incomplete. Before his death Wun had arranged for unedited copies of the text to be privately circulated, along with something even more valuable—Martian "pharmaceuticals," including the drug that would add some thirty or more years to an average human life span, the so-called Fourth treatment by which Lise's father had presumably been tempted.

There were supposedly lots of native Fourths on Earth now, though they lacked the elaborate social structures that constrained the lives of their Martian cousins. Taking the treatment was illegal under a UN accord signed by virtually every member nation. Most of what the Department of Genomic Security did back in the States was shutting down Fourth cults both genuine and fraudulent—that, and policing the booming trade in human and animal genetic enhancements. These were the folks Lise's ex-husband worked for.

"**Y**ou know," she said, "we haven't talked much about this."

"We haven't talked nearly enough about anything at all, seems to me."

Her smile, though brief, was pleasing.

She said, "Do you know any Fourths?"

"Wouldn't recognize one if I saw one." And if that was an evasion, she didn't appear to notice.

"Because it's different here in the Port," she said, "here in the New World. The laws aren't enforced the way they are back on Earth."

"That's changing, I hear."

"Which is why I want to look at what my father was interested in before it all gets erased. People say there's a Fourth underground in the city. Maybe more than one."

"Yeah, I've heard that. I've heard a lot of things. Not all true."

"I can do all the secondhand research I want, but what I really need is to talk to someone who's had direct experience with the Fourth community here."

"Right. Maybe Brian can arrange it for you, next time DGS arrests somebody."

He was immediately sorry he'd said it, or said it so bluntly. She tightened up. "Brian and I are divorced, and I'm not responsible for what Genomic Security does."

"But he's looking for the same people you're looking for."

"For different reasons."

"Do you ever wonder about that? Whether he might be using you as some kind of cat's paw? Riding on your research?"

"I don't show my work to Brian—to anyone."

"Not even when he's baiting you with the woman who maybe took away your father?"

"I'm not sure you have the right—"

"Forget it. I'm just, you know, concerned."

She was obviously on the verge of handing that right back to him, but she cocked her head and thought about it first. That was one of the things Turk had noticed about her right away, the habit she had of stepping outside the moment before she rendered a verdict.

She said, "Don't make assumptions about me and Brian. Just because we're still on speaking terms doesn't mean I'm doing him favors."

"Just so we know where we are," he said.

The sky was gray again by noon, but the clouds were rain clouds, nothing exotic, and they brought a drenching, unseasonable downpour. Turk guessed the rain might ultimately be a boon—it would wash some of this ash into the soil or out to sea, maybe help salvage the season's crops, if that was possible. But it did nothing to ease the drive south from the Port, once he recovered his car from the parking lot at Harley's. Glistening washes of gray ash made the pavement treacherous. Creeks and rivers had turned the color of clay and ran turgidly in their beds. When the road crossed the high ridges Turk could see a bloom of silt tailing into the sea from a dozen muddy deltas.

He left the coast road at an unmarked exit toward a place most English-speakers called New Delhi Flats, a shanty settlement on a plateau between two creeks, under a sheer bluff that crumbled a little every rainy season. The alleys between the rows of cheap Chinese-branded prefab housing were unpaved, and the fair-weather huts had been improved with tarpaper roofing and sheets of insulation hauled in from cheapjack factories up-coast. There were no police in the Flats, no real authority beyond what could be leveraged by the churches, temples, and mosques. The earthmovers hadn't been anywhere near the Flats, and the narrower alleys were congested with sloggy wet dunes. But a passage had been shoveled along the main avenue, and it took Turk only a few extra minutes to reach Tomas Ginn's undistinguished home—an arsenic-green hovel squeezed between two just like it.

He parked and waded through a thin gruel of wet ash to Tomas's door. He knocked. When there was no answer he knocked again. A lined face appeared briefly at the small curtained window to his left. Then the door swung open.

"Turk!" Tomas Ginn had a voice that sounded as if it had been filtered through bedrock, an old man's voice, but firmer than it had been when Turk first encountered him. "Didn't expect to see you. Specially in the middle of all this trouble. Come on in. Place is a fuckin' mess but I can pour you a drink, anyhow."

Turk stepped inside. Tomas's home was little more than a single thin-walled room with a raggedy sofa and table at one end and a miniature kitchen at the other, all dimly lit. The Port Magellan Power Authority hadn't strung any cables out this way. The only electricity came from an array of Sinotec photovoltaics on the roof, and their efficiency had been slashed by the dustfall. The place had a lingering aroma of sulfur and talc, but that was mostly the ash Turk had tracked in with him. Tomas was a fastidious housekeeper, in his own way. A "fuckin' mess," in Tomas's vocabulary, meant there were a couple of empty beer bottles undisposed-of on a narrow counter.

"Sit on down," Tomas said, settling himself on a chair with a dent in the seat that had been worn into a mirror image of his bony ass. Turk selected the least-tattered cushion on his friend's ancient sofa. "Can you believe this shit falling out of the sky? I mean, who asked for *that*? I had to shovel my way out of the house yesterday just to go out and get groceries."

Pretty unbelievable, Turk acknowledged.

"So what brings you here? Something more than neighborliness, I expect, given the weather. If you can call it weather."

"Got a question to ask," Turk said.

"A question or a favor?"

"Well—starts with a question, anyway."

"Serious?"

"It might be."

"So you want a beer? Get the dust out of your throat?"

"Not a bad idea," Turk said.

Turk had met Tomas aboard an ancient single-hulled tanker bound for Breaker Beach on its final voyage.

The ship, called *Kestrel,* had been Turk's ticket to the New World. Turk had signed on as an able-bodied seaman at negligible wages. All the crew had, because it was a one-way trip. Across the Arch, in Equatoria, the market for scrap iron and steel was booming. On Earth a leviathan like the *Kestrel* was a liability, too old to meet international standards and useless for anything but the poorest kind of coastal trade, prohibitively expensive to scrap. But in the New World the same rusty hulk would be a source of valuable raw material, stripped and diced by the acetylene-wielding armies of Thai and Indian laborers who made their living unrestrained by environmental regulations—the professional breakers of Breaker Beach, located some hundred miles north of Port Magellan.

Turk and Tomas had shared a mess on that voyage and learned a few things about each other. Tomas claimed to have been born in Bolivia, but he had been raised, he said, in Biloxi, and had worked the docks in that city and then New Orleans as a boy and young man. He had been at sea off and on for decades, during the tumultuous years of the Spin, when the U.S. government had revived the old Merchant Marine as a gesture toward national security, and afterward, when trade across the Arch created fresh demand for new shipping.

Tomas had joined *Kestrel* for the same reason Turk had signed on: it was a one-way ticket to the promised land. Or what they both liked to imagine was a promised land. Tomas wasn't naïve: he had crossed the Arch five times before, had spent months in Port Magellan, knew the town's vices firsthand, and had seen how cruelly the town could treat newcomers. But it was a freer, more open, more casually polyglot city than any on Earth—a seaman's town, much of it built by expatriate sailors, and it was where he wanted to spend the last years of his life, looking at a landscape on which human hands had only recently been laid. (Turk had signed on for much the same reason, though it would be his first trip cross-Arch. He had wanted to get as far from Texas as it was practical to get, for reasons he didn't care to dwell on.)

The trouble with *Kestrel* was that, because it had no future, it had been poorly maintained and was barely seaworthy. Everyone aboard was aware of that fact, from the Filipino captain down to the illiterate Syrian teenager who stewarded the crew mess. It made for a dangerous transit. Bad weather had scuttled many a vessel bound for Breaker Beach, and more than one rusty keel had gone to rest under the Arch of the Hypotheticals.

But the weather in the Indian Ocean had been reassuringly benign, and because this was Turk's first passage he had risked the derision of his shipmates by arranging to be on deck when the crossing happened. A night crossing of the Arch. He staked out a place aft of the forecastle out of the breeze, made a pillow from a hank of rag stiff with dried paint, stretched out and gazed at the stars. The stars had been scattered by the four billion years of galactic evolution that had transpired while the Earth was enclosed in its Spin membrane, and they remained nameless after thirty years, but they were the only stars Turk had ever known. He had been barely five years old when the Spin ended. His generation had grown up in the post-Spin world, accustomed to the idea that a person could ride an ocean vessel from one planet to another. Unlike some, however, Turk had never been able to make that fact seem prosaic. It was still a wonder to him.

The Arch of the Hypotheticals was a structure vastly larger than anything human engineering could have produced. By the scale of stars and planets, the scale on which the Hypotheticals were assumed to operate, it was a relatively small thing . . . but it was the biggest *made* thing Turk imagined he would ever encounter. He had seen it often enough in photographs, on video, in representative diagrams in schoolbooks, but none of those did justice to the real item.

He had first seen it with his own eyes from the Sumatran port where he joined the *Kestrel*. The Arch's eastern leg had been visible on clear days and especially at sunset, when the last light climbed that pale thread and burnished it to a fine golden line. But now he was almost directly beneath the apex, a different view entirely. The Arch had been compared to a thousand-mile-wide wedding ring dropped into the Indian Ocean, half of it embedded in the bedrock of the planet and the other half projecting above the atmosphere into naked space. From the deck of the *Kestrel* he couldn't see either leg where it entered the sea, but he could see the peak of the Arch reflecting the last light of the sun, a brushstroke of silvery-blue fading to dusky red at its eastern and western extremities. It quivered in the heat of the evening air.

Up close, people said, if you sailed within hailing proximity of either leg, it looked as plain as a pillar of concrete rising from the surface of the sea, except that the enormously wide pillar didn't *stop* rising, simply vanished from sight. But the Arch wasn't an inert object no matter how static it appeared. It was a machine. It communicated with a copy of itself—or the other half of itself, perhaps—set in the compatible ocean of the New World, many light-years distant. Maybe it orbited one of the stars Turk could see from the deck of the *Kestrel:* there was a shivery thought. The Arch might appear to be inanimate, but in fact it was watching the near surface of both worlds, conducting two-way traffic. Because that was what it did: that was its function. If a bird, a storm-tossed tree limb, or an ocean current passed beneath the Arch it would continue on its way unmolested. The waters of Earth and the New World never mingled. But if a manned ocean vessel crossed under the Arch it would be picked up and translated across an unimaginable distance. By all reports the transition was so easy as to be almost anticlimactic, but Turk wanted to experience it out here in the open, not down in crew quarters where he wouldn't even know it had happened until the ship sounded its ritual horn.

He checked his watch. Almost time. He was still waiting when Tomas stepped out of the shadows into the glare of a deck light, grinning at him.

"First time, yeah," Turk said, forestalling the inevitable comment.

"Fuck," Tomas said, "you don't need to explain. I come out every time I pass. Day or night. Like paying respects."

Respects to whom? The Hypotheticals? But Turk didn't ask.

"And, oh my!" Tomas said, aiming his old face at the sky. "Here it comes."

So Turk braced himself—unnecessarily—and watched the stars dim and swirl around the peak of the Arch like watery reflections stirred by the prow of a boat. Then suddenly there was fog all around the *Kestrel,* or a mistiness that reminded him of fog although it had no scent or taste of moisture to it—a transient dizziness, a pressure in his ears. Then the stars came back, but they were different stars, thicker and brighter in what seemed like a blacker sky; and now the air *did* taste and smell subtly different, and a gust of it swirled around the hard steel angles of the topdeck as if to introduce itself, air warm and salt-scented and bracingly fresh. And up on the high bridge of the *Kestrel,* the compass needle must have swung on its pivot, as compasses did at every crossing of the Arch, because the ship's horn sounded one long wail—punishingly loud but sounding almost tentative across an ocean only lately acquainted with human beings.

"The New World," Turk said, thinking, That's it? As easy as that?

"Equatoria," Tomas said, confusing the continent with the planet as most people did. "How's it feel to be a spaceman, Turk?"

But Turk couldn't answer, because two crewmen who had been stealthily pacing the topdeck rounded on Turk with a bucket of saltwater and doused him, laughing. Another rite of passage, a christening for the virgin sailor. He had crossed, at last, the world's strangest meridian. And he had no intention of going back, no real home to go back to.

Tomas had been frail with age when he boarded the Kestrel, and he was injured when the beaching of the vessel went bad.

There were no docks or quays at Breaker Beach. Turk had seen it from the deck rail, his first real look at the coast of Equatoria. The continent loomed out of the horizon like a mirage, pink with morning light, though hardly untouched by human hands. The three decades since the end of the Spin had transformed the western fringe of Equatoria from a wilderness into a chaos of fishing villages, lumber camps, primitive industry, slash-and-burn farmland, hasty roads, a dozen booming towns, and one city through which most of the hinterland's rich resources were channeled. Breaker Beach, almost a hundred nautical miles north of Port Magellan, was possibly the ugliest occupied territory on the coast—Turk could hardly say, but the Filipino cargomaster insisted it was, and the argument was plausible. The broad white beach, protected from the surf by a pebbly headland, was littered with the corpses of broken vessels and smudged with the smoke and ash of a thousand fires. Turk spotted a double-hulled tanker not unlike the *Kestrel,* a score of coastal tankers, even a military vessel stripped of all identifying flags and markings. These were recent arrivals, the work of their deconstruction hardly begun. For many miles more the beach was crowded with steel frames denuded of hull plating, cavernous half-ships in which the acetylene glare of the breakers' torches made a fitful light.

Beyond that lay the scrap-metal huts and forges and toolsheds and machine shops of the breakers, mostly Indian and Malaysian men working out the contracts that had bought them passage under the Arch. Farther on, hazy in the morning air, forested hills unrolled into the blue-gray foothills of the mountains.

He couldn't stay on deck during the beaching. The standard way to deliver a large vessel to Breaker Beach was simply to run it up the littoral and strand it there. The breakers would do the rest, swarming over the ship once the crew had been evacuated. The ship's steel would end up in re-rolling mills downcoast, the ship's miles of wiring and aluminum piping would be extracted and sold in bulk lots, even the ship's bells, Turk had heard, would be marketed to local Buddhist temples. This was Equatoria, and any manmade thing would find a use. It didn't matter that beaching a vessel as enormous as the *Kestrel* could be a violent, destructive process. None of these ships would ever float again.

He went belowdecks when the signal sounded and found Tomas waiting in the crew mess, grinning. Turk had grown fond of Tomas's bony grin—demented-looking but genuine. "End of the road for *Kestrel,*" Tomas said, "and the end of the road for me, too. Every chicken comes home to roost, I guess."

"We're positioned off the beach," Turk said. Soon the captain would start the engines and engage the screws and send the ship dead for shore. The engines would be shut down at the last practical moment and the prow of the ship would gully into the sand while the tide was high. Then the crew would drop rope ladders and scurry down the hull; their kit bags would be lowered; Turk would take his first steps in the grit and wash of Breaker Beach. Within a month *Kestrel* would be little more than a memory and a few thousand tons of recycled iron, steel, and aluminum.

"Every death is a birth," said Tomas, who was old enough to get away with such pronouncements.

"I wouldn't know about that."

"No. You strike me as somebody who knows more than he lets on. End of *Kestrel.* But your first time in the New World. That's a death and a birth right there."

"If you say so, Tomas."

Turk felt the ship's elderly engines begin to throb. The beaching would be violent, inevitably. All the loose gear in the ship had already been stowed or dismounted and sent ashore along with the lifeboats. Half the crew was already ashore. "Whoa," Tomas exclaimed as the vibration came up through the deck plating and the chair legs. "Making some speed now, you bet."

The prow of the ship would be cutting a knife-edge through the water, Turk thought, as it did whenever the vessel began to throb and surge like this. Except they weren't in open water anymore. Their slot on the beach was dead ahead, the continent rising beneath them. The captain was in radio contact with a shore pilot who would call in minor course corrections and tell him when to cut the engines.

Soon, Turk hoped. He liked being at sea, and he didn't mind being belowdecks, but he found he very much disliked being in a windowless room when a deliberately-engineered disaster was only moments away. "You done this before?"

"Well, no," Tomas said, "not from this end. But I was at a wreckers' beach near Goa a few years ago and I watched an old container ship ground itself. Ship not much smaller than this one. Kind of a poetry to it, actually. It rode up the tideline like one of those turtles trying to lay an egg. I mean, I guess you want to brace yourself for it, but it wasn't *violent*." A few minutes later Tomas looked at the watch that hung like a bracelet on his skinny wrist and said, "About time to cut engines."

"You got it timed?"

"I got eyes and ears. I know where we were anchored and I can tell by listening what kind of speed we're making."

This sounded to Turk like one of Tomas's boasts, but it might be true. Turk wiped his palms on the knees of his jeans. He was nervous, but what could go wrong? At this point it was all ballistics.

What *did* go wrong—as he sorted it out afterward—was that at a critical moment *Kestrel*'s bridge lost electrical power, due to some short or component failure in the antique circuitry, so that the captain could neither hear the shore pilot's instructions nor relay his orders to the engine room. *Kestrel* should have come in coasting, but she beached under power instead. Turk was thrown from his chair as the ship ground into the littoral and listed grotesquely to starboard. He was alert enough to see the brushed-steel cutlery locker break loose from the near wall and tumble toward him. The locker was the size of a coffin and about as heavy, and he tried to crawl away from it, but there wasn't time to pull himself out of the way. But here was Tomas, somehow still upright, grabbing for the screeching metal box and managing to snag the corner of it as it slid by, giving Turk enough time to scramble aside. He fetched up against a chair as *Kestrel* stopped moving and the ship's engines finally, mercifully, died. The old tanker's hull gave a ratcheting, prehistoric groan and fell silent. Beached. No harm done . . .

Except to Tomas, who had briefly taken the full weight of the locker and whose left arm had been sliced open below the elbow, deep enough to show bone.

Tomas cradled the injury in his blood-soaked lap, looking startled. Turk applied a handkerchief as a tourniquet and told his friend to stop cursing and keep still while he went for help. It took him ten minutes to find an officer who would listen to him.

The ship's doctor had already gone ashore and the infirmary had been stripped of drugs, so Tomas had to be lowered from the deck in an improvised rope-and-basket litter with only a couple of aspirin to dull the pain. The *Kestrel*'s captain, in the end, refused to admit liability, collected his pay from the breaker boss, and caught a bus for Port Magellan before sunset. So Turk was left to look after Tomas until an off-shift Malay welder could be convinced to summon a genuine doctor. Or what passed for a doctor in this part of the New

World. A woman, the skinny Malay said in broken English. A good doctor, a Western doctor, very kind to the breakers. She was white but had lived for years in a Minang fishing village not far upcoast.

Her name, he said, was Diane.

CHAPTER SIX

Turk told Tomas Ginn about Lise—a little bit about her. How they had connected when they were stranded in the mountains; how he couldn't get her out of his mind even when they were back in civilization, even when she stopped returning his calls; how they got back together during the ashfall.

Tomas listened from his tattered easy chair, sipping beer from a green glass bottle and smiling placidly, as if he had discovered some kind of windless place inside his head. "Sounds like you hardly know this lady."

"I know as much as I need to. Some people, it isn't that hard to tell whether you trust them or not."

"Trust her, do you?"

"Yeah."

Tomas cupped the crotch of his baggy jeans. "This is what you trust. Every inch a sailor."

"It's not like that."

"It never is. But it always is. So why you want to drive up here and tell me about this woman?"

"Actually, I was thinking maybe I could introduce her to you."

"To me? I ain't your daddy, Turk."

"No, and you're not what you used to be, either."

"Don't see what that's got to do with it."

Turk had to tread carefully here. With the utmost delicacy, insofar as he was capable of it. "Well . . . she's curious about Fourths."

"Oh, my Christ." Tomas rolled his eyes. "*Curious?*"

"She's got reasons to be."

"So you want to serve *me* up to her? Exhibit A or whatever?"

"No. What I really want to do is let her talk to Diane. But I want your opinion first."

Diane—the Western doctor, or nurse, as she insisted on calling herself—had hiked to Breaker Beach from some inland village to treat Tomas's slashed arm.

At first Turk was suspicious of her. In Equatoria, especially out here in the backwoods, nobody was checking anybody's medical license. At least that was the impression he got. If you owned a syringe and a bottle of distilled water you could call yourself a doctor, and the breaker bosses would naturally endorse any self-appointed physician who worked for free, regardless of results. So Turk sat with Tomas inside a vacant hut waiting for this woman to arrive, making occasional conversation until the older man fell asleep despite the blood still leaking into his makeshift bandage. The hut was made of some local wood, round barked branches knobbed like bamboo holding up a flat tin roof. It smelled of stale cooking and tobacco and human sweat. It was hot inside, though the screened door admitted an occasional slow sigh of air.

The sun was going down when the doctor finally walked up the plank steps to the platform floor, tugging aside a layer of bug netting.

She wore a tunic and loose pants of a cloth the color

and texture of raw muslin. She wasn't a young woman. Far from it. Her hair was so white it seemed almost transparent. "Who's the patient?" she asked, squinting. "And light a lamp, please—I can hardly see."

"My name's Turk Findley," Turk said.

"Are you the patient?"

"No, I—"

"Show me the patient."

So he turned up the wick of an oil lamp and escorted her through another layer of netting to the yellowed mattress where Tomas slept. Out in the dusk, insect choruses were warming up. They sounded like no insects he had heard before, but you could tell that's what it was, that steely staccato buzzing. From the beach came the sound of hammering, the clatter of sheet metal, the chug and whine of diesel motors.

Tomas snored, oblivious. The doctor—Diane— looked at the bandage on his arm with an expression of contempt. "How did this happen?"

Turk told her how it had happened.

"So he sacrificed himself for you?"

"Sacrificed a chunk of his arm, anyhow."

"You're lucky to have a friend like that."

"Wake him up first. Then tell me whether I'm lucky."

She nudged Tomas's shoulder and Tomas opened his eyes and promptly cursed. Old curses, Creole curses, pungent as gumbo. He tried to sit up, then thought better of it. Finally he fixed his attention on Diane. "And who the fuck might you be?"

"I'm a nurse. Calm down. Who bandaged you?"

"Guy on the ship."

"He did a lousy job. Let me see."

"Well, I guess it was his first time. He—*ow!* Jesus! Turk, is this a real nurse?"

"Don't be an infant," Diane said. "And hold still. I can't help you if I can't see what's wrong." A pause.

"Ah. Well. You're lucky you didn't cut an artery." She took a syringe from her kit and filled it. "Something for the pain before I clean and stitch."

Tomas started to protest, but that was for show. He looked relieved when the needle went in.

Turk backed away and tried to give Diane room to work, not that there was a whole lot of space in this little hut. He wondered what it must be like to make a living as a breaker—to sleep under a tin roof praying you wouldn't be hurt or killed before your contract played out, before you got the payoff they promised you, a year's wages and a bus ticket to the Port. There was an official camp physician, the breaker boss had explained, but he only came in twice a week, usually to fill out forms. Diane did most of the routine cut-and-stitch duty.

Turk watched her as she worked, a silhouette cast by lamplight on the gauzy bug screen. She was skinny and she moved with the calculated caution of the very old. But she was strong, too. She worked methodically and smoothly, occasionally muttering to herself. She might be around Tomas's age, which the sailor variously gave as sixty or seventy—maybe older.

She worked, and from time to time Tomas swore with fierce intent but a certain drugged lethargy. There was a stink of antiseptic, and Turk stepped out into the rising dark. His first night in the New World. In the near distance there was a stand of flowering bushes he couldn't name, six-fingered leaves moving in an offshore breeze. The flowers were blue and smelled like cloves or cinnamon or some other Christmas spice. Farther off, the lights and fires of the industrial beach guttered like lit fuses. And beyond the beach the ocean rolled in faint green phosphorescence, and the alien stars turned grand slow circles.

"There's a potential complication," Diane said when she had finished with Tomas.

She came and sat with Turk on the edge of the wooden platform that held the floor a foot or so above the ground. She had worked hard cleaning and closing Tomas's wound, and she mopped her forehead with a handkerchief. Her accent was American, Turk thought. A shade southern—Maryland, maybe, or those parts.

He asked her what kind of complications those might be.

"With luck, nothing serious. But Equatoria is a completely novel microbial environment—do you understand?"

"I may be dumb, but I'm not ignorant."

She laughed at that. "I apologize, Mr.—?"

"Findley, but call me Turk."

"Your parents named you Turk?"

"No, ma'am. But the family lived in Istanbul for a couple years when I was a kid. I picked up a little Turkish. And a nickname. So what are you saying—Tomas might come down with some local disease?"

"There are no native human beings on this planet, no hominids, no primates, nothing remotely like us. Most local diseases can't touch us. But there are bacteria and fungi that thrive in moist, warm environments, including the human body. Nothing we can't adjust to, Mr. Findley—Turk—and nothing so dangerous or communicable that it could be carried back to Earth. But it's still not a good idea to arrive in the New World with a challenged immune system or, in Mr. Ginn's case, an open wound bandaged by an idiot."

"Can't you give him some kind of antibiotic?"

"I did. But the local microorganisms don't necessarily respond to standard pharmaceuticals. Don't misunderstand. He's not ill, and in all likelihood he won't become ill, but there's a certain unavoidable risk. Are you a close friend of Mr. Ginn?"

"Not exactly. But like I said, he was trying to help me out when he got hurt."

"I'd prefer to keep him here a few days, under my observation. Is that all right?"

"Fine by me, but you might have to go some to convince Tomas. I'm not his keeper."

"Where are you headed, if you don't mind me asking?"

"Downcoast to the city."

"Any particular address? A number where I can reach you?"

"No, ma'am. I'm new here. But you can tell Tomas I'll look for him at the union hall when he makes it down to Port Magellan."

She seemed disappointed. "I see."

"Or maybe I can call you."

She turned and gazed at him for a long moment. Scrutinized him, actually. Turk started to feel a little awkward under that relentless stare. Then she said, "Okay. Let me give you a number."

She found a pencil in her kit bag and scribbled the number on the back of a Coast & Urban Coach Lines ticket stub.

"**S**he was evaluating you," Tomas said.

"I know that."

"Good instincts, that woman."

"Yeah. That's the point," Turk said.

So Turk found a place to live in the Port and lived on his savings for a while and dropped by the Seaman's Union every now and then to look for Tomas. But Tomas never showed. Which, at first, didn't worry him much. Tomas could be anywhere. Tomas could have taken it into his head to cross the mountains, for all he knew. So Turk would have dinner or a drink and forget about his messmate; but when a month had passed he dug out the ticket stub and keyed the number scribbled on it.

What he got was an automated message that the number had been discontinued.

Which piqued his curiosity as well as his sense of obligation. His money was running out and he was getting ready to sign up for pipeline work, but he caught a ride upcoast and hiked a couple of miles to the breaker compound and started asking questions. One of the breaker bosses remembered Turk's face and told him his friend had got sick, and that was too bad, but they couldn't let a sick sailor take up time and attention, so *Ibu* Diane and some Minang fishermen had hauled the old man back to their village.

Turk bought dinner at a tin-roofed Chinese restaurant at the crossroads, then hitched a ride farther upcoast, to a horseshoe bay turning gaudy colors under the long Equatorian dusk. The driver, a salesman for some West African import firm, pointed Turk at an unpaved road and a sign marked in a curvilinear language Turk couldn't read. Minang village down that way, he said. Turk walked a couple of miles through the forest, and just as the stars were turning bright and the insects bothersome he found himself between a row of wooden houses with buffalo-horn eaves and a lantern-lit general store where men in box caps sat at cable-spool tables drinking coffee. He put on his best smile and asked a local for directions to Doctor Diane's clinic.

The pedestrian smiled back and nodded and called out to the coffee house. Two muscular young men hurried out and positioned themselves on each side of Turk. "We'll take you there," they said in English when Turk repeated his request—and they smiled, too, but Turk had the uneasy feeling he'd been politely but firmly taken into custody.

"I guess I was pretty fucked-up when you finally saw me," Tomas said.

"You don't remember?"

"Not much of it, no."

"Yeah," Turk said. "You were pretty fucked-up."

Pretty fucked-up, which in this case meant Tomas was bedridden, emaciated, gasping for breath in the back room of the big wooden building Diane called her "clinic." Turk had looked at his friend with something approaching horror.

"Jesus Christ, what happened to him?"

"Calm down," *Ibu* Diane said. *Ibu* was what the villagers called her. He gathered it was some kind of honorific.

"Is he dying?"

"No. Appearances to the contrary, he's getting well."

"All this from a cut on his arm?"

Tomas looked as if someone had stuck a hose down his throat and siphoned out his insides. Turk thought he had never seen a thinner man.

"It's more complicated than that. Sit down and I'll explain."

Outside the window of Diane's clinic, the Minang village was lively in the dark. Lanterns hung swaying from eaves and he could hear the sound of recorded music playing tinnily. Diane made coffee with an electric kettle and a French press, and the resulting brew was hot and dense.

There used to be two real doctors at the clinic, she said. Her husband and a Minang woman, both of whom had lately died of natural causes. Only Diane was left,

and the only medicine she knew was what she had
learned while acting as a nurse. Enough to keep the
clinic going: it was an indispensable resource not only
for this village but for a half-dozen nearby villages and
for the impoverished breakers. Any condition she
couldn't treat she referred to the Red Crescent clinic up
the coast or the Catholic charity hospital in Port Magellan, though that was a long trip. In matters of cuts,
cleanly broken bones, and common disorders, she was
perfectly competent. She consulted regularly with a
traveling physician from the Port who understood her
situation and made sure she was supplied with basic
medicines, sterile bandages, and so forth.

"So maybe you should have sent Tomas downcoast,"
Turk said. "He looks seriously ill to me."

"The cut on his arm was the least of his problems.
Did Tomas tell you he had cancer?"

"Jesus, no. Cancer? Does he?"

"We brought him back here because his wound was
infected, but the cancer showed up in simple blood tests.
I don't have much in the way of diagnostic equipment,
but I do have a portable imager—ten years old but it
works like a charm. It confirmed the diagnosis, and the
prognosis was very grave. Cancer is hardly an untreat-
able disease, but your friend had been avoiding doctors
for far too long. He was deeply metastasized."

"So he *is* dying."

"No." Diane paused. Once again she riveted him
with that stare, fierce and a little uncanny. Turk made an
effort not to avert his own eyes. It was like playing
stare-down with a cat. "I offered him an unconventional
treatment."

"Like what, radiation or something?"

"I offered to make him a Fourth."

For a moment he was too startled to speak. Outside,
the music played on, something tunelessly alien beaten

out of a wooden xylophone and funneled through a cheap loudspeaker.

He said, "You can do that?"

"I can. I have."

Turk wondered what he had gotten himself into and how he could most efficiently extract himself from it. "Well . . . I guess it's not illegal here . . ."

"You guess wrong. It's just easier to get away with. And we have to be discreet. An extra few decades of life isn't something you advertise, Turk."

"So why tell me?"

"Because Tomas is going to need some help as he recovers. And because I think I can trust you."

"How could you possibly know that?"

"Because you came here looking for him." She startled him by smiling. "Call it an educated guess. You understand that the Fourth treatment isn't just about longevity? The Martians were deeply ambivalent about tinkering with human biology. They didn't want to create a community of powerful elders. The Fourth treatment gives and it takes away. It gives you an extra thirty or forty years of life—and I'm a case in point, if you haven't guessed—but it also rearranges certain human traits."

"Traits," Turk said, dry-mouthed. He had never, to his knowledge, spoken to a Fourth before. And that was what this woman claimed to be. How old *was* she? Ninety years? One hundred?

"Am I so frightening?"

"No, ma'am, not at all, but—"

"Not even a little?" Still smiling.

"Well, I—"

"What I mean to say, Turk, is that as a Fourth I'm more sensitive to certain social and behavioral cues than the majority of unmodified people. I can generally tell when someone's lying or being disingenuous, at least when we're face-to-face. Although, against *sincere* lies I have no defense. I'm not omniscient, I'm not especially wise, and I can't read minds. The most you might say is that my bullshit detector has been turned up a notch or two. And since any group of Fourths is necessarily under siege— from the police or from criminals, or both—that's a useful faculty to have. No, I don't know you well enough to say I trust you, but I *perceive* you clearly enough to say that I'm *willing* to trust you . . . do you understand?"

"I suppose so. I mean, I don't have anything against Fourths. Never thought much about it either way."

"That comfortable innocence is over. Your friend won't die of cancer, but he can't stay here, and he has a lot of adjustments to make. What I would like to do is discharge him into your care."

"Ma'am—uh, Diane—I don't know the first thing about taking care of a sick man, much less a Fourth."

"He won't be sick for long. But he'll need an understanding friend. Will you be that person for him?"

"Well, I mean, you know, I'm willing, I suppose, but it might be better to make some other arrangement, because I'm in a difficult position, financially and all—"

"I wouldn't have asked you if I could think of anything better. It was a blessing that you showed up when you did." She added, "If I hadn't wanted you to find me I would have been much more difficult to find."

"I tried calling, but—"

"I had to discontinue that number." She frowned but didn't offer to explain.

"Well—" Well, fuck, he thought. "I guess I wouldn't turn out a stray dog in a rainstorm."

Her smile returned. "That's what I thought."

"I guess you learned a few things about Fourths since then," Tomas said.

"I don't know," Turk said. "You're the only close sample I've got. Not too inspiring, actually."

"Did she actually say that, about a bullshit detector?"

"More or less. What do you think, Tomas, is it true?"

Tomas had recovered from his illness—from the genetic rebuild that constituted the Fourth treatment—as quickly as Diane had predicted. His psychological adjustment was another matter. He was a man who had come to Equatoria prepared to die, and instead he had found himself staring down another three or more decades for which he had no plan or ambition.

Physically, though, it had been a liberation. After a week of recovery Tomas could have passed for a man much younger. His crabbed way of walking became more supple, his appetite was suddenly bottomless. This was almost too strange for Turk to deal with, as if Tomas had shed his old body the way a snake sheds its skin. "Fuck, it's just me," Tomas would proclaim whenever Turk became too uncomfortably conscious of the distance between the old Tomas and the new. Tomas clearly relished his newfound health. The only drawback, he said, was that the treatment had erased his tattoos. Half his history had been written in those tattoos, he said.

"Is it true that I have an improved bullshit detector? Well, that's in the eye of the beholder. It's been ten years, Turk. What do you think?"

"We never talked much about this."

"I would of been happy to keep it that way."

"Can you tell when you're being lied to?"

"There's no drug that'll make a stupid man smart. And I'm not a particularly smart man. I'm no lie detector, either. But I can generally tell when somebody's trying to sell me something."

"Because I think Lise has been lied to. Her business with Fourths is legitimate, but I think she's being used. Also she has some information Diane might like to hear."

Tomas was silent for a while. He tipped up his beer to drain it and put the bottle on a tray table next to his chair. He gave Turk a look uneasily reminiscent of Diane's evaluative stare.

"You're in some difficult territory here," he said.

"I know that," Turk said.

"Could get dangerous."

"I guess that's what I'm afraid of."

"Can you give me some time to think this over?"

"Guess so," Turk said.

"Okay. I'll ask around. Call me in a couple of days."

"I appreciate it," Turk said. "Thank you."

"Don't thank me yet," Tomas said. "Maybe I'll change my mind."

CHAPTER SEVEN

The node in Lise's car announced new mail as she was driving to the Consulate. "From?" Lise asked.

"Susan Adams," the node replied.

These days Lise could not think of her mother without visualizing that calendar-box of pharmaceuticals on her kitchen counter, assorted by day and hour, the clockwork of her mortality. Pills for depression, pills to adjust her blood cholesterol, pills to avert the Alzheimer's for which she carried a suspect gene. "Read," she said, grimly.

Dear Lise. The node's voice was male, indifferent, offering up the text with all the liveliness of a frozen fish. *Thank you for your latest. It is somewhat reassuring after what I've seen on the news.*

The ashfall, she meant, which still clogged the side streets and had caused thousands of tourists to flee to their cruise ships, begging for a quick ride home. People who had come to Equatoria hoping to find a landscape pleasingly strange, but who had stumbled into something altogether different—*real* strangeness, the kind that didn't negotiate with human preconceptions.

Precisely how her mother would have reacted, Lise thought.

All I can think of is how far away you are and how inaccessible you have made yourself. No, I won't start that old argument again. And I won't say a word about your separation from Brian.

Susan Adams had argued fiercely against the divorce—ironically, since she had argued almost as fiercely against the marriage. At first, Lise's mother had disliked Brian because he worked for Genomic Security— Genomic Security, in Susan Adams' mind, being represented by the terse and unhelpful men who had hovered around her after her husband's incomprehensible disappearance. Lise must not marry one of these compassionless monsters, she had insisted; but Brian was not compassionless, in fact Brian had charmed Lise's mother, had patiently dismantled her objections until he became a welcome presence. Brian had quickly learned the paramount rule in dealing with Lise's mother, that one did not mention the New World, the Hypotheticals, the Spin, or the disappearance of Robert Adams. In Susan Adams' household these subjects had acquired the power of profanity. Which was one reason Lise had been so anxious to leave that household behind.

And there had been much anxiety and resistance after the wedding, when Brian was transferred to Port Magellan. *You must not go,* Lise's mother had said, as if the New World were some ghostly otherness from which no one emerged undamaged. No, not even for the sake of Brian's career should they enter that perdition.

This was, of course, an ongoing act of denial, a forcible exile of unacceptable truths, a strategy her mother had devised for containing and channeling her unvented grief. But that was precisely why Lise resented it. Lise hated the dark space into which her mother had walled these memories. Memory was all that was left of Lise's father, and that memory surely included his wide-eyed fascination with the Hypotheticals and his love of the planet into which they had opened their perplexing doorway.

Even the ashfall would have fascinated him, Lise thought: those cogs and seashells embedded in the dust, pieces in a grand puzzle . . .

I simply hope that these events convince you of the wisdom of coming home. Lise, if money is a problem, let me book you a ticket. I admit that California is not what it once was, but we can still see the ocean from the kitchen window, and although the summers are warm and the winter storms more intense than I remember them being, surely that's a small thing compared to what you are presently enduring.

You don't know, Lise thought, what I'm enduring. You don't care to know.

In the afternoon sunlight the American Consulate looked like a benevolent fortress set behind a moat of wrought-iron fences. Someone had planted a garden along the runnels of the fence, but the recent ashfall hadn't been kind to the flowers—native flowers, because you weren't supposed to bring terrestrial plants over the Arch, not that the ban was especially effective. The flowers that had survived the ashfall were sturdy red whore's-lips (in the crude taxonomy of the first settlers), stems like enamelled chopsticks and leaves like Victorian collars enfolding the tattered blooms.

There was a guard at the consulate door next to a sign that advised visitors to check all weapons, personal electronics, and unsealed bottles or containers. This was not a new drill for Lise, who had regularly visited Brian at the Genomic Security offices before the divorce. And she remembered riding past the consulate as a teenager during her father's time here; remembered how reassuring and strong the building had seemed with its high white walls and narrow embrasures.

The guard called Brian's office for confirmation and issued her a visitor's badge. She rode the elevator to the fifth floor, mid-building, a tiled windowless hallway, the labyrinth of bureaucracy.

Brian stepped into the corridor as she approached and held open the door marked simply 507 DGS. Brian, she thought, was somehow changeless: carefully dressed, still trim in his mid-thirties, tanned; he took weekend hikes in the hills above the Port. He smiled briefly as a way of greeting her, but his demeanor today was stiff—sort of a whole-body frown, Lise thought. She braced herself for whatever was coming. Brian bossed a staff of three people but none of them was present. "Come on in," he said, "sit down, we have to have a little discussion. I'm sorry, but we'll get this out of the way as quickly as possible."

Even at this juncture he was unfailingly nice, the quality she had found most frustrating in him. The marriage had been bad from the beginning. Not a disaster so much as a bad choice compounded by more bad choices, some of which she was reluctant to admit even to herself. Worse because she couldn't confess her unhappiness in any way Brian was liable to understand. Brian went to church every Sunday, Brian believed in decency and propriety, and Brian despised the complexity and weirdness of the post-Spin world. And that, ultimately, was what Lise could not abide. She had had enough of that from her mother. She wanted, instead, the quality her father had tried so hard to communicate to her on those nights when they looked at the stars: awe, or, failing that, at least courage.

Brian had occasional charm, he had earnestness, he had, buried in him, a deep and poignant seriousness of purpose. But he was afraid of what the world had become, and that, in the end, she could not abide.

She sat down. He pulled a second chair across the carpet and sat facing her knee-to-knee. "This might not be the pleasantest conversation we ever had," he said. "But we're having it for your sake, Lise. Please try to remember that."

Turk arrived at the airport that afternoon still pondering his talk with Tomas and intending to inspect his aircraft before he went home for the night. Turk's little Skyrex twin-engine fixed-wing prop plane was nearly five years old and needed repairs and maintenance more often than it used to. It had lately been fitted with a new fuel injector, and Turk wanted to see for himself what the mechanics had done. So he parked in his usual space behind the cargo building and crossed a patch of tarmac turned woolen-gray by ash and rain, but when he reached the hangar he found the door padlocked. Tucked behind the latch was a note advising him to see Mike Arundji.

Not much question what this was about. Turk owed two months' rent on his hangar space and was in arrears for maintenance.

But he was friendly with Mike Arundji—most of the time, anyhow—and he walked into the owner's office rehearsing his usual excuses. It was a ritual dance: the demand, the apology, the token payment (though even that was going to be tight), another reprieve . . . although the padlock was a new touch.

This time the older man looked up from his desk with an expression of deep regret. "The lock," he said immediately, "yeah, I'm sorry about that, but I don't have a choice here. I have to run my business like a business."

"It's the ash," Turk said. "I lost a couple of charters to it. Otherwise you'd be paid by now."

"So you say, and I'm not disputing it. But what difference would a couple of charters make, long-term? You have to ask yourself. This isn't the only small airport in the district. I've got competition. In the old days it was okay to be a little loose, cut everybody some slack. It was all semi-amateurs, independents like you. Now there are corporate charter companies bidding up hangar space. Even if the books balanced I'd be taking a loss on you. That's just a fact."

"I can't make money if I can't fly my plane, Mike."

"The trouble is, I can't make money whether you fly it or not."

"Seems like you do okay."

"I have a payroll to meet. I have a whole new raft of regulations coming down from the Provisional Government. If you looked at my spreadsheets you wouldn't tell me I'm doing okay. My accountant doesn't come in here and tell me I'm doing okay."

And you probably don't call your accountant an amateur, Turk thought. Mike Arundji was an old hand: he had opened up this strip when there was nothing south of Port Magellan but fishing villages and squatters' camps. Even a half-dozen years ago the word "spreadsheet" would have been foreign to his vocabulary.

That was the kind of environment in which Turk had arranged for the import—at eye-bulging expense—of his six-seater Skyrex. And it had made him a modest little living, at least until recently. He no longer owed money on it. Unfortunately, he seemed to owe money on everything else. "So what do I have to do to get my plane back in the air?"

Arundji shifted in his chair and wouldn't meet Turk's eye. "Come in tomorrow, we'll talk about it. Worse comes to worst, it wouldn't be hard to find a buyer."

"Find—what?"

"A buyer. A *buyer,* you know! People are interested. Sell the plane, pay your debts, start fresh. People do that. It happens all the time."

Turk said, "Not to me."

"Calm down. We don't necessarily have conflicting interests here. I can help you get a premium price. I mean, *if it comes to that.* And shit, Turk, you're the one who's always talking about hiring onto a research boat and sailing somewhere. Maybe this is the time. Who knows?"

"Your confidence is inspiring."

"Think about it, is what I'm saying. Talk to me in the morning."

"I can pay what I owe you."

"Can you? Okay. No problem. Bring me a certified check and we'll forget about it."

To which Turk had no answer.

"Go home," Arundji said. "You look tired, buddy."

"First," Brian said, "I know you were with Turk Findley."

"What the hell?" Lise said promptly.

"Hold on, let me finish—"

"What, you had somebody *follow* me?"

"I couldn't do that if I wanted to, Lise."

"What, then?"

Brian took a breath. His pursed lips and narrowed eyes were meant to announce that he found this as unpleasant as she did. "Lise, there are other people at work here."

She made an effort to control her own breathing. She was already angry. And in a way the anger was not unwelcome. It beat feeling guilty, the mood in which her encounters usually left her. "What people?"

"Let me just remind you of the larger issues," he said. "Bear with me. It's easy to forget what's at stake. The nature and definition of the human genome, of what we are as a people, all of us. That's been put at risk by everything from the cloning trade to these Martian longevity cults, and there are people in every government in the world who spend a lot of time thinking about that."

His credo, the same justification, Lise recalled, that he had once offered to her mother. "What does that have to do with me?" Or Turk, for that matter.

"You came to me with an old snapshot taken at one of your dad's faculty parties, so I ran it through the database—"

"You *offered* to run it through the database."

"I offered, okay, and we pulled an image from the dockland security cameras. But when you run a check like that, the query gets bumped around a little bit. And I guess something rang a bell somewhere. Within the last week we've had people from Washington show up here—"

"What do you mean, DGS people?"

"DGS people, right, but very senior, people working out of levels of the department light-years above what we do here. People who are deeply interested in finding the woman in the picture. People interested enough to sail out of Djakarta and knock on my door."

Lise sat back in her chair and tried to absorb all this.

After a long moment she said, "My mother showed the same snapshot to DGS back when my father disappeared. Nobody made a fuss about it then."

"That was a decade ago. Other information has turned up since. The same face in a different context. More than that I can't say."

"I'd like to talk to these people. If they know anything about Sulean Moi—"

"Nothing that would help you find out what happened to your father."

"How can you be sure of that?"

"Try to put it in perspective, Lise. These people are doing an important job. They mean business. I went out of my way to convince these guys *not* to talk to you."

"But you gave them my name?"

"I told them everything I know about you, because

otherwise they might think you're involved in—well, what they're investigating. Which would be a waste of their time and a hardship for you. Honestly, Lise. You have to keep a low profile on this one."

"They're watching me. Is that what you're trying to say? They're watching me and they know I was with Turk."

He winced at the name, but nodded. "They know those things. Yes."

"Jesus, Brian!"

He raised his hands in a gesture that looked like surrender. "All I'm saying is, when I stand back from all this—from what our relationship is and what I would like it to be—when I ask myself what would really be best for you—my advice is to let this go. Stop asking questions. Maybe even think about heading back home, back to California."

"I don't want to go home."

"Think about it, is all I'm saying. There's only so much I can do to protect you."

"I never asked you to protect me."

"Maybe we can talk about this again when you've given it some consideration."

She stood up. "Or maybe not."

"And maybe we can talk about Turk Findley and what's going on in that department."

In that department. Poor Brian, unfailingly prim, even when he was rebuking her.

She thought about defending herself. She could say, *We were having dinner when the ash fell.* She could say, *Of course he came home with me, what was he supposed to do, sleep in his car?* She could lie and say, *We're just friends.* Or she could say, *I went to bed with him because he's unafraid and unpredictable and his fingernails aren't impeccably clean and he doesn't work for the fucking DGS.*

She was angry, humiliated, not a little guilt-stricken. "It's not your business anymore. You need to figure that out, Brian."

And turned, and left.

Turk went home to fix himself dinner, some shiftless meal appropriate to his mood. He lived in a two-room bungalow set among similar cabins on a barely-paved road near Arundji's airfield, on a bluff overlooking the sea. Maybe someday this would be expensive real estate. Currently it was off-grid. The toilet fed a cesspool and his electricity came from sunlight and a generator in a back shed. Every summer he repaired his shingles, and every winter they leaked from a new angle.

The sun was setting over the foothills west of him, and to the east the sea had turned an inky shade of blue. A few fishing boats straggled toward the harbor to the north. The air was cool and there was a breeze to carry off the remnant stink of the ash.

The ash had settled in windrows around the foundations of the cabin, but the roof seemed to have borne up under the strain. His shelter was intact. There wasn't much food in the kitchen cupboards, however. Less than he remembered. It was canned beans or go out for groceries. Or spend money he didn't have in some restaurant he couldn't afford.

Lost my plane, he thought. But no, not really, not yet; the plane was only embargoed, not yet sold. But there was nothing in his bank account to offer a convincing counter-argument. So that little mantra had been running through his head since he left Mike Arundji's office: *Lost my plane.*

He wanted to talk to Lise. But he didn't want to dump his problems on her. It still seemed unlikely that he had hooked up with her at all. His relationship with Lise was something fortune had dropped in his lap. Fortune had done him few favors in the past, and he wasn't sure he trusted it.

Cornmeal, coffee, beer . . .

He decided to give Tomas another call. Maybe he hadn't explained too well what it was he wanted. There was only one real favor he could do Lise, and that was to help her understand why her father had gone Fourth—which Turk assumed was what had happened. And if anyone could explain that to her or put it in a sane perspective it might be Tomas and, if Tomas would put in a word for him, *Ibu* Diane, the Fourth nurse who lived with the Minang upcoast.

He ticked Tomas's number into his phone.

But there was no answer, nor was the call dumped to voice mail. Which was odd because Tomas carried his phone everywhere. It was probably his most valuable possession.

Turk thought about what to do next. He could go over his accounts and try to rig up some accommodation with Mike Arundji. Or he could drive back into town, maybe see Lise, if she wasn't sick of him—maybe check up on Tomas on the way. The sensible thing, he guessed, would be to stay home and take care of business.

If he had any real business to take care of.

He turned off the lights as he left.

Lise drove away from the consulate feeling scalded. That was the word precisely. Scalded, dipped in hot water, burned raw. She drove aimlessly for more than an hour until the car registered the sunset and switched on its lights. The sky had gone red, one of those long Equatorian sunsets, made gaudier by the fine ash still lingering in the air. She drove through the Arab district, past souks and coffee shops under piebald awnings and strings of colored lights, the crowds dense this evening, making up for time lost during the ashfall; then up into the foothills, the pricey neighborhoods where wealthy men and women from Beijing or Tokyo or London or New York built faux-Mediterranean palaces in pastel shades. Belatedly, she realized she was driving down the street where she had lived with her parents during her four adolescent years in this city.

And here was the house where she had lived when her family was still whole. She slowed the car as she passed. The house was smaller than she remembered and noticeably smaller than the would-be palaces that had grown up around it, a cloth coat among minks. She dreaded to think what it must rent for nowadays. The white-painted veranda was drenched in evening shadow, and had been furnished by strangers.

"This is where we'll be living for the next little while," her mother had told her when they moved here from California. But to Lise it was never "my house," even when she was talking to friends at the American school. It was "where we're staying," her mother's preferred formulation. At thirteen Lise had been a little frightened of the foreign places she had seen on television, and Port Magellan was all those foreign places jumbled together in a single overbrimming gumbo. At least at first, she had longed for lost California.

Now she longed for—what?

Truth. Memory. The extraction of truth from memory.

The roof of the house was dark with ash. Lise could not help picturing herself on the veranda in the old days, sitting with her father. She wished she could sit there with him now, not to discuss Brian or her problems but to speculate about the ashfall, to talk about what Robert Adams had liked to call (inevitably smiling as he said it) the *Very Large Subjects*, the mysteries that lay beyond the boundary of the respectable world.

It was dark when she finally got home. The apartment was still in disarray, the dishes unwashed in the sink, the bed unmade, a little of Turk's aura still lingering. She poured herself a glass of red wine and tried to think coherently about what Brian had said. About powerful people and their interest in the woman who had (perhaps, in some way) seduced her father away from home.

Was Brian right when he said she should leave? Was there really anything meaningful left to extract from the shards of her father's life?

Or maybe she was closer than she realized to some fundamental truth, and maybe that was why she was in trouble.

Turk guessed there was something wrong when Tomas failed to answer the second and third calls he placed from the car. Tomas might have been drinking—he still drank, though rarely to excess—but even drunk, Tomas usually answered his phone.

So Turk approached the old man's trailer with some apprehension, snaking his car through the dust-choked alleys of the Flats at a cautious speed. Tomas was a Fourth, hence fairly hearty, but not immortal. Even Fourths grew old. Even Fourths died. Tomas might be sick. Or he might be in some other kind of trouble. There was often trouble in the Flats. A couple of Filipino gangs operated out of the area, and there were drug houses scattered through the neighborhood. Unpleasant things happened from time to time.

He parked his car by a noisy bodega and walked the last few yards to the corner of Tomas's muddy little street. It was only just dark and there were plenty of people around, canned music yammering from every other doorway. But Tomas's trailer was dark, the windows unlit. Could be the old man was asleep. But no. The door was unlocked and ajar.

Turk knocked before he stepped inside, even though

he had a sour certainty that the gesture was pointless. No answer.

He reached to his left, switched on the overhead light and blinked. The room had been trashed. The table next to Tomas's chair was lying legs-up, the lamp in pieces on the floor. The air still smelled of stale masculine sweat. He made a cursory check of the back bedroom, but it was likewise empty.

After a moment's thought, he left Tomas's small home and knocked at the door of the trailer next door. An obese woman in a gray shift answered: a Mrs. Goudy, lately widowed. Tomas had introduced her to Turk once or twice, and Mrs. Goudy had been known to share a drink with the old man. No, Mrs. Goudy hadn't heard from Tomas lately, but she had noticed a white van parked outside his trailer a little while ago . . . was anything wrong?

"I hope not. When exactly did you see this van, Mrs. Goudy?"

"Hour ago, maybe two."

"Thank you, Mrs. Goudy. I wouldn't worry about it. Best to keep your door locked, though."

"Don't I know it," Mrs. Goudy said.

He went back to Tomas's place and closed the door, making sure it was secure this time. A wind had come up, and it rattled the makeshift streetlight where Tomas's short walkway met the road. Shadows swayed fitfully.

He took his phone out of his pocket and called Lise, praying she would answer.

Back at the apartment, Lise had her home node read aloud the remainder of her mother's letter. The home unit, at least, had a female voice, slightly if unconvincingly modulated.

Please don't misunderstand, Lise. I'm just worried about you in the usual motherly way. I can't help thinking of you alone in that city—

Alone. Yes. Trust her mother to strike at her vulnerable place. Alone—because it was so hard to make anyone else understand what she wanted here and why it was so important to her.

—putting yourself in danger—

A danger that seemed so much more real when you were, as she said, *alone . . .*

—when you could be here at home, safe, or even with Brian, who—

Who would show the same puzzled condescension that radiated from her mother's message.

—would surely agree—

No doubt.

—that there's no use digging up the dead past.

But what if the past wasn't dead? What if she simply lacked the courage or callousness to put the past behind her, had no choice but to pursue it until it yielded its last dividend of pain or satisfaction?

"Pause," she said to the media node. She couldn't take too much of this at one time. Not with everything else that was happening. Not when an alien dust had dropped out of the sky. Not when she was being tracked and possibly bugged by DGS, for reasons not even Brian would explain. Not when she was, yes, thanks Mom for that little reminder, *alone*.

She checked her other text messages.

They were junk, except for one, which turned out to be gold. It was a note and an attachment sent by one Scott Cleland, whom she had been trying to contact for months. Scott Cleland was the only one of her father's old university associates she hadn't yet succeeded in talking to. He was an astronomer, working with the Geophysical Survey at the observatory on Mt. Mahdi. She had just about given up on him. But here at last was a response to her mail, and a friendly one: the node read it to her, adopting a male voice to suit the given name.

Dear Lise Adams: I'm sorry to have been so slow in responding to your queries. The reason for this is not just procrastination. It took a little searching to find the attached document, which may interest you.

I wasn't close to Dr. Adams but we respected each other's work. As for the details of his life at that time, and the other questions you asked, I'm afraid I can't help you. Our connection was purely professional.

At the time of his disappearance, however, and as you probably know, he had begun work on a book to be called *Planet as Artifact*. He asked me to read the brief introduction he had written, which I did, but I found no errors and could suggest no significant improvements (apart from a catchier title).

In case there was no copy of this among his papers, I enclose the one he sent me.

Robert Adams' disappearance was a great loss to all of us at the university. He often spoke affectionately about his family, and I hope your research brings you some comfort.

Lise had the household node print the document. Contrary to what Cleland suspected, her father had not left a copy of the introduction with his papers. Or, if he had, Lise's mother had shredded it. Susan Adams had shredded or discarded all of her husband's papers and had donated his books to the university. Part of what Lise had come to think of as the Ritual Cleansing of the Adams Household.

She turned off her phone and poured a glass of wine and took the wine and the six pages of printed text out to the balcony. The night was warm, she had swept away the ash this morning, and the indoor lamps cast enough light to read by.

After a few minutes she went back inside to fetch a pen, came out again and began to underline certain phrases. She underlined them not because they were new to her but because they were familiar.

Many things changed during the interval we call the Spin, but perhaps the most far-reaching change is also the most overlooked. The Earth was held in stasis for more than four billion years, which means we now live in a universe vastly more ancient—and more complexly evolved—than the one to which we were accustomed.

Familiar because, in more polished prose, these were the things he had often said to her when they sat on the veranda and looked out at the darkness and the stars.

Any real understanding of the nature of the Hypotheticals must take this into account. They were ancient when we first encountered them, and they are more ancient now. Since they cannot be observed directly, we must make our deductions about them based on their work in the universe, by the clues they leave behind them, by their vast and abiding footprints.

Here was the excitement she learned from him at an early age, an outward-looking curiosity that contrasted with her mother's habitual caution and timidity. She could hear his voice in the words.

Of their works, one of the most immediately obvious is the Indian Ocean Arch that links the Earth to the New World—and the Arch that connects the New World to another less hospitable planet, and so on, as far as we have been able to explore: a chain of increasingly hostile environments made available to us for reasons we do not yet understand.

Sail to the other side of this world, he had told Lise, and you'll find a second Arch, and beyond it a rocky, stormy planet with barely breathable air; and beyond that—a journey that had to be undertaken on ocean vessels sealed and pressurized as if they were spaceships— a third world, its atmosphere poisoned with methane, the oceans oily and acidic.

But the Arch is not the only artifact at hand. The planet "next door to Earth," from which I write these words, is also an artifact. There is evidence that it was constructed or at least modified over the course of many millions of years with the objective of making it a congenial environment for human beings.

Planet as artifact.

Many have speculated about the purpose of this eons-long work. Is the New World a gift or is it a trap? Have we entered a maze, as laboratory mice, or have we been offered a new and splendid destiny? Does the fact that our own Earth is still protected from the deadly radiation of its expanded sun mean that the Hypotheticals take an interest in our survival as a species, and if so, why?

I cannot claim to have answered any of these questions, but I mean to give the reader an overview of the work that has already been done and of the thoughts and speculations of the men and women who are devoting their professional lives to that work. . . .

And, later in the piece, this:

We are in the position of a coma patient waking from a sleep as long as the lifetime of a star. What we cannot remember, we must rediscover.

She underlined that twice. She wished she could text it to her mother, wished she could write it on a banner and wave it in Brian's face. This was all she had ever meant to say to them: an answer to their genteel silences, to the almost surgical elision of Robert Adams from the lives of his survivors, to the gently troubled poor-Lise expressions they wore on their faces whenever she insisted on mentioning her vanished father. It was as if Robert Adams himself had stepped out of obscurity to whisper a reassuring word. *What we cannot remember, we must rediscover.*

She had put the pages aside and was heading for bed when she checked her phone one last time.

Three messages were stacked there, all tagged urgent, all from Turk. A fourth came in while the phone was still in her hand.

PART TWO

THE
OCULAR
ROSE

CHAPTER EIGHT

After the fall of the luminous dust—after the skies had cleared and the courtyard had been swept and the desert or the wind had absorbed what was left behind—news of another mystery came to the compound where the boy Isaac lived.

The ash had been terrifying when it fell and had been a topic for endless talk and speculation when it stopped. The newer mystery arrived more prosaically, as a news report relayed from the city across the mountains. It was less immediately frightening, but it touched uneasily on one of Isaac's secrets.

He had overheard two of the adults, Mr. Nowotny and Mr. Fisk, discussing it in the corridor outside the dining hall. Commercial flights to the oil wastes of the Rub al-Khali had been canceled or re-routed for days even before the ashfall, and now the Provisional Government and the oil powers had issued an explanation: there had been an earthquake.

This was a mystery, Mr. Nowotny went on to say, because there were no known faults beneath that part of the Rub al-Khali: it was a geologically stable desert craton that had persisted unchanged for millions of years. There should never have been even a minor tremor so deep in the Rub al-Khali.

But what had happened was more than a tremor. Oil production had been shut down for more than a week, and the wells and pipelines had been expensively damaged.

"We know less about this planet than we thought we did," Mr. Nowotny said.

It was slightly less mysterious to Isaac. He knew, though he could not say how, that something was stirring under the sedate sands of the deep western desert. He felt it in his mind, his body. Something was stirring, and it spoke in cadences he didn't understand, and he could point to it with his eyes closed even though it was hundreds of miles away, still only half-waking from a slumber as long as the lives of mountains.

For two days during and after the ashfall everyone had stayed inside, doors closed and windows locked, until Dr. Dvali announced that the ash wasn't particularly harmful. Eventually Mrs. Rebka told Isaac he could go out at least as far as the courtyard gardens, as long as he wore a cloth mask. The courtyard had been cleaned but there might still be remnant dust in the air, and she didn't want him inhaling particulate matter. He must not put himself at risk, she said.

Isaac agreed to wear the mask even though it was sweatily warm across his mouth and nose. All that remained of the dust was a grainy residue silted against the brick walls and the rail fences made of nevergreen wood. Under a relentless afternoon sun, Isaac stooped over one of these small windrows and sifted the ash with his hand.

The ash, according to Dr. Dvali, contained tiny fragments of broken machines.

Not much remained of these machines, to Isaac's eyes, but he liked the grittiness of the ash and the way it pooled in his palm and slipped like talc between his fingers. He liked the way it compressed into a flaky lump when he squeezed it and dissolved into the air when he opened his fist.

The ash glittered. In fact it glowed. That wasn't exactly the right word, Isaac knew. It wasn't the sort of glow you could see with your eyes, and he understood that no one else in the compound could see it the way he did. It was a different kind of glow, differently perceived. He thought perhaps Sulean Moi would be able to explain, if he could find a way to pose the question.

Isaac had a lot of questions he wanted to ask Sulean. But she had been busy since the ashfall, often in conference with the adults, and he had to wait his turn.

At dinner Isaac noticed that when the adults discussed the ashfall or its origins they tended to direct their questions to Sulean Moi, which surprised him, because for years he had assumed the adults with whom he lived were more or less all-knowing.

Certainly they were wiser than average people. He could not say this by direct experience—Isaac had never met any average people—but he had seen them in videos and read about them in books. Average people seldom talked about anything interesting and often hurt each other savagely. Here in the compound, the talk was occasionally intense but the arguments never drew blood. Everyone was wise (or seemed to be), everyone was calm (or struggled to give that impression), and, except for Isaac, everyone was old.

Sulean Moi was apparently not an average person either. Somehow, she knew *more* than the other adults. She was smarter than the people to whom Isaac had always deferred, and—even more perplexing—she didn't seem to like them very much. But she tolerated their questions politely.

Dr. Dvali said, "Of course it implicates the Hypotheticals," talking about the ashfall, and asked Sulean, "Don't you agree?"

"It's an obvious conclusion to draw." The old woman probed the contents of her bowl with a fork. The adults theoretically took turns cooking, though a handful volunteered more often than the rest. Tonight Mr. Posell had taken kitchen duty. Mr. Posell was a geologist, but as a chef he was more enthusiastic than talented. Isaac's vegetable bowl tasted of garlic, gulley-seed oil, and something dreadfully burnt.

"Have you seen or heard of anything like it," Dr. Dvali asked, "in your own experience?"

There was no formal hierarchy among the adults at the commune, but it was usually Dr. Dvali who took the lead when large issues arose, Dr. Dvali whose pronouncements, when he made them, were considered final. He had always paid close attention to Isaac. The hair on his head was white and silky-fine. His eyes were large and brown, his eyebrows wild as abandoned hedges. Isaac had always tolerated him indifferently. Lately, however, and for reasons he didn't understand, Isaac had begun to dislike him.

Sulean said, "Nothing exactly like this. But my people have had a little more experience with the post-Spin world than yours, Dr. Dvali. Unusual things do fall out of the sky from time to time."

And who were "my people," and what sky was she talking about?

"One of these things conspicuously absent from the Martian Archives," Dr. Dvali said, "is any discussion of the nature of the Hypotheticals."

"Perhaps there was nothing substantive to say."

"You must have an opinion, Ms. Moi."

"The self-replicating devices that constitute the Hypotheticals are equivalent in many ways to living creatures. They process their environment. They build complicated structures out of rock and ice and perhaps even empty space. And their byproducts aren't immune to the process of decay. Their physical structures grow old and corrupt and are systematically replaced. That would explain the detritus in the dust."

Corrupt machines have fallen on us, Isaac thought.

"But the sheer tonnage of it," Dr. Dvali said, "distributed over so many square kilometers—"

"Is that so surprising? Given the great age of the Hypotheticals, it's no more surprising that decomposed mechanisms should fall out of the sky than that your garden should generate organic mulch."

She sounded so sure of herself. But how did Sulean know such things? Isaac was determined to find out.

That night the quick southern winds grew even quicker, and Isaac lay in bed listening to his window rattle in its casement. Beyond the glass the stars were obscured by fine sand blown aloft from the wastelands of the Rub al-Khali.

Old, old, old: the universe was old. It had generated many miracles, including the Hypotheticals, but not least Isaac himself—his body, his very thoughts.

Who was his father? Who was his mother? His teachers had never really answered the question. Dr. Dvali would say, *You're not like other children, Isaac. You belong to all of us.* Or Mrs. Rebka would say, *We're all your parents now,* even though it was inevitably Mrs. Rebka who tucked him into bed, who made sure he was fed and bathed. It was true that everyone at the commune had taken a hand in raising him, but it was Dr. Dvali and Mrs. Rebka he pictured when he imagined what it might be like to have a particular mother and father.

Was that what made him feel different from the people around him? Yes, but not just that. He didn't think the way other people thought. And although he had many keepers, he had no friends. Except, perhaps, Sulean Moi.

Isaac tried to sleep but couldn't. He was restless tonight. It wasn't an ordinary restlessness, more like an appetite without an object, and after he had lain in bed for long hours listening to the hot wind rattle and whisper, he dressed and left his room.

Midnight had come and gone. The commune was quiet, the corridors and wooden stairs echoing the sound of his footsteps. Probably there was no one awake except Dr. Taira, the historian, who did her best reading (he had heard her say) late at night. But Dr. Taira was a pale, skinny woman who kept to herself, and if she happened to be awake she didn't notice when Isaac shuffled past her door. From the lower commons room he entered the open courtyard, unobserved.

His shoes crunched on the wind-blown grit underfoot. The small moon hung over the eastern mountains and cast a diffuse light through the dust-obscured darkness. Isaac could see well enough to walk, at least if he was careful, and he knew the environment around the commune so completely that he could have navigated blind. He opened the squeaky gate in the courtyard fence and headed west. He let his wordless impulses lead him and the wind carry away his doubts.

There was no road here, just pebbly desert and a series of shallow, serpentine ridges. The moon aimed his shadow like an arrow in front of him. But he was headed in the right direction: he felt the rightness of it in the center of himself, like the sense of relief he felt when he solved some vexing mathematical problem. He deliberately set aside the noise of his own thinking and gave his attention to the sounds that came out of the darkness— his feet on the sandpaper gravel and the wind and the sounds of small nocturnal creatures foraging in the creviced landscape. He walked in a state of blissful emptiness.

He walked for a long time. He could not have said how long or far he had walked when he came at last to the rose. The rose startled him into a sudden awareness.

Had he had been walking in his sleep? The moon, which had been above the mountains when he left home, now lit the flat western horizon like a watchman's lantern. Although the night air was relatively cool he felt hot and exhausted.

He looked away from the moon and back at the rose, which grew from the desert at his feet.

"Rose" was his own word. It was what came to mind when he saw the thick stem rooted in the dry ground, the glassy crimson bulb that could pass in the moonlight for a flower.

Of course it wasn't really a flower. Flowers didn't grow in isolation in arid deserts, and their petals weren't made of what appeared to be translucent red crystals.

"Hello," Isaac said, his voice sounding small and foolish in the darkness. "What are you doing here?"

The rose, which had been leaning toward the moonlit west, promptly swiveled to face him. There was an eye in the middle of the bloom, a small eye black as obsidian, and it regarded him coolly.

Perhaps not surprisingly—Isaac wasn't surprised—it was Sulean Moi who eventually found him.

It was a still, hot morning by the time she arrived, and he sat on the ground as if the desert were a vast curved bowl and he had slid to the center of it. He cradled his head in his hands and rested his elbows on his knees. He heard the sound of her shuffling approach but he didn't look up. He didn't have to. He had hoped she would come for him.

"Isaac," Sulean Moi said, her voice dry but gentle.

He didn't answer.

"People are worried about you," she said. "They've been looking everywhere."

"I'm sorry."

She put her small hand on his shoulder. "What caused you to come all this way from home? What were you after?"

"I don't know." He gestured at the rose. "But I found this."

Now Sulean knelt to look at it—slowly, slowly, her old knees crackling.

The rose had suffered by daylight. Its dark green stem had buckled at dawn. The crystalline bulb was no longer radiant and the eye had lost its luster. Last night, Isaac thought, it had been something like alive. Now it was something like dead.

Sulean gazed at it thoughtfully a long while before she asked, "What is it, Isaac?"

"I don't know."

"Is this what you came out here for?"

"No . . . I don't think so." That was an incomplete answer. The rose, yes, but not only the rose . . . something the rose represented.

"It's remarkable," she said. "Shall we tell anyone about this, Isaac? Or shall we keep it secret?"

He shrugged.

"Well. We do have to go back, you know."

"I know."

He didn't mind leaving—the rose wouldn't last much longer.

"Will you walk with me?"

"Yes," Isaac said. "If I can ask you some questions."

"All right. I hope I can answer them. I'll try."

So they turned away from the ocular rose and began to walk eastward at the old woman's pace, and Sulean was patient while Isaac began to assemble all the uncertain-ties that had come into his head, not least the question of the rose itself. Although he hadn't slept, he wasn't tired. He was wide awake—as awake as he had ever been, and more curious.

"Where are you from?" he finally asked.

There was a brief hitch in the rhythm of her foot-steps. He thought for a moment she might not answer. Then:

"I was born on Mars," she said.

That felt like a true answer. It wasn't the answer he had expected and he had the feeling it was a truth she would have preferred not to reveal. Isaac accepted it without comment. Mars, he thought.

A moment later he asked, "How much do you know about the Hypotheticals?"

"That's odd," the old woman said, smiling faintly and regarding him with what he took to be affection. "That's exactly what I came all this way to ask you."

They talked until noon, when they reached the com-pound, and Isaac learned a number of new things from their conversation. Then, before stepping past the gate, he paused and looked back the way he had come. The rose was out there, but not just the rose. The rose was only— what? An incomplete fragment of something much larger.

Something that interested him deeply. And some-thing that was interested in him.

CHAPTER NINE

Turk drove through one of the older parts of the city, frame houses painted firetruck-red by Chinese settlers, squat three- and four-story apartment buildings of ochre brick quarried from the cliffs above Candle Bay. It was late enough now that the streets were empty. Overhead, an occasional shooting star wrote lines against the dark.

Half an hour ago he had finally gotten through to Lise. He couldn't say what he needed to say over the phone, but she seemed to catch on after a couple of awkward questions. "Meet me where we met," he said. "Twenty minutes."

Where they had met was a 24-hour bar-and-grill called La Rive Gauche, located in the retail district west of the docks. Lise had shown up there six months ago with a crowd from the consulate. A friend of Turk's had spotted a friend at the table and hauled him over for introductions. Turk noticed Lise because she was unescorted and because she was attractive in the way he found women attractive at first glance, based on the depth and availability of her laughter as much as anything else. He was wary of women who laughed too easily and unnerved by women who never laughed at all. Lise laughed gently but wholeheartedly, and when she joked there was nothing mean or competitive in it. And he liked her eyes, the way they turned up at the corners, the pale aqua of the irises, what they looked at and lingered on.

Later she started talking about a trip she was planning across the mountains to Kubelick's Grave, and Turk gave her one of his business cards. "Makes more sense than driving," he said. "Really. You'd have to go by way of the Mahdi Pass, but the road isn't a hundred percent reliable this time of year. There's a bus, but it's crowded and it slides into a gully every now and then."

He asked her what she wanted in a crapped-out little filling-station town like Kubelick's Grave, and she said she was trying to locate an old colleague of her father's, a man named Dvali, but she wouldn't elaborate. And that was probably the end of it, Turk thought, strangers in the night, passing ships, et cetera, but she had called a couple of days later and booked a flight.

He hadn't been looking for a lover—no more than he ever was. He just liked the way she smiled and the way he felt when he smiled back, and when they were forced to wait out that off-season storm on the shore of a mountain lake it was as if they had been granted a free pass from God.

Which had been revoked, apparently. Karma had come calling.

There was only the night staff at the bar and all the tables were empty, and the waitress who brought Turk a menu looked irritable and eager to go off-shift.

Lise showed up a few minutes later. Turk immediately wanted to tell her about Tomas's disappearance and what that might mean, the possibility that his connection with Lise had led someone nasty to Tomas. But he hadn't started to rehearse the words when she launched into the story of her run-in with her ex-husband Brian Gately—which was also pertinent.

Turk had met Brian Gately a couple of times. That was the interesting thing about docklands places like La Rive Gauche: you saw American businessmen sitting next to merchant sailors, Saudi oil executives sharing gossip with Chinese salarymen or unwashed artists from the arrondissements. Brian Gately had seemed like one of those temporary transplants common enough in this part of town, a guy who could travel around the world—two worlds—without really leaving Dubuque, or wherever it was he had been raised. Nice enough, in a bland way, as long as you didn't challenge any of his preconceptions.

But tonight Lise said Brian had threatened her. She described her meeting with him and finished, "So yes, it was a threat, not from Brian directly, but he was communicating what he'd been told, and it adds up to a threat."

"So there are DGS people in town who have a particular interest in Fourths. Especially the woman in the photo."

"And they know where I've been and who I've talked to. The implications of that are fairly obvious. I mean, I don't think anyone followed me here. But they might have. Or planted a locator in my car or something. I have no way of knowing."

All that was possible, Turk thought.

"Lise," he said gently, "it might be worse."

"Worse?"

"There's a friend of mine, a guy I've known a long time. His name is Tomas Ginn. He's a Fourth. That's not public information, but he's pretty upfront about it if he trusts a person. I thought you might like to talk to him. But I had to clear that with him first. I visited him this morning; he promised to think about it. But when I called him tonight I couldn't get hold of him, and when

I went to his place he was gone. Abducted. Apparently some people in a white van took him away."

She looked at him wide-eyed and said, "Oh, Christ." She shook her head. "He was what, arrested?"

"Not formally arrested, no. Only the Provisional Government has the power to make an arrest, and they don't do plainclothes warrantless raids—not to my knowledge."

"So he was kidnapped? That's a reportable crime."

"I'm sure it is, but the police are never going to hear about it. Tomas is vulnerable because of what he is. A blood test would prove he's a Fourth, and that in itself is enough to get him shipped back to the States and put on permanent probation or worse. A neighbor told me about the men in the van, but she'd never say any of that to a government official. Where my friend lives, his neighbors are generally people with a lot of exposure on legal grounds—a lot of what people do for a living in Tomas's neighborhood is prohibited under the Accords, and most of them are squatting on land they don't have title to."

"You think Brian knows something about this?"

"Maybe. Or maybe not. It sounds like Brian's pretty far down the pecking order."

"The Genomic Security office at the consulate is kind of a joke compared to what they do back home. They run facial-recognition software at the ports and occasionally serve a warrant on some fugitive dog-cloner or black-market gene-enhancer, but that's about it. At least until now." She paused. "What he told me was that it would be smart for me to go home. Back to the States."

"Maybe he's right."

"You think I should leave?"

"If you're concerned about your safety. And probably you ought to be."

She sat up straighter. "Obviously I'm concerned

about my safety. But I'm concerned about other things, too. I'm here for a reason."

"Clearly these people don't fuck around, Lise. They followed you, and it would be wise to assume they're the people who kidnapped Tomas."

"And they're interested in the woman in the photograph, Sulean Moi."

"So they might imagine you're involved in some way. That's the danger. That's what Brian was trying to tell you."

"I *am* involved."

Turk registered her determination and decided he wouldn't press her on it, at least not tonight. "Well, maybe you don't have to leave. Maybe you just need to lay low for a little while."

"If I hide, I can't do my work."

"If you mean talking to people who knew your father and asking questions about Fourths, no, you can't do that, obviously. But there's no disgrace in keeping quiet until we figure this out."

"Is that what you'd do?"

Fuck no, Turk thought. What I would do is pack my case and catch the next bus out of town. Which was what he had always done when he felt threatened. No point in saying that to Lise, though.

Briefly, he wondered if that was why Lise's father had vanished. Maybe the idea of Fourthness had seemed like a door out of whatever secret sin he couldn't endure. Or maybe he didn't take up the offer of artificial longevity at all. Maybe he just walked. People did.

Turk shrugged.

Lise was looking at him with a sad intensity he felt in his throat. "So you're telling me Brian's right and I ought to go back to the States."

"I regret every minute we're not together. But I hate the idea of you getting hurt."

She looked at him a while longer. Two more couples had just come through the door—probably tourists, but who could tell? Their privacy was compromised. She reached across the table and touched his hand. "Let's go for a walk," she said.

Really, he thought, all we know about each other is a handful of stories and thumbnail sketches: the short version of everything. Before tonight, it was all that had seemed necessary. Their best conversations had been wordless. Suddenly that wasn't enough.

"Where are you parked?" she asked.

"The lot around the corner."

"Me too. But I don't know if I should use my car. It might be tagged with a tracking device or something."

"More likely they bugged mine. If they were following me this morning I would have led them straight to Tomas." And Tomas, an old man living hand-to-mouth out in the Flats, would have been an easy target. A quick blood test—no doubt forcibly applied—would have revealed him as a Fourth. And then all bets were off.

"Why would they do that, though? Why take him away?"

"To interrogate him. I can't think of any other reason."

"They think he knows something?"

"If they're serious they would have given him a hemo test as soon as they were through the door."

"No. Genomic Security—if we're assuming that's who's responsible—doesn't work like that. Even here, there are limits. You can't steal people away and interrogate them for no reason."

"Well, I guess they thought they had a reason. But, Lise, what you read about Genomic Security in press releases isn't the whole story. That agency's bigger than Brian's little piece of it. When they break up a cloning ring or bust some longevity scam it makes the news, but they do other things that aren't so public."

"You know this for a fact?"

"It's what I've heard."

"From Fourths?"

"Well—from Tomas, for example."

"Unofficial kidnappings. This is insane."

To which he had no answer.

"I don't want to go back to my apartment," she said. "And I guess it wouldn't be any safer at your place."

"And I haven't dusted," Turk said, just to see a ghost of a smile pass across her lips. "We could rent a room."

"That doesn't guarantee they won't find us."

"If they want us, Lise, they can probably have us. It may be possible to change that, but for now we're better off assuming they know where we are. But I doubt they'll do anything drastic, at least not right away. It's not you they're after, and you're not the kind of person they can just pick up and work over. So what do you want to do, Lise? What's your next step?"

"I want to do what I should have done months ago."

"What's that?"

"I want to find Avram Dvali."

They walked along the undulating pavement toward the harbor lights and the faint clang of cargo containers cycling through the quays. The streets were empty and lonesome, and the remnant dust caked on curbs and walls muffled the sound of their footsteps.

Turk said, "You want to go to Kubelick's Grave."

"Yes. All the way this time. Will you take me there?"

"Maybe. But there's someone we ought to talk to first. And, Lise, there are things you ought to do if you're serious about this. Let someone you trust know where you are and what's happening. Take out enough cash to keep you for a while and then don't touch your e-credit. Things like that."

She gave him that half-smile again. "What did you do, take a course in criminal behavior?"

"It comes naturally."

"Another thing. I can afford the time and money it takes to go underground for a while. But you have work to do, you have a business to run."

"That's not a problem."

"I'm serious."

"So am I."

And that's the difference between us, Turk thought. She had a purpose: she was committed to finishing this post-mortem on her father's disappearance. He was just putting on his shoes and walking. Not for the first time, and in all likelihood not for the last.

He wondered if she knew that about him.

CHAPTER TEN

The senior Genomic Security operatives who had lately arrived from the States were named Sigmund and Weil, and Brian Gately's teeth clenched every time the two men came to the DGS offices at the consulate.

They came in this morning not half an hour after Brian arrived for work. He felt his molars grinding.

Sigmund was tall, sepulchral, flinty. Weil was six inches shorter and stout enough that he probably bought his pants at a specialty store. Weil was capable of smiling. Sigmund was not.

They advanced toward Brian where he stood by the water cooler. "Mr. Gately," Sigmund said, and Weil said, "Can we talk to you privately?"

"In my office."

Brian's office wasn't large but it had a window overlooking the consulate's walled garden. The cubicle was equipped with a filing cabinet, a desk of native wood, enough floating memory to accommodate the Library of Congress a few times over, and a plastic ficus. The desk was covered with correspondence between Genomic Security and the Provisional Government, one small tributary of the information stream that circulated between the two domains like an eternal sludgy Nile. Brian sat in his customary chair. Weil plumped down in the guest chair and Sigmund stood with his back to the door like a carrion bird, sinister in his patience.

"You talked to your ex-wife," Weil said.

"I did. I told her what you asked me to tell her."

"It doesn't seem to have done any good. Do I have to tell you she reconnected with Turk Findley?"

"No," Brian said flatly. "I don't suppose you do."

"They're together right now," Sigmund said. Sigmund was a man of few words, all of them unwelcome. "In all probability. Her and him."

"But the point," Weil said, "is that we can't currently locate either of them."

Brian wasn't sure whether to believe that. Weil and Sigmund represented the Executive Action Committee of the Department of Genomic Security. Much of what the Executive Action Committee did was highly classified, hence the stuff of legend. Back home, they could write themselves constitutional waivers with more or less automatic judicial approval. Here in Equatoria—in the overlapping magisteria of the United Nations Provisional Government, contending national interests, and monied oil powers—their work was at least theoretically more constrained.

Brian wasn't an idealist. He knew there were levels and echelons of Genomic Security to which he would never be admitted, realms where policy was made and rules were defined. But on the scale at which he worked Brian thought he performed useful if unexciting work. Criminals often fled from the U.S. to Equatoria, criminals whose misdeeds fell under the aegis of Genomic Security—cloning racketeers, peddlers of false or lethal longevity treatments, Fourth cultists of a radical stripe, purveyors of "enhancements" to couples willing to pay for superior children. Brian did not pursue or apprehend those criminals, but what he did do—liaising with the Provisional Government, smoothing ruffled feathers when jurisdictional disputes arose—was essential to their apprehension. It was tricky, the relationship between a quasi-police organization attached to a national consulate and the UN-sponsored local government. You had to be polite. You had to make certain reciprocal gestures. You couldn't just wade in and offend everybody.

Although apparently these guys could. And that was disappointing, because Brian believed in the rule of law. The inevitably imperfect, confusing, grindingly inefficient, occasionally corrupt, but absolutely essential rule of law. That without which we are no better than the beasts, etc. He had run his office that way: carefully, cleanly.

And now here came Sigmund and Weil, the tall one sour as Angostina bitters and the short one hard but hale, like a velvet-wrapped bowling ball, to remind him that at altitudes more vertiginous than his own the law could be tailored to suit a circumstance.

"You've already been a big help," Weil said.

"Well, I hope so. I want to be."

"Putting us in touch with the right people at the Provisional Government. And of course this thing with Lise Adams. The fact that you had a personal relationship with this woman—I mean, 'awkward' is hardly the word for it."

"Thank you for noticing," Brian said, stupidly grateful even though he knew he was being played.

"And I can assure you again that we don't want to arrest her or even necessarily talk to her directly. Lise is definitely not the target in this case."

"You're looking for the woman in the photograph."

"Which of course is why we don't want Lise getting underfoot. We hoped you could get that idea across to her . . ."

"I tried."

"I know, and we appreciate it. But let me tell you how this works, Brian, so you understand what our concerns are. Because when your image search came up on our database, it definitely raised eyebrows. You said Lise explained to you why she's interested in Sulean Moi—"

"Sulean Moi was seen with Lise's father before he disappeared, and she wasn't connected to the university or anyone else in the family's social circle. Given Lise's father's interest in Fourths, it's an obvious connection to make. Lise suspects the woman was a recruiter or something."

"The truth is a little more bizarre. You deal with Fourths on a regular basis, legally speaking. No surprises for you there. But the longevity treatment is only one of the medical modifications that were brought to Earth by our Martian cousins."

Brian nodded.

"We're after something a little bigger than the usual Fourth cultist here," Weil said. "Details are scarce, and I'm not a scientist, but it involves a biologically mediated attempt at communicating with the Hypotheticals."

Like many of his generation Brian tended to wince at mention of the Hypotheticals, or for that matter the Spin. The Spin had ended before he was old enough to attend school, and the Hypotheticals were simply one of the more abstruse facts of daily life, an important but airy abstraction, like electromagnetism or the motions of the tides.

But like everyone else he had been raised and educated by Spin survivors, people who believed they had lived through the most momentous turning point in human history. And maybe they had. The aftershocks of the Spin—wars, religious movements and counter-movements, a generalized human insecurity and a corrosive global cynicism—were still shaping the world.

Mars was an inhabited planet and mankind had been admitted into a labyrinth as large as the sky itself. All these changes had no doubt been confounding to those who endured them and would be felt for centuries to come.

But they had also become a license for an entire generation's lunacy, and that was less easy for Brian to excuse. Many millions of otherwise rational men and women had reacted to the Spin with a shocking display of irrationality, mutual distrust, and outright viciousness. Now those same people felt entitled to the respect of anyone Brian's age or younger.

They didn't deserve it. Lunacy wasn't a virtue and decency didn't boast. "Decency," in fact, was what Brian's generation had been left to rebuild. Decency, trust, and a certain decorum in human behavior.

The Hypotheticals were the causal agent behind the Spin: Why would anyone want to communicate with them? What would that even mean? And how could it be achieved by a biological modification, even a Martian one?

"What this technology does," Sigmund said, "is modify a human nervous system to make it sensitive to the signals the Hypotheticals use to communicate among themselves. Basically, they create a kind of human intermediary. A communicant who can translate between our species and whatever the Hypotheticals are."

"They actually did this?"

"The Martians won't say. It may have been attempted on their planet, maybe more than once. But we believe the technology, like the longevity treatment, was carried to Earth by Wun Ngo Wen and released into the general population."

"So why haven't I heard more about it?"

"Because it's not something universally desirable, like an extra forty years of life. If our intelligence is correct, it's lethal if attempted on an adult human being. It may be what killed Jason Lawton, way back when."

"So what good is it if it's lethal?"

"It may not be lethal," Weil said, "if the pharmaceuticals are delivered to a human being *in utero*. The developing embryo builds itself around the biotech. The human and the alien growing together."

"Jesus," Brian said. "To do that to a child—"

"It's profoundly unethical, obviously. You know, at the Department we spend a lot of time worrying about Fourths, about the harm that can come from cultists engineering changes in human biology. And that's a real, legitimate problem. But this is so much more shocking. Really, deeply . . . *evil* is the only word for it."

"Has anybody actually done this on Earth?"

"Well, that's what we're looking into. So far we have very little hard evidence or eyewitness testimony. But where we do, one person appears. Many names, but just one person, one face. You want to guess who that is?"

The woman in the photograph. The woman who had been seen with Lise's father.

"So Sulean Moi shows up on facial-recognition data from the docks at Port Magellan, and when we arrive to investigate we find Lise, who has a prior connection, has been going over this same ground, talking to her father's old colleagues and so forth. For perfectly legitimate reasons, granted. She's curious, it's a family mystery, she thinks knowing the truth would make her feel better. But that leaves us with a problem. Do we interfere with her? Do we let her go on doing what she's doing, and just sort of supervise? Do we warn her that she's in dangerous territory?"

"Warning her didn't work," Brian said.

"So we have to make use of her in some other way."

"Make use of her?"

"Instead of physically arresting her—which is what some of my superiors have been advocating—we think a wait-and-watch approach might be more informative in the long run. She's already connected with other persons of interest. One of them is Turk Findley."

Turk Findley, the freelance pilot and general fuck-up. Bad as it was that Brian had not been able to sustain his marriage to Lise, how much worse that she had taken up with someone so wayward, dysfunctional, and generally useless to his fellow man? Turk Findley was another variety of fallout from the Spin, Brian thought. A maladapted human being. A purposeless drifter. Possibly something worse, if Sigmund's implication was correct.

"You're saying Turk Findley has some connection to this elderly woman, apart from the fact that she once chartered a flight with him?"

"Well, that's certainly suggestive right there. But Turk has other contacts almost as suspicious. Known and suspected Fourths. And he's a criminal. Did you know that? He left the United States with a warrant on him."

"Warrant for what?"

"He was a person of interest in a warehouse fire."

"What are you telling me, he's an arsonist?"

"The case lapsed, but he may have burned down his old man's business."

"I thought his father was an oil man."

"His father worked in Turkey at one time and had some connections with Aramco, but he made most of his money on an import business. Some kind of bad blood between the two, the old man's warehouse burns down, Turk skips the country. You can draw your own conclusions."

It just gets worse, Brian thought. "So we have to get Lise away from him. She might be in danger."

"We suspect she's been drawn into something she doesn't understand. We doubt she's under any kind of duress. She's cooperating with this man. It was probably Turk who told her to stop taking calls."

"But you can find them, right?"

"Sooner or later. But we're not magicians, we can't just conjure them out of the void."

"Then tell me how I can help." Brian couldn't help adding, "If you'd been straight with me about this before I talked to her—"

"Would you have done anything differently? We can't just hand out this kind of information. And neither can you, Brian. Just so you know. We're taking you into our confidence here. None of this is to be discussed except between you, me, and Sigmund."

"Of course not, but—"

"What we'd like you to do is keep trying to get in touch with her. She may be aware of your calls even if she isn't answering them. She might eventually feel guilty or lonely and decide to talk to you."

"And if she does?"

"All we want right now is a clue to her location. If you can talk her into meeting you, with or without Turk, that would be even better."

Much as he disliked the idea of handing her over to the Executive Action Committee, surely that was better than letting her get more deeply involved in some criminal enterprise. "I'll do what I can," Brian said.

"Great." Weil grinned. "We appreciate that."

The two men shook Brian's hand and left him alone in his office. He sat there a long time, thinking.

CHAPTER ELEVEN

The up-coast roads hadn't been entirely cleared of the ashfall (or the muck it made when it mixed with rain), so Turk had to pull over at a truckstop and rent a room while the route was plowed at some critical switchback by the overworked road crews of the Provisional Government.

The motel was a cinderblock barracks cut into the boundary of the forest, dwarfed by spire willows that leaned across the building like sorrowing giants. It was designed to cater to truckers and loggers, Lise gathered, not tourists. She ran her finger along the sill of their room's small window and showed Turk the line of dust.

"Probably from last week," he said. "They don't spend a lot of money on housekeeping out this way."

Dust of the gods, then. The debris of ancient Hypothetical constructions. That's what they were saying about it now. The video news was full of poorly-interpreted facts about the ashfall: fragments of things that might once have been machines, fragments of things that might once have been living organisms, molecular arrangements of unprecedented complexity.

Lise could hear voices from the room next door arguing in what sounded like Filipino. She took out her phone, wanting another fix of the local broadcast news. Turk watched her closely and said, "Remember—"

"No calls in or out. I know."

"We should reach the village by this time tomorrow," Turk said, "as long as the road's cleared overnight. Then we might actually learn something."

"You have a lot of faith in this woman—Diane, you said her name was?"

"Not faith exactly. She needs to know about Tomas. She might be able to do something to help him. And she's been hooked into the local Fourth network for a long time—it's even possible she knows something about your father."

She had asked him how long he had been connected with Fourths. Not connected, exactly, he said. But this Diane woman trusted him, and he had done favors for her in the past. It had been Diane, apparently, who suggested Turk's charter business as a way of getting Sulean Moi to the mountains as discreetly as possible. More than that Turk did not know; had not wanted to know.

Lise looked again at the windowsill, the dust. "Lately I feel like it's all connected. Everything weird that's been happening—the ash, Tomas, whatever's going on out west . . ."

The news broadcasts had begun reporting on the earthquake that had temporarily shut down the oil complexes of the Rub al-Khali.

"It's not necessarily connected," Turk said. "It's just triple-strange."

"What?"

"Something Tomas used to say. Weirdness comes in clusters. Like this time we were crewing a freighter in the Strait of Malacca. One day we had engine trouble and had to anchor for repairs. Next day freakish weather, a monsoon nobody'd predicted. Day after that the sky was clear but we were hosing Malay pirates off the deck. Once things get strange, Tomas used to say, you can pretty much count on triple-strange."

How comforting, Lise thought.

They shared a bed that night but they didn't make love. Both of them were tired and both of them, Lise thought, were coming to terms with the truth that this wasn't a tent by a mountain lake and they weren't having a harmless weekend adventure. Larger forces had been engaged. People had been hurt. And, thinking about her father, she began to wonder whether he might have stumbled into some similar wonderland of triple-strangeness. Maybe his disappearance had not been selfish or even voluntary: maybe he'd been abducted, like Turk's friend Tomas, by anonymous men in an unmarked van.

Turk was asleep as soon as he hit the mattress, typically. Nevertheless it was good to lie beside him, to feel his bulk at her side. He had showered before bed and the smell of soap and maleness emanated from him like a benevolent aura. Had Brian ever smelled like that?

Not that she could recall. Brian had no particular smell beyond the chemical tang of whatever deodorant he happened to be using. Probably took some small degree of pride in being odor-free.

No, that wasn't fair. There was more to Brian than that. Brian believed in an ordered life. That didn't make him a monster or a villain, and she couldn't believe he had been personally involved in tracking her movements or abducting Tomas. That wasn't playing by the book. Brian always played by the book.

Not necessarily a bad thing. If it made him less adventurous than Turk, it also made him more reliable. Brian would never fly a plane across a mountain or hire himself out as an able-bodied seaman on some rust-riddled merchant vessel. Nor would he break a promise or violate an oath. Which was why it had been so hard to negotiate the conclusion of their hasty and unwise marriage. Lise had met Brian when she was doing a journalism degree at Columbia and he was a junior functionary in the New York offices of the DGS. It was his gentleness and his sympathy that had won her over, and she had only belatedly understood that Brian would always be *at* her side but never quite *on* her side—that in the end he was one more in the chorus of voices advising her to ignore her own history because its lacunae might conceal some unbearable truth.

But he had loved her, innocently, doggedly. Claimed he still did. She opened her eyes and saw her phone where she had left it on the bedside table, faintly glowing. It had already registered several attempted calls from Brian. She had answered none of them. That was also unfair. Necessary, maybe. She was willing to take Turk's word on that. But not fair, and not kind. Brian deserved better.

By morning a lane had been opened and they drove north for another four hours, passing buses, jitneys painted like circus caravans, logging trucks, freight trucks, tank trucks loaded with refined oil or gasoline, until Turk turned west on one of the poorly-maintained side roads that diced through this part of the country like the lines on an old man's palm.

And suddenly they were in the wilderness. The Equatorian forest closed on them like a mouth. It was only here, away from the city and the farms and refineries and busy harbors, that Lise felt the alienness of this world, the intrinsic and ancient strangeness that had fascinated her father. The towering trees and dense, ferny undergrowth—plants for which Lise did not know the folk names, much less their provisional binomials—were supposedly related to terrestrial life: their DNA contained evidence of terrestrial ancestry. The planet had been stocked and seeded by the Hypotheticals, supposedly to make it habitable for human beings. But the plans of the Hypotheticals were long-term, to say the least. They calculated events in the billions of years. Evolution must be a perceptible event to them.

Maybe they couldn't even directly experience events as brief, in their eyes—if they *had* eyes—as a human life. Lise found that idea oddly comforting. She could see and feel things that for the Hypotheticals must be vanishingly evanescent: things as commonplace as the swaying of these strange trees above the road and the sunlight that speckled their shadows on the forest floor. That was a gift, she thought. Our mortal genius.

The sun tracked through finely-feathered or fernlike leaves. The underbrush was populated with wildlife, much of which had not (even yet) learned to fear human beings. She caught glimpses of jack dogs, a striped ghoti, a flock of spidermice, the names usually referring to some Earthly animal although the resemblance was often fanciful. There were insects, too, humming or whining in the emerald shadows. Worst were the carrion wasps, not dangerous but big and foul-smelling. Gnats, which looked exactly like the gnats that used to hover in shady places back home, swarmed among the mossy tree trunks.

Turk drove with close attention to the unpaved road. Fortunately the dustfall here had been light and the canopy of the forest had absorbed most of it. When the driving was critical Turk was silent. On the straightaways, he asked about her father. She had discussed this with him before, but that had been before the dustfall and the strange events of the last few days.

"How old were you exactly when your father disappeared?"

"Fifteen." A young fifteen. Naïve, and clinging to

American fashions as a rebuke to the world into which she had been unwillingly imported. Braces on her teeth, for God's sake.

"The authorities take it seriously?"

"How do you mean?"

"Just, you know, he wouldn't be the first guy to walk out on his family. No offense."

"He wasn't the type to walk out on us. I know everybody says that in cases like this. 'It was so unexpected.' And I was the loyal, naïve daughter—I couldn't imagine him doing anything bad or thoughtless. But it's not just me. He was fully engaged in his work at the university. If he was leading a double life I don't know where he found the time for it."

"Supporting his family on a teacher's salary?"

"We had money from my mother's side."

"So I guess it wasn't hard to get the attention of the Provisional Government when he disappeared."

"We had ex-Interpol men interviewing everybody, an open police file, but nothing ever came of it."

"So your family contacted Genomic Security."

"No. They contacted us."

Turk nodded and looked thoughtful while he maneuvered the vehicle through a shallow washout. A three-wheeled motorcycle passed in the opposite direction—balloon tires, high carriage, a basket of vegetables strapped to the rear rack. The driver, some skinny local, glanced at them incuriously.

"Anybody find that odd," Turk asked, "that Genomic Security came calling?"

"My father was researching Fourth activity in the New World, among other things, so they were aware of him. He'd had talks with them before."

"Researching Fourths for what purpose?"

"Personal interest," she said, cringing at how incriminating that sounded. "Really, it was part of his whole fascination with the post-Spin world—how people were adapting to it. And I think he was convinced the Martians knew more about the Hypotheticals than they included in their Archives, and maybe some of that knowledge had been passed around by Fourths along with the chemical and biological stuff."

"But the Genomic Security people didn't turn up anything either."

"No. They kept the file open for a while longer, or so they claimed, but in the end they didn't have any more luck than the PG had. The conclusion they obviously reached was that his research had gotten the better of him—that at some point he was offered the longevity treatment and took it."

"Okay, but that doesn't mean he had to disappear."

"People do, though. They take the treatment and assume a new identity. It means not so many awkward questions when your peers start to die off and you still look like the picture in your grad book. The idea of starting a new life is attractive for a lot of people, especially if they're in some kind of personal or financial bind. But my father wasn't like that."

"People can carry around a fear of death and never let on, Lise. They just live with it. But if you show them a way out, who knows how they might behave?"

Or who they might leave behind. Lise was silent for a moment. Over the hum of the car's engine she heard a minor-key melody trilling from the high canopy of the forest, some bird she couldn't identify.

She said, "When I came back here I was prepared for that possibility. I'm far from convinced that he just walked out on us, but I'm not omniscient, I can't know for sure what was going on in his mind. If that's what happened, okay. I'll deal with it. I don't want revenge, and if he did take the treatment—if he's living somewhere under a new name—I can deal with that, too. I don't need to see him. I just need to know. Or find somebody who does."

"Like the woman in the photograph. Sulean Moi."

"The woman you flew to Kubelick's Grave. Or like this Diane, who sent her to you."

"I don't know how much Diane can tell you. More than I can, anyhow. I made it a point not to ask questions. The Fourths I've met . . . they're easy to like, they don't strike me as sinister, and as far as I can tell they're not doing anything to put the rest of us in danger. Contrary to all that Genomic Security bullshit you hear on the news, they're just people."

"People who know how to keep secrets."

"I'll grant you that," Turk said.

Moments later they passed a crude wooden sign on which the name of the village had been written in several languages: DESA NEW SARANDIB TOWN, in approximate English. Half a mile farther on a skinny kid, not much more than twenty years old, Lise guessed, if that, stepped into the road and waved them down. He came to Turk's side of the car and leaned into the window.

"Going to Sarandib?" The kid's shrill voice made him seem even younger than he looked. His breath smelled like rancid cinnamon.

"Headed that way," Turk said.

"You got business there?"

"Yeah."

"What kind of business?"

"Personal business."

"You want to buy ky? Not a good place to buy ky."

Ky was the hallucinogenic wax produced by some kind of native hive insect, lately a big deal in the Port Magellan clubs. "I don't want any ky. Thanks anyhow." Turk stepped on the gas—not hard enough to injure the kid, who ducked away promptly, but hard enough to win him a nasty look. Lise glanced back and saw the kid still standing in the road, glaring after them. She asked Turk what that was all about.

"Lately you get townies driving around the boondocks trying to score a gram or two, getting robbed, getting into trouble."

"You think he wanted to sell us some?"

"I don't know what he wanted."

But the kid must have had a phone on him, and he must have called ahead, because as soon as they passed the first few inhabited shacks along the road and before they reached the town center the local *gendarmerie*, two big men wearing improvised uniforms and driving a years-old utility truck, forced Turk's vehicle to the side of the road. Lise sat still and let Turk do the talking.

"You have business here?" one of the men asked.

"We need to see *Ibu* Diane."

Long pause. "No such person here."

"Okay," Turk said. "I must have made a wrong turn. We'll stop and have lunch, and then, since there's no such person, we'll be on our way."

The cop—if you could call him that, Lise thought, because these small-town constabularies had no standing with the Provisional Government—gave Turk a long sour look. "You have a name?"

"Turk Findley."

"You can get a tea across the road. I don't know about lunch." He held up a single finger. "One hour."

They were seated at a table that appeared to have been made from an enormous discarded cable spool, sweating in the afternoon heat and drinking tea from chipped ceramic cups while the other patrons of the café avoided their eyes, when the curtains parted and a woman entered the room.

An old, old woman. Her hair was the color and texture of dandelion fluff, her skin so pale that it seemed in danger of tearing. Her eyes were unusually large and blue, framed inside the stark contours of her skull. She came to the table and said, "Hello, Turk."

"Diane."

"You know, you really shouldn't have come back here. This is a bad time."

"I know," Turk said. "Tomas was arrested, or kidnapped or something."

The woman displayed no reaction beyond a barely-perceptible flinch.

"And we have a couple of questions to ask, if that's okay."

"Since you're here, we may as well talk." She pulled up a chair and said, "Introduce me to your friend."

This woman is a Fourth, Lise thought. Maybe that was why she generated this odd, fragile authority, to which strong men apparently deferred. Turk introduced her as *Ibu* Diane Dupree, using the Minang honorific, and Lise accepted the woman's small, brittle hand. It was like handling some unexpectedly muscular small bird.

"Lise," Diane said. "And you have a question for me?"

"Show her the picture," Turk said.

So Lise fumbled nervously in her pack until she came up with the envelope containing the photo of Sulean Moi.

Diane opened the envelope and looked at the photograph for a long moment. Then she handed it back. Her expression was mournful.

"So can we talk?" Turk asked.

"I think we have to. But somewhere more private than this. Follow me."

Ibu Diane led them away from the café, down a lane between a makeshift grocery store and a wooden municipal building with buffalo-horn eaves, past a gas station where the pumps were painted carnival colors. Lise would have expected a slow walk, given Diane's age and the heat of the day, but the older woman moved briskly and at one point reached out and took Lise's hand to urge her along. It was a strange gesture and it made Lise feel like a little girl.

She took them to a cinderblock bunker on which a multilingual sign announced, in its English portion, MEDICAL CLINIC. Lise said, "Are you a doctor?"

"I'm not even a registered nurse. But my husband was a physician and he cared for these people for years, long before the Red Crescent showed up in any of these villages. I learned basic medicine from him, and the villagers wouldn't let me retire after he died. I can take care of minor injuries and sicknesses, administer antibiotics, salve a rash, bind a wound. For anything more serious I send people to the clinic down the highway. Have a seat."

They sat in the reception area of Diane's clinic. It was fitted out like a village parlor with wicker furniture and wooden slat blinds clattering in the breeze. Everything was painted or upholstered in faded green. There was a watercolor picture of the ocean on one wall.

Ibu Diane smoothed her plain white muslin dress. "May I ask how you came to possess a photograph of this woman?"

Get to the point, in other words. "Her name is Sulean Moi."

"I know."

"You know her?"

"I've met her. I recommended Turk's charter service to her."

"Tell her about your father," Turk suggested, and Lise did. And she brought the story up to date: how she had come back determined to learn more about the disappearance; Brian Gately's connection to Genomic Security;

how he had run her old snapshot of Sulean Moi through the Agency's facial-recognition software and learned that the woman had re-entered Port Magellan only months earlier.

"That must have been the trigger," Diane said.

"Trigger?"

"Your inquiries—or your ex-husband's—probably brought Ms. Moi to someone's attention back in the States. Genomic Security has been looking for Sulean Moi for a long time."

"Why? What's so important about her?"

"I'll tell you what I know, but would you answer some questions of mine first? It might clarify matters."

"Go ahead," Lise said.

"How did you meet Turk?"

"I hired him to fly me over the mountains. One of my father's colleagues was known to have visited Kubelick's Grave. At the time it was the only lead I had. So I hired Turk . . . but we never made it across the mountains."

"Bad weather," Turk said, and coughed into his hand.

"I see."

"Then," Lise said, "when Brian told me Sulean Moi had chartered a small plane just a few weeks before—"

"How did Brian know this? Oh, I suppose he arranged a search of the air traffic manifests. Or something like that."

Lise said, "It was a lead I intended to follow up . . . although Brian urged me not to. Even then, he thought I was getting in too deep."

"While Turk, of course, was fearless."

"That's me," Turk said. "Fearless."

"But I hadn't got around to it, and then there was the ashfall, and then—"

"And then," Turk said, "Tomas got himself disappeared, and we found out Lise was being followed and her phone service was tapped. And I'm sorry, Diane, but all I could think of was to come here. I was hoping you could—"

"What? Intervene on your behalf? What magic do you think I possess?"

"I *thought*," Turk said, "you might be able to explain. I also didn't rule out the possibility of some useful advice."

Diane nodded and tapped her chin with her forefinger. Her sandal-clad foot counted a parallel rhythm on the wooden floor.

"You could start," Lise said, "by telling us who Sulean Moi really is."

"The first relevant fact about her," Diane said, "is that she's a Martian."

The human civilization on Mars had been a great disappointment to Lise's father.

That was another thing they had discussed, those nights on the veranda when the sky had opened like a book above them.

Robert Adams had been a young man—an undergraduate at Cal Tech during the lean years of the Spin, facing what had looked like the inevitable destruction of the world he knew—when Wun Ngo Wen arrived on Earth.

The most spectacular success story of the Spin had been the terraforming and colonization of Mars. Using the expanding sun and the passage of millions of years in the external solar system as a kind of temporal lever, Mars had been rendered at least marginally habitable and seed colonies of human beings had been established there. While a scant few years passed on Earth behind its Spin membrane, civilizations on Mars had risen and fallen.

(Even those bare facts—unmentionable in the presence of Lise's mother, who had lost her parents to the dislocations of the Spin and would brook no discussion of it—had raised the hackles on Lise's neck. She had learned all this in school, of course, but without the attendant sense of awe. In Robert Adams' hushed discourse the numbers had not been just numbers: When he said *a million years* she could hear the distant roar of mountains rising from the sea.)

A vastly old and vastly strange human civilization had arisen on Mars during the time it took, on the enclosed Earth, for Lise to walk to school and back.

That civilization had been wrapped by the Hypotheticals in its own envelope of slow time—an enclosure that brought Mars into synchronization with the Earth and ended when the Earth's enclosure ended. But before that happened, the Martians had sent a manned spacecraft to Earth. Its sole occupant had been Wun Ngo Wen, the so-called Martian Ambassador.

Lise would ask—they had this conversation on more than one starry summer night—"Did you ever meet him?"

"No." Wun had been killed in a roadside attack during the worst years of the Spin. "But I watched his address to the United Nations. He seemed . . . likable."

(Lise had seen historical footage of Wun Ngo Wen from an early age. As a child she had imagined having him for a friend: a sort of intellectual Munchkin, no taller than herself.)

But the Martians had been coy from the beginning, her father told her. They had given the Earth their Archives, a compendium of their knowledge of the physical sciences, in some areas more advanced than earthly science. But it said very little about their work in human biology—the work that had produced their caste of long-lived Fourths—or about the Hypotheticals. To Lise's father these were unforgivable omissions. "They've known about the Hypotheticals for hundreds if not thousands of years," he said. "They must have had *something* to say, even if it was only speculation."

When the Spin ended, and both Earth and Mars were restored to the customary flow of time, radio communication with the Martians had flourished for a time. There had even been a second Martian expedition to Earth, more ambitious than the first, and a group of Martian legates had been installed in a fortresslike building attached to the old United Nations complex in New York—the Martian Embassy, it came to be called. When their scheduled five-year tenure expired, they were returned home aboard a terrestrial spacecraft jointly engineered by the major industrial powers and launched from Xichang.

There was never a second delegation. Plans to send a reciprocal terrestrial expedition to Mars broke down in multinational negotiations, and in any case the Martians had shown little enthusiasm for it. "I suspect," Lise's father said, "they were a little bit appalled by us." Mars had never been a resource-rich world, even after the ecopoeisis, and its civilization had survived through a sort of meticulous collective parsimony. Earth—with its vast but polluted bodies of water, its inefficient industries and collapsing ecosystems—would have horrified the visitors. "They must have been glad," Robert Adams said, "to put a few million miles between them and us."

And they had their own post-Spin crises to deal with. The Hypotheticals had also installed an Arch on Mars. It rose above the equatorial desert, and it opened on a similar small, rocky planet, hospitable but uninhabited, orbiting a distant star.

Communications between Earth and Mars had slowed to a perfunctory trickle.

And there were no more Martians on Earth. They had

all gone home when the diplomatic mission ended. Lise had never heard otherwise.

So how could Sulean Moi be a Martian?

"**S**he doesn't even look like a Martian," Lise said. Martians were four to five feet tall at most and their skin was deeply ridged and wrinkled. Sulean Moi, as she appeared in the original snapshot from her father's house in Port Magellan, had been only ordinarily short and not especially wrinkly.

"Sulean Moi has a unique history," Diane said. "As you might imagine. Would you like a cold drink? I think I would—my throat's a little dry."

"I'll fetch," Turk said.

"Fine. Thank you. As to Sulean Moi . . . I'm afraid I have to tell you something about myself before I can explain." She hesitated and closed her eyes briefly. "My husband was Tyler Dupree. My brother was Jason Lawton."

A second passed before Lise placed the names. They were names out of history books, Spin-era names. Jason Lawton was the man who had helped seed the barren deserts of Mars, the man who had set the replicator launches in motion, the man to whom Wun Ngo Wen had entrusted his collection of Martian pharmaceuticals. It was Jason Lawton who had defied the U.S. government by distributing those drugs, and the techniques for reproducing them, among a scattered group of academics and scientists who would become the first Terrestrial Fourths.

And Tyler Dupree, if she recalled correctly, had been Jason Lawton's personal physician.

"Is that possible?" Lise whispered.

"I'm not trying to impress you with my age," Diane said. "Just establish my credentials. I'm a Fourth, of course, and I've been a part of that community since its inception. That's why Sulean Moi came to see me, a few months ago."

"But—if she's a Martian, how did she get here? Why doesn't she look like a Martian?"

"She was born on Mars. When she was very young she nearly died in a catastrophic flood—she suffered injuries, including tissue death in the brain, that could only be treated by a radical reconstruction using the same drugs that extend life. Given at such an early age, the treatment has a rather dire side effect—a sort of genetic recidivism. She never acquired the wrinkles most Martians develop at puberty, and she continued growing past the point at which they ordinarily stop. Which left her looking almost like an Earthling—a throwback, as they would have seen it, to her earliest ancestors. Because she lost most of her immediate family, and because she was considered grotesquely deformed, she was raised by a community of ascetic Fourths. They gave her an impeccable education, if nothing else. No doubt because of her appearance, she was fascinated by Earth and devoted herself to scholarship in what we would call 'Terrestrial Studies'—I have no idea what the Martians called it."

"An expert on Earth," Lise said.

"Which was why, eventually, she was selected as one of the Martian legates."

"If that's true, her photograph would have been everywhere."

"She was kept away from the press. Her existence was a carefully guarded secret. Do you understand why?"

"Well—if she looked so much like an Earthling—"

"She could pass unnoticed in a crowd and she had taught herself to speak at least three terrestrial languages like a native."

"So she was what, a spy?"

"Not exactly. The Martians knew there were Fourths on Earth. Sulean Moi was their diplomatic mission to *us*."

Turk handed out glasses of ice water. Lise sipped eagerly—her throat was dry.

"And when the Martians left," Diane said, "Sulean Moi chose to stay behind. She traded places with a woman, a Terrestrial Fourth who happened to resemble her. When the legation went back to Mars that woman went with them—our own secret ambassador, in a way."

"Why did Sulean Moi stay?"

"Because she was shocked by what she found here. On Mars, of course, the Fourths have existed for centuries, constrained by laws and institutions that don't exist on Earth. Martian Fourths buy their longevity with a variety of compromises. They don't reproduce, for instance, and they don't participate in government except as observers and adjudicators. Whereas all *our* Fourths are outlaws—both endangered and potentially dangerous. She hoped to bring Martian formality to the chaos."

"I gather she didn't succeed."

"Let's say her successes have been modest. There are Fourths and Fourths. Those of us who are sympathetic to her goals have funded and encouraged her over the years. Others resent her meddling."

"Meddling in what?"

"In their efforts to create a human being who can communicate with the Hypotheticals."

"I know how grotesque that must sound," Diane Dupree said. "But it's true." She added, in a more subdued voice, "It's what killed my brother Jason."

What made this unquestionable, Lise thought, was the woman's obvious sincerity. That, and the wind rattling the blinds, and the human noise of the villagers going about their business, a dog barking aimlessly in the distance, Turk sipping his ice water as if these assertions were old news.

"That was how Jason Lawton died?" In the books

Lise had read, Jason Lawton had been a casualty of the anarchic last days of the Spin. Hundreds of thousands had died in the panic.

"The process," Diane said calmly, "is deadly in an adult. It rebuilds much of the human nervous system and it renders it vulnerable to further manipulation by the networked intelligences of the Hypotheticals. There is—well, a sort of communication can take place. But it kills the communicant. Theoretically, the procedure might be more stable if it was applied to a human fetus *in vivo*. An unborn child in the womb."

"But that would be—"

"Indefensible," Diane said. "Morally and ethically monstrous. But it's been a terrible temptation for one faction of our community. It holds out the possibility of a real understanding of the mystery of the Hypotheticals, what they want from us and why they've done what they've done. And maybe something more, not just communication but a sort of communion. Commingling the human and the divine, if I can use those words."

"And the Martians want to stop this from happening?"

Diane looked subtly ashamed. "The Martian Fourths were the first to try it."

"What—they modified a human fetus?"

"The project was unsuccessful. The child didn't survive past puberty. The experiment was conducted by the same group of ascetic Fourths who raised Sulean Moi—she was there when the child died."

"The Martians allowed this?"

"Only once. Sulean Moi meant to prevent the same thing happening among our own Fourths, who are even less constrained by law and custom—or to interrupt the process if it had already begun."

The breeze was warm, but Lise shivered. "And has it? Begun, I mean?"

"The technology and the pharmaceuticals were

distributed by Jason along with everything else Wun
Ngo Wen brought to Earth. We've had the capability for
decades, but there was no real interest in pursuing it
except among a few . . . you might say, rogue groups."

"I thought Fourths had some kind of built-in inhibi-
tion," Turk said. "For instance, Tomas. Once he took the
treatment he stopped drinking anything stronger than
beer and he quit picking bar fights."

"We're inhibited against obvious aggression, but not
so much so that we lack the capacity for moral choice—
or self-defense. And this isn't aggression, exactly, Turk.
It's callous, it's inexcusable, but it's also, in a sense,
abstract. Pushing a needle into the vein of a pregnant
volunteer isn't a *perceived* act of violence, especially if
you're convinced of the necessity of it."

Lise said, "And that's why Genomic Security is interested in Sulean Moi."

"Yes. Genomic Security and every similar agency.
It isn't just Americans who fear Fourths, you know. In
the Islamic world the prejudice is especially strong.
Nowhere is safe. For decades Genomic Security has
been attempting to track down and secure every extant
trace of forbidden Martian biotechnology. Probably less
to destroy it than to monopolize it. They haven't succeeded and probably never will succeed. The genie is
out of the bottle. But they've learned a few things in the
course of their work. They learned about Sulean Moi,
obviously. And the idea of Fourths interceding with the
Hypotheticals scares the hell out of them."

"For the same reason you're afraid of it?"

"Some of the same reasons," Diane said. She drank
from her glass of ice water. "Some."

The village muezzin called the faithful to prayer.
Diane ignored the sound.

Lise said, "Sulean was in Port Magellan at least once
before. Twelve years ago."

"Yes."

"Going about the same business?"

"Yes."

"Successfully? I mean, did she stop—whoever was involved—from doing this thing?"

Ibu Diane looked at Lise, looked away. "No, she was not successful."

"My father knew her."

"Sulean Moi knows a lot of people. What was your father's name?"

"Robert Adams," Lise said, her heart beating harder.

Diane shook her head. "The name isn't familiar. But you said you were looking for one of his colleagues in the town of Kubelick's Grave?"

"A man named Avram Dvali."

"Avram Dvali." *Ibu* Diane's expression became somber. Lise felt her excitement peak.

"Dvali was a Fourth?"

"He was. He is. He's also, in my opinion, just slightly insane."

CHAPTER TWELVE

After walking Isaac back to the compound Sulean Moi told Dr. Dvali about the flower.

The story seemed so improbable that it became necessary to mount an expedition and set out in search of the thing. Sulean didn't participate but she gave explicit directions. Dr. Dvali took three other men and one of the commune's vehicles and drove off into the desert. Dvali's excitement was predictable, Sulean thought. He was in love with the Hypotheticals—with what he imagined them to be. He could hardly resist the gift of an alien flower.

They were back by late afternoon. Dvali hadn't been able to find the sighted rose, but the expedition wasn't fruitless. There had been other unusual things growing in the dry wastes. He had collected three samples in a cotton bag, and he displayed them to Sulean and several other observers on a table in the common room.

One of his prizes was a spongy green disk shaped like a miniature bicycle wheel, with twig-like spokes and a gnarl of roots still attached to the hub. One was a translucent tube a centimeter in diameter and as long as

Sulean's forearm. The last was a viscid, knobby lump resembling a clenched fist, blue veined with red.

None of these things looked healthy, although arguably they might once have been alive. The bicycle wheel was blackened and crumbling in places. The hollow tube had fractured along its axis. The fist was pallid and had begun to emit an unpleasant odor.

Mrs. Rebka said, "Did these things fall with the ash?"

Dvali shook his head. "They were all rooted."

"They grew out there? Out in the desert?"

"I can't explain it. I would guess they're associated with the ashfall in some way."

Dvali looked expectantly at Sulean.

Sulean had nothing to say.

In the morning Sulean went to see Isaac, but his door was closed and Mrs. Rebka stood outside, her arms crossed. "He's not well," she said.

"I'll speak to him briefly," Sulean said.

"I'd prefer to let him rest. He's running a fever. I think you and I have to talk, Ms. Moi."

The two women walked out into the courtyard. They kept to the shade of the main building and sat together on a stone bench with a view of the garden. The air was hot and still, and sunlight fell on the fenced flowerbed as if it had an immense invisible weight. Sulean waited for Mrs. Rebka to speak. In fact Sulean had expected something hostile from Mrs. Rebka sooner or later. She was the closest thing Isaac had to a mother, though Isaac's nature had precluded any real emotional warmth, at least on his part.

"He's never been sick before," Mrs. Rebka said. "Not once. But since you arrived . . . he's not the same. He wanders, he eats less. He's taken a ferocious interest in books, and at first I thought that was a good thing. But I wonder if it isn't just another symptom."

"Symptom of what?"

"Don't be evasive." Mrs. Rebka was a large woman. To Sulean all these people seemed large—Sulean herself barely topped five foot three—but Mrs. Rebka was especially large and seemed to want to appear intimidating. "I know who you are, as well as anyone does. Everyone in the community has been aware of you for years. We weren't surprised when you knocked at the door. Only surprised that it had taken so long. We're prepared to let you observe Isaac and even interact with him. The only condition is that you don't interfere."

"*Have* I interfered?"

"He's changed since you got here. You can't deny that."

"That has nothing to do with me."

"Doesn't it? I hope you're right. But you've seen this before, haven't you? Before you came to Earth."

Sulean had never made a secret of it. The story had spread among these Terrestrial Fourths—especially those, like Dvali, who were obsessed with the Hypotheticals. She nodded.

"A child like Isaac," Mrs. Rebka said.

"In some ways like him. A boy. He was Isaac's age when he—"

"When he died."

"Yes."

"Died of his . . . condition?"

Sulean didn't answer immediately. She hated calling up these memories, instructive as they inevitably were. "He died in the desert." A different desert. The Martian desert. "He was trying to find his way, but he got lost." She closed her eyes. Behind her eyelids the world was an infinite redness, thanks to this insufferably bright sunlight. "I would have stopped you if I could. You know that. But I came too late, and you were all very clever about concealing yourselves. Now I'm as helpless as you are, Mrs. Rebka."

"I won't let you hurt him." The fervor in Mrs. Rebka's voice was as startling as the accusation.

"I wouldn't do anything to harm him!"

"Possibly not. But I think, on some level, you're frightened of him."

"Mrs. Rebka, have you misunderstood so completely? Of course I'm afraid of him! Aren't you?"

Mrs. Rebka didn't answer, only stood up and walked slowly back into the compound.

That night Isaac was still feverish and was confined to his room. Sulean lay awake in her own room, gazing past the sand-scuffed windowpane at the stars.

At the Hypotheticals, to use that wonderfully ambiguous name bestowed upon them by English-speaking people. They had been called that even before their existence was well-established: the hypothetical entities who had enclosed the Earth in a strange temporal barrier, so that a million years might pass while a man walked his dog or a woman brushed her hair. They were a network of self-reproducing semibiological machines distributed throughout the galaxy. They intervened in human affairs, and perhaps the affairs of innumerable other sentient civilizations, for reasons not well-understood. Or for no reason at all.

She was looking at them, though they were of course invisible. They permeated the night sky. They contained worlds. They were everywhere.

Beyond that, what could one say? A network so vast it spanned a galaxy was indistinguishable from a natural force. It could not be bargained with. It could not even be spoken to. It interacted with humanity over inhuman spans of time. Its words were decades and its conversations were indistinguishable from the process of evolution.

Did it think, in any meaningful sense? Did it wonder,

did it argue with itself, did it fabricate ideas and act on them? Was it an *entity*, in other words, or just a huge and complex *process*?

The Martians had argued over this for centuries. Sulean had spent much of her childhood listening to elderly Fourths debate the question. Sulean didn't have a conclusive answer—no one did—but her suspicion was that the Hypotheticals had no center, no operative intelligence. They did complex, unpredictable things—but so did evolution. Evolution had produced vastly complex and interdependent biological systems without any central direction. Once self-reproducing machines had been unleashed on the galaxy (by some long lost ancient species, perhaps, long before Earth or Mars had condensed from stellar dust), they had been subject to the same inexorable logic of competition and mutation. What might that not have bred, over billions of years? Machines of immense scale and power, semi-autonomous, "intelligent" in a certain sense—the Arch, the temporal barrier that had surrounded the Earth—all that, yes. But a central motivating consciousness? A mind? Sulean had come to doubt it. The Hypotheticals were not one entity. They were just what happened when the logic of self-reproduction engulfed the vastnesses of space.

The dust of ancient machines had fallen on the desert, and from that dust had grown strange, abortive fragments. A wheel, a hollow tube, a rose with a coal-dark eye. And Isaac was interested in the west, the far west. What did that mean? Did it have a discernible meaning?

It meant, Sulean thought, that Isaac was being sacrificed to a force as mindless and indifferent as the wind.

In the morning Mrs. Rebka allowed Sulean to visit the boy's room. "You'll see," she said grimly, "why we're all so concerned."

Isaac was limp under a tangle of blankets. His eyes were closed. Sulean touched his forehead and felt the radiant heat of fever.

"Isaac," she sighed, as much to herself as to the boy. His pale inertness provoked too many memories. There had been another boy, yes, another fever, another desert.

"The rose," Isaac said, startling her.

"What's that?" she said.

"I remember the rose. And the rose, the rose remembers."

As if asleep, eyes still shut, he pulled himself into a sitting position, his pillow compressed under the small of his back and his head knocking the backboard of the bed. His hair was lank with sweat. How immortal human beings seem when they can walk, run, jump, Sulean thought. And how fragile when they can't.

Then the boy did something that shocked even Sulean.

He opened his eyes and the irises were newly discolored, as if their pale uniform blue had been spattered with gold paint. He looked at her directly and he smiled.

Then he spoke, and he spoke a language Sulean had not heard for decades, a Martian dialect from the sparsely inhabited southern wastes.

He said, "It's you, big sister! Where have you been?"

Then, just as quickly, he slept again, and Sulean was left shivering in the terrible echo of his words.

CHAPTER THIRTEEN

The next morning a helicopter flew low over the Mi-nang village, and while that might have been innocuous—logging companies had been surveying these hills for the past couple of months—it unsettled the villagers and caused *Ibu* Diane to suggest that they move quickly. Staying was riskier than leaving, she said.

"Where are we going?" Lise asked.

"Over the mountains. Kubelick's Grave. Turk will fly us there, won't you, Turk?"

He appeared to think about it. "I might need a crow-bar," he said, cryptically. "But yeah."

"We'll take one of the village cars back to the city," *Ibu* Diane said. "Something inconspicuous. The car you came in is a liability. I'll ask one of the villagers to drive it up the coast road and leave it somewhere."

"Do I get it back when all this is finished?"

"I doubt it."

"Well, that figures," Turk said.

The authorities had ways of tracking people in whom they were interested, Lise knew. Tiny RF tags could be planted on a vehicle or even in an item of clothing. And there were more arcane, even subtler devices available. The Minang villager who drove their car north also took with him their clothing and other possessions. Lise changed into a floral-print blouse and muslin pants from the village store, Turk into a pair of jeans and a white shirt. Both of them showered in Ibu Diane's clinic. "Be especially careful of your hair," Diane had instructed them. "Things can be hidden in hair."

Feeling simultaneously purified and paranoid, Lise climbed into the rust-spackled vehicle Diane had arranged for them to drive. Turk took the driver's seat, Lise buckled in next to him, and they waited while Diane said goodbye to a dozen villagers who had gathered around her.

"Popular woman," Lise observed.

"She's known in every village up the north coast," Turk said. "She moves between a whole bunch of these communities, expat Malays and Tamils and Minang, season by season, helping out. They all keep a place for her and they're all protective of her."

"They know she's a Fourth?"

"Sure. And she's not the only one. A bunch of these village elders are more elderly than you might think."

The world was changing, Lise thought, and no amount of rhetoric about the sanctity of the human genome was going to stop it. She pictured herself trying to communicate that truth to Brian. A truth he would no doubt refuse or deny. Brian was adept at patching cracks in the foundation of his faith in the good works of Genomic Security. But the cracks kept coming. The edifice trembled.

Ibu Diane Dupree levered herself into the car with elaborate caution and fastened her threadbare seat belt. Turk drove slowly, and the crowd of villagers followed for a few yards, filling the narrow street.

"They don't like to see me go," Diane said. "They're afraid I might not come back."

Lise shrank a little every time they passed another vehicle, but Turk drove cheerfully once they were back on the paved roads, a cloth cap pulled low over his eyes, humming to himself. Ibu Diane sat patiently, watching the world scroll past.

Lise decided to break Diane's silence. She turned her head and said, "Tell me about Avram Dvali."

"It might be easier if you told me what you already know."

"Well—he taught at the American University, but he was secretive and not especially well-liked by the faculty. He left his teaching position without an explanation less than a year before my father vanished. Someone at the chancery office told me his last paycheck had been forwarded by letter mail to a box address in Kubelick's Grave. According to my mother," at least on the rare and emotionally difficult occasions when Lise had pressed her to talk about the past, "he visited the house several times before he quit his job. There's no listed address for him in Kubelick's Grave, but a search on his name didn't turn up any contemporary address, anywhere. I meant to go to Kubelick's Grave and see if the box address still worked or if there was any record of who had rented it. But it seemed like a long shot."

"You were very close to something you didn't understand. I'm not surprised Genomic Security took an interest in you."

"So Dvali was involved in one of these communicant cults."

"Not *involved* in it. It was *his*. He created it."

Dvali, she said, had taken his Fourth treatment in New Delhi years before he immigrated to the New World. "I met him not long after he was hired by the university.

There are literally thousands of Fourths in the area around Port Magellan—not including those who choose to live out their extended lives quietly and in isolation. Some of us are more organized than others. We don't hold conventions, for obvious reasons, but I meet most of the known Fourths, sooner or later, and I can sort out the cliques and subgroups."

"Dvali had his own group?"

"So I gather. Like-minded people. A few of them." She hesitated. "We're called Fourths, you know, because on Mars the treatment is equivalent to entering a fourth stage of life, an adulthood beyond adulthood. But the treatment doesn't guarantee any special maturity. That's built into the institutions surrounding it as much as into the treatment itself. Avram Dvali brought his own obsession into his Fourthness."

"What obsession?"

"With the Hypotheticals. With the transcendent forces of the universe. Some people chafe at their humanity. They want to be redeemed by something larger than themselves, to ratify their sense of their own unique value. They want to touch God. The paradox of Fourthness is that it's a magnet for such people. We try to contain them, but—" She shrugged. "We don't have the tools the Martians put in place."

"So he organized around the idea of creating a, a—"

"A communicant, a human interface with the Hypotheticals. He was very serious about it. He recruited his group from among our community and then did his best to seal them away from us. They became much more secretive once the process was underway."

"You couldn't stop him?"

"We tried, of course. Dvali's project wasn't the first such attempt. In the past, the intervention of other Fourths was enough to quell the effort—abetted, when necessary, by Sulean Moi, whose authority among *most* Fourths is unquestionable. But Dr. Dvali was immune to moral suasion, and by the time Sulean Moi arrived, he and his group were in hiding. We've had very sporadic contact with them since—too little and too late to stop them."

"You mean there's a child?"

"Yes. His name, I'm told, is Isaac. He would be twelve years old by now."

"My father disappeared twelve years ago. You think he might have joined this group?"

"No—from your description of him and my knowledge of Dvali's recruiting, no, I'm sorry, he's not among them."

"Then maybe he knew something dangerous about them—maybe they abducted him."

"As Fourths we're inhibited against that kind of violence. What you're suggesting isn't *impossible,* but it's extremely unlikely. I've never heard even a rumor that Dvali was capable of such a thing. If anything like that happened to your father, it was more likely the work of Genomic Security. They were sniffing at Dvali's heels even then."

"Why would DGS kidnap my father?"

"Presumably to interrogate him. If he resisted—" Diane shrugged unhappily.

"Why would he resist?"

"I don't know. I never met your father. I can't answer that."

"They interrogated him and then, what, killed him?"

"I don't know."

Turk said, "They have what they call Executive Action Committees in DGS, Lise. They write their own legal ticket and they do what they want. I'm pretty sure that's who took Tomas Ginn. Tomas is a Fourth, and Fourths are notoriously hard to interrogate—they're not especially afraid of death and they have a high tolerance to pain. Getting any information out of a stubborn

Fourth means putting him through a process that's usually, in the end, fatal."

"They killed Tomas?"

"I expect so. Or transported him to some secret prison to kill him a little more slowly."

Could Brian have known about this, learned about it at work? Lise had a brief but horrifying vision of the DGS staff at the consulate laughing at her, at her naïve quest to uncover the truth about her father. She had been walking over an abyss on a skin of thin ice, nothing to protect her but her own ignorance.

But—no. As an institution, Genomic Security might be capable of that; Brian was not. Unhappy as she had been in her marriage, she knew Brian intimately. Brian was many things. But he was not a murderer.

Clever as *Ibu* Diane had been about discarding cars and clothing, Turk seemed to lose some of his confidence as they left the wooded lands and entered the industrialized outskirts of Port Magellan. Coming past the oil refineries at dusk, the ocean on the left and the refineries emitting a kind of fungal glow, he said, "There's a couple of vehicles I keep seeing ever since we got on the main road. Like they're pacing us. But it could be my imagination."

"Then we shouldn't go directly to Arundji's," Diane said. "In fact we should get off the highway as soon as possible."

"I'm not saying we're being followed. It's just something I noticed."

"Assume the worst. Take the next exit. Find a gas station or somewhere we can stop without arousing suspicion."

"I know people around here," Turk said. "People I can trust, if we need a place to stay overnight."

"Thank you, Turk, but I don't think we should

endanger anyone else. And I doubt Lise is anxious to make the acquaintance of one of your old girlfriends."

"Didn't say anything about a girlfriend," Turk said, but he blushed.

He pulled into a filling station attached to a retail store. This was the part of Port Magellan where the refinery workers lived, lots of prefabricated bungalows assembled in haste during the boom years and gone shabby since. He parked away from the pumps, under an umbrella tree. The last daylight had gone and there was only the yellow-orange glare of the street lamps.

"If you want to dump the car," Turk said, "there's a bus station a couple of blocks down. We can catch the bus to Rice Bay and walk to Arundji's. Won't get there till midnight, though."

"Maybe that's best," Diane said.

"Hate to abandon another vehicle, though. Who's paying for all this transportation?"

"Friends and friends of friends," Diane said. "Don't worry about it. Don't take anything out of the car."

Lise begged permission to go into the small store and buy something to eat—they hadn't stopped for a meal since breakfast—while Turk and Diane unscrewed and discarded the vehicle's license plates.

She bought cheese, crackers, and bottled water for the bus trip. At the counter she noticed a stack of disposable utility phones, the kind you pick up when you've lost your personal unit, also favored, or so she had read, by drug dealers seeking anonymity. She grabbed one and added it to the groceries. Then she walked around the back of the store, bag in one hand and phone in the other.

She tapped out Brian's home number.

He picked up almost immediately. "Yes?"

Lise was briefly paralyzed by the sound of his voice. She thought about clicking off. Then she said, "Brian? I can't talk right now, but I want you to know I'm okay."

"Lise . . . please, tell me where you are."

"I can't. But one thing. This is important. There's a man named Tomas Ginn—that's T-O-M-A-S, G-I-N-N—who was taken into custody a couple of days ago. Presumably without a warrant or any legal record. It's possible he's being held by Genomic Security or somebody claiming to be DGS. Can you check on this? I mean, is it okay with you that people are being kidnapped? If not, is there anything you can do to get this man set free?"

"Listen to me, Lise. Listen. You don't know what you're involved in. You're with Turk Findley, right? Did he tell you he's a criminal? That's why he fled the States, Lise. He—"

She turned and saw Turk come around the corner of the store. Too late to hide. She closed the phone, but that was a useless gesture. She could see the anger on his face in the stark artificial light. Wordlessly, he took the phone from her hand and threw it into the air.

The phone sailed past a lamp standard and fluttered like a huge moth before disappearing down the embankment of a ravine.

Too shocked to speak, Lise turned to face him. Turk's face was livid. She had never seen him like this. He said, "You have no fucking clue, do you? No idea what's at stake here."

"Turk—"

He didn't listen. He grabbed her wrist and began to pull her toward the street. She managed to break his grip, though she dropped the bag of cheese and crackers.

"Goddamnit, I'm not a child!"

"Fucking prove it," he said.

The bus ride wasn't exactly pleasant.

Lise sat sullenly apart from Turk, watching the night roll by in the frame of the window. She was determined not to think about what Turk had done, or what she might have done wrong, or what Brian had said, at least until she calmed down. But as the anger abated she simply felt desolate. The last bus south was half-empty, the only other passengers a few grim-faced men in khaki pants and blue shirts, probably shift workers who lived downcoast to save the cost of city rent. The man in the seat behind her was muttering in Farsi, possibly to himself.

The bus stopped periodically at concrete-block terminals and storefront depots off the highway, a world populated by forlorn men and flickering lights. Then the city was behind them and there was only the highway and the horizonless dark of the sea.

Diane Dupree came across the aisle and took the seat next to Lise.

"Turk thinks you need to take the risk more seriously," the old woman said.

"Did he tell you that?"

"I surmised."

"I do take it seriously."

"The phone was a bad idea. In all likelihood the call can't be traced, but who knows what technology the police or Genomic Security might bring to bear? It's better not to make assumptions."

"I do take it seriously," Lise insisted again, "it's just . . ."

But she couldn't finish, couldn't find the words for the sudden awareness of exactly how much of life as she had known it was slipping away under the wheels of the bus.

By the time the bus reached a depot near Arundji's airport Turk had stopped gnashing his teeth and had begun to look a little sheepish. He gave Lise an apologetic sidelong glance, which she ignored.

"It's a good half mile to Arundji's," he said. "You two up for the walk?"

"Yes," Diane said. Lise just nodded.

The road from the depot was rural and sparsely lit. As they walked Lise listened to the crackle of her footsteps on the barely-paved verge of the road, the rush of wind raking scrubby, treeless lots. Off in the high grass some insect buzzed—she could have mistaken it for a cricket except for the mournful tone of its creaking, like a disconsolate man running his thumbnail over the teeth of a comb.

They approached the fenced territory of Arundji's at a back entrance, away from the main gate. Turk fished a key out of his pocket and swung open a chain-link gate, saying, "You might want to stay inconspicuous from here on in. The terminal shuts down after ten o'clock, but we've got a maintenance crew on site and security guards out where they're grading the new runway."

Lise said, "Don't you have a right to be here?"

"Sort of. But it would be best not to attract too much attention."

She followed Turk and Diane to an aluminum-sheet hangar, one of dozens lined up at the rear of the terminal. Its huge doors were chained shut and Turk said, "I wasn't kidding about that crowbar. I'll need something to spring this."

"You're locked out of your own hangar?"

"Kind of a funny story." He walked off, apparently looking for a tool.

Lise was sweaty and her calves ached from the walk and she needed to pee. She no longer owned a change of clothes.

"Forgive Turk," Diane said. "It isn't that he distrusts you. He's afraid for you. He—"

"Are you going to do this from now on? Make these guru-like pronouncements? Because it's getting kind of tiresome."

Diane stared, wide-eyed. Then, somewhat to Lise's relief, she laughed. Lise said, "I mean, I'm sorry, but—"

"No! Don't apologize. You're absolutely right. It's one of the hazards of great age, the temptation to pronounce judgments."

"I know what Turk is afraid of. Turk is burning his bridges behind him. My bridges are still there. I have a life I can go back to."

"Nevertheless," Diane said, "here you are." She smiled again. "Speaks the guru."

Turk came back with a piece of rebar from the construction site and used it to lever off the latch, which was flimsier than the padlock attached to it and came away from the door with a concussive twang. He rolled open the big steel doors and switched on the interior light.

His plane was inside. His twin-engine Skyrex. Lise remembered this aircraft from their abortive flight across the mountains—ages ago, it seemed.

Lise and Diane used the grimy employees' restroom while Turk did his preflight checks. When Lise came back from the rear of the hangar she found him in a heated discussion with a uniformed man. The man in the uniform was short, balding, and conspicuously unhappy. "I have to call Mr. Arundji," he said, "you *know* that, Turk," and Turk said, "Give me a few minutes, that's all I ask—haven't I bought enough rounds over the last few years to earn me that?"

"I'm advising you that this is not allowed."

"Fine. No problem. Fifteen minutes, then you can call anybody you want."

"I'm giving you notice here. Nobody can say I let you get away with this."

"Nobody'll say any such thing."

"Fifteen minutes. More like ten."

The guard turned and walked away.

In the old days, Turk said, an airport was anywhere in Equatoria you could carve out a landing strip. A little four-seater prop plane would get you places you couldn't otherwise go, and nobody worried about filing a flight plan. But that had changed under the relentless pressure of the Provisional Government and the air-travel conglomerates. Big business and big government would drive places like Arundji's into the ground, Turk said, sooner or later. Even now, he said, it wasn't exactly legal to be making this kind of after-hours departure from a closed strip. Probably it would cost him his license. But he was being squeezed out anyhow. Nothing to lose, he said. Nothing much. Then he pivoted the plane onto a vacant runway and started his takeoff run.

This was Turk doing what he claimed to do best, Lise thought: putting on his shoes and walking away from something. He believed in the redemptive power of distant horizons. It was a faith she couldn't bring herself to share.

The aircraft left the ground swaying like a kite, its huge feathered props pulling them toward the moonlit mountains, the engine purring. *Ibu* Diane peered out the window and murmured something about "how much quieter these things are than they used to be—oh, years ago now, years ago."

Lise watched the arc of the coast tilt to starboard and the distant smudge of Port Magellan grow even smaller. She waited patiently for Turk to say something, maybe even to apologize, but he didn't speak—only pointed once, abruptly; and Lise looked up in time to see the white-hot trail of a shooting star flash over the peaks and passes of the mountains toward the emptiness of the western desert.

CHAPTER FOURTEEN

Brian Gately wasn't prepared for the violent image that popped out of his mailbox that morning. It provoked an unpleasant memory.

In the summer of his thirteenth year Brian had done volunteer work at the Episcopal church where his family worshipped. He had not been a particularly devout teenager—doctrinal matters confused him, he avoided Bible Study—but the church, both the institution and the physical building, possessed a reassuring weight, a quality he later learned to call "gravitas." The church put a sensible boundary on things. That was why his parents, who had lived through the economic and religious uncertainties of the Spin, went to church every week, and that was why Brian liked it. That, and the pinewood smell of the newly-built chapel, and the way the stained-glass windows broke the morning light into colors. So he had volunteered for summer work and had spent a few drowsy days sweeping the chapel or opening doors for elderly parishioners or running errands for the pastor or the choirmaster, and in mid-August he was recruited to help set up tables for the annual picnic.

The suburb in which Brian lived was graced with a number of well-maintained parks and wooded ravines. The annual church picnic—an institution so quaint the words themselves had a sort of horse-and-buggy aura about them—was held in the largest of these parks. More than a picnic, it was (according to the flyer in the Sunday bulletin) a Day of Family Communion, and there were plenty of families there to commune with, three generations in some cases, and Brian was kept busy laying out plastic tablecloths and lugging coolers of ice and soft drinks until the event was well under way, hot dogs circulating freely, kids he barely knew tossing Frisbees, toddlers underfoot, and it was the perfect day for it, sunny but not too hot, a breeze to carry off the smoke of the grills. Even at the age of thirteen Brian had appreciated the slightly narcotic atmosphere of the picnic, an afternoon suspended in time.

Then his friends Lyle and Kev showed up and tempted him away from the adults. Down through the woods there was a creek where stones might be skipped or tadpoles captured. Brian begged a break from his volunteer work and went off with them into the green shade of the forest. Down by the verge of the creek, which flowed in a shallow ribbon over gravel tilled by ancient glaciers, they found not just stones to throw but, surprisingly, a habitation: a scrap of canvas tent, all awry, and plastic grocery bags, rusted cans (pork and beans, animal food), empty bottles and brown flasks, a corroded shopping cart, and finally, between two oak trees whose roots had grown out of the ground and twined together like a fist, a bundle of old clothes— which, examined more closely, was not a bundle of old clothes at all, but a dead man.

The dead homeless man must have been there for days, undiscovered. He looked both bloated, a tattered red cotton shirt stretched taut across his enormous belly, and shrunken, as if something essential had been sucked out of him. The exposed parts of him had been nibbled by animals, there were bugs on his milky-white eyes, and when the wind came around the smell was so bad that Brian's friend Kev turned and promptly vomited into the glassy water of the creek.

The three of them ran back to the friendly part of the park and told Pastor Carlysle what they'd found, and that was the end of the picnic. The police were called, an ambulance came to retrieve the body, and the suddenly somber gathering broke up.

Kev and Lyle, over the course of the next six months, stopped showing up for Sunday services, as if the church and dead man had become associated one with the other, but Brian had the opposite reaction. He believed in the protective power of the chapel, precisely because he had seen what lay beyond it. He had seen unhallowed death.

He had seen death, and death shouldn't have surprised him: nevertheless he was shocked by what popped out of his mailbox twenty years later, within the sanctified walls of his office and the carefully-defined if crumbling boundaries of his adult life.

Two days before he had received the brief, aborted phone call from Lise.

It had come late in the late evening. Brian had been on his way home from one of those tedious consulate social nights, drinks at the ambassador's residence and small talk with the usual suspects. Brian didn't drink much but what he did drink went to his head, and he let his car do the driving on the way home. Slowly, then— the car was idiotically literal-minded about speed limits and restricted to the few streets with automated driving grids—but safely, he came back to the apartment he had once shared with Lise, with its attendant atmosphere of claustrophobia and something that might have been desperation had it been less comfortably furnished. He showered before bed, and as he toweled off he listened to the silence of the city night and thought: am I inside the circle or out of it?

The phone rang as he turned out the lights. He put the slate wedge to his ear and registered her distant voice.

He tried to warn her. She said things he didn't immediately understand.

And then the connection was broken.

Probably he should have gone to Sigmund and Weil with this, but he didn't. Couldn't. The message was personal. It was meant for him and for him alone. Sigmund and Weil could get along without it. Early the next day he sat in his office thinking about Lise, his failed marriage. Then he picked up the phone and called Pieter Kirchberg, his contact at the Security and Law Enforcement Division of the UN Provisional Government.

Kirchberg had done him a number of small favors in the past and Brian had done more than a few in return. The settled eastern coast of Equatoria was a United Nations protectorate, at least nominally, with a complicated set of laws established and constantly revised by international committees. The closest thing to a fully-established police force was Interpol, though blue-helmeted soldiers did most of the daily enforcement. The result was a bureaucracy that created more paperwork than justice and existed mainly to smooth over conflicts between hostile national interests. To get anything done, you had to know people. Kirchberg was one of the people Brian knew.

Kirchberg answered promptly and Brian listened to his inevitable complaints—the weather, the bullying oil cartels, his boneheaded underlings—before getting down to business. Finally, as Kirchberg wound down, he said, "I want to give you a name."

"Fine," he said. "Just what I need. More work. Whose name?"

"Tomas Ginn." He spelled it.

"And why are you interested in this person?"

"Departmental matter," Brian said.

"Some desperate American criminal? A better-baby salesman, a renegade organ-vendor?"

"Something like that."

"I'll run it when I can. You owe me a drink."

"Anytime," Brian said.

He didn't tell Sigmund and Weil about that, either.

It was the following morning that the photograph rolled out of his printer, along with an unsigned note from Kirchberg.

Brian looked at the photograph, then put it face down on his desk, then picked it up again.

He had seen worse things. What he thought about immediately and involuntarily was the body he had discovered beyond the outer limits of the church picnic a quarter of a century ago, the body which had lain among the exposed roots of two trees with its eyes gone milky white and its skin traversed by feckless ants. He felt the same involuntary lurch of his stomach.

The photograph was of an old man's body broken on a salt-encrusted rock. The marks on the body might have been massive bruises or simply the effects of decomposition. But there was no mistaking the bullet wound in the forehead.

Kirchberg's unsigned note said: *Washed up near South Point two days ago; no papers but identified as Tomas W. Ginn (U.S. Merchant Marine DNA database). One of yours?*

Mr. Ginn had wandered outside the boundaries of the

picnic, it seemed. And so, he thought with sickly dismay, had Lise.

In the afternoon he called Pieter Kirchberg again. This time Kirchberg was less chatty.

"I got what you sent me," Brian said.

"No need to thank me."

"One of ours, you said. What did you mean by that?"

"I'd just as soon not discuss it."

"An American, you mean?"

No answer. *One of yours.* So, yes, an American, or was Pieter suggesting that Tomas Ginn belonged to Genomic Security? Or that his death did? Maybe he meant *one of your killings.*

"Is there anything else?" Kirchberg asked. "Because I have a lot of work waiting for me. . . ."

"One more favor," Brian said. "If you don't mind, Pieter. Another name."

PART THREE

INTO
THE
WEST

CHAPTER FIFTEEN

Before he could say anything more—in Martian or in English—the boy Isaac stopped speaking and fell into a sleep from which he could not be aroused. The Fourths continued to tend to his needs but were unable to treat or diagnose his condition. His vital signs were stable and he seemed to be in no immediate danger.

Sulean Moi sat with the child in his room as the sun shone on the desert beyond the window, clocking shadows across the alkaline grit. Two days passed. One morning, as occasionally happened this time of year, a storm blew out of the mountains, a shelf of coal-black clouds that produced much lightning and thunder but only a little rain. By sunset the storm had gone and the sky in its wake was a radiant, purified turquoise. The air smelled fresh and astringent. Still the boy slept.

Out in the western wastes spindly plants were provoked by the brief rain to flower. Perhaps other things, too, bloomed in the emptiness. Things like Isaac's ocular rose.

Outwardly calm, Sulean was terrified.

The boy had spoken with Esh's voice.

She wondered if this was what religious texts meant when they talked about trembling in the presence of God. The Hypotheticals weren't gods—if she understood what that simple but strangely elastic word meant—but they were just as powerful and just as inscrutable. She didn't believe they possessed conscious intent, and even the word "they" was a misnomer, a crude anthropomorphism. But when "they" manifested themselves, the natural human response was to cower and hide—the instinctive reaction of the rabbit to the fox, the fox to the hunter.

Twice in a lifetime, Sulean thought: that's my special burden, to witness this twice in a lifetime.

At times she napped in the chair next to the bed where Isaac lay, his chest rising and falling with the cadence of his breath. Often she dreamed—more fiercely and deeply than she had dreamed since she was a child—and in her dreams she was in a different desert, where the horizon was close and the sky a dark and penetrating blue. In this desert there were rocks and sand and also a number of brightly-colored tubular or angular growths, like a madman's hallucinations come to life. And of course there was the boy. Not Isaac. The other boy, the first one. He was more frail than Isaac, his skin was darker, but his eyes, like Isaac's, had become gold-flecked and strange. He was lying where he had fallen in a stupor of exhaustion, and although Sulean was in the company of a number of grown men she was the first who dared approach him.

The boy opened his eyes. He could not otherwise move, because his legs, arms, and torso had been bound with pliant ropes or vines. The strange growths had pinned him there, and some of them had pierced his body.

Surely he must be dead. How could anyone survive such an impalement?

But he opened his eyes. He opened his eyes and whispered, "*Sulean*—"

She woke in the chair next to Isaac's bed, sweating in the dry heat. Mrs. Rebka had come into the room and was staring at her.

"We're having a meeting in the common room," Mrs. Rebka said. "We would like you to be there, Ms. Moi."

"All right. Yes."

"Has his condition changed?"

"No," Sulean said.

Thinking: *Not yet.*

It wasn't really a coma. It was only sleep, though a profound one that lasted many days. Isaac woke from it that evening, and when he did, he was alone in his room.

He felt . . . different.

More alert than usual: not only awake but more awake than he had ever been. His vision seemed sharper and more focused. He felt as if he could count the dust motes in the air, if he wanted, even though there was only the light of his bedside lamp to see by.

He wanted to go west. He felt the attraction of what was out there, although there was no word for it, no word he knew. A presence, rising; and it wanted him, and he wanted it, with an urgency akin to love or lust.

But he wouldn't leave the compound, not tonight. Isaac's first and purely instinctive long walk had come to nothing—apart from the discovery of the rose—and there was no use repeating it. Not until he was stronger. Still, he did need to get away from the narrow confinement of his room. To smell the air and feel it on his skin.

He stood, dressed, and walked downstairs past the closed doors of the large central room from which emanated the solemn voices of adults. He went out to the courtyard. A guard had been posted at the far gate, presumably to keep him from wandering away again. But he stayed on the other side of the houses, in the walled garden.

The air was cool tonight and the garden was lush. He stepped in among the plants, following the gardener's cobbled path. The night-blooming succulents had put out blossoms, richly colorful even in the faint moonlight.

Other things, small things, stirred in the soil where the ash had been driven down by the rain.

Isaac put his hand palm-down on a bare patch of earth. The soil was warm, retaining what it had conserved of the day's heat.

Overhead, the stars were crystal-bright. Isaac looked a long time at the stars. They were symbols hovering on the brink of intelligibility, letters that made words that made sentences he could almost (not quite) read.

Something touched his hand where it rested on the rich garden loam, and Isaac looked down again. When he pulled his hand away he saw the earth swell and crumble minutely—*a worm,* he thought; but it wasn't a worm. It wasn't anything he had ever seen before. It shrugged itself slowly from the soil like a knuckled, fleshy finger. Maybe some kind of root, but it grew too quickly to be natural. It extended itself toward Isaac's hand as if it sensed his warmth.

He wasn't afraid of it. Well, no, that wasn't true. Part of him *was* afraid of it, almost paralyzed with terror. The everyday part of him wanted to recoil and run back to the safety of his room. But above and enclosing the everyday part of him was this new sense of himself, bold and confident, and to the new Isaac the pale green finger wasn't frightening or even unfamiliar. He recognized it, although he couldn't name it.

He allowed it to touch him. Slowly, the green finger encircled his wrist. Isaac drew a curious strength from it, and it from him, he suspected, and he looked back at the sky where the stars which were suns glimmered brightly. Now each star seemed as familiar as a face, each with its own color and weight and distance and identity, known but not named. And like an animal scenting the air, he faced once more to the west.

Two things were obvious to Sulean as she entered the common room. One was that much discussion had taken place in her absence—she had been called here to testify, not to deliberate.

The second obvious thing was an atmosphere of collective sadness, almost mourning, as if these people understood that the life they had created for themselves was coming to an end. And that was no doubt true. This community couldn't exist much longer. It had been created for the purpose of birthing and nurturing Isaac, and that process would soon be finished . . . one way or another.

The majority of these people must have been born before the Spin, Sulean thought. Like other Terrestrial Fourths, a large percentage of them had come from the academic community, but not all; there were technicians who helped maintain the cryogenic incubators; there was a mechanic, a gardener. Like Martian Fourths, these people had separated themselves from the general community. They were not like the Fourths among whom Sulean had been raised . . . but they *were* Fourths; they stank of Fourthness. So glum, so self-important, so blind to their own arrogance.

Avram Dvali, of course, was chairing the meeting. He waved Sulean to a chair at the front of the room. "We'd like you to explain a few things, Ms. Moi, before the crisis proceeds any further."

Sulean sat primly erect. "Of course I'm happy to help in any way I can."

Mrs. Rebka, who sat at Dr. Dvali's right at the head table, gave her a sharply skeptical look. "I hope that's true. You know, when we took on the task of raising Isaac thirteen years ago we faced some opposition—"

"*Raising* him, Mrs. Rebka, or *creating* him?"

Mrs. Rebka ignored the remark. "Opposition from other members of the Fourth community. We acted on convictions not everyone shared. We know we're a minority, a minority within a minority. And we knew you were out there, Ms. Moi, doing whatever work you do for the Martians. We knew you might eventually find us, and we were prepared to be frank and open with you. We respect your connection to a community far older than our own."

"Thank you," Sulean said, not concealing her own skepticism.

"But we had hoped you would be as frank with us as we were with you."

"If you have a question, please ask it."

"The procedure that created Isaac has been attempted before."

"It has been," Sulean admitted, "yes."

"And is it true that you have some personal experience of that?"

This time she wasn't quite so quick to answer. "Yes." The story of her upbringing had circulated widely among the Terrestrial Fourths.

"Would you share that experience with us?"

"If I'm reluctant to talk about it, the reasons are largely personal. The memory isn't pleasant."

"Nevertheless," Mrs. Rebka said.

Sulean closed her eyes. She didn't want to recall these events. The memory came to her, unbidden, all too often. But Mrs. Rebka was right, as much as Sulean hated to admit it. The time had come.

The boy.

The boy in the desert. The boy in the Martian desert. The boy had died in the dry southern province of Bar

Kea, some distance from the biological research station where he had been born and where he had lived all his life.

Sulean was the same age as the boy. She had not been born at the Bar Kea Desert Station but she could remember no other home. Her life before Bar Kea was little more than a story she had been told by her teachers: a story about a girl who had been washed away, along with her family, by a flood along the Paia River, and who had been rescued from the intake filter of a dam three miles downstream. Her parents had died and the small girl, this unremembered Sulean, had been so grievously wounded that she could only be saved by profound biotechnical intervention.

Specifically, the child Sulean had to be rebuilt using the same process that was used to extend life and create Fourths.

The treatment was more or less successful. Her damaged body and brain were reconstructed according to templates written in her DNA. For obvious reasons, she remembered nothing of her life before the accident. Her salvation was a second birth, and Sulean had relearned the world the way an infant learns it, acquiring language a second time and crawling before she took her first (or second) tentative steps.

But there was a drawback to the treatment, which was why it was so rarely used as a medical intervention. It conferred its customary longevity, but it also interrupted the natural cycle of her life. At puberty, every Martian child developed the deep wrinkles that made Martians appear so distinctive to Terrestrials. But that didn't happen to Sulean. She remained, by Martian standards, sexless and grotesquely smooth-skinned, an overgrown infant. When she looked in a mirror, even today, Sulean was inevitably reminded of something pink and unformed: a grub writhing in a rotten stump. To protect her from humiliation she had been sheltered and nurtured by the Fourths who saved her life, the Fourths of Bar Kea Desert Station. At the Station she had a hundred indulgent, caring parents, and she had the dry hills of Bar Kea for a playground.

The only other child at the Station was the boy named Esh.

They had not given him any other name, only Esh.

Esh had been built to communicate with the Hypotheticals, though it seemed to Sulean he could barely communicate even with the people around him. Even with Sulean, whose company he obviously enjoyed, he seldom spoke more than a few words. Esh was kept apart, and Sulean was allowed to see him only at appointed times.

Nevertheless she was his friend. It didn't matter to Sulean that the boy's nervous system was supposedly receptive to the obscure signals of alien beings, any more than it mattered to Esh that she was as pink as a stillborn fetus. Their uniquenesses made them alike and had thus become irrelevant.

The Fourths at Bar Kea Desert Station encouraged the friendship. They had been disappointed by Esh's refractory silences and his outward display of dull-normal intelligence. He was studious but incurious. He sat wide-eyed in the classrooms the adults had designed for him, and he absorbed a reasonable amount of information, but he was indifferent to it all. The sky was full of stars and the desert was full of sand, but stars and sand might have traded places for all it mattered to Esh. Whether he spoke to the Hypotheticals, or they to him, no one could say. He was stubbornly silent on the subject.

Esh was at his liveliest when he was alone with Sulean. They were allowed to leave the station on certain days to explore the nearby desert. They were supervised, of course—an adult was always within sight—but compared to the closeted spaces of the Station this was wild freedom. Bar Kea was formidably dry, but the scarce spring rains sometimes pooled among the rocks, and Sulean delighted in the small creatures that swam in these short-lived ponds. There were tiny fish that encased themselves in hibernatory cysts, like seeds, when the water dried, and sprang back to life during the rare rains. She liked to cup the populated water in her hands, Esh watching with silent wonder as the wriggling things slipped between her fingers.

Esh never asked questions, but Sulean pretended he did. At the Station she was always being taught, always being encouraged to listen; alone with Esh she became the teacher, he the rapt and silent audience. Often she would explain to him what she had learned that day or week.

People had not always lived on Mars, she told him one day as they wandered among sunlit, dusty rocks. Years and centuries ago their ancestors had come from Earth, a planet closer to the sun. You couldn't see Earth directly, because the Hypotheticals had enclosed it in a lightless barrier—but you knew it was there, because it had a moon that circled it.

She mentioned the Hypotheticals (called by Martians *Ab-ashken*, a word compounded of the root-words for "powerful" and "remote"), cautiously at first, wondering how Esh would react. She knew he was part Hypothetical himself and she didn't want to offend him. But the name provoked no special response, only his usual blank indifference. So Sulean was free to lecture, imagine, dream. Even then the Hypotheticals had fascinated her.

They live among the stars, as far as anyone knows, she told the boy.

Esh, of course, said nothing in return.

They're not exactly animals, they're more like machines, but they grow and reproduce themselves.

They do things for no apparent reason, she told him. *They put the Earth inside a slow-time bubble millions of years ago, but no one knows why.*

No one has talked to them, she said, *unless you have, I suppose, and no one has seen them. But pieces of them fall out of the sky from time to time, and strange things happen. . . .*

Pieces of them fall from the sky: this last piece of information caused considerable consternation among Dr. Dvali's Fourths.

Dvali cleared his throat and said, "There's nothing about such an event in the Martian Archives."

"No," Sulean admitted. "Nor did we ever mention it in direct communication with the Earth. Even on Mars it's a rare occurrence—something that happens once every two or three hundred years."

Mrs. Rebka said, "Excuse me, but *what* happens? I don't understand."

"The Hypotheticals exist in a kind of ecology, Mrs. Rebka. They bloom, flourish, and die back, only to repeat the cycle again, over and over."

"By the Hypotheticals," Dr. Dvali said, "I presume you mean their machines."

"That may not be a meaningful distinction. There's no evidence that their self-reproducing machines are under the control of anything but their own networked intelligence and their own contingent evolution. Naturally, the detritus of their lives circulates through the solar system. Periodically the debris is captured by the gravitation of an inner planet."

"Why haven't these things fallen on the Earth?"

"Before the Spin the Earth existed in a much younger solar system. Five billion years ago the Hypotheticals had barely established themselves in the Kuiper Belt. If their machines did occasionally enter the Earth's atmosphere it would have been an isolated, rare event. There are enough reports of hovering lights or strange aerial objects to suggest that perhaps it *did* happen, now and then, though no one recognized it as such. When the Spin barrier was put in place it excluded any such fall-through, and even now the Earth is protected from the excessive radiation of the sun by a different kind of membrane. Mars, for good or ill, is more exposed. Martians didn't arrive in the modern day as strangers, Dr. Dvali. We've grown and evolved for millennia with the knowledge that the Hypotheticals exist and that the solar system is, in effect, their property."

"The ash that fell on us," Mrs. Rebka said, her voice throaty with a kind of hostile urgency, "was that the same phenomenon?"

"Presumably. And the growths in the desert. It's only natural to assume that *this* solar system has also hosted Hypotheticals for countless centuries. The annual meteor showers are more likely their detritus than the simple remains of ancient rocks. The ashfall was just a particularly dense example, perhaps from a recent exfoliation. As if we had passed through a cloud of, of—"

"Of their discarded cells," Dr. Dvali said.

"Cells, in a sense, shed, perhaps discarded, but not necessarily inert or entirely dead. Some partial metabolism persists." Hence the ocular rose and the other abortive, short-lived growths.

"Your people must have studied these remains."

"Oh yes," Sulean said. "In fact we cultivated them. Much of our biological technology was derived from the study of them. Even the longevity treatment is remotely derived from Hypothetical sources. Most of our pharmaceuticals entail some element of Hypothetical technology—that's why we grow them at cryogenic temperatures, simulating the outer solar system."

"And the Martian boy—and Isaac as well, I suppose—"

"The treatment *they* received is much more closely related to the raw matter of Hypothetical devices. I suppose you thought it was some purely human pharmaceutical? Another example of marvelous Martian biotech? And in a sense it is. But it's something more, too. Something inhuman, inherently uncontrollable."

"And yet Wun Ngo Wen brought the seed stock to Earth."

"If Wun had discovered the older, wiser culture we all assumed must exist on Earth, I'm sure he would have been frank about the origins of it. But he found something quite different, unfortunately. He entrusted many of our secrets to Jason Lawton, who rashly experimented on himself—and Jason Lawton circulated the secrets to people *he* trusted, who proved no more prudent."

Sulean was aware of the shock in the room. These were names, Wun Ngo Wen and Jason Lawton, reverently spoken among Terrestrial Fourths. But they were mortal men, after all. Susceptible to doubt, fear, greed, and hasty decisions repented at leisure.

"Still," Dr. Dvali said at last, "your people could have told us—"

"These are *Fourth* things!" Sulean was surprised by the vehemence in her own voice. "You don't understand. It's not *zuret*—" She couldn't exactly translate the word and all its nuances. "It's not correct, it's not *proper*, to share them with the unaltered. The unaltered don't want to know; these things are for the very old to worry about; by accepting the burden of longevity they accept *this* burden too. But I would have shared them with *you*, Dr. Dvali, before you began this project, if you hadn't hidden yourself so well."

But the people she was addressing, born in the raucous jungle that was Earth, couldn't be expected to understand.

Even their Fourthness was alien. The last estate of life, the elective decades, meant nothing more to them than a few more years in which to draw breath. On Mars all Fourths were ritually separated from the rest of the population. When you entered the Fourth Age—unless you entered it, as Sulean had, under exceptional circumstances—you accepted its constraints and agreed to live according to its cloistered traditions. The Terrestrial Fourths had attempted to re-create some of those traditions, and this group had even withdrawn to a kind of desert sanctuary, but it wasn't the same . . . they didn't understand the burden of it; they hadn't been initiated into the sacral knowledge.

They lacked, perversely, the terrible dry monasticism of the Martian Fourths. It was what Sulean had hated about the Fourths who raised her. On Mars the Fourths moved as if through the invisible corridors of some ancient labyrinth. They had traded joy for a dusty *gravitas*. But even that was better than this anarchic recklessness— all the vices of terrestrial humanity, needlessly prolonged.

Dr. Dvali, perhaps sensing her agitation, said, "But what about the child? Tell us what happened to Esh, Ms. Moi."

What happened to the boy was both simple and terrible. It began with an infall of Hypothetical debris from the outer system.

This was not entirely unexpected. Martian astronomers had tracked the movement of the dust cloud for days before its arrival. There was some general excitement about the event. Sulean had been granted permission to climb the stairs to a high parapet of Bar Kea Desert Station, which had served as a fortress in the last of the wars five hundred years ago, to watch the fiery infall.

There had been no such event in two lifetimes, and Sulean wasn't the only one who climbed up on the walls to watch. Bar Kea Station had been built with its back to the spine of the Omod Mountains, and the dry southern plains, where much of the debris would fall, stretched roadless and mysterious in the starlight. That night the sky was shot through with falling stars like threaded fire, and Sulean stared at the show with rapt attention until an unwelcome sleepiness overcame her and one of her minders put a hand on her shoulder and escorted her back to bed.

Esh had come up to the parapet too, and although he watched the green and golden glow of the infalling debris he betrayed no reaction.

Back in bed Sulean found her sleepiness had evaporated. She lay awake for a long time thinking of what she had seen. She thought about the accumulated debris of Ab-ashken devices, things that ate ice and rock and lived and died over the course of long millennia in lonely places far from the sun, the remnants of them burning as they fell through the atmosphere. In some of these events enough of the debris had survived that it began a kind of abortive new life—the history books described curious growths of an incomplete and oddly mechanical nature, unsuited to the heat and (to them) corrosive air of this planet. Would that happen again? If so, would she witness it? Astronomers said the bulk of the material would fall not terribly far from Bar Kea Station. Fascinated as she was by the Hypotheticals, Sulean longed to see a living example.

So, apparently, did Esh.

There was considerable excitement in the station the next morning. Esh was in an agitated state—had cried for the first time since infancy, and one of his tenders had found him knocking his head against the southern wall of his sleeping chamber. Some invisible influence had shattered his customary complacency.

Sulean wanted to see him—*demanded* to be allowed

to see him, when she heard the news—but she was refused, for days on end. Doctors were called in to examine Esh. The boy slipped in and out of fevers and deep,
impenetrable sleeps. Whenever he was awake he demanded to be allowed to go outside.

He had stopped eating, and by the time Sulean was allowed into his chamber she hardly recognized him. Esh
had been chubby, round-cheeked, young for his age. Now
he had grown gaunt, and his eyes, strangely flecked with
gold, had retreated into the bony contours of his skull.

She asked him what was wrong, not expecting an answer, but he startled her by saying, "I want to go see
them."

"What? *Who?* Who do you want to see?"

"The Ab-ashken."

The boy's timid voice made the word sound even
stranger than it otherwise might have. Sulean felt a chill
creep up from the small of her spine to the crown of her
head.

"What do you mean, you want to go see them?"

"Out in the desert," Esh said.

"There's nothing out there."

"Yes, there is. The Ab-ashken."

Then he began to cry, and Sulean had to leave the
room. The nurse who had been attending Esh followed
her into the corridor and said, "He's been asking for
days to leave the building. But this is the first time he
mentioned the Ab-ashken."

Were they really out there, the Hypotheticals, the Ab-
ashken, or at least the fragmentary remains of them?
Sulean posed the question to one of her caretakers, a
fragile elder who had been an astronomer before he became a Fourth. Yes, he said, there had been some activity to the south, and he showed her a set of aerial
photographs that had been taken over the previous few
days.

Here was a wasteland not very different from the landscape beyond the gates of Bar Kea Station—sand, dust, and rocks. But cradled in a broad declivity was a clump of objects so unnatural as to defy description. Half-built, crazily incomplete things, it seemed to Sulean—brightly-colored pipes, silvered hexagonal mirrors, chambered spheres, many of these things linked to one another like the parts of an enormous, impossible insect.

"This must be where he wants to go," Sulean said.

"Possibly. But we can't allow that. The risk is too great. He might come to harm."

"He's coming to harm *here*. He looks like he's dying!"

Her tutor shrugged. "The decision's neither mine nor yours."

Perhaps not. But Sulean was afraid for Esh. As a friend he wasn't much, but he was all she had. He shouldn't be held captive against his will, and Sulean longed to release him. She tried to imagine how she might do that, how she might sneak into his room and smuggle him outside . . . but the corridors of Bar Kea Station were never empty, and Esh was always under guard.

Nor was she often allowed to see him, and Sulean's life seemed empty without his mute presence. Sometimes she walked past his room and winced when she heard him crying or shouting.

The situation remained unchanged for more endless, sunny days. Out in the wasteland, her tutor said, the Abashken growths had bloomed and were beginning to wither, unsuited as they were to this environment. But Esh's frantic anxiety only increased.

Dr. Dvali said, "These growths, were they dangerous?"

"No. There was never anything more than a temporary kind of life to them."

Like hothouse flowers, Sulean thought, transplanted to the wrong climate and soil.

The last time she saw Esh alive was a day later.

Sulean was outside that morning, walking where she used to walk with him. Her minder stood at a discreet distance, mindful that Sulean was troubled and might want time to herself.

It was another sunny day. The rocks cast deep shadows across the sand. Sulean wandered aimlessly near the Station's gates, not really thinking about anything—in fact trying hard not to think about Esh—when she saw him, as startling as a mirage, squatting in the shade of a boulder looking south.

This was inexplicable. Sulean glanced back at her minder, another venerable Fourth. He had paused to rest in the shade of Bar Kea Station's southern wall. The old Fourth had not seen Esh, and Sulean did nothing to betray his presence.

She walked slowly closer, careful not to hurry and make herself conspicuous. Esh looked up plaintively from his hiding place.

She bent down as if examining a piece of shale or a scuttling sandbug and whispered, "How did you get away?"

"Don't tell," Esh demanded.

"I won't, of course I won't. But how—"

"No one was looking. I stole a robe," he added, lifting his arms in the voluminous whiteness of some larger person's desert garb. "I came over the north parapet where it touches the rock wall and climbed down."

"But what are you doing out here? It'll be dark in a couple of hours."

"I'm doing what I have to."

"You need food and water."

"I can do without."

"No you can't." Sulean insisted on giving him her water bottle, which she always carried when she left the shelter of the Station, and a bar of pressed meal she had been saving for herself.

"They'll know I'm gone," Esh said. "Don't tell them you saw me."

This was more conversation than Sulean had ever had with Esh, a comparative flood of words. She said, "I will. I mean, I won't. I won't tell anyone."

"Thank you, Sulean."

Another startling novelty: the first time he had ever said her name, maybe the first time he had said anyone's name. This wasn't just Esh crouching in the sand in front of her, this was Esh plus something else.

The Ab-ashken, Sulean thought.

The Hypotheticals were inside him, looking out through his altered eyes.

Somewhere in the Station a bell began to ring, and Sulean's sleepy minder looked alert and called her name. "Run," she whispered.

But she didn't wait to see if the boy took her advice. She turned back to the Station, pretending nothing had happened, and went to her keeper, and said nothing at all, as if the silence in which Esh had dwelt for so many years had entered her throat and stilled her voice.

"What was it he wanted?" Dvali asked. "To find the fallen artifacts, presumably—but what then?"

"I don't know," Sulean said. "I suppose like calls to like. The same instinct or programming that causes the Hypothetical replicators to cluster and share information and reproduce may have operated equally on the boy Esh. The crisis was caused by his proximity to these devices."

"As is Isaac's?" Mrs. Rebka asked.

"Possibly."

"Your people must have asked these questions."

"Without finding any answers, unfortunately."

Dvali said, "You told us the boy died."

"Yes."

"Tell us how."

Sulean thought: *Must I? Must I endure this yet again?*
Of course she must. Today, as every other day.

He had been gone from the Station for hours and it was
well after dark when Sulean's resolve broke. Frightened
by the thought of Esh alone in the night, and shaken by
the anxiety and alarms that ran through the Station like
electricity in the absence of the boy, she sought out the
man she considered the kindest of her mentors, her astronomy instructor, who used the single name Lochis.
She had seen Esh this afternoon, she told him through a
gush of guilty tears. When Lochis finally understood, he
ordered her to stay where she was while he assembled a
search party.

A group of five men and three women, all experienced in the hazards and geography of the desert, left
the Station at dawn. They rode in a cart pulled by one of
the Station's few large machines—large machines were
a luxury on a resource-poor planet—and Sulean was allowed to ride along to point out where she had last seen
Esh and perhaps to help convince him to return to the
Station, should they find him.

More sophisticated machines, lighter-than-air remote
viewing devices and the like, had already been sent
from the nearest large city, but they wouldn't arrive for
another day. Until then, Lochis told her, it would be a
labor of eyesight and intuition. Fortunately Esh had not
been able to conceal his tracks, and it was obvious that
he was heading for the most concentrated infall of Ab-
ashken remains.

As the expedition crossed a line of low hills into the
low basinland of the southern desert, Sulean saw the

decaying evidence of that infall. The machine-drawn cart passed close to a clump of dried and decaying . . . well, *things,* was the only word Sulean could apply to it. A wide-mouthed tube, yellowish-white and more than two people high, towered over a cluster of orbs, pyramids, and slivered mirrors. All these things had simply grown out of the pebbly desert floor and died. Or almost died. A few feathery tendrils, like enormous bird feathers, stirred feebly amidst the surrealistic rubble. Or maybe it was the faint dry wind that made them move.

Sulean's first confrontation with the Hypotheticals had been when she looked into Esh's altered eyes. This was her second. She shivered despite the heat and shrank back against Lochis's protective bulk.

"Don't be afraid," he said. "There's nothing dangerous here."

But she wasn't afraid, not exactly. It was a different emotion that had overtaken her. Fascination, dread— some dizzying combination of the two. Here were pieces of the Ab-ashken, fragments of things that had overgrown the stars themselves, bone and sinew from the body of a god.

"It's as if I can feel them," she whispered.

Or perhaps it was her own future she felt, bearing down on her like the waters of a swollen river.

"Again, Ms. Moi," Dr. Dvali said sternly. "How did the boy die?"

Sulean allowed a few moments to tick away in the silence of the common room. It was late. All was quiet. She imagined she could hear the sound of the desert wind pulsing in her ears.

"It was probably exhaustion that brought him to a stop. We found him at last in a small depression, invisible until we came very close. He was prostrate, barely breathing. All around him . . ."

She hated this image. It had haunted her all her long life.

"Go on," Dvali said.

"All around him, things had grown. He was enclosed in a sort of grove of Hypothetical remnants. They were spiky, dangerous-looking things, spears of some brittle green substance, incomplete, of course, obviously not sustainable, but still motile . . . still *alive,* if you accept that description."

"And they had surrounded him?" Mrs. Rebka asked, her voice gentler now.

"Or they had grown up around him while he slept, or he had deliberately gone to them. Some of them had . . . pierced him." She touched her ribs, her abdomen, to show them where.

"Killed him?"

"He was still conscious when we found him."

Sulean had torn herself away from Lochis and run thoughtlessly toward Esh, who was impaled on the picket of alien growths. She ignored the frightened voices calling her back.

Because this was her fault. She should never have helped Esh escape the Station. As unhappy as he had been there, he had at least been safe. Now something dreadful had overtaken him.

She felt no particular fear of the Ab-ashken growths, peculiar as they were. They had grown around the boy's body like a ring of sharpened fenceposts. She could smell them, although she was barely aware of it—a sharply chemical smell, sulfurous and rank. The growths were not healthy; they were mazed with cracks and fissures and in places blackened with something like rot. Their stalks shifted slightly when she moved among them, as if they were aware of her presence. And maybe they were.

They were certainly aware of Esh. Several of the tallest growths had arched into half-circles and pierced the boy with their sharpened tips. They had penetrated his chest and abdomen in three places, leaving little circles of dry blood on his clothing. Sulean couldn't tell at first whether he was dead or, somehow, still alive.

Then he opened his eyes and looked at her and—impossibly—*smiled.*

"Sulean," he said. "I found it."

Then he closed his eyes for the last time.

The silence in the common room was interrupted by a timid knock.

There was only one person at the commune who hadn't attended this meeting. Mrs. Rebka hurried to open the door.

Isaac stood outside, still wearing his night clothes, the knees of his pajamas soiled, his hands dirty, his expression somber.

"Someone's coming," he said.

CHAPTER SIXTEEN

The door to Brian Gately's office opened just as a news summary popped up on his desktop. The visitor was the chubby DGS man named Weil. The press release was something about the recent ashfall.

Weil had left his sullen friend Sigmund elsewhere, and he was grinning—though his cheerfulness, under the circumstances, struck Brian as vaguely obscene.

"You forwarded this?" Brian asked, gesturing at the release.

"Read it. I'll wait."

Brian tried to focus on the document, but his mind's eye insisted on reviewing the photograph Pieter Kirchberg had sent. The corpse of Tomas Ginn on a rocky beach, much worse for wear. He wondered whether Weil had seen the photo. Or ordered the killing.

He was tempted to ask. He dared not. He blinked and read the press service release.

PORT MAGELLAN / REUTERS.ET: Scientists at the Mt. Mahdi Observatory today made the startling announcement that the recent Equatorian "ashfall," which affected the eastern coast and desert inland of that continent, was "not entirely inert."

The ashes and the microscopic structures the ash contained, believed to be the degraded remnants of Hypothetical structures from the outer reaches of the local solar system, have apparently shown signs of life.

In a joint press conference held today at the Observatory, representatives of the American University, the United Nations Geophysical Survey, and the Provisional Government displayed photographs and samples of "incompletely self-replicating and self-assembling quasi-organic objects" recovered from the western extremes of the dry inland basin that stretches from the coastal mountains to the western sea.

These objects, ranging from a pea-sized hollow sphere to an assembly of what appeared to be tubes and wires as large as a man's head, were said to be unstable in a planetary environment and hence posed no threat to human life.

"The 'space-plague' scenario is a non-starter," senior astronomer Scott Cleland said. "The infalling material was ancient and probably already corrupted by wear and tear before it entered the atmosphere. The vast majority of it was sterilized by a violent passage that left only a few nano-scale elements intact. A very few of these retained enough molecular integrity to re-initiate the process of growth. But they were designed to flourish in the extreme cold and vacuum of deep space. In a hot, oxygen-rich desert they simply can't survive for long."

Asked whether any of these structures remained active today, Dr. Cleland said, "None that we've sampled. By far the greatest number of active clusters occurred deep in the Rub al-Khali," the oil-rich far western desert. "Residents of the coastal cities are unlikely to find alien plants in their gardens."

Because harmful effects cannot be entirely ruled out, however, a loose quarantine has been established between the oil concessions and the western coast of Equatoria. This formidable terrain has attracted no substantial settlements, although tourists occasionally visit the canyonlands and the oil consortia maintain a constant presence. "Travel is being monitored and alerts have been issued," said Paul Nissom of the Provisional Government's Territorial Authority. "We want to keep out the casually curious and facilitate the work of the researchers who need to study and understand this important phenomenon."

There were a couple of further paragraphs with trivial details and contact numbers, but Brian figured he had the gist. He gave Weil a well-what-about-it look.

"Works out nicely for us," Weil said.

"What are you talking about?"

"Ordinarily the Provisional Government isn't much more than a half-assed nanny. Since the ashfall, and especially this weird shit out west, they finally started paying attention to who goes where. Monitoring air traffic, especially."

There were more private planes per capita in Equatoria than anywhere back on Earth, most of them small craft, and an equally large number of casual airstrips. For years the traffic had been unregulated, ferrying passengers between bush communities or oil geologists to the desert.

"The bad news," Weil continued, "is that Turk Findley made it to his plane, along with Lise Adams and an unidentified third party. They flew out last night."

Brian felt an expanding hollowness in his chest. Some

of it was jealousy. Some of it was fear for Lise, who was digging herself into deeper trouble by the hour.

"The *good* news," Weil said, his smile broadening, "is that we know where they went. And we're going there. And we want you to come with us."

CHAPTER SEVENTEEN

Turk had expected to land his aircraft at a familiar strip a couple of miles outside of Kubelick's Grave, west of the foothills on the highway to the oil allotments. His plane might be confiscated if Mike Arundji had called ahead and was prepared to press charges. But that was probably inevitable anyway.

Diane surprised him, as the plane began the long glide down the western slopes of the divide toward the desert, by suggesting a different destination. "Do you remember where you took Sulean Moi?"

"More or less."

"Take us there, please."

Lise craned her head to look back at Diane. "You know where to find Dvali?"

"I've heard a few things over the years. These foothills are riddled with little utopian communities and religious retreats of every imaginable kind. Avram Dvali disguised his compound as one of those."

"But if you knew where he was—"

"We didn't, not at first. But even a community like Dvali's is porous. People arrive, people leave. He was hidden from us when it was critical for him to hide, before the child was born."

It meant another half hour in the air. After yet more simmering silence Turk said, "I'm sorry about that phone thing back in the city. What were you doing, trying to get a message to your mom back in the States, something like that?"

"Something like that." She was pleased that he had apologized and she didn't want to make it worse by admitting she'd called Brian Gately, even in an attempt to get Tomas Ginn out of custody. "Can I ask you a question?"

"Go ahead."

"How come you had to steal your own plane?"

"I owed some money to the guy who owns the airstrip. The business hasn't been going too well."

"You could have told me that."

"Didn't seem like a good way to impress a rich American divorcée."

"Hardly rich, Turk."

"Looked that way from where I stood."

"So how were you planning to get out of hock?"

"Didn't have what you could call an actual plan. Worst case, I figured I'd sell the plane and bank whatever I didn't owe and find a berth on one of those research ships that sail out past the Second Arch."

"There's nothing past the Second Arch but rocks and bad air."

"Thought I'd like to see for myself. That, or—"

"Or what?"

"Or if something worked out between you and me, I thought I'd stay in the Port and get a job. There's always pipeline work."

She was briefly startled. Also pleased.

"Not that it matters now," he added. "Once we're done here—and whether you find out anything about your father or not—you're going to have to head back to the States. You'll be okay there. You come from a respectable family and you're well-connected enough that they won't arrest and interrogate you."

"What about you?"

"I can disappear on my own terms."

"You could, you know, come back with me. Come back to the States."

"Wouldn't be safe, Lise. The trouble we're in right now isn't the first trouble I've had. There are good reasons why I can't go back."

Tell me, she thought. Don't make me ask. *Did he tell you he's a criminal? That's why he fled the States.* So tell me. She said, "Legal problems?"

"You don't want to know."

"Yeah, I do."

He was flying low across the desert, the moonlit foothills hanging off his right wing. He said, "I burned down a building. My father's warehouse."

"You told me your father was in the oil business."

"He was, at one time. But he didn't like being overseas. When we left Turkey he went into my uncle's import business. They brought in nickel-and-dime shit from Middle Eastern factories, rugs and souvenirs and things like that."

"Why'd you burn down the warehouse?"

"I was nineteen years old, Lise. I was pissed off and I wanted to do some damage to my old man."

She said as gently as possible, "How come?"

He allowed another silent moment to pass, looking at the desert, his instruments, anywhere but at her. "There was this girl I'd been seeing. We were going to get married. It was that serious. But my old man and my uncle didn't want it to happen. They were old-fashioned about, you know, race."

"Your girlfriend wasn't white?"

"Hispanic."

"Did you really care what your father thought?"

"Not at that point, no. I hated him. He was a brutal little shit, frankly. Drove my mother to her grave, in my opinion. I didn't give a fuck what he thought. But he knew that. So he didn't say a word to me. What he did was, he went to my girlfriend's family and offered to pay a year's tuition on her college education if she would stay away from me. I guess it sounded like a good deal. I never saw her again. But she felt bad enough to send me a letter and explain what happened."

"So you burned his warehouse."

"Took a couple cans of paint stripper out of the garage and went down to the industrial district and dumped it on the truck bay doors. It was after midnight. The place was three-quarters in flames by the time the fire department got there."

"So you had your revenge."

"What I didn't know was that there was a night guard in the building. He spent six months in a burn ward because of me."

Lise said nothing.

"What made it worse," Turk said, "was that my old man covered it up. Cooked up some arrangement with the insurance company. He tracked me down and told me that. How he'd taken this huge financial hit in order to save me from legal action. He said it was because I was family, that was why he did what he did about my girlfriend, because family mattered, whether I knew it or not."

"He expected you to be *grateful*?"

"Hard as that is to believe, yeah, I think he honestly expected me to be grateful."

"Were you?"

"No," Turk said. "I was not grateful."

He landed the Skyrex where he had landed it for Sulean Moi some months before, on a little strip of pavement that appeared to be in the middle of nowhere but was, Diane insisted, less than a mile from Dvali's compound, a hikeable distance.

They hiked, carrying flashlights.

He could smell the commune before he could see it. It smelled like water and flowers against the flat mineral essence of the desert. Then they crossed a little hill and there it was, a few lights still burning: four buildings and a courtyard, terracotta roofs like some kind of transplanted hacienda. There was a garden, and a gate, and Turk saw what looked like a young boy standing behind the ornate ironwork. As soon as the boy spotted them he ran inside, and by the time they reached the gate many more lights had come on and a crowd of ten or fifteen people was waiting for them.

"Let me talk to them," Diane said, a suggestion Turk was happy to accept. He stood a few paces back with Lise while the old woman approached the fence. Turk tried to study the crowd of Fourths, but the light was behind them and they weren't much more than silhouettes.

Diane shaded her eyes. "Mrs. Rebka?" she said abruptly.

A woman stepped out of the crowd. All Turk could see of this Mrs. Rebka was that she was a little plump and that her hair was fine and made a white halo around her head.

"Diane Dupree," the woman named Mrs. Rebka said.

"I'm afraid I've brought uninvited guests."

"And you're one yourself. What brings you here, Diane?"

"Do you have to ask?"

"I suppose not."

"Turn us away, then, or let us in. I'm tired. And I doubt we'll have much time to talk before we're disturbed again."

Isaac wanted to stay and see the visitors—unexpected visitors being as rare a phenomenon in Isaac's life as the ashfall had been—but his fever had returned and he was escorted back to bed, where he lay sleepless and sweating for several hours more.

He knew that the tendril that had reached up from the garden and touched his hand was a Hypothetical device. A biological machine. It was incomplete and unsuited to this environment, but Isaac had experienced a deep and thrilling sense of rightness as it circled his wrist. Some fraction of the unfulfilled need inside him had been briefly satisfied.

But that contact was over, and the need was worse for its absence. He wanted the western desert, and he wanted it badly. He was, of course, also afraid—afraid of the vast dry land and of what he might find there, afraid of the need that had overtaken him with such compulsive force. But it was a need that could be sated. He knew that now.

He watched the dawn as it drove the stars away, the planet turning like a flower to the sun.

Two of the Fourths escorted Lise and Turk to a dormitory room in which several bunks had been set up. The bedclothes were clean enough but had the smell of long-undisturbed linen.

The Fourths who accompanied them were aloof but seemed reasonably friendly, given the circumstances. Both were women. The younger of them said, "The bathroom is down the hall when you want it."

Lise said, "I need to talk to Dr. Dvali—will you tell him I want to see him?"

The Fourths exchanged glances. "In the morning," the younger one said.

Lise lay down on the nearest bunk. Turk stretched out on another, and almost immediately his breathing settled into long snores.

She tried to suppress her resentment.

Her head was full of thoughts, all raucous, all screaming for attention. She was a little shocked that she had come this far, that she had been party to what amounted to a theft and was accepting the hospitality of a community of rogue Fourths. Avram Dvali was only a few rooms away, and she might be exactly that close to understanding the mystery that had haunted her family for a dozen years.

Understanding it, she thought, or being trapped in it. She wondered how close her father had actually gotten to these dangerous truths.

She left her bunk, tiptoed across the room, and slipped under Turk's blanket. She curled against him, one hand on his shoulder and the other snaked under his pillow, hoping his audacity or his anger would seep into her and make her less afraid.

Diane sat with Mrs. Rebka—Anna Rebka, whose husband Joshua had died before she became a Fourth—in a room full of tables and chairs recently abandoned by the community's residents. Water glasses had been left on the rough wooden tabletops to marinate in their own condensation. It was late, and the night air of the desert moved through the room and chilled her feet.

So this is their compound, Diane thought. Comfortable enough, if austere. But there was an atmosphere of monasticism about it. A sacral hush. It was uneasily familiar—she had spent much of her youth among the intemperately religious.

She knew or could imagine much of what went on

here. The compound no doubt functioned like other such communities, apart from their experiment with the child. Hidden somewhere, probably underground, were the ultra-low-temperature bioreactors in which Martian "pharmaceuticals" were propagated and stored. She had already seen the pottery kilns that functioned as camouflage: an uninvited visitor would be offered crude crockery and utopian tracts and sent away none the wiser.

Diane had known or met most of the founding members. Only one of the original founders had not been a Fourth, and that was Mrs. Rebka herself. Presumably she had taken the treatment since.

"What I have to tell you," Diane said, "is that Genomic Security is in Port Magellan, apparently in force. And they'll find you before long. They've been following the Martian woman."

Mrs. Rebka maintained a steely calm. "Haven't they always been following the Martian woman?"

"Apparently they're getting better at it."

"Do they know she's here?"

"If they don't, they soon will."

"And your coming here might have led them to us. Did you think about that, Diane?"

"They've already connected Sulean Moi with Kubelick's Grave. They have Dvali's name. From there, how hard would it be for them to locate this place?"

"Not hard," Mrs. Rebka admitted, staring at the tabletop. "We're modest about our presence here, but still . . ."

"Still," Diane said, dryly. "Have you planned for this contingency?"

"Of course we have. We can be gone within hours. If we must."

"What about the boy?"

"We'll keep him safe."

"And how's the experiment going, Anna? Are you in touch with the Hypotheticals? Do they talk to you?"

"The boy is sick." Mrs. Rebka raised her head and frowned. "Spare me your disapproval."

"Did you ever consider what you were creating here?"

"With due respect, if what you say is true, we don't have time to *debate*."

Diane said—more gently—"Has it been what you hoped?"

Anna Rebka stood, and Diane thought she wasn't going to answer. But she paused at the door and looked back.

"No," she said flatly. "It hasn't."

Lise woke when sunlight from the window touched her cheek like a feverish hand.

She was alone in the room. Turk had gone off somewhere, probably taking a pee or inquiring about breakfast.

She dressed in the generic shirt and jeans the Fourths had provided for her, thinking about Avram Dvali, framing the questions she wanted to ask him. She needed to talk to him as soon as possible, as soon as she washed up and had something to eat. But there were hurried footsteps from the corridor beyond her door, and when she looked out the window she saw a dozen vehicles being loaded with supplies. She drew the obvious conclusion: these people were getting ready to abandon the compound. Lise could think of dozens of good reasons why they might want to. But she was suddenly afraid Dvali would be gone before she could talk to him; she hurried into the corridor and asked the first person who passed where she could find him.

Probably the common room, the passing Fourth advised her, down the corridor and left off the courtyard—but he might also be supervising the loading. She finally located him by the garden gate, where he was consulting some kind of written list.

Avram Dvali. She must have glimpsed him at the faculty parties her parents used to hold in Port Magellan, but she had seen so many unintroduced adults at those events that their faces had been blenderized by memory. Did he look familiar? No. Or only vaguely, from photographs. Because he had taken the Fourth treatment he probably looked much as he had twelve years ago: a bearded man, big eyes in a rounded face. His eyes were shaded by a broad-brimmed desert hat. Easy to imagine him circulating through the Adams living room, one more middle-aged professor of something-or-other, a drink in one hand and the other prospecting in the pretzel bowl.

She suppressed her anxiety and walked straight toward him. He looked up as she approached.

"Miss Adams," he said.

He had been warned. She nodded. "Call me Lise," she said—to quell his suspicions, not because she wanted to be on a first-name basis with a man who had created and confined a human child for purposes of scientific research.

"Diane Dupree said you wanted to speak to me. Unfortunately, at the moment—"

"You're busy," she said. "What's going on?"

"We're leaving."

"Where are you going?"

"Here and there. It's not safe to stay, for reasons I imagine you understand."

"I really just need a few minutes. I want to ask you about—"

"Your father. And I'd be happy to talk to you, Miss Adams—Lise—but do you understand what's happening here? Not only do we have to leave with all deliberate speed, we need to destroy much of what we've built. The bioreactors and their contents, documents and cultures, anything we don't want to fall into the hands of our persecutors." He consulted a printed paper, then made a checkmark as two men dragged a dolly of cardboard boxes to one of the trucks. "Once we're ready to go, you and your friends can ride with me for a while. We'll talk. But for now I need to attend to business." He added, "Your father was a brave and principled man, Miss Adams. We disagreed about some things, but I held him in the highest regard."

That was something, at least, Lise thought.

Turk had gotten up early.

The sound of hurried footsteps in the hall woke him, and he was careful to roll out of bed without disturbing Lise, who had climbed in with him sometime during the night. She was half-wrapped in a blanket and softly snoring, tender as the creation of some benevolent god. He wondered how she would react to what he had told her about himself. Not the CV she'd been hoping for. More than enough to chase her back to her family in California, maybe.

He went to find *Ibu* Diane, meaning to offer his help if help was needed: everybody seemed to be carrying something. The Fourths were obviously getting ready to abandon the place. But Diane, when he found her in the common room, told him all the duties had been assigned and were being performed in some meticulous order by the Fourths, so he made himself breakfast. When he figured it was time to wake up Lise, if she wasn't up already, he headed back to their room.

He was intercepted by a young boy peering out of a doorway down the corridor. It could only be the boy Diane was so worked up about—the half-Hypothetical boy. Turk had pictured some freakish hybrid, but what stood in front of him was just a babyfaced twelve-year-old, his face flushed and his eyes a little wide.

"Hey there," Turk said cautiously.

"You're new," the boy said.

"Yeah, I got here last night. My name's Turk."

"I saw you from the garden. You and the other two." The boy added, "I'm Isaac."

"Hi, Isaac. Looks like everybody's pretty busy this morning."

"Not me. They didn't give me anything to do."

"Me neither," Turk said.

"They're going to blow up the bioreactors," the boy confided.

"Are they?"

"Yes. Because—"

But suddenly the boy stiffened. His eyes widened until Turk could see the small uncanny flecks of gold around the irises. "Whoa, hey—you all right?"

A terrified whisper: "Because I remember—"

The boy began to topple over. Turk caught him in his arms and called for help.

"Because I remember—"

"What, Isaac? What do you remember?"

"Too much," the boy said, and wept.

CHAPTER EIGHTEEN

By dawn Brian Gately was on a transport plane lofting out of Port Magellan's major airport, strapped into a bench seat with Weil on one side of him and Sigmund on the other. Elsewhere in the plane was a group of armed men—not quite soldiers, since they wore no insignia on their flak jackets. The interior of the plane was stripped-down and possessed all the homely comfort of an industrial warehouse. Brian could tell day was breaking by the red glow coming through the porthole-sized windows.

Weil had ordered him to the airport well before dawn. "In the event that we get involved in negotiations," he had said, "or in any other talking-type situation—a post-event interrogation, say—we'd like you to be the one who interacts with Lise Adams. We think you'd be better than someone she doesn't know. How do you feel about that?"

How did he feel about that? Shitty, basically. But he could hardly say no. He might be in a position to protect her. He certainly didn't want her questioned by some hostile DGS functionary or one of these mercenaries.

She was in the wrong place for the wrong reasons, but that didn't make her a criminal, and with luck Brian might be able to defend her from the threat of prison. Or worse. His memory of the photo of Tomas Ginn's body throbbed in his head like a fragile aneurysm.

What he told Weil was, "I'll help if I can."

"Thank you. We appreciate that. I know it's not what you signed up for."

Not what he had signed up for. That was becoming a joke. He had signed up with Genomic Security because he possessed a talent for administration and because one of his father's cousins, a DGS bureau chief in Kansas City, had opened the door for him. He had believed in the work of Genomic Security, at least to the degree to which it was professionally necessary to believe. The Department's mission statement had made sense to him, the idea of preserving the human biological heritage against black-market cloning, unlicensed human modification, and imported Martian biotech. Most nations had similar bureaus and they followed the broad guidelines set down by the United Nations under the Stuttgart Accords. All clean and aboveboard.

And if there were bureaucratic nooks at the more carefully classified levels of DGS, hidden aeries in which less politically palatable attacks on the enemies of human genetic continuity were planned and carried out—was that so surprising? Those who were required to know, knew. Brian had never been required to know. Ignorance was his preferred mode of consciousness, at least when it came to the Executive Action Committee. Of course not everything could be done legally or visibly. As an adult, one understood this.

But he didn't like it. It was Brian's nature to prefer rules to anarchy. Law was the gardener of human behavior, and what lay beyond was brutal, red in tooth and claw. What lay beyond the garden was Sigmund and

Weil and their uncommunicative smiles and their cadres of armed men. What lay beyond, fundamentally, was the battered body of Tomas Ginn.

The aircraft lurched as it rose to cross the coastal mountains that absorbed most of Equatoria's rainfall and made the inland a desert. "We'll be in Kubelick's Grave in an hour," Weil said. Brian had passed through Kubelick's Grave once before, part of an orientation tour he had taken when he was newly-arrived from the States. It was a nothing town, an adobe armpit that existed for the sole purpose of refueling land traffic bound for the oil sands of the Rub al-Khali or back through the Mahdi Pass to the coast. Weil said there was a community of robed eccentrics living in the desert foothills north and east of Kubelick's Grave: rogue Fourths, in fact, since aerial photographs taken in the past few hours showed Turk Findley's little bush plane nearby.

And now the site would be seized and secured, Brian thought, and would the seizure be violent? There was a large number of weapons on hand, he hoped, mainly for show. To make a plausible threat. Because Fourths were supposed to be nonviolent, gentled by the same tech that granted them longevity. No killing would be necessary, surely. And if there was any killing involved, it wouldn't involve Lise. He would see to that. In his intentions, at least, he was brave.

It all happened quickly.

The airport at Kubelick's Grave was barely large enough to accommodate the transport. As soon as it had settled at the end of a cracked concrete runway, the rear cargo door dropped and the armed men trooped off in military order. A handful of lightly armored vehicles waited in the coppery morning sunlight. Brian joined Sigmund and Weil in one of those open-topped desert vehicles the locals called "roosters" for the way they bounced over the landscape like flightless birds. Sigmund took the driver's seat and they drove off at the back of the convoy. Not a comfortable ride. The heat and sun were oppressive even at this hour. All he saw of Kubelick's Grave was a garage and gas depot where rusty automobile parts lay scattered, the drive train of an ancient truck abandoned on the gravel like the spine of some Jurassic creature. Then they were off the main road, rattling over a hardpan trail parallel to the mountains.

An hour passed, broken only by the hoarse shouting of Sigmund as he attempted to converse with someone over a field radio. The talk, what Brian could hear of it, consisted of codewords and incomprehensible commands. Then the convoy came over the peak of a small rill and the Fourth compound was suddenly dead ahead. The military vehicles put on a burst of speed, big tires kicking up geysers of dust, but Weil pulled up short and killed the engine, leaving Brian's ears ringing in the relative silence.

Sigmund began yelling again, first into his radio and then at Weil: something about "too late" and an order to "abort."

"They abandoned the compound," Weil said to Brian. "Fresh tracks. Must have been a good two dozen vehicles."

"Can't you secure the site, at least?"

"Not until we can defuse whatever ordnance they left behind. What happens in these cases, they—"

He was interrupted by a burst of distant light.

Brian looked at the Fourth compound. A moment before it had been a cluster of small buildings around a central courtyard. Now it was an expanding cloud of dust and smoke.

"Shit," Weil had time to say. The concussion reached them a fraction of a second later, a noise that seemed to swell his lungs until his chest hurt. Brian closed his eyes. A second shockwave, like the beat of a hot wing, washed over him.

The compound was gone. Brian told himself that Lise wasn't inside: no one had been inside.

". . . rig it . . ." Weil was saying.

"What?"

"They rig it to destroy their technical gear and keep us from taking samples. We got here late." Weil's complexion had turned pale with dust kicked up by the explosion. Sigmund's assault team had turned back, hastily.

"Is Lise—?"

"We have to assume she left with the others."

"Going where?"

"They won't all be traveling together. From the tracks it looks like a couple dozen vehicles headed in different directions. We'll run down a few of them. With luck we'll pick up Lise and the other major targets. With a little more warning we would have had drones in the air to keep watch. But we didn't have time and anyway every drone on the continent has been shipped to the far west, surveying the fucking oil allotments for earthquake damage."

Sigmund was still growling into his handset. Then he switched it off and said to Weil, "The plane's gone."

Turk Findley's bush plane, presumably. Gone. Escaped. Should he be pleased about that?

"The aircraft, at least, we can track," Weil said.

And Lise along with it.

Brian looked back at the ruins of the compound. Black smoke gushed from collapsed foundations and small fires burned fitfully in the surrounding desert. Of the brick and adobe buildings that had once stood there, nothing remained.

They spent the night in what passed for public accommodations in Kubelick's Grave, a tile-roofed motel in which Brian shared a unit with Sigmund and Weil. Two beds and a cot—Brian got the cot.

Most of the afternoon and evening he spent listening to Sigmund make and take calls. The name of the Executive Action Committee was frequently invoked.

That night, unable to sleep in his cot, cold despite the banging antique electric heater, it occurred to Brian to wonder whether they had found out about Lise's last call to him.

Were his calls tapped for audio? Lise's callback code had been unfamiliar to him, probably a disposable loaded with anonymous minutes, so they wouldn't have been able to trace it. And there hadn't been anything really incriminating about the call. Apart from the fact that Brian had failed to report it. Which would suggest that his loyalties were divided. That he might not be a trustworthy DGS man.

He wanted to be angry with Lise. Hated her pointless personal involvement in this fucking mess, her obsessive need to sort out her father's disappearance and turn the story into some kind of memoir.

He wanted to be angry with her, and he was angry with himself when he didn't succeed.

Reports on the round-up of fugitive Fourths began to come in before dawn, Sigmund shouting into his phone while Brian hurriedly dressed.

Success had been mixed, he gathered.

"At least half the population of the compound is still at large," Weil said. "Our guys intercepted three vehicles carrying a total of fifteen people, none of them the major players. The *good* news—"

Brian braced himself.

"The *good* news is, a small plane registered to Turk Findley attempted to refuel at a little utility airport a

couple of hundred miles west of here. The airport manager recognized the plane from a legal bulletin—Mr.
Findley's former employer wants it impounded for back
rent. He called the Provisional Government and somebody there was kind enough to refer the matter to us.
Our guys arrived and detained the pilot and passengers.
One male, three females, all refusing to identify themselves."

"And one of them is Lise?" Brian asked.

"Maybe. That's not confirmed. And there may be
higher-value targets along with her."

"She's not a target. I wouldn't call her a target."

"She made herself a target when she ran."

But not high value, he thought, clinging to that. "Can
I see her?"

"We can be there by noon if we get a move on," Weil
said.

It occurred to Brian to wonder, as the town of Kubelick's
Grave vanished behind them, who Kubelick might have
been and why he was buried out here in the badlands; but
nobody in the car had an answer to that question. Then
the little cluster of buildings was behind them, Sigmund
driving away from the mountains toward the razor-flat
western horizon. The road ahead quivered in the morning heat like a figment of the imagination.

Sigmund couldn't make his phone work, though he
kept banging it with one hand while he steered with the
other. Even communication between the widely-spaced
cars of the convoy—this vehicle plus three heavy trucks
containing hired soldiers—was intermittent and unreli-
able. Weil couldn't explain it: "A half-dozen aerostats
anchored between here and the west coast and not one of
the fucking things doing what it's supposed to do. Lucky
we got the news from the airfield when we did. Jesus!"

And it was not only the ruptured communication that seemed remarkable to Brian. He called attention to the steady flow of traffic in the opposite direction, not just oil-company traffic but a number of private vehicles, some so sand-pitted and sun-scarred that they looked barely functional. As if they were evacuating the inhabited outposts of the Rub al-Khali, and maybe they were—some new tremor, maybe.

Sixty miles farther on the convoy pulled onto the gravel verge and stopped. Sigmund and Weil went forward to talk to the leader of the paramilitary company. It looked more like an argument than a conversation, but Brian couldn't make out the words. He stood at the roadside watching the eastbound traffic. Eerie, he thought, how much this part of Equatoria looked like Utah: the same dusty blue horizon, the same torpid daytime heat. Had the Hypotheticals designed this desert when they assembled the planet, and if so, why? But Brian doubted they paid that kind of attention to details—the Hypotheticals, it seemed to him, were firm believers in the long result. Plant a seed (or seed a planet) and let nature do the rest. Until the harvest . . . whatever that meant or might one day mean.

Not much grew out here, just the peculiar woody tufts the locals called cactus grass, and even this looked dehydrated to Brian's eye. But among the umber patches of cactus grass at his feet he spotted a place where something more colorful had taken root. He crouched to look, for lack of anything better to do. What had caught his attention was a red flower: he was no botanist, but the bloom looked out of place in this barren scrub. He put out his hand and touched it. The plant was cold, fleshy . . . and it seemed almost to cringe. The stem bent away from him; the flower, if it *was* a flower, lowered its head.

Was that normal?

He hated this fucking planet, its endless strangeness. It was a nightmare, he thought, masquerading as normalcy.

They came at last to the airfield off the highway, a couple of quonset-hut structures and two paved landing strips at contrary angles to one another, a bank of fuel pumps, a two-story adobe control tower with a radar bubble. Ordinarily the airstrip's customers would have been oil company planes ferrying executives to and from the Rub al-Khali. Today there was just one plane visible on the tarmac: Turk Findley's aircraft, a sturdy little blue-and-white Skyrex baking in the sun.

The Genomic Security caravan parked in front of the nearest pavilion. Brian was a little shaky getting out of the car, his fears surfacing again. Fear for Lise, and under that a fear *of* Lise—of what she might say to him and what she might deduce, correctly or not, about his presence in the company of men such as Sigmund and Weil.

Maybe he could help her. He clung to that thought. She was in trouble, deep and perilous trouble, but she could still keep herself afloat if she said the right things, denied complicity, shifted the blame, and cooperated with the inquiry. If she was willing to do that, Brian might be able to keep her out of prison. She would have to go back home, of course, forget about Equatoria and her little journalistic hobby. Given the events of the last few days, though, she might not be so haughty at the prospect of a trip back to the States. She might even learn to appreciate what he had done, and was willing to do, on her behalf.

He hurried to keep up with Sigmund and Weil, who brushed past a cluster of airstrip employees and hurried down a makeshift corridor to the door of a tiny office guarded by an airport security guy in a dusty blue uniform. "The suspects are inside?" Sigmund asked.

"All four of 'em."

"Let's see them."

The guard opened the door, Sigmund went through first, Weil behind him, Brian in the rear. The two DGS men stopped short and Brian had to crane to see over their shoulders.

"Fuck!" Sigmund said.

Three women and one man sat at a stained conference table in the middle of the room. Each of them had been handcuffed to a chair.

The male was maybe sixty years old, judging by his looks. Probably older, since he was a Fourth. He was white-haired, he was skinny, he was dark-complexioned . . . what he was *not* was Turk Findley.

The three women were of similar age. None of them looked like Sulean Moi. And certainly none of them was Lise Adams.

"Decoys," Weil said, his voice turgid with disgust.

"Find out who they are and what they know," Sigmund told the armed men waiting in the corridor.

Weil pulled Brian out after him. "Are you all right?"

"Just . . . yes," Brian managed. "I mean, I'm fine."

He wasn't fine. He was picturing the four prisoners with bullet-raddled skulls, washed up, perhaps, on some distant beach, or just buried in the desert, bodies shriveled under a layer of grit, paying the butcher's bill for their longevity.

CHAPTER NINETEEN

Dvali drove the car that took them north until night-fall, and in her less distracted moments Lise made a study of him.

He was—above all else—protective of the child, Isaac.

Lise and Turk had been hustled into a big utility vehicle, the kind with sprung-metal wheels that could cope with all kinds of terrain. The car had been built to accommodate six people comfortably but they had squeezed in seven: Dvali, Lise and Turk, Diane, Mrs. Rebka, Sulean Moi—and Isaac.

Turk had advocated taking the Skyrex, but Dvali and Mrs. Rebka argued him out of it. An aircraft would be easier to trace and harder to hide than one land vehicle among many. They would use the plane as a diversion, Dr. Dvali said. Four of the compound's eldest Fourths, one of whom was a qualified pilot, volunteered to take it west. Probably they would be captured. But they knew what they were doing, Dr. Dvali had insisted. They weren't afraid to die, if it came to that. One of the ironies of the Martian treatment was that it quelled the fear of death even as it extended life. Turk asked if they had a cure for the fear of insolvency.

So they drove away, and a dozen or so land vehicles left the compound after them, scattering in multiple directions on the available roads or across the raw desert. The compound had been rigged with explosives to keep it from falling into the hands of the authorities and to destroy any evidence that might lead to their eventual capture. Lise and company had been too far down the road to see the actual explosion, but at one point she had spotted a plume of smoke on the horizon. She asked Dr. Dvali whether anyone might have been hurt—if DGS agents had arrived before the timed detonation, wouldn't they have been killed?

"DGS knows what to expect in situations like this. If they found the compound deserted they would have known it was rigged to detonate."

But if they'd been careless, or the timing had been bad?

Dvali shrugged. "Nothing is guaranteed in this life."

"I thought Fourths were supposed to be nonviolent."

"We're more sensitive than unaltered people to the suffering of others. That makes us vulnerable. It doesn't make us stupid, and it doesn't prevent us from taking risks."

"Even risks with other people's lives?"

Sulean Moi—who was, according to Diane, a deformed Martian, but who looked to Lise like a skinny Appalachian apple doll—had smiled sardonically at that. "We aren't saints. That should be obvious by now. We make moral choices. Often the wrong ones."

Dvali wanted to drive through the night, but Turk convinced him to stop and make camp in a glade of the scrubby finger pines that forested the western slope of the mountainous Equatorian divide. Because of the elevation rain fell fairly regularly here, and there was even a clean-running creek from which they could draw potable water. The water was cold and Lise guessed it came from the glaciers that clung to the valleys of the highest passes. The chill provoked a pleasant memory of the time (she had been ten years old) when her father took her skiing at Gstaad. Sunlight on snow, the mechanical groan of the lifts and the sound of laughter cutting the cold air: far away now, worlds and years away.

She helped Turk warm up a canned meat and vegetable stew over a propane stove. He wanted to have dinner ready and the stove cooled off by nightfall in case there were drones overhead looking for their heat signature. Dr. Dvali said he doubted their pursuers would go to such lengths, especially since most such surveillance equipment had been co-opted for use in the crisis in the oilpatch. Turk nodded but said it was better to take a useless precaution than give themselves away.

On the road north along the foothills they had discussed their plans. Turk, at least, had discussed his plans; the Fourths were less forthcoming. Turk and Lise would ride as far north as the town of New Cumberland; from there they would catch a bus over the Pharoah Pass to the coast. The Fourths would continue on to—well, to wherever it was they meant to go.

Someplace where they could take care of the boy, Lise hoped. He was a strange-looking child. His hair was rusty red, cut short by whoever passed for the compound's barber, probably Mrs. Rebka with a pair of kitchen scissors. His eyes were widely spaced, giving him a birdlike aspect, and the pupils were flecked with gold. He hadn't said much all day, and most of that had been in the morning, but he was uncomfortable in some way Lise couldn't quite understand: whenever the road curved he would either frown and moan or sigh with relief. By late afternoon he was feverish—"again," she heard Mrs. Rebka say.

Now Isaac was sleeping in one of the rear seats of the car, windows open to let the alpine air flow through. Hot day, but the sunlight had grown horizontal, and she had been told the air might turn uncomfortably cold during the night. There were only six sleeping bags in the vehicle but they were the expensive kind, thermally efficient, and someone could sleep in the car if necessary. It didn't seem likely to rain but Turk had already strung a tarp among the trees for what meager protection or concealment it could offer.

She stirred the pot of stew while Turk made coffee. "It's too bad about the plane."

"I would have lost it anyway."

"What are you going to do when you get back to the coast?"

"Depends," he said.

"On what?"

"A lot of things." He looked at her as if from a distance, squinting. "Probably go back to sea . . . if nothing else turns up."

"Or we could go back to the States," she said, wondering how he'd read that *we*. "The legal trouble you were in, that's essentially over, right?"

"It could heat up again."

"So we'll do something else." The pronoun hanging in the air like an unbroken piñata.

"Guess we have to."

We.

They served out dinner while the sun met the horizon in a reddening haze. Turk ate quickly and said little. Diane Dupree sat on a distant log with the Martian woman Sulean Moi, conversing intently but inaudibly, while Mrs. Rebka hovered over Isaac, who had to be coaxed to eat.

Which left Dr. Dvali, and Lise's first real opportunity to speak to him with any degree of privacy. She abandoned

Turk to the camp stove and the pots and went to sit next to him. Dvali looked at her querulously, like a large brown bird, but made no objection when she joined him. "You want to talk about your father," he said.

She could only nod.

"We were friends." It was as if Dvali had rehearsed this speech. "What I admired most about your father was that he loved his work, but not in a narrow way. He was in love with it because he saw it in the broader context. Do you know what I mean?"

"No." Yes. But she wanted to hear it from him. "Not exactly."

Dvali reached down and scooped a handful of dirt. "What do I have in my hand?"

"Topsoil. Old leaves. Probably a few bugs."

"Topsoil, mineral residue, silts, decaying biomass broken down to elemental nutrients, feeding itself back to itself. Bacteria, fungal spores—and no doubt some insects." He brushed it away. "Much like Earth, but subtly different in the details. On the geological level the resemblance between the two planets is even more obvious. Granite is granite, schist is schist, but they exist here in different proportions. There's less vulcanism here than on Earth. The continental plates drift and erode at a different speed, the thermocline between the equator and the poles is less steep. But what's really distinctive about this world is how fundamentally *similar* it is to Earth."

"Because the Hypotheticals built this planet for us."

"Maybe not for us, exactly, but yes, they built it, or at least modified it, and that turns our study of this world into a whole new discipline—not just biology or geology but a kind of planetary *archaeology*. This world was profoundly influenced by the Hypotheticals long before modern human beings evolved, millions of years before the Spin, millions of years before the Arch was put in place. That tells us something about their methods and their extraordinary capacity for very long-term planning. It may also tell us something about their ultimate goals, if we ask the right question. That was the context in which your father worked. He never lost sight of that larger truth, never ceased to marvel at it."

"Planet as artifact," Lise said.

"The book he was writing." Dvali nodded. "Have you read it?"

"All I've seen of it is the introduction." And a few notes, salvaged from one of her mother's convulsive fits of radical housecleaning.

"I wish there had been more. It would have been an important work."

"Is that what you talked about with him?"

"Often enough, yes."

"But not always."

"Obviously, we talked about the Martians and what they might know about the Hypotheticals. He knew I was a Fourth—"

"You told him?"

"I took him into my confidence."

"May I ask why?"

"Because of his obvious interest. Because he was trustworthy. Because he understood the nature of the world." Dvali smiled. "Basically, because I liked him."

"He was okay with that, with your—Fourthness?"

"He was curious about it."

"Did he talk about taking the treatment himself?"

"I won't say he didn't consider it. But he never made the request to me or, so far as I know, anyone else. He loved his family, Miss Adams—I don't need to tell you that. I was as shocked as anyone else when I heard about his disappearance."

"Did you confide in him about this project of yours, too? About Isaac?"

"When it was in the planning stage, yes, I talked to

him about it." Dvali sipped his coffee. "He hated the idea."

"But he didn't inform on you. He didn't do anything to stop it."

"No, he didn't inform on us, but we argued bitterly over it—the friendship was strained at that point."

"Strained, but not broken."

"Because despite our disagreement, he understood why the work seemed necessary. Urgently necessary." Dvali leaned closer to her and for a moment Lise was afraid he would reach out and take her hands. She wasn't sure she could stand that. "The idea of any tangible contact with the Hypotheticals—with the motivating spirit behind their vast network of machines—fascinated him as much as it fascinated me. He knew how important it was, not just for our generation but for generations to come, for humanity as a species."

"You must have been disappointed when he wouldn't cooperate."

"I didn't need his cooperation. I would have liked his approval. I was disappointed when he withheld it. After a time we simply stopped talking about it—we talked about other things. And when the project began in earnest I left Port Magellan. I never saw your father again."

"That was six months before he disappeared."

"Yes."

"Do you know anything about that?"

"About his disappearance? No. Genomic Security was in the Port at the time—looking for me, among others, since rumors of the project had reached them—and when I heard Robert Adams had gone missing I assumed he'd been picked up and interrogated by Genomic Security. But I don't know that for certain. I wasn't there."

"Most of the people who are interrogated by Genomic Security walk away from it, Dr. Dvali." Although she knew better.

"Not all," Dvali said.

"He wasn't a Fourth. Why would they hurt him?" *Kill him*, she couldn't bring herself to say.

"He would have resisted on principle and out of personal loyalty."

"You knew him well enough to say that?"

"I took the treatment in Bangalore, Miss Adams, twenty years ago. I'm not omniscient, but I'm a good judge of human character. Not that there was anything especially occult about Robert Adams. He wore his sincerity on his sleeve."

He was murdered. That had always been the most likely explanation, though the details might be uglier than Lise had imagined. Robert Adams had been murdered and the men who murdered him would never come to trial for it. But there was another story inside the story. The story of his curiosity, his idealism, the strength of his convictions.

Some of these thoughts must have shown on her face. Dvali was radiating a sympathetic concern. "I know that isn't much help. I'm sorry."

Lise stood up. All she felt at the moment was cold. "May I ask you one more thing?"

"If you like."

"How *do* you justify it? The fate of humanity aside, how do you justify putting an innocent child in Isaac's position?

Dvali turned up his cup and emptied the last of his coffee on the ground. "Isaac was never an innocent child. Isaac has never been anything other than what he is now. And I would trade places with him, Miss Adams, if I could. Eagerly."

She came across the campground to the circle of light in which Turk was sitting, fiddling with a pocket telecom receiver. Turk, her avatar of disappearances: Turk, who had vanished from many lives. "Radio broken?"

"Nothing coming in over the aerostats. Nothing from Port Magellan. Last I heard they were talking about another tremor out west." Oil revenue, of course, being the Port's perennial obsession. In the Trusts we trust. Turk gave her a second look. "Are you all right?"

"Just tired," she said.

She brewed another pot of coffee and drank enough to keep her alert, even as the others began to settle in for the night. At last—as she had hoped—there was no one up and moving except herself and the Martian woman, Sulean Moi.

Lise was intimidated by Sulean Moi, even though she looked like the kind of elderly woman you might help across the street at a stoplight. She wore her age and the distance she had traveled as a kind of invisible aura. It took a certain amount of courage to join her at the guttering campfire, where the logs had worn down to radiant hollows and red chambers.

"Don't be afraid," the old woman said.

Lise was startled. "Are you reading my mind?"

"Reading your face."

"I'm not really afraid." Not much.

Sulean smiled, exposing her small white teeth. "I think I would be, in your position—given what you must have heard about me. I know the stories they tell. The grim elder Martian, victim of a childhood injury." She tapped her skull. "My supposed moral authority. My unusual history."

"Is that how you see yourself?"

"No, but I recognize the caricature. You spent a good deal of time and energy looking for me, Miss Adams."

"Call me Lise."

"Lise, then. Do you still have that photograph you've been showing around?"

"No." She had destroyed it back in the Minang village, at Diane's urging.

"Just as well. So here we are. No one to overhear us. We can talk."

"When I started looking for you I had no idea—"

"That it would inconvenience me? Or that it would attract the attention of Genomic Security? Don't apologize. You knew what you knew, and what you didn't know could hardly enter into your calculations. You want to ask me about Robert Adams and how and why he died."

"Do you know for a fact that he's dead?"

"I didn't witness the killing, but I've spoken with people who saw him abducted and I can't imagine any other outcome. If he had been able to come home he would have done so. I'm sorry if that seems blunt."

Blunt but increasingly self-evident, Lise thought. "It's true that he was taken by Genomic Security?"

"By one of what they call their Executive Action Groups."

"And they were hunting for Dr. Dvali and his group."

"Yes."

"And so were you."

"Yes. For slightly different reasons."

"You wanted to stop him from creating Isaac."

"I wanted to stop him from performing a needlessly cruel and probably useless human experiment, yes."

"Isn't that what Genomic Security wanted?"

"Only in their press releases. Do you really believe organizations like Genomic Security operate within their mission statements? If Genomic Security could acquire the tools they would have secret bunkers full of multiple Isaacs—wired to machines, under armed guard."

Lise shook her head to order her thoughts. "How did you meet my father?"

"The first useful person I met in Equatoria was Diane Dupree. There's no formal hierarchy among Terrestrial Fourths, but in every Fourth community there's some pivotal figure who figures in every major decision. Diane played that role in coastal Equatoria. I told her why I wanted to find Dvali and she gave me the names of people who might be useful—not all of them Fourths. Dr. Dvali had befriended your father. I befriended him too."

"Dr. Dvali said my father was trustworthy."

"Your father had a striking faith in fundamental human goodness. That didn't always work to his advantage."

"You think Dvali took advantage of him?"

"I think it took him a long time to see Dr. Dvali for what he was."

"Which is?"

"A man with grandiose ambitions, profound insecurities, and a dangerously malleable conscience. Your father was reluctant to reveal Dr. Dvali's announced plans and whereabouts, even to me."

"Did he, though?"

"Once we got to know each other. We spent a lot of time discussing cosmology first. I think that was your father's unique way of evaluating people. You can tell a lot about a person, he once said, by the way they look at the stars."

"If he told you what he knew, why couldn't you find Dvali and stop him?"

"Because Dr. Dvali was wise enough to change his plans once he left Port Magellan. Your father believed Dvali was establishing a compound on the far west coast of Equatoria—still mostly a wilderness even today, apart from a few fishing villages. That's what he told me, and that's no doubt what he told Genomic Security when they interrogated him."

"Dvali thinks my father refused to talk—that that was why they killed him."

"I'm sure he resisted. I doubt he succeeded, given what I know about their interrogation techniques. I know it hurts you to hear that, Lise, and I'm sorry, but it's the truth. Your father told me what he knew because he believed Dvali ought to be stopped and he believed I had the authority to intervene without doing violence to Dvali or the Fourth community in general. If he told these things to Genomic Security, he would have done so only under duress. But, Lise, it didn't matter. Dvali wasn't on the west coast. He never had been. Genomic Security lost track of him, and by the time I found out where he had truly gone it was far too late—years had passed. Isaac was a living child. He couldn't be called back into the womb."

"I see."

In the ensuing silence Lise could hear the crackle of the smoldering fire.

"Lise," Sulean Moi said softly. "I lost my parents when I was very young. I expect Diane told you that. I lost my parents, but, worse than that, I lost my memory of them. It was as if they had never existed at all."

"I'm sorry."

"I'm not asking for sympathy. What I want to tell you is that, at a certain age, I made it my business to educate myself about them—to learn who they were, and how they had come to live beside a certain river before it flooded, and what warnings they might have heeded or ignored. I think I wanted to know whether I ought to love them for trying to rescue me or hate them for failing. I found out a lot of things, mostly irrelevant, including a number of painful truths about their personal lives, but the only *important* thing I learned was that they were blameless. It was a very small consolation, but it was all there would ever be, and in a way it was enough. Lise—your father was blameless."

"Thank you," Lise said hoarsely.

"And now we should try to sleep," Sulean Moi said, "before the sun comes up again."

Lise slept better than she had in several nights—even though she was in a sleeping bag, on uneven ground, in a strange forest—but it wasn't the sun that woke her, it was Turk's hand on her shoulder. Still dark out, she registered groggily. "We have to go," Turk said. "Hurry up, Lise."

"Why—?"

"The ash is falling again in Port Magellan, more and heavier, and it'll cross the mountains before too long. We need to get under shelter."

CHAPTER TWENTY

Isaac woke to see the clouds billowing through the passes behind the moving car, clouds shot through with luminous particles, clouds like the clouds of August 34th. But the sudden and breathtaking hurt obscured all that.

What he felt wasn't pain, exactly, but something very much like it, a sensitivity that made light and noise intolerable, as if the exposed blade of the world had been thrust into his skull.

Isaac understood his own specialness. He knew he had been created in an attempt to communicate with the Hypotheticals, and he knew he had been a disappointment to the adults around him. He knew other things, too. He knew the vacuum of space wasn't empty: it was populated by ghost particles that existed too briefly to interact with the world of tangible things; but the Hypotheticals could manipulate these ephemeral particles and use them to send and receive information. The Martian technology embedded in Isaac had attuned his nervous system to this kind of signaling. But it never resolved into anything like the comfortable linearity of words. Most of the time it was a sense of distant, inexpressible urgency. Sometimes—now—it was more like pain. And the pain was connected with the approaching cloud of dust and ash: the unseen world heaved with an invisible tumult, and Isaac's mind and body vibrated in concert.

He was aware, too, of being lifted into the rear seat of the car, of being strapped in by hands not his own, of the voices and concerns of his old and new friends. They were afraid for him. And they were afraid for themselves. He was aware of Dr. Dvali ordering everyone into the car, the slamming doors, the revving engine. And he was glad it was not Dr. Dvali who held his head and soothed him (it was Mrs. Rebka), because he had come to dislike Dr. Dvali, almost to hate Dr. Dvali, for reasons he didn't understand.

Mrs. Rebka wasn't a physician but she had trained herself in basic medicine, as had the other Fourths, and Lise watched as she administered a sedative, pricking the boy's arm with an old-fashioned syringe. Isaac began to breathe more deeply and his screaming eventually ebbed to a sigh.

They drove. The vehicle's headlights cut columns of light into the falling dust. Turk was doing the driving on behalf of the Fourths, trying to get out of the foothills before the roads became impassable. Lise had asked whether they shouldn't take Isaac to a hospital, but Mrs. Rebka shook her head: "There's nothing a hospital can do for him. Nothing we can't do for him ourselves."

Diane Dupree watched the boy with wide, anxious eyes. Sulean Moi also watched him, but her expression was more inscrutable—some combination, it seemed to Lise, of resignation and terror.

But it was Mrs. Rebka who allowed Isaac to rest his head on her shoulder, who reassured him with a word or the silent pressure of her hand when the bounce and rattle of the car disturbed him. She smoothed his hair and dabbed his forehead with a damp cloth. Before long the sedative put him to sleep.

There was an obvious question Lise had been wanting to ask since they arrived at the Fourth compound, and since no one else had anything to say—and because the noise of the windshield wipers scraping dust across glass was driving her slightly crazy—she drew a breath and asked, "Is Isaac's mother still alive?"

"Yes," Mrs. Rebka said.

Lise turned to face her. "Are you his mother?"

"I am," Mrs. Rebka said.

What do you see, Isaac?

Much later, as he was waking up from the sleep they had injected into him, Isaac pondered the question.

Mrs. Rebka was the one who had asked it. He tried to formulate an answer before the pain came back and stole his words. But the question was hard to answer because he was having a hard time seeing anything at all. He was aware of the vehicle and the people in it, the ash falling beyond the windows, but they all seemed vague and unreal. Was it daytime yet? But now the car had stopped, and before he answered Mrs. Rebka's question he asked one of his own: "Where are we?"

Up front, the man named Turk Findley said, "Little town called Bustee. We might be staying here a while."

Outside there were small buildings visible through the fog of dust. He could see them plainly enough. But that wasn't what Mrs. Rebka had meant by her question.

"Isaac? Can you walk?"

Yes, he could, for now, though the sedative was wearing off and the blade of the world was beginning to draw blood again. He climbed out of the car with one hand on Mrs. Rebka's arm. Dust sifted across his face. The dust smelled like something burned. Mrs. Rebka steered him toward the nearest small building, which was one wing of a motel. Isaac heard Turk say he had rented the last available room, for more money than it was worth. Lots of people were sheltering in Bustee tonight, Turk said.

Then he was inside, on a bed, on his back, and the air was less dusty, though it still stank, and Mrs. Rebka brought a fresh cloth and began to dab the grime from his face. "Isaac," she said again gently, "what are you looking at? What do you *see*?"

Because he kept turning his head in one direction— west, of course—and staring.

What did he see?

"A light."

"Here in the room?"

No. "A long way away. Farther than the horizon."

"But you can see it from here? You can see it through the walls?"

He nodded.

"What does it look like?"

Many words crowded Isaac's mind, many answers. A fire in a faraway place. An explosion. Sunrise. Sunset. The place where the stars fall and burn in their eagerness to live. And the thing deep underground that knows and welcomes them.

But what he said was simply, truthfully, "I don't know."

Only Turk had been to Bustee before. The name, he said, was derived from a Hindi word for "slum." It wasn't a slum, but it was a greasy little road town on the edge of the Rub al-Khali, catering to traffic along the northernmost route to and from the oil lands. Cinderblock buildings and a few timber-framed houses; a store that sold tire gauges, maps and compasses, sunblock, cheap novels, disposable phones. Three gas stations and four restaurants.

None of which Lise could see from the window of the

motel room. The ashfall sifted down in gray, stinking curtains. Power lines down or transformers shorted by dust, she guessed, and repairs wouldn't be quick, not out here in low-priority-land. It was a miracle they had made it here at all, even in their big all-terrain all-weather vehicle. Someone from the motel office knocked at the door and handed out flashlights and a warning not to attempt candles or any kind of open flame. But the Fourths had packed their own flashlights, and there was nothing to see anyway, only dingy walls and patchwork wallpaper. Lise kept a flashlight at hand for navigating her way to the bathroom when the need arose.

The boy Isaac slept, driven more by exhaustion than sedatives now, Lise guessed. The adults had huddled for conversation. Dr. Dvali was speculating about the ashfall in his persuasive and gently-modulated voice. "It might be a cyclical event. There's evidence in the geological record—this was some of your father's work, Miss Adams, though we never knew how to interpret it. Very thin ash layers compressed into the rock at intervals of ten thousand years or so."

"What does that mean," Turk asked, "it happens every ten thousand years? Everything gets buried in ash?"

"Not everything. Not everywhere. You find evidence of it mainly in the far west."

"Wouldn't it have to be a pretty thick layer to leave traces like that?"

"Thick, or persistent over a long period of time."

"Because these buildings aren't built to hold up anything much more than their own weight."

Roofs crushed, dust entombing the survivors: a cold Pompeii, Lise thought. That was chilling. But she had another thought. She said, "And Isaac—is the dustfall connected with what's happening to Isaac?"

Sulean Moi gave her a sad look. "Of course it is," she said.

Isaac understood it best in his dreams, where knowledge was rendered in wordless shapes and colors and textures.

In his dreams, planets and species arose like vagrant thoughts, were dismissed or committed to memory, evolved as thoughts evolved. His sleeping mind worked the way the universe worked—how could it be otherwise?

Half-heard phrases filtered into his floating awareness. *Ten thousand years.* The dust had fallen before, ten thousand years before and ten thousand years before that. Vast structures seeded space with their residue, feeding cyclical processes that turned and turned like faceted diamonds. The dust fell in the west because the west was calling it, as the west called Isaac. This planet wasn't Earth. It was older, it existed in an older universe, old things lived inside it. Things lived inside it: things that were not mindful but listened and spoke and pulsed in slow, millennial rhythms.

He could hear their voices. Some were close to him. Closer than they had ever been before.

The groan of the hotel's stressed beams and timbers continued after dusk and through the night—management sent a crew up to shovel the roof—but the ashfall tapered off, and by dawn the air had cleared to a gritty semitransparency. Lise had fallen asleep despite her best efforts to stay awake, curled on a foam mattress with the stink of the dust in her nostrils and sweat streaking her face.

She was the last to wake. She opened her eyes and saw that the Fourths were up and had gathered at the room's two windows. The light coming in was less bright than a rainy autumn glow, but it was more than she had dared hope for while the dust was still falling.

She sat up. She was wearing yesterday's clothes and her skin was encrusted with yesterday's dirt. Also her throat. Turk had noticed her movement; he handed her a bottle of water and she gulped it gratefully. "What time is it?"

"About eight." Eight o'clock by the long Equatorian reckoning of the hours. "Sun's been up for a while now. The dust stopped falling but it's still settling. A lot of fine powder in the air."

"How's Isaac?"

"He's not screaming, anyway. We're okay . . . but you might want to take a look outside."

Mrs. Rebka stepped back to tend to Isaac and allowed Lise to take her place at the window. Lise looked outside reluctantly.

But there seemed to be nothing unexpected. Just a road drifted over with ash, the same road they had crept along yesterday, pushing their vehicle to the limit of its endurance. The car was where they had left it, dust duned on the windward side. Its webbed steel wheels were still dilated, as big as the tires on the industrial rigs parked in sheltering rows beyond it. The daylight was dim and gritty, but she could see all the way to the gas station some hundred or so yards to the south. The road was empty of pedestrians, but other faces peered from other windows. Nothing moved.

No . . . that wasn't quite true.

The *dust* moved.

Beyond the courtyard, in the gray emptiness of the road, something like a whirlpool began to form as she watched. A region of ash the size of a dinner table began to turn a slow clockwise circle.

"What *is* that?"

Dr. Dvali, standing next to Turk, said, "Watch."

Turk put a hand on her left shoulder and her own right hand moved to cover it. The ash turned more quickly, dimpled at the center of the vortex, slowed again. Lise didn't like what she was seeing. It was unnatural, threatening, or maybe that was just the vibe she was picking up from the others: they knew what to expect, they had seen this before. Whatever it was.

Then the dust exploded—*like a geyser,* Lise thought. It shot a plume about ten feet into the air. She gasped and took an involuntary step back.

The ejected dust became a rooster-tail in the wind and eventually faded into the general miasma of the air, but as it cleared it became obvious that the geyser had left something behind . . . something shiny.

It looked like a flower. A ruby-colored flower, Lise marveled, smooth-stemmed and with a texture that made her think of the skin of a newborn infant. Stem and head were the same shade of deep, hypnotic red.

Turk said, "That's the closest one yet."

The flower—a word to which Lise's frantic thoughts automatically defaulted, because it really *did* look like a flower, with a gargantuan stem and a crown of petals, and she realized she was thinking of the sunflowers in her mother's garden in California, which had been just about this tall when they went to seed—began to arch and twist, turning its convex head to some rhythmless, inaudible tune.

She said, "There are *more* of these?"

"There were."

"Where? What happened to them?"

"Wait," Turk said.

The flower turned its head toward the hotel. Lise stifled another small gasp, because in the center of the bloom there was something that looked like an eye. It was round, and it glittered wetly, and it contained a sort of pupil, obsidian-black. For one awful moment it appeared to look directly at her.

"Is this what it was like on Mars?" Dr. Dvali said to Sulean Moi.

"Mars is countless light-years away. Where we are now, the Hypotheticals have been active for much longer. The things that grew on Mars were much less active, different in appearance. But if you're asking me whether this is a similar phenomenon, then yes, probably it is."

The ocular sunflower abruptly stopped moving. The inundated town of Bustee was still and silent, as if holding its breath.

Then there was, to Lise's horror, more motion in the dust, bumped-up rills and puffs of ash converging on the flower. Something—several things—leaped onto the stalk of it with frightening speed. They moved continuously and she could only form a vague impression of their nature, things crab-like, sea-green, many-legged, and what they did to the sunflower was—

They ate it.

They nipped at its stalk until the writhing thing toppled; then they were on it like piranhas on a carcass, and when the manic flurry of their devouring was finished they disappeared, or became inert once more, camouflaged in the fallen ash.

Nothing was left behind. No evidence whatsoever.

"This," Dr. Dvali said, "is why we're reluctant to leave the room."

CHAPTER TWENTY-ONE

Turk spent the rest of the morning at the window, cataloging the varieties of peculiar life that sprang out of the dust. Know your enemy, he thought. Lise stood next to him much of the time, asking brief but pertinent questions about what he had seen before she woke up. Dr. Dvali had switched on their little wireless telecom receiver and was drawing down sporadic reports from Port Magellan, a useful activity in Turk's opinion, but the other Fourths did nothing but talk: endlessly and to little purpose. It was one of the failings of Fourths, Turk decided. They might occasionally be wise. But they were incurably talky.

Right now they were picking on the Martian woman, Sulean Moi, who seemed to know more than the rest of them about the ashfall but who was reluctant to share her knowledge. Mrs. Rebka was particularly insistent. "Your taboos aren't relevant here," she said. "We need all the information we can get. You owe it to us . . . to the boy, at least."

Temperate as it sounded, this was, by Fourth standards, nearly a fistfight.

The Martian woman, dressed in oversized denim pants that made her look like some implausibly skinny oil-rig jock, sat on the floor hugging her knees. "If you have a question," she said sullenly, "ask it."

"You said the ashfall on Mars generated peculiar forms of, of—"

"Of life, Mrs. Rebka. Call it by its name. Why not?"

"Lifeforms like what we're seeing outside?"

"I don't recognize the flowers or the predators that consume them. In that sense, there's no similarity. But that's to be expected. A forest in Ecuador doesn't look like a forest in Finland. But both are forests."

"The purpose of it, though," Mrs. Rebka said.

"I've studied the Hypotheticals since childhood and I've listened to a lot of highly-informed speculation and I still can't guess the 'purpose' of it. The Martian ashfalls are isolated events. The life they generate is vegetative, always short-lived, and unstable in the long term. What conclusions can be drawn from such isolated examples? Very few." She hesitated, frowning. "The Hypotheticals—whatever else they are—are almost certainly not discreet entities but a collation of vastly many interconnected processes. They are an ecology, in other words. These manifestations either play some explicit role in that process or are an unintended consequence of it. I don't believe they represent any kind of deliberate strategy on the part of a higher consciousness."

"Yes," Mrs. Rebka said impatiently, "but if your people understood enough to engineer Hypothetical technology into human beings—"

"You possess that ability too." Sulean Moi looked pointedly at Isaac.

"Because it was given to us by Wun Ngo Wen."

"Our work on Mars has always been purely pragmatic. We were able to culture samples from the ashfall and observe their ability to interact with human protein at the cellular level. Centuries of that kind of observation produced some insight into the ways human biology might be manipulated."

"But you engineered what you admit is Hypothetical technology."

"Technology or biology—in this case I'm not sure the distinction is meaningful. Yes, we cultured alien life, or technology if you prefer that word, at the microscopic level. Because it grows, reproduces, and dies, we were able to select and manipulate certain strains for certain traits. Over the course of a great many years we generated the modified cultures that enhance human longevity. And other germ lines as well. One of the most radical of which is the treatment you applied to Isaac while he was still in the womb. In *your* womb, Mrs. Rebka."

Mrs. Rebka reddened.

Turk understood the significance of what they were discussing, and he guessed it was important, but it seemed ridiculously remote at a time when real problems were percolating so close to hand. Right outside the door, in fact. Was it safe to go outside? That was the question they ought to be asking. Because sooner or later they would have to leave this room. Because they had very little in the way of food.

He begged the loan of Dr. Dvali's little radio and pushed the nodes into his ears, blocking out the querulous Fourths and inducing other voices.

The available broadcast was a narrowband thing from Port Magellan, two guys from one of the local media collectives reading UN advisories and updated reports. This ashfall had been only a little worse than the first, at least in terms of weight and duration. A few roofs had collapsed to the south of the city. Most roads were currently impassable. People with respiratory problems had been sickened by ash inhalation, and even healthy people were spitting gray residue, but that wasn't what had everybody scared. What had everybody scared were the peculiar things growing out of the ash. The announcers called these things "growths" and reported that they had appeared randomly across the city, but especially where the ash was deep or had drifted. They sprang from the dust, in other words, like seedlings from mulch. Although they lived only briefly and were quickly "reabsorbed" into the local environment, a few of them—"objects resembling trees or enormous mushrooms"—had erupted to impressive heights.

There was a dreamlike (or nightmare-like) aspect to these reports. A "pink cylinder" fifty feet in length was blocking traffic at a downtown intersection. "Something witnesses describe as an immense spiky bubble, like a piece of coral," had sprouted from the roof of the Chinese consulate. Reports of small motile forms were yet to be officially confirmed.

Terrifying as this was, the manifestations were dangerous only if you happened to be in the wrong place at the wrong time—if one of them fell on you, for example. Still, residents were advised to stay indoors and keep windows closed. The ash had stopped falling, an offshore breeze was dispersing the lightest of the particles, and work crews were prepped to hose down the streets again ("growths" and all, Turk supposed) as soon as that was practical.

Unless this began to happen repeatedly, the city would recover. But the city was on the far side of a chain of mountains pierced by a few currently useless passes, and Bustee, like every other tin-and-tarpaper road town between the foothills and the Rub al-Khali, depended on the coast for supplies. How long till the passes were cleared? Weeks, minimum, Turk guessed. The last ashfall had been hard on these towns but this one had been worse, locally much denser, and the weird-ass plant life (or whatever it was) would surely impede the work necessary to

get commerce up and running. So food would run short:
what about water? He wasn't sure how these desert settlements were supplied. You turned on the tap, but where
was the reservoir? Up in the foothills? Was the water still
potable, and would it stay that way?

At least there was food and bottled water in the car,
enough to last them a while. What Turk didn't like was
that the vehicle was sitting out in the parking lot of this
motel where someone might be tempted to break in and
share the wealth. Here, at least, was a problem he could
confront. He stood up and said, "I'm going outside."

The others turned to look goggle-eyed at him. Dvali
said, "What are you talking about?"

He explained about the food. "Even if no one else is
hungry, I am."

"It might not be safe," Dvali said.

Turk had seen a couple of other people out in the street
with handkerchiefs tied over their mouths. One of them
had been within fifteen feet of a "lifeform" when it
sprouted from the dust, but the flower hadn't interfered
with the man and the man had shown absolutely no incli-
nation to fuck with the flower. Which jibed with what the
news was saying about Port Magellan. "Just to the car
and back. But I'd like somebody in the doorway watching
out for me, and I need something to use for a mask."

There was no debate, to Turk's relief. Dr. Dvali used
a pocketknife to cut off a corner of the bedsheet, which
Turk tied over his nose and mouth. Turk took the vehicle's keycard from Mrs. Rebka while Lise volunteered
for door duty.

"Don't stay out any longer than you need to," she
said.

"Don't worry," he said.

The sky was blue, made chalky by the ash that gave the
air a sour, sulfuric tang. No telling what this was doing

to everybody's lungs. If the dust contained alien spores—which was what all the talk seemed to imply—might they not take root in the moist interior of a human body? But they didn't seem to need much moisture, Turk thought, if they could grow on the paved street of a desert town in a dry September. In any case, there had been no reports of purely ash-related deaths. He shook off these concerns and tried to concentrate on the task at hand.

He felt lonely as soon as he stepped outside. The motel parking lot was a paved half-moon with an empty ceramic fountain in the middle of it. Beyond it was the main street, really just a stretch of Highway 7 heading into the Rub al-Khali. Across the street there was a row of one-story brick commercial buildings. All of this was ash-coated, windows dust-encrusted, traffic signs and billboards rendered illegible. The silence was unbroken.

The Fourths' vehicle, recognizable by its boxy shape and sprung-steel wheels, was parked a dozen yards to Turk's left. He stood a moment and looked back at Lise, who was holding the door open a crack. He gave her a little wave and she nodded. All clear. Onward.

He took long deliberate steps, trying not to stir up too much dust. His shoes impacted the drifted ash and left finely-detailed prints under chalky clouds.

He reached the car without incident and was only slightly unnerved by the distance that had opened up between himself and the room where Lise was waiting. He used his forearm to brush a layer of ash off the rear of the vehicle, the baggage compartment where the groceries were stored. He took Dr. Dvali's keycard out of his pocket and applied it to the security slot. Tendrils of dust rose up around his hands.

He paused and lifted the cloth that covered his mouth long enough to spit. The spittle plopped inelegantly on

the surface of the ash-covered sidewalk, and he half
expected something to rise up from beneath, like a fish
rising to bait, and snatch it away.

He opened the cargo door and selected a cooler full
of bottled water and a box of canned goods—the kind
of thing you could eat without cooking if you had to—
and that, plus a few stacks of flatbread, was all he could
carry. Enough for now. Or he could get in the car and
drive it closer to the room: but that would block the
route around the courtyard and maybe attract unwanted
attention . . .

"Turk!" Lise yelled from the doorway. He looked
back at her. The door was wide open and she was leaning forward, her hair framing her face. She pointed with
obvious urgency: "Turk! *In the street*—"

He saw it at once.

It didn't look threatening. Whatever it was. In fact it
looked like nothing more than a scrap of loose paper or
sheet plastic caught in a gust of wind, fluttering at head
level above the dust-duned highway by the diner. It
flapped, but you couldn't really say it was flying, not in
the purposeful way a bird flies.

But it wasn't a sheet of paper; it was something
stranger than that. It was colored glassy blue at the center, red at its four extremities. And although it was
clumsy in the air, it appeared to move by design, slip-
sliding up the center of the road.

Then it seemed to hesitate, its four wing-tips pumping simultaneously to loft it a few feet higher. The next
time it moved, it moved in a new direction.

It moved toward Turk.

"Get the fuck back here!" Lise was screaming.

They said these things weren't dangerous. Turk
hoped that was true. He dropped everything but the carton of canned goods and began to run. About halfway to

the door he glanced back over his shoulder. The flapping thing was right behind him, a yard to his right—way too close. He dropped the last carton and broke into a full-out sprint.

The thing was bigger than it had looked from a distance. And louder: it sounded like a bedsheet on a laundry line in a windstorm. He didn't know whether it could hurt him but it was clearly *interested* in him. He ran, and because the ash here was six inches deep, in places deeper, it was like running on a sandy beach. Or in a nightmare.

Lise threw the door wide open.

Soon Turk could see the flapping thing in his peripheral vision, beating the air like a piston. All it had to do was veer right and it would be on him. But it kept its steady if erratic course, paralleling him, almost as if it was racing him. Racing him—

To the open door.

He slowed down. The flapper rattled past him.

"Turk!"

Lise was still posed in the doorway. Turk ripped the cloth from his mouth and took a deep breath: bad move, because his throat was instantly clogged. "Close it," he croaked, but she couldn't hear him. He gagged and spat. "The door, dammit, close the fuckin' door!"

Whether or not she heard him, the danger dawned on Lise. She stepped back and simultaneously made a grab for the doorknob, missed, lost her balance and fell. The flapping thing, no longer awkward in the air, homed in on her as if it were laser-guided. Turk began sprinting again, but she was too far away.

She sat halfway up, balanced on an elbow, eyes wide, and Turk felt a stab of fear under his ribs sharp as a thorn to the heart. She raised an arm to fend off the thing. But it ignored her as it had ignored Turk. It slid past her into the room.

Turk couldn't see what happened next. He heard a muted scream, and then Mrs. Rebka's voice, a keening wail, more shocking because it came from a Fourth. She was calling Isaac's name.

CHAPTER TWENTY-TWO

Lise sat stunned on the floor, not sure exactly what had happened. The thing, the flying thing, the thing she had thought was about to attack Turk, had come inside the room. For a single dazed moment she heard the sound of it subside to a moist fluttering. Then the sound stopped altogether, and Mrs. Rebka began shouting.

Lise struggled to her feet.

"Shut the door!" Dr. Dvali roared.

But no. Not yet. She waited for Turk, who came barreling in along with a cloud of dust. Then she slammed the door and looked around warily for the flying creature. Idiotically, she was thinking of the summer her parents had taken her on vacation to a cabin in the Adirondacks: one night a bat had come down the chimney and fluttered around in the darkness, terrifying her. She recalled with supernatural clarity the feeling that at any moment something hot and alive would tangle itself in her hair and begin to bite.

But the flapping thing had already alighted, she realized.

The Fourths gathered around the bed where Isaac lay, because—

Because the flying creature had landed *on the boy's face*.

The terrified boy had turned his head against the pillow. The animal, or creature or whatever it was called or ought to be called, covered his left cheek like a fleshy red poultice. One corner of it matted the hair above his temple while another enclosed his neck and shoulder. Isaac's mouth and nose remained free, although the gelid body of the thing had adhered to his trembling lower lip. His left eye was dimly visible through the creature's translucent body. His other eye was wide open.

Mrs. Rebka went on calling the boy's name. She reached for the creature as if to pull it away, but Dvali caught her hand. "Don't touch it, Anna," he said.

Anna. Mrs. Rebka's name was Anna. Some idiotically calm fraction of Lise's mind filed that fact away. *Anna Rebka,* who was also the boy's mother.

"We need to get it off him!"

"Something to handle it with," Dvali said. "Gloves, a stick, a piece of paper—"

Turk yanked a pillowcase from one of the spare pillows and wrapped it around his right hand.

Strange, Lise thought, how the flying thing had ignored Turk in the street, how it had ignored Lise, for that matter, and the other adults, all easy targets, but had lighted without hesitation on Isaac. Did that mean something? Whatever the flying thing truly was—and she did not doubt that it had sprung from the ash, like the ocular flower or the host of carnival objects the news was reporting from Port Magellan—was it possible it had *chosen* Isaac?

The others stood back from the bed as Turk reached

toward the creature with his wrapped hand. But then another strange thing happened:

The flying thing disappeared.

"The hell?" Turk said.

Isaac gasped and sat suddenly upright, put his hand to his face and felt the freshly revealed skin.

Lise blinked and tried to replay the memory in her mind's eye. The flapping thing had dissolved—or at least that's how it had looked. It had turned to liquid all at once and instantly evaporated. Or, no, it had *seeped away,* like a puddle of water drawn into moist earth. There wasn't even a wisp of vapor where it had been. It was as if it had drained directly into Isaac's flesh.

She set aside that troubling thought.

Mrs. Rebka pushed past Turk and reached for the boy—fell on the bed beside him and took him into her arms. Isaac, still gasping, bent his body against her and ducked his head into her shoulder. He began to sob.

When it became obvious nothing more was about to happen—nothing monstrous, at least—Dvali asked the others to step back. "Give them some room." Lise retreated and grabbed Turk's hand. His hand was sweaty and dusty but infinitely reassuring. She couldn't begin to guess what had just happened, but the aftermath was utterly comprehensible: a frightened child was being comforted by his mother. For the first time Lise began to see Mrs. Rebka as something more than a spooky, emotionally distant Fourth. For Mrs. Rebka, at least, Isaac wasn't a biology experiment. Isaac was her son.

"What the fuck," Turk repeated. "Is the kid all right?"

That remained to be seen. Sulean Moi and Diane Dupree sequestered themselves in the motel room's tiny kitchen nook, talking fervently but quietly. Dr. Dvali watched Mrs. Rebka from a careful distance. Gradually Isaac's breathing grew steadier. At last he pulled away from Mrs. Rebka and looked around. His peculiar gold-flecked eyes were large and wet, and he hiccupped a couple of times.

Diane Dupree emerged from her conference with the Martian woman and said, "Let me examine him."

She was the closest thing to a medical doctor in the room, so Mrs. Rebka reluctantly allowed Diane to sit with the boy, measuring his pulse and thumping his chest, doing these things, Lise suspected, more to reassure Isaac than to diagnose him. She did look closely at his left cheek and forehead where the creature had touched him, but there was no obvious rash or irritation. Lastly she looked into Isaac's eyes—those strange eyes—and seemed to find nothing extraordinary there.

Isaac mustered enough courage to ask, "Are you a doctor?"

"Just a nurse. And you can call me Diane."

"Am I all right, Diane?"

"You seem all right to me."

"What happened?"

"I don't know. A lot of strange things are happening right now. That was just one of them. How do you feel?"

The boy paused as if taking inventory. "Better," he said finally.

"Not scared?"

"No. Well. Not as much."

In fact he was speaking more coherently than he had for a couple of days. "May I ask you a question?"

The boy nodded.

"Last night you said you could see through the walls. You said there was a light only you could see. Do you still see it?"

He nodded again.

"Where? Can you point at it?"

Haltingly, Isaac did so.

"Turk," Diane said. "Do you have your compass?"

Turk carried a brass-encased compass in his pocket—he had refused to abandon it back in the Minang village, much to *Ibu* Diane's annoyance. He took it out and sighted along Isaac's arm toward his extended index finger.

"This is nothing new," Mrs. Rebka said impatiently. "He always points the same way. A little north of west."

"Just about due west now. Tending to the south, if anything." Turk looked up and registered their expressions. "Why? Is that important?"

By mid-afternoon the street was more nearly normal. Nothing had grown out of the ashfall for a couple of hours. There were occasional eddies in the dust, but that could have been the wind—a gusty wind had come up, clouding the air and piling gray windrows against exposed vertical surfaces. But it swept away some of the ashfall and even exposed the asphalt in places.

Only a few of the bizarre growths had lasted out the morning. Most, like the flower with an eye in its bloom, were attacked (*eaten*, Lise thought, might as well use the word) by smaller and more mobile entities, which then faded and vanished. Some of the larger growths were still more or less intact. She had seen a sort of technicolor tumbleweed blowing down the street, obviously the husk of something no longer vital. And there was a fretwork of brittle white tubules clinging to one of the buildings opposite the motel, obscuring a sign that had once announced AUTO PARTS but was no longer legible under the pale fretwork.

The relative calm drew people out of their hiding places. A few big-tired vehicles clanked past, more or less managing the dustfall. The motel clerk knocked on the door and asked whether everyone was okay—he had seen a little of the morning's drama. Turk said they were fine and he even ventured outside again (door firmly closed behind him, Lise at the window concealing her anxiety) and came back from the car with enough groceries to last a couple of days.

Mrs. Rebka continued hovering over Isaac, who was alert and not obviously suffering. He was sitting up now, facing the western wall of the room as if he were praying to some backward Mecca. This wasn't new behavior, Lise understood, but it was still deeply spooky. When Mrs. Rebka took a bathroom break, Lise went to the boy's bedside and sat with him.

She said hello. He looked at her briefly, then turned his head back to the wall.

Lise said, "What is it, Isaac?"

"It lives underground," the boy said.

And Lise suppressed a shiver and backed away.

Turk and Dr. Dvali conferred over a map.

It was the standard fold-up map of the topography and sparse roads of Equatoria west of the mountains. Lise peeked over Turk's shoulder as he marked lines with a pen and a ruler. "What's this about?"

"We're triangulating," Turk said.

"Triangulating what?"

Dvali, with only slightly strained patience, pointed at a dot on the map. "This is the compound where you met us, Miss Adams. We left there and we traveled north about two hundred miles—here." A flyspeck marked *Bustee*. "Back at the compound Isaac's obsession was with a very specific compass point, which we've drawn out." A long line into the west. "But where we are now, his directional sense appears to have altered slightly." Another long line, not quite parallel to the first. The lines moved closer across the amber-colored vastness of the desert, deep into the marked boundaries of the international mineral-rights concessions. They intersected in the Rub al-Khali, the sandy tableland that comprised the western quarter of Equatoria.

"That's what he's pointing at?"

"That's what he's been pointing at all summer—more urgently in the last few weeks."

"So what is it? What's there?"

"As far as I know, nothing. Nothing's there."

"But it's where he wants to go."

"Yes." Dr. Dvali looked past Lise at the other Fourths. "And that's where we're going to take him."

The Fourth women said nothing, only stared.

It was Mrs. Rebka who finally, reluctantly, nodded her consent.

Lise couldn't sleep that night. She tossed on her mattress listening to the sounds the others made. Whatever else the Fourth treatment might cure, it did nothing for snoring. And yet they slept. And she did not.

Eventually, well past midnight, she got up, stepped over sleeping bodies on her way to the bathroom, and splashed her face with lukewarm water. Instead of going back to bed she went to the window, where Turk was sitting in a chair keeping the night watch.

"Can't sleep," she whispered.

Turk kept his gaze fixed on the street outside, a ghostly void by the light of the dust-dimmed moon. Nothing was happening. The peculiar eruptions from the ashfall showed no sign of resuming. Finally he said, "You want to talk?"

"I don't want to wake anybody up."

"Come out to the car." Turk and Dr. Dvali had moved the car closer to the room, where it would be easier to keep an eye on. "We can sit there awhile. It's safe enough now."

Lise had not left the room since they arrived and the

idea appealed to her. She was wearing her only pair of jeans and an oversized shirt she had borrowed from the Fourth compound. She pulled her shoes onto her bare feet.

Turk opened the door and eased it shut when they had stepped outside. The smell of the ash was instantly stronger. Sulfur, or something bitter like that—why did the ash smell like sulfur? Hypothetical machines grew in cold places, or so Lise had learned in school: distant asteroids, the frozen moons of frozen planets. Was there sulfur out there? She had heard of sulfur on the moons of, was it, Jupiter? The New World's solar system had a planet like that, a cold radioactive giant, far from the sun.

The wind had died with nightfall. The sky was hazy but she could see a few stars. Even when she was very young her father had loved to show her the stars. The stars need names, he would say, and together they would name them. *Big Blue. Point of the Triangle.* Or silly names. *Belinda. Grapefruit. Antelope.*

She slid into the front seat next to Turk.

"We need to talk about what happens next," he said.

Yes. That was undeniably true. She said, "The Fourths are taking Isaac west."

"Right. I don't know what they hope to accomplish. "

"They think he can talk to the Hypotheticals."

"Great—what's he going to say? Greetings from the human race? Please stop dropping shit on us from outer space?"

"They're hoping to learn something profound."

"You believe that?"

"No. But *they* do. Dvali does, at least."

"Fourths are generally pretty reasonable people, but would *you* put a bet on that outcome? I wouldn't."

It was like religion, Lise supposed. You didn't lay odds on the sacred, you just looked for it with an open heart and hoped for the best. But she didn't say that to

Turk. "So what do we do when they take off for the desert?"

He said, "I'm thinking of going with them."

"You're—what?"

"Wait, it makes sense. You saw the map, right? The place they're headed is three-quarters of the way to the west coast. From there there's a decent road all the way to the sea. The west coast, Lise, that's nothing but fishing villages and research outposts. Catch a boat on the southern route back to Port Magellan and by the time I get there nobody's looking for me anymore, the whole Fourth thing is over and Genomic Security has probably figured that out. I have enough friends in the Fourth community that I can probably get myself a whole new set of identity documents."

Nights got chilly in the desert this time of year. The upholstery was cold and their talk had made condensation on the window. "I can see a couple of problems with that."

"So can I—what's your list?"

She tried to be logical. "Well, the ashfall. Even if the roads are passable, even with a good vehicle, you could get stalled, run out of gas, have engine problems."

"It's a risk," he admitted, "but you can plan for it, carry tools and parts and fuel and so on."

"And the Fourths aren't a free ride. They expect to find something out there. What if they're right? I mean, look at the way that flying thing went after Isaac. Maybe he *is* special, maybe he has some special attraction to the, uh, whatever grows out of the ash, and, if so, that could be a major obstacle."

"I thought about that too. But I haven't heard of anyone being seriously hurt by those things, except accidentally. Even Isaac. Whatever happened to him, it doesn't seem to have made him worse."

"It landed on his *face,* Turk. It sank into his skin."

"He's sitting up, he's not feverish, he's no sicker than he was before."

"You wouldn't say that if it had been you."

"That's the point—it *wasn't* me; whatever that thing was, I'm not what it wanted."

"So we just tag along and when they're finished with Isaac—whatever that means—we go on to the coast? That's the plan?"

He said with an embarrassment Lise could feel even in the shadows of the car, "Doesn't have to be both of us. If you want you can stick here and try to catch a ride over the pass when the ash clears. You have options I don't have. Probably safer to do that, from the objective point of view."

The objective point of view. Doubtless Turk imagined he was giving her the latitude to back out graciously from a reckless plan. He led the kind of life that allowed for sudden reversals of fortune and heavy wagers against fate. She didn't. That was the implication, and it was, of course, true, by and large—though not lately.

"I'll think about it," she said, and stepped out of the car into the moonlit night, wishing she had been able to sleep.

Come morning there was a degree of near-normality in Bustee: a few pedestrians in the street, a few capable vehicles beginning to head toward the larger towns to the south. Locals gawked at the remains of alien life clinging to the facades of buildings or littering the sidewalks like broken, once-brightly-colored toys. Life reassembling itself, Lise thought, despite the strangeness. Her own life, more deeply unraveled, was slower to knit.

The Fourths, now that they had reached a consensus, set out to procure supplies. A party of four—Dr. Dvali, Sulean Moi, Diane Dupree, and Turk—went to see what money could still buy at the local shops. Turk was even talking about a second vehicle, if they could procure one.

Lise stayed in the motel room with Mrs. Rebka and Isaac, hoping to catch another couple of hours of sleep. Which turned out to be difficult, because Isaac was agitated again. Not because of the flying thing that had attacked him—that seemed to have passed from his mind as promptly as a bad dream—but out of a new sense of urgency, a need to hurry to the heart of whatever was happening out west. Mrs. Rebka had asked a few tentative questions. What did he mean when he talked about something "underground"? But Isaac couldn't answer and grew frustrated when he tried.

So Mrs. Rebka told him they were going west, they *were* going west, as soon as they possibly could; and eventually Isaac accepted this consolation and fell back to sleep.

Mrs. Rebka left the bedside and moved to a chair. Lise pulled her own chair closer.

Mrs. Rebka looked about fifty years old. Lise had assumed she was older. She was a Fourth, and Fourths could appear "about fifty" for decades. But if Isaac was hers, she couldn't be much older than she looked. And anyway, Lise thought, wasn't it true that Fourths were biologically unable to conceive? So Mrs. Rebka's pregnancy must have begun before her conversion.

The obvious question was difficult but Lise was determined to ask it, and she wasn't likely to have a better opportunity. "How did it happen, Mrs. Rebka? The boy, I mean. How did he . . . I mean, if this isn't too personal."

Mrs. Rebka closed her eyes. Fatigue was written all over her face, fatigue or some deep, intractable despair. "What are you asking, Miss Adams? How he was altered or why he was conceived?"

Lise fumbled for an answer but Mrs. Rebka waved it off. "A brief and not especially interesting story. My husband was a lecturer temporarily seconded to the American University. Not a Fourth, but friendly toward them. He might have considered the treatment himself except that he was a devout, Orthodox Jew—his religious principles forbade it. And he died for the lack of it. He had an aneurism in his brain, inoperable. The treatment was the only thing that might have saved him. I begged him to take it, but he refused. In my grief I hated him a little for that. Because . . ."

"Because you were pregnant."

"Yes."

"Did he know?"

"By the time I was certain of it the aneurism had burst. He lived a few days but he was comatose."

"That child was Isaac?"

Mrs. Rebka closed her eyes. "That was fetal tissue that became Isaac. I know how brutal that sounds. But I couldn't tolerate the idea of raising the child alone. I meant to have an abortion. It was Dr. Dvali who convinced me otherwise. He had been one of my husband's closest friends and he became mine. He admitted that he was a Fourth. He talked to me about the controversies in the Fourth community, what it was like being— at least in some sense—a better kind of human being. And he talked to me about the Hypotheticals, a subject that had always interested me. He introduced me to others in his community. They were supportive."

"They talked you into doing what they wanted you to do."

"Nothing as crude as that. They didn't feed me propaganda. I *liked* these people—I liked them better than all the unchanged people who visited me out of a sense of duty, who were relentlessly sympathetic and secretly indifferent. The Fourths were authentic. They said what they believed. And one of the things Avram Dvali believed in was the possibility of communicating with the

Hypotheticals. He led me very gradually to the idea that I might have something to contribute to that very important work, because I was unchanged. And pregnant."

"So you gave him Isaac?"

"Not *Isaac*! I gave him the *possibility* of Isaac. Otherwise I would never have carried the child to term." She breathed in, breathed out, and the sound, to Lise's ears, was like the sound of the tide retreating from an ancient beach. "It wasn't any more complicated than the ordeal of becoming a Fourth. The customary injection, and then, when the process was underway, an intrauterine injection to keep the altered infant from being rejected by my body. I was tranquilized much of the time. I honestly remember very little of the pregnancy itself. He came to term in seven months."

"And afterward."

Mrs. Rebka looked away. "Avram was adamant that he should be raised by the community, not exclusively by me. He said it would be better if I didn't bond too closely with the child."

"Better for you or better for Isaac?"

"Both. We weren't sure he would survive to maturity. Isaac was—is—an *experiment*, Miss Adams. Avram was protecting me from what could have been an even more traumatic episode of grief. And beyond that . . . as much as I wanted to be a parent to Isaac, the boy has a difficult personality. He refused close contact with anyone. As a baby he wouldn't consent to be held. It really was as if he belonged to some new species, as if on the most fundamental biological level he knew he wasn't one of us."

"Because you made him that way," Lise could not help saying.

"True. The responsibility is all ours. And the guilt, of course. All I can say is that we hoped his contribution to our understanding of the universe would redeem the ugliness of his creation."

"Was that something you believed, or something they told you to believe?"

"Thank you for making excuses for me, Miss Adams, but yes, I believed it; all of us believed in it to one degree or another. That's why we came together in the first place. But none of us believed it as confidently and as— I'm tempted to say as *heroically*—as Avram Dvali. We had doubts, of course we did; we had moments of remorse. It isn't a pleasant story, is it? I'm sure you're asking yourself how we could have contemplated such a thing, much less carried it out. But people are capable of all kinds of acts, Miss Adams. Even Fourths. You ought to remember that." Mrs. Rebka closed her eyes. "And now I'm tired, and I don't have anything further to say."

The others came back with food, bottled water, spare parts, and (miraculously) a second vehicle—another big-tired utility vehicle purchased, Turk said, at ridiculous expense from a larcenous local dealer. The Fourths had more cash than good sense, Turk said, or maybe the sense to know when cash was no good.

She helped Turk load supplies into the vehicles. He moved with easy muscularity, loose-hipped and unself-conscious. There was a certain pleasure in doing the work with him, not thinking about Mrs. Rebka or Isaac or Dr. Dvali or what might be waiting out in the Rub al-Khali.

"So are you riding with us," he finally asked, "or are you waiting for a bus back to the Port?"

She didn't grace him with an answer. He didn't deserve one.

Because of course she was going with him. Into the big unknown, or wherever it was good people went when they disappeared.

PART FOUR

**RUB
AL-KHALI**

CHAPTER TWENTY-THREE

Brian Gately was safely back in Port Magellan when the second ashfall struck.

Sigmund and Weil had done something remarkable as they flew with Brian across the Bodhi Pass and down to the coastal plain: they had admitted defeat. The Fourths were scattered, Weil said, and the burned compound had yielded no evidence beyond the charred remains of a bioreactor hidden in a basement. Nothing incriminating had been discovered in Turk Findley's purloined aircraft, and the four captives were obviously decoys, elderly even by the standards of Fourths.

"So what, then," Brian asked as their aircraft overflew a canyon along which, far below, a lone oil tanker was navigating the switchbacks, "you just go home?"

"Of course we don't give up. We do what we've been doing for years, monitor communications, run software on strategic surveillance sites. Sooner or later something turns up. And in the meantime there's one less bioreactor to worry about. If nothing else, somebody's plans have been seriously fucked with."

"For this," Brian asked, "people die?"

"Who died, Brian? I don't remember anyone dying."

So he came at last to his small apartment in the polyglot city and was alone there when for the second time the sky filled with the luminous debris of ancient, incomprehensible machines.

He watched the local news broadcasts with a vague indifference. The newscasters used words like "strange" and "unprecedented," but Brian wasn't impressed: it was only a kind of celestial rot, the rubble of a vast disintegration. The Hypotheticals had built their intelligences in the cold places around and between countless stars, and they built them to last, no doubt, but any made thing had a lifetime. The pyramids of Egypt eroded; the Roman aqueducts were stumps of broken stone. So must the constructions of the Hypotheticals break down once they had served their dozen or their million allotted years.

The ashes birthed monstrosities, some of which he could see from his own window. A dozen yards down the road, where the Arabic commercial district declined into a structureless maze of souks and tea shops, a green tubule as big as a sewer pipe writhed as if in a strong wind and then tumbled over to barricade the street.

In his mind he played back Lise's final phone call. Where was she now? Not even Sigmund and Weil had been able to answer that question. She had fled with the rogue Fourths, victim of her own wild sympathies. Free, perhaps, in some distasteful sense of the word. Unbroken. Not yet fallen to earth like an ancient machine.

The ashfall took longer to clean up than it had the first time. And because it had happened twice, the people on television were asking themselves somber questions. Was this the end of it or would it happen again? Would the effects follow some exponential curve, each time more peculiar and disastrous, until Port Magellan was entirely buried under a mass of what looked like enormous children's toys?

Part of Brian wanted to deny the possibility while another part of him relished it. This was, after all, an alien planet, and how credulous we were, he thought, to imagine we could simply move in unmolested and conduct our lives as if it were a second Earth.

But the civil authorities, ant-like, methodically cleared the debris and reestablished their pheromonic lines of communication. When he could no longer avoid it Brian drove from his apartment along the smudged avenues to the American district, to the consulate building, to the offices of the Department of Genomic Security, Port Magellan Branch.

He walked past his own office to the door of his immediate superior, a consular legate named Larry Diesenhall. Diesenhall was a fifty-five-year-old career man with a shaved head and eyes so delicately colored they appeared to have been drawn in crayon. Diesenhall looked up at Brian and smiled. "Good to see you back, Brian."

Back at last. The prodigal son. Brian took an envelope out of his jacket pocket and dropped it on Diesenhall's immaculate desktop.

"What's this?"

"Have a look."

The envelope contained a pair of photographs—the photographs Pieter Kirchberg had sent him, extra copies of which Brian had run off on his printer this morning. He averted his eyes while Diesenhall opened the envelope.

"Jesus!" Diesenhall said. "Christ! What am I looking at here?"

The dead, Brian thought. The dead, who are customarily absent from church picnics and polite offices. He

sat down and explained about Tomas Ginn and about
Sigmund and Weil and the burning compound in the
desert and the four unlucky Fourths who had been
found in Turk Findley's aircraft and might or might not
have been tortured in an attempt to extract their confes-
sions. On several occasions Diesenhall tried to interrupt, but Brian talked over him, compulsively, a flood of
words too powerful to be dammed.

By the time he finished Diesenhall was staring at
him, gape-jawed.

"Brian . . . this is upsetting."

One way of describing it, Brian thought.

"I mean, wow. Do you realize how tenuous your position is here? You come to me with these complaints
about Sigmund and Weil, but I don't have anything to
do with them. What the Executive Action Committee
does is outside the public mandate. Neither you nor I are
members of that committee, Brian. And that community
isn't answerable to the likes of us. You had a relationship with a woman who was apparently deeply involved
with known Fourths, and for you, and I hope you realize
this, the outcome could have been much worse. Questions were asked about you. About your loyalty. And I
stood up for you. I was happy to do that. So now you
come to me with these allegations and with this—" The
photographs. "This *obscenity*. What do you expect me
to do?"

"I don't know. Get upset. Complain. File a report."

"Really? Do you really want me to do *any* of that? Do
you have any idea what that would mean for *both* of us?
And do you think it would make any kind of difference?
That any *good* would come of it? That anything would
change, except for us?"

Brian thought about that. He didn't have a counter-
argument. Probably Diesenhall was right.

He took a second envelope from his jacket and dropped it on Diesenhall's desktop. Diesenhall promptly recoiled, his hands scuttling back to the edge of the desk. "Christ, what's this?"

"My resignation," Brian said.

CHAPTER TWENTY-FOUR

The last human being they saw west of Bustee was a stout woman who was locking up a Sinopec gas station. She had already shut down the pumps, but she opened them long enough to refuel both vehicles while she lectured Dr. Dvali in a Cantonese accent about the foolishness of heading deeper into the desert. Nobody left out there, she said. Even the riggers and pipeline workers, even the hired men with no money but what they hoped to be paid, they had all gone east after the first ashfall. "It was worse out there," she said.

"Worse in what way?"

"Just worse. And the earthquakes."

"Earthquakes?"

"Little earthquakes. Damaged things. All that has to be fixed, when it's safe to come back, if."

Dr. Dvali frowned. Turk said, "We're on our way to the west coast, actually, other side of the desert."

"Stupid way to get there," the Cantonese woman said, to which Turk could only nod and shrug.

* * *

Extraterrestrial dust mixed with ordinary sand had duned against the sun-white planking of the depot. The wind came from the south, hot and dry. A talcum-powdered world, Lise thought. She thought of what Turk had said about the west coast, the other side of the desert. She imagined waves breaking on a beach, a few adventurous fishing trawlers anchored in some natural harbor. Rainfall and greenness and the smell of water.

As opposed to this merciless, sun-stricken horizon.

Stupid way to get there. Well, yes, no doubt.

During the long drive, Sulean Moi watched the way Avram Dvali and Anna Rebka conducted themselves around the boy.

Mrs. Rebka, the boy's mother almost despite herself, was the most attentive. Dvali was less directly involved—Isaac had begun to shrink from his touch—but his attention always circled back to the child.

Dvali was an idolater, Sulean thought. He worshipped a monstrosity. He believed Isaac held the key to—what? Not "communication with the Hypotheticals." That neat and linear goal had been abandoned long ago. A leap of cognition, an intimacy with the immense forces that had shaped the mundane and celestial worlds. Dvali wanted Isaac to be a god, or at least god-touched, and he wanted to touch the hem of his robes in turn and be enlightened.

And me, Sulean thought. What do *I* want with Isaac? Above all she had wanted to forestall his birth. It was to prevent such tragedies that she had left the Martian embassy in New York. She had made herself a dark, often unwelcome presence in the community of Terrestrial Fourths, subsisting on their charity while scolding them for their hubris. Don't worship the Hypotheticals: they are not gods. Don't contrive to bridge the divide between the Hypotheticals and the human: that gap cannot be bridged. We know. We tried. We failed. And in the process we committed what can only be called a crime. We shaped a human life for our own purposes and produced, in the end, only pain, only death.

Twice in her wanderings on Earth she had forestalled such a project. Two rogue communities of Fourths, one in Vermont and one in rural Denmark, had been on the verge of attempting to create a hybrid child. In both cases Sulean had alerted more conservative Fourths and exerted the moral weight they accorded her as a Martian Fourth. In both cases she had succeeded in preventing tragedies. Here she had failed. She was a dozen years too late.

And yet she insisted on accompanying the child on what was no doubt his final journey, when she could have walked away and continued her work elsewhere. Why? She allowed herself to wonder whether she might be as susceptible as Dr. Dvali to the seductive lure of contact . . . even though she knew it was impossible and absurd.

More likely it was because the boy Isaac had spoken a few words in a language he couldn't possibly have known.

That is to say: because she was afraid of him.

"**Y**ou make much of that," Turk asked, "what the lady said about earthquakes?"

He rode in the lead vehicle with Dvali, who had taken the wheel. The wind still pushed snaketrails of dust across the road, but most of the ash seemed to have been blown away—or had been absorbed into the earth, the same way that flapping thing had been absorbed into Isaac's skin.

Another day of driving and they would reach the outskirts of the oil concessions. The target they had triangulated was a couple hundred miles west of there.

"I don't disbelieve her," Dr. Dvali said evenly. "Was there anything in the news?"

Turk had been keeping Dr. Dvali's radio plugged into one ear, though reception was intermittent. They were a long way from the aerostats. "Nothing about earthquakes. But I wouldn't rule it out." He wouldn't rule out munchkins or dinosaurs, at this point. "They say it could happen again, the ashfall. You think that's possible?"

"I don't know," Dr. Dvali said. "No one knows."

Except maybe Isaac, Turk thought.

They stopped for the night at a gas-food-lodging complex that had once catered to tanker drivers but was now deserted.

There was no mystery about why it had been abandoned. Alien growths were festooned across the building's roof. These were gaudy tubular things, turned to lacework by their own decomposition. But they must once have been heavy, because pieces of the roof had collapsed under their weight. And that wasn't all: a filigree of blue tendrils had invaded the restaurant, covering everything within a few yards of the door (floor, ceiling, tables, chairs, a busboy's cart) in randomly interwoven ropes and strings. These, too, were decaying. Touch them and they turned to rancid powder.

Turk located room keys and opened doors until he found enough undamaged rooms to allow them all some welcome privacy. Turk and Lise took one room, Dvali another. Sulean Moi consented to share a suite with Diane, Mrs. Rebka, and the boy Isaac.

Sulean wasn't unhappy with the room arrangements. She couldn't bring herself to like Mrs. Rebka, but she hoped to be allowed a few moments alone with the boy.

The opportunity came that evening. Dvali summoned everyone for what he called "a community meeting."

Isaac, of course, couldn't participate, and Sulean volunteered to stay with him—she had nothing to contribute to the talking, she said.

Mrs. Rebka agreed, reluctantly. As soon as she had left the room, Sulean went to the boy's bedside.

He wasn't feverish, he was even alert at times, and he could sit up, walk, take food. He had been blessedly quiet in the car, as if some of the dreadful inhuman neediness had passed from him since the flying thing attacked him. Dvali was loathe to discuss that event, since he didn't understand it, but it was the boy's first deeply personal contact with the semiliving creations of the Hypotheticals. Sulean wondered what it had felt like. Was the thing still in his body even now, had it disassembled itself into molecular fragments in order to circulate through his blood? And if so, why? Was there even a reason, or was it just another mindless tropism evolved over uncountable millions of years?

She wished she could ask Isaac. But there was only time for the most pressing questions.

She forced herself to smile at the boy. Isaac smiled back as readily as he ever had. I'm his friend, she thought. His Martian friend. "I knew someone like you," she said, "a long time ago."

"I remember," Isaac said.

Sulean felt a fluttering in her chest.

"Do you know who I'm talking about?"

One word. "Esh."

"You know about Esh?"

Isaac nodded solemnly, his gold-flecked eyes gone distant.

"What do you know about him?"

Isaac began to tell the story of Esh's brief childhood at Bar Kea Station, and Sulean was astonished to hear the boy speaking Esh's Martian dialect again.

She felt dizzy. "Esh," she whispered.

Isaac said, in English, "He can't hear you."

"But *you* can hear *him*?"

"He can't talk, Sulean. He's dead. You know that."

Of course she knew that. She had held his dying body in her arms, sick with the knowledge that she had helped him escape to the desert, to the thing he had so desperately wanted, the same thing Isaac wanted, which was the Hypotheticals, which was death.

She said, "But you can speak in his voice."

"Because I remember him."

"You *remember* him?"

"That is, he—I don't know how to explain!"

The boy was becoming anxious. Sulean suppressed her own terror and forced what she hoped was a reassuring smile. "You don't have to explain. It's a mystery. I don't understand it either. Just tell me how it feels."

"I know what I am, I know what they made me to be, Dr. Dvali, Mrs. Rebka, they want me to talk to the Hypotheticals, but I can't do that. I'm sorry, but I can't. But there's something in me—" He pointed to his ribs. "And out there—" The desert. "—something that remembers a million things and Esh is only one of them, but because he's *like* me it remembers him *to* me—I mean—"

Sulean stroked the boy's head. His hair was lank and gritty. All this traveling and no water for baths. Poor child. "Please don't be upset."

"The thing in me remembers Esh and I remember what Esh remembered. I look at you and I see both."

"Both?"

"The way you are now. And the way you were then."

Quite a contrast, Sulean imagined.

"And Esh can see me, too?"

"No, I told you, he's dead, he can't see anything. He's not here. But I know what he would say if he *was* here."

"And what would he say, Isaac?"

"He would say," and Isaac slipped into the Martian

language again, his inflections shockingly familiar even after all these long and arduous years: "He would say, *Hello, big sister.*"

Esh's voice, undeniably.

"And he would say . . ."

"What? Tell me."

"He would say, *Don't be afraid.*"

Oh, but that I cannot do, Sulean thought, and she retreated from the bed, almost to the door where, although she had not heard him arrive, Dr. Dvali was standing and listening, his face red with an emotion that was as much jealousy as anger.

"How long have you known this about him?"

Dvali had insisted on walking a short distance from the truck stop, away from the others, into the intimidating landscape that had surrounded them for days, as if the deserts of Mars had been re-created on this hotter alien world. A huge sky domed the evening emptiness, and of the works of man there was only the most tawdry.

Esh, Esh, she thought. Such a distance to come to hear his voice again. "A few weeks," she managed to say.

"Weeks! And were you planning to share this information with us?"

"There was never any *information.* Only a possibility."

"The significant possibility that Isaac is somehow sharing memories with your Martian experiment, this Esh—"

"Esh wasn't an experiment. He was a child, Dr. Dvali. And he was my friend."

"You're evading the issue."

"I'm evading nothing. I'm not an accessory to your work. Had it been possible, I would have prevented you from beginning it."

"But you didn't, and you're here now. I think you

should examine your own motives, Ms. Moi. I think you're here for the same reason we created Isaac. Because you've spent a lifetime trying to understand the Hypotheticals, and after—what, eighty years? Ninety?—you're no farther ahead than you were when you were young."

Certainly the Hypotheticals had never been far from her thoughts, not since they devoured Esh. An obsession, yes, maybe, but it had never influenced her judgment—had it?

As to whether she *understood* the Hypotheticals . . .

"They don't exist," she said.

"Excuse me?"

"The Hypotheticals. They don't exist, not the way you imagine them. What do you picture when you think about them? Some great wise ancient presence? Beings of infinite wisdom inscrutable to our petty minds? That was the mistake the Martian Fourths made. What risk would not be justified by the possibility of conversing with God? But they don't exist! There is nothing in all the starry sky but some vast operative logic connecting one thoughtless machine to the next. It's ancient, it's complex, but it isn't a *mind*."

"If that's so," Dvali said, "then who were you just talking to?"

Sulean opened her mouth and then closed it.

That night, for the first time in many days, Lise and Turk made love. The privacy of a separate room was an instant aphrodisiac. They didn't discuss it, didn't need to discuss it; in the candlelit darkness Lise had undressed and watched Turk undress, and then she had blown out the candle and found him by the faint light of the dust-dimmed moon. He smelled rank, and so did she. It didn't matter. Here was the communication at which they always excelled. Briefly she wondered whether, elsewhere in this ruin, the Fourths could hear the creak of the bedsprings. Probably, she thought. Probably good for them if they did hear it. It might enliven their old, juiceless lives.

Turk eventually fell asleep with his arm across her ribs and she was content to lie with him in the fading glow.

At last, though, she had to shift herself out of the embrace. Despite everything, she couldn't sleep. She thought about how far they had come, and she remembered a line she had read in some old book: *The thin end of nowhere, whittled down to a fine point.*

The night was cold. She curled against Turk again, seeking his warmth.

She was still awake when the building began to tremble.

Diane Dupree was awake in the room she shared with Sulean Moi, Mrs. Rebka, Isaac.

She focused her attention on the sound of Isaac's breathing, thinking how strange life must have been for Isaac, raised motherless—Mrs. Rebka had been something less than a mother—and fatherless—unless you counted Dr. Dvali's sinister hoverings—but indifferent, by all accounts, to affection. A difficult, refractory child.

She had overheard a little of Sulean Moi's argument with Dr. Dvali earlier today. It had raised uneasy questions in her mind.

The Martian woman was right, of course. Dr. Dvali and Mrs. Rebka weren't scientists, studying the Hypotheticals by unconventional means. They were on a pilgrimage. And at the end of it they expected something holy, something redemptive.

The same longing—years and years ago now—had carried her almost to her death. Diane had wrapped herself in her first husband's faith, and he had taken her to a religious retreat where she contracted an illness that nearly killed her. The cure had been her conversion to what the Martian Wun Ngo Wen had called the Fourth state, the adulthood beyond adulthood.

She thought she had left that longing behind her when she became a Fourth. It was as if, after the longevity treatment, something cool and methodically rational had risen up and taken control of her life. Something soothing, if a little deadening. No more reckless storming of Heaven. She had lived a steady, useful life.

Could she have been wrong, though, about how much she had left behind and how much she still carried with her, unsuspected? When the lines had intersected on the map, the triangulation of Isaac's urges, Diane had felt a familiar longing for the first time in . . . oh, many years.

She felt it again when she found out that Isaac could gain access to the memories of a long-dead Martian child he had never known.

The Hypotheticals had remembered Esh, Diane thought.

What else might the Hypotheticals have remembered?

Her brother Jason had died in a state of attempted communion with the Hypotheticals. Did they remember *that*? Did they in fact remember Jason?

And if she asked, would Isaac speak with Jason's voice?

She sat upright, almost guiltily, when the building began to tremble and shake. Fortifications breached, she thought dazedly: the walls of Heaven tumbling down.

By the time Turk managed to light a candle, the shaking had stopped.

The old Chinese lady was right, he thought. Earthquakes!

He turned back to Lise, who sat up in bed with the blanket pooled around her waist. He said, "You okay? It's just a tremor."

"Promise we won't stop," she said.

Turk blinked. Her skin by candlelight was pale, unearthly. "Stop?"

"When they get where they're going," and he understood by a toss of her head that she meant the Fourths, "we don't *stop,* right? We keep on heading for the west coast? Like you said?"

"Of course. What are you worried about? This was just a tremor, Lise. You lived in California, you must have felt little quakes like that."

"Because they're crazy, Turk. They sound rational, but they have this big carnival of craziness planned. I don't want any part of it."

Turk went to the window just to make sure the stars hadn't exploded or anything, because she was right, lunacy was on the march. But there was only the central Equatorian desert stretched out under its meager moon. That was a sight to make you feel small, he thought, that desert.

And another little tremor rattled the useless lamp on the side table.

Isaac felt the tremor but it didn't quite wake him. He had been sleeping a lot lately. He had lost some of his ability to distinguish between sleeping and waking.

The clock of the stars turned relentlessly inside him. In the darkness he dreamed things for which he had no words. There were many things for which he had no words. And there were words he knew but didn't understand and couldn't define: for instance, *love.*

I love you, Mrs. Rebka had whispered to him when no one but Isaac could hear.

He hadn't known what to say in return. But that was

all right. She didn't seem to need an answer. *I love you, Isaac, my only son,* she had whispered, and then turned her face away.

What did that mean?

What did it mean when he closed his eyes and saw the cycling stars or the banked fires of an invisible thing deep in the western desert? What did it mean that he felt its liveliness and power?

What did it mean that he could hear a million voices, more voices than there were stars in the sky? What did it mean that out of that multitude he could call up the voice of Esh, a dead Martian boy? Was he remembering Esh or was something remembering Esh *through him*— remembering Esh's voice with the air in Isaac's lungs?

Because—and here was something Isaac *did* know— the act to which he had been summoned, to which all the tumbling fragments of Hypothetical machinery had been summoned from their lazy courses in the sky, was a remembering.

A remembering larger than the world itself.

He felt it coming. The crust of the planet trembled, its shivering rose up through the foundation of this old building, through the floor, the joists, the beams, through the bed frame and the mattress, until Isaac trembled along with it, the motion filling him with a heatless joy, memory and annihilation advancing with giant steps, with strides as long as continents, until at last he asked himself:

Is this love?

PART FIVE

IN THE
COMPANY OF THE
UNSPEAKABLE

CHAPTER TWENTY-FIVE

They had reached the outskirts of the oil concessions—the desolate, thin end of nowhere—when the third and most intense ashfall began.

There had been some warning, conveyed by Dr. Dvali's intermittently-functional telecom receiver. The precipitation had been relatively light in Port Magellan, but dense waves of it were falling in the west, as if focused there.

By the time Dr. Dvali announced this news, the threat was ominously visible. Lise, looking through the back window of the vehicle as it sped down the highway between two equally flat horizons, saw clouds the color of boiling slate materialize from a chalk-blue sky.

"We'll need to get under cover again," she heard Turk say.

To the southwest Turk could just make out the silver-black silhouettes of the Aramco drilling and pumping complex. Evacuated, presumably—a couple of the far towers seemed to be leaning off vertical, though that could be an illusion—but Turk guessed the site would still be guarded, both by machines and by armed men.

Fortunately they didn't need to head in that direction. The oil concessions had grown a ring of commerce around them, businesses run by lonely men for lonely men, strip clubs and bars and porn vendors, which meant that not far down the road they would find more respectable commercial concessions and housing for the hired workers. Which appeared as the two cars raced the black cloud flowing from the east: a gated side road, the gate unchained; a mall (grocery store, media retailers, a multi-mart); and a number of sturdy concrete buildings in which one- or two-room utility apartments were stacked like boxes.

Turk, in the lead car with Lise and Dr. Dvali, looked back and saw the second vehicle pulling into the mall lot. Dvali swung around and intercepted them in front of the grocery store.

"Supplies," Diane explained.

"We don't have time," Dvali said sternly. "We need to get under cover."

"Such as the building up ahead? I would suggest you break in or whatever you need to do, and we'll follow as soon as we find food."

Dvali clearly didn't like this idea, but just as clearly, Turk thought, it made sense: they had been running low on essentials and the ash storm might maroon them for a good long time. "Be quick about it," Dvali said unhappily.

Whoever designed this workers' barracks had made no attempt to disguise the institutional nature of the project. On the outside the building was weathered concrete and cracked pavement and an empty parking lot adjoining a tennis court enclosed in a chain-link fence, its net slumped in disarray. The door Turk approached was hollow steel painted industrial yellow, no doubt battered by the boots of hundreds of shit-drunk oil-riggers over the years, and it was locked, but the lock was fragile and gave way after some leverage with a tire-iron. Dvali fidgeted while Turk performed this task, glancing back at the approaching storm. The light was thinning already, the disc of the sun growing weak and obscure.

The door sprang loose and Turk stepped into the interior darkness, followed by Dr. Dvali and finally Lise.

"Uck!" Lise said. "God, it stinks!"

The evacuation must have been hurried. In many of the apartments that opened onto this hallway—more like cells, with their small high windows and cubicle bathrooms—food had been left to rot, toilets had been abandoned unflushed. They set about finding the most presentable first-floor residences and settled on three spaces, two adjoining and one cross-hall, from which the previous residents had removed the most obvious perishables. Lise reached up to swing open a window, but Dvali said, "No, not with the dust coming. We'll have to live with the stench."

There was no electricity, and the light was fading fast. Turk and Dvali unloaded their gear from the car, by which time the afternoon had turned into a smudgy twilight and the ash had begun to fall like snow. Dvali said, "Where are the others?"

"I could go hurry them up," Turk offered.

"No . . . they know where to find us."

Diane and Sulean Moi left Mrs. Rebka in the car with Isaac while they scrounged for groceries. The store had been nearly stripped, but in a stockroom in the back they discovered a few boxes of canned soups, not especially appetizing but possibly vital if the storm locked them indoors for any length of time. They ferried a few of these cartons out to the vehicle as the sky darkened. "One more box," Diane said at last, assessing the oncoming ash cloud, "and then we should get under cover."

A skylight above the aisles of the grocery store cast pale illumination on the empty shelves, some of which had been tumbled down by a previous tremor. Diane and Sulean each picked up a final carton and headed for the door, feet crunching on glass and litter.

As soon they reached the sidewalk they heard Isaac's screams. Diane dropped her carton instantly, spilling cans of creamed this-and-that down the sidewalk, and yanked open the passenger-side door and then craned her head back. "Help me!"

The boy's screaming was interrupted only by gasps for breath, and Diane couldn't help thinking that it must hurt simply to make such a noise, that a child's lungs shouldn't be capable of this awful sound. He thrashed and kicked and she grabbed his wrists and pinned them, which required more strength than she would have imagined. Mrs. Rebka was up front, fumbling the key-card into its slot. "He just started screaming—I can't calm him down!"

The important thing now was to get under shelter. "Start the car," Diane said.

"I tried! It won't!"

Now the storm was on top of them: not just a few ominous dustflakes anymore but a roiling front that came out of the desert with shocking speed and solidity. It broke before Diane could say another word, and as quick as that they were engulfed in it, choking in it.

Literally choking. She gagged, and even Isaac fell silent as soon as he drew a deep breath full of the dust. All light faded and the air became impenetrably dark and dense. Diane spat out a gagging mouthful of foulness and managed to shout, "We have to take him inside!"

Had Mrs. Rebka heard? Had Sulean? Evidently she had; Sulean, little more than a dimly-perceptible shape, helped Diane lift the boy and take him from the car into the grocery store, while Mrs. Rebka followed, her hand on Diane's back.

Being inside the store wasn't much improvement. The broken skylight admitted huge gusts of ash. They managed to get Isaac upright between them and he even supported his own weight as they groped for the stockroom. And found it, and closed themselves inside, in absolute darkness now, waiting for the dust to settle enough to allow a decent breath, registering how much worse this was than they had anticipated, Diane thinking: After all these years, is this where I've come to die?

CHAPTER TWENTY-SIX

It was obvious as soon as the storm broke that Isaac and the Fourth women had been stranded elsewhere.

Because "storm" was not just an abstraction this time. This wasn't a loose fall of dust, Lise thought, like some early-autumn snow shower in Vermont. Nor was it a puzzling astrophysical phenomenon that could be swept away by morning light. If this had happened in Port Magellan the city would have been shut down for months. It was a deluge, an inundation, no less so because it was taking place in the evacuated far west, where there were few eyes to see and no one to send help.

The darkness was the worst of it. Because the expedition was divided, they had only the two flashlights from the vehicle Dvali had been driving. The flashlights were fully-charged and guaranteed (the label said) for a hundred hours, but even their cumulative power made for a dismally small zone of light in a large and stifling darkness. Turk and Dr. Dvali insisted on combing through all three stories of the residence to make sure the accessible windows were sealed against the dust. It was a scary, arduous task, an ongoing reminder of how alone they were in this hollow wind-screaming building. And even after that the ash managed to get inside, invading the inevitable chinks and gaps, spilling out of the stairwells. Particles of it hovered in the flashlight beams, and the stink infused the air, their clothes, their bodies.

Finally they settled down in a room on the third floor, with a window from which they could assess the situation outside (if morning ever came, Lise thought; if the sun's light reached them ever again), and Turk opened a can of corned beef with his pocketknife and served it out on some plastic dishes he found in one of the kitchen cupboards.

Oil riggers lived like university freshmen, Lise had concluded. Angry, depressive university freshmen. Exhibits A, B, C: the empty bottles randomly scattered, the heaps of clothes abandoned in corners, the stripped mattresses and tattered paper shrines to the World's Biggest Breasts.

Dvali was talking about Isaac. He had been talking about Isaac for hours, it seemed to Lise, fretting over his absence and what this fresh starfall might mean "to his status as a communicant." It all began to sound more than slightly mad, until she was moved to ask, "If you care so much about him, couldn't you have given him a last name?"

Dvali looked sideways at her. "We raised him communally. Mrs. Rebka named him Isaac, and that seemed sufficient."

"You could have called him Isaac Hypothetical," Turk said. "Given his paternity."

"I don't find that funny," Dvali said. But at least he shut up.

The ash was falling thicker than ever. She could see it outside the window when she pointed a flashlight that way, but only as an undifferentiated wash of glittery gray. More than in Port Magellan, she thought. More than in Bustee.

She didn't care to consider what might be growing in it.

It took a long while for the air in the poorly-sealed grocery store stockroom to settle, and it never settled completely, but eventually Diane noticed that her lungs were less painful, her throat less raw, her vertigo slowly becoming bearable.

How much time had passed since the storm began? Two hours, a dozen? She couldn't be sure. There was no sunlight anymore, in fact no light whatsoever. There hadn't been time to rescue flashlights from the vehicle, or anything else for that matter. There had only been time to search the narrow stockroom (by touch and from memory) for something to rinse the ash out of their mouths: a cache of carbonated soft drinks in plastic bottles. Warm, the liquid foamed on the tongue and mixed with the inhaled particles until it tasted like charred flannel. But drink enough of it and you could speak, at least.

The three women were gathered around Isaac, who lay on the concrete floor breathing noisily. Isaac had become their touchstone, Diane thought. He had sipped several times from one of the bottles, but he was feverish—a new, frightening heat baked off his skin—and since the ashfall began he hadn't spoken or been able to speak.

We're like the witches in *Macbeth,* Diane thought, and Isaac is our cauldron, boiling.

"Isaac," Anna Rebka said. "Isaac, can you hear me?"

Isaac's response was a stirring in his limbs, a faint murmur that might have been assent.

Diane knew they might die here, all of them. The thought wasn't extraordinarily troubling to her, though she dreaded the pain and discomfort. One of the benefits of Fourthness (and they were all Fourths in this room, even, in his way, Isaac), was this muting of the anxiety about one's death. She had lived, after all, a very long time. She carried memories of the Spinless world, the vanished Earth as she had seen it as a child and on its last night: a house, a lawn, the sky. Back when she had believed in god, a god who made sense of the world by loving it.

The god she missed, perhaps even the god Dr. Dvali had been unconsciously invoking when he created Isaac. Oh, she had seen it all before, the fractured longing for redemption: she had lived with it, lived it. It had driven her brother Jason just as it had driven Diane. Jason's obsession had not been very different from Dvali's—the difference being that Jason, in the end, had offered himself on the altar, not a child.

Isaac's breathing began to deepen and his body cooled slightly. Diane wondered about his reaction to the ashfall. The link, of course, was through the Hypothetical machines, the half-living things that generated and inhabited and arose from the fallen dust. But what did that mean, what was the point of it, what was it meant to accomplish?

She must have spoken that last aloud—her mind was still a little muddled—because Sulean Moi said, "Nothing, it's meant to accomplish nothing." Her voice was a raw croak. "That's the truth Dr. Dvali wants to deny. The Hypotheticals are comprised of a network of self-reproducing machines. That much we all more or less agree upon. But they aren't a *mind,* Diane. They can't talk to Isaac, not the way I'm talking to you."

"That's smug," Mrs. Rebka said from her corner of the darkness. "And not true. You talked to the dead boy, Esh, through Isaac. Wouldn't you call that communication?"

The Martian woman was silent. How strange it was to be having this conversation in the absolute darkness,

Diane thought. And how Fourth of us. How would she have reacted to this predicament before her own treatment? Probably the fear would have overwhelmed her. Fear, and claustrophobia, and the steady awful sifting sound of ash (but it was so much *more* than ash) settling on the roof and stressing the building's beams and timbers.

"He told me he *remembers* Esh," Sulean said. "Memory is also an attribute of machines. A modern telephone has a larger memory than some mammals. I suspect the first Hypothetical machines were sent out into the universe for the purpose of gathering data, and I suspect they still do that, in infinitely subtler ways. Somehow, Esh's memory became available to the machines that killed him. He became a datum, which Isaac is able to access."

"Then I suppose Isaac will become a datum too," Mrs. Rebka said, suddenly meek, and here, Diane thought, was the heart of her revealed. Mrs. Rebka knew that Isaac would die, that there was no other possible outcome of his transaction with the Hypotheticals, and some part of her had accepted that dreadful truth.

"As he probably remembers Jason Lawton," Sulean Moi said. "Isn't that the question on your mind, Diane?"

Hateful in her perceptiveness, this Martian hag. Doomed to exile from her planet, her people, even her Fourthness. She was steeped in bitterness. Worse, she was right. It was the question Diane had dared not ask. "Maybe I'd rather not know."

"And Dr. Dvali wouldn't stand for it. He would prefer to keep Isaac's epiphanies to himself. But Dr. Dvali isn't here."

"That doesn't matter," Diane said, faintly panicky.

"Isaac," Sulean Moi said.

"Stop," Mrs. Rebka said.

"Isaac, can you hear me?"

Mrs. Rebka said *Stop* again, but Isaac's voice came faintly, a whisper: "Yes."

"Isaac," Sulean Moi said, "do you remember Jason Lawton?"

Please, no, Diane thought.

But the boy said, "Yes."

"And what would he say, if he were here?"

Isaac cleared his throat, a moist, froggy sound.

"He would say, 'Hello, Diane.' He would say—"

"No more," Diane begged. "Please."

"He would say, 'Be careful, Diane.' Because it's about to happen. The last thing."

What last thing? But there wasn't even time to pose the question before the last thing came up from the limestone and bedrock far underground. It shook the building, it rocked the floor, it quenched all thought, and it didn't stop.

CHAPTER TWENTY-SEVEN

Only Isaac saw it happening, because only Isaac had eyes that could see it.

He could see many things, few of which he had described even to Mrs. Rebka or Sulean Moi, his most trusted friends.

For instance, he could see himself. He saw himself more clearly than ever before in the absolute darkness of the buried stockroom. Not his body exactly, but when he looked down he could see the silver skein of the Hypothetical presence inside him. It shared his nervous system, made glowing traceries of ever-finer filaments joined in bundles to the shimmering rod of his spine. Had the others been able to see him this way they probably would have been horrified. Some fraction of Isaac, the merely human part, was also horrified. But that voice was a diminishing presence, and a dissenting voice thought he was beautiful. He looked like electricity. He looked like fireworks.

The women—Mrs. Rebka, Sulean Moi, Diane—were also visible to him, but they shone with a much fainter light. Isaac guessed the Fourth treatment had done that to them, that it had infected them with a little bit (but only a little bit) of Hypothetical life. It was as if they were timid lamps in a fog, while Isaac . . . Isaac was a searchlight, glaring.

And he could see other things, too, beyond the walls.

He saw the ashfall. To Isaac's eyes it was a storm of stars, each grain distinctly bright and merging into a general brightness, an atmosphere of luminosity. Bright, yes, but also, somehow, transparent: he could see *through* it—especially to the west.

The infinitely tiny Hypothetical machines weren't falling at random. Taken together, their trajectories were focused on the place where something old was rising from the bedrock of the desert. It had stirred in its sleep like a lazy behemoth and the ground had trembled, canting the oil derricks and shattering pumps and pipelines. It had stirred and stirred again as more ash fell, triggered by unknowable cues into new activity.

And it stirred again now, ferociously. The earth didn't just shake this time, it roared, and although the merely human part of Isaac was blind in the darkness he heard quite clearly the groan of deep rock stressed to the fracturing point, the slap and crack of collapsing walls. He felt a rush of foul air, and his breath became labored and painful again.

But none of that mattered to the part of him that could see.

This is a machine, he thought, watching the great device heave itself out of the night desert a hundred and more miles to the west. Machine, yes, but it was alive . . . it was both. The words did not exclude one another. The voice in him that had been Jason Lawton's voice said: a living cell is a machine made of protein. What falls from the sky and what rises from the earth is just life by other means.

The giant structure shouldering itself out of the

ground in the west resembled the Arch, or at least the pictures Isaac had seen of the Arch. It was a huge half-ring made of the same stuff as the dust that was falling from beyond the sky, condensed and differently arranged, its molecules and its unusual atoms subverting natural laws for which Isaac had no name but to which Jason Lawton's memory attached words like "strong force" and "weak force." It was lovely in its intrinsic glow, a rainbow shining in colors without names. It was an Arch for things to pass through; but it didn't lead to another planet.

Things were passing through it now. From the utter blackness inside it, where even Isaac couldn't see, luminous clouds ascended to the stars.

The thought of Jason lingered in Diane's mind even after she was hurt.

The earthquake happened in a series of jolting shocks, almost unbearable in the darkness. That much she understood, and she had been able to suppress her fear at least for the first few moments. Then the building began to collapse.

Or so she intuited from the fact that she felt a sharp blow to her right shoulder and neck, followed by dazed unconsciousness, followed by an awakening to pain, nausea, and a terrifying inability to draw breath. She gasped. A little air entered her lungs, but not enough. Not nearly enough.

"Lie still." The voice was a guttural croak. Mrs. Rebka? No, she thought it must be Sulean Moi. Diane tried to answer but couldn't. Her lungs wouldn't do anything but spasm in feeble attempts to draw air. She tried to sit up, or at least turn to one side, in order to avoid vomiting on herself.

That was when she discovered that the left side of her body was numb, dead, useless.

"Part of the ceiling came down on you," Sulean Moi said.

Diane gagged and retched, but nothing came up, for which she was thankful. And the tremors in the earth had stopped, that was good. She tried to evaluate her own injuries but couldn't think clearly enough to do so, not when her body was pulling so hard for air. She hurt. And she was frightened. She had no particular fear of death, but this, oh, this was less bearable than death itself: this was why people *elected* to die, to make an end to this kind of suffering.

She thought of Jason again—why had she been thinking of Jason?—and then of Tyler, her lost husband. Then even these thoughts became too weighty to sustain, and she passed out again.

Isaac could see that Diane had been badly hurt. Even in the dark it was possible to see that. Her dim glow had been nearly extinguished. Compared to Sulean Moi, Diane was a guttering candle.

It was hard to pay attention. He was mesmerized by the invisible landscape all around him. Mesmerized because he was a part of it, he was *becoming* it . . . but that could wait. Now that the new Arch had assembled itself in the west—from Hypothetical molecules, granite, magma, memory—there was a kind of pause. All around him for many miles the fresh blanket of dust began to undergo a new stage of metabolism. That would take time. Isaac could afford to be patient.

He surprised Sulean Moi and Mrs. Rebka by crawling over fallen beams, fragments of drywall, scattered foam insulation and collapsed aluminum venting to the place where Diane Dupree lay trapped beneath a heavy joist. His lungs labored and his mouth was foul with dust, but he could breathe, at least, which Diane apparently could not, not easily. And he could tell when he reached out to touch her that the falling debris had hurt her head. He meant to stroke her hair, the way Mrs. Rebka stroked his hair when he was ill, but the place above Diane's left ear yielded to his touch, and his hand came away sticky.

Tyler Dupree had died one day in August, the long Equatorian August, two years ago, the long Equatorian years.

Diane had hiked with him up one of the steep, rolling ridges of the coast, for no other reason than to sit at its summit and watch the forest drop like a deep green broadcloth to the sea.

Neither of them was young; both had lived out most of their extended lives as Fourths. Lately Tyler complained from time to time of fatigue, but he had gone on seeing patients, mainly the young men who worked as breakers (their injuries could be horrendous) and the Minang villagers among whom she and Tyler had settled. Today he had said he felt fine, and he had insisted on the long hike—he called it "the closest thing to a vacation I'm likely to get." So Diane had gone with him, relishing the dimness beneath the trees and the brightness of the high meadows, but also vigilant, watching him.

The Fourth metabolism was powerful but finely balanced. It could be pushed hard, but like any other physical thing it had a breaking point. Age couldn't be indefinitely deferred because the treatment itself aged. When Fourths failed, they tended to fail all at once.

Which was how Tyler had failed.

She thought he might have known it was happening. That was why he had insisted on this hike. They came to a place he loved but seldom had time to visit, a broad swath of granite and mountain grass. They put out a blanket, and Diane opened her backpack and withdrew the treasures she had stored for this occasion: Australian wine, bread from the bakeries of Port Magellan, cold roast beef, things foreign to the Minang diet to which they had become accustomed. But Tyler wasn't hungry. He lay down on his back and pillowed his head against a bump of moss. He was thin these days, his skin was pale despite exposure to the sun, and he looked, Diane thought, almost elfin.

"I think I'll sleep," he said. And it was at that moment, in the August sunlight and surrounded by the smell of rock and water and black earth, that she had known he was dying.

Some atavistic part of her wanted to rescue him, to carry him down the mountain the way he had once carried her across much of the continental United States when she was mortally ill. But there was no cure; the Fourth treatment could be taken only once.

Time later for grief. She knelt beside him and stroked his head. She said, "Can I get you anything?" And he said, "I'm happy right here."

So she lay down beside him and held him in her arms as the afternoon waned. Much later, much too soon, the sun went down, and it was time to go home, but only Diane stood up.

I'm happy right here.

But was this Jason with her in the darkness? Her brother Jason who had died so many years ago? No: it was the strange boy Isaac, but he sounded so much like Jason . . .

"I can remember you, Diane. If that's what you want, I can do it."

She understood what he was offering. The Hypotheticals remembered Jason, and so did she, but the long slow memory of the Hypotheticals was less perishable; it persisted over billions of years. Did she want to join him in that immensity?

She tried to turn her head but could not. She drew a breath, just enough to force out a single word:

"No," she said.

CHAPTER TWENTY-EIGHT

Turk was asleep when the earthquake struck. He and Lise and Dr. Dvali had spread mattresses on the concrete floor and slept, or tried to sleep, and at some point in the darkness Lise had scooted up next to him, both of them still wearing the reeking clothes they had worn for days, not that it mattered. She curled against the small of his back and cupped her knees to his knees, her breath warming his neck and raising the small hairs there. Then the floor heaved like a live thing and the air filled with a clamorous roar, the only distinguishable element of which was Lise's scream, audible because it was next to his ear. He managed somehow to roll over and hold her—they held each other—while the noise reached an unthinkable crescendo and the room's carefully-sealed window kicked out of its flanges and shattered on the floor. Nothing to do but hold on as the floor itself slanted away from horizontal, bucking like a car that had slipped its gears.

They held each other until it stopped. How long a time that was Turk couldn't say. A medium-sized eternity. It left his ears ringing, his body bruised. He drew enough good air to ask Lise whether she was okay, and she drew enough good air to say, "I guess." So Turk called out to Dr. Dvali, who answered belatedly: "My leg's hurt. Other than that I'm all right."

The noise and vertigo went on well after the shaking ceased, but Turk began to recover some composure. He thought about aftershocks. "Maybe we should try to get outside," he said, but Dvali said no, not in the ash storm.

Turk separated himself from Lise and began to grope through the litter on the floor, finally locating the flashlight he had left beside the mattress: it had rolled all the way to the window-side wall. Switched on, it lit up a column of dust motes and debris. The room was intact, but barely. Lise huddled on the mattress, ghost-white, and Dvali, just as pale, sat propped in a corner. His left leg was bleeding where something sharp had fallen on it, but the wound didn't seem serious.

"So what *do* we do?" Lise asked.

Dvali said, "Wait until dawn and hope it doesn't happen again."

If dawn ever came, Turk thought. If anything like sunlight ever again reached this godforsaken badland.

Lise said, "I hate to be practical here, but I have to pee. Really badly."

Turk swung the flashlight beam toward the adjoining bathroom. "Looks like the throne's intact, but I wouldn't try to flush. And the door's off entirely."

"So look the other way," Lise said, gathering her blankets around her, and Turk thought how much easier all this would be if he didn't love her so much.

"There's light coming in the window," she said an hour or so later, and Turk made his way over there, treading cautiously on the broken glass.

The ash had stopped falling: that much was obvious. Had the dustfall been as thick as it was yesterday they would have choked on it. But only a few stray flakes had drifted in, and Turk thought the air smelled fresher and less sulfurous, unless he was just getting used to it.

The light to which Lise had drawn his attention was real enough—it became obvious when he switched off the flashlight. But it was too early for dawn, and this light wasn't coming from the sky. It was coming from down below.

From the streets of this little corporate outpost, from the roofs of damaged buildings, the desert, anywhere the ash had fallen. He called Lise and Dvali over to look.

A few nights when he was at sea Turk had seen his vessel's wake glowing where bioluminescent algae had been stirred up by the passage of the ship. Always an eerie thing to see, and this reminded him of it, but what was happening here was stranger still. The desert, or the interplanetary dust that had fallen on it, was aglow with a phosphorescence of many colors: gemstone reds, glassy yellows, glistening blues. And the colors weren't stationary but constantly shifting, like a polar aurora.

"What do you think it is?" Lise asked.

Dr. Dvali's face was bathed in the reflected colors. He said, a little breathlessly, "I think we're as close as anyone has come to seeing the face of the Hypotheticals."

Turk said, "So what are they doing out there?"

But even Dr. Dvali couldn't answer that question.

Come dawn, it was apparent that they had been lucky.

Most of the north wing of the building had collapsed. Corridors ended in masses of rubble or open air. If we'd turned left instead of right, Turk thought, we'd be buried in there.

As soon as there was enough light to navigate they made their way downstairs. The structure wouldn't survive another shaking—"And we need to find Isaac," Dvali said.

But Turk was a little uncertain about how to proceed, because another thing was obvious by daylight: the situation on the ground had changed.

Where there had been desert, there was a forest.

Or something like a forest.

Dvali was limping conspicuously by the time they descended the stairwell to the door at the intact end of the building, though he refused to stop and rest. It was essential, he said, that they find Isaac and the others. "The others" being a sort of footnote in Dvali's mind, Lise suspected. For Dvali there was only Isaac, Isaac and the apotheosis of the Hypotheticals, whatever that might turn out to mean.

"Go on, open it," Dvali said, waving at the door.

Lise and Turk had agreed that the most useful thing they could do was to try to reach the local mall where they had left Isaac and the Fourth women. How to get there was an open question. When Lise had looked out into the light of dawn she had seen a landscape utterly transformed—had seen what she might have called a canopy of trees, if trees were made of glossy tubes and iridescent beach balls.

And she asked the same stupid, irrepressible question: "*Why?* What's it for? Why now, why here?"

"We may yet find out," Dr. Dvali said.

If the past was any guide, Turk thought, the Hypothetical growths would ignore human beings (with the obvious exception of Isaac, who was only partly human)—but was that still true?

He cracked the door a narrow inch, and when nothing came rushing in he risked a look outside.

Cool air touched his face. The sulfuric stench of the ashfall was gone. So was the ash itself. It had all turned into a Technicolor forest. Compared to this, the growths in Bustee had been daffodils withering in a cold breeze. This was high summer. This was some kind of Hypothetical Eden.

He drew the door fully open and waited. Lise and Dr. Dvali crowded him from behind.

The ash had turned itself into a forest of stalks bearing globular fruit instead of leaves. The stalks, of several colors but predominantly a cyanotic blue, lofted up twenty or thirty feet into the air and were so closely spaced that a person would have to turn sideways to pass between them. The globes that comprised the canopy ranged in size from goldfish bowl to beach ball to something a man might climb inside and stand upright in without bumping his head. They pressed up against each other, gently yielding where they touched, to make a nearly solid but translucent mass. The sunlight that came through was dim and shiftingly iridescent.

Turk took a tentative step. From here he could see along the wall of the workers' barracks to the point at which it had collapsed, the three floors of the north wing pancaked into something less than one. God help us if we'd been in there, he thought. And God help Isaac and the women, wherever they might have found shelter.

The trunks (as he began to think of them) of the strange trees (though you could call them lampposts just as accurately) were rooted in the ground—where there had been pavement they had cracked and penetrated it—and Turk couldn't see far enough in any direction to really get his bearings. Everything faded, forty or fifty yards out, to a shimmering blue vagueness. To find the mall where the women and Isaac had last been seen they would have to navigate by compass and the clues directly under their feet.

"What do they live on?" Lise asked in a hushed voice. "There's no water here."

"Maybe more water than they're used to getting out where they usually grow," Turk said.

Dvali said, "Or they're using some catalytic process that doesn't need water, a completely different kind of metabolism. They must have evolved for a billion years in an environment far harsher than this."

A billion years of evolution. If that was true, Turk thought, then these things, as a species, if that word applied, were older than the human race itself.

They moved in silence through the Hypothetical forest, though it was not entirely a silent place. No wind reached them at street level, but there must have been a wind blowing, Turk guessed, because the iridescent globes that crowned the tubular trunks occasionally bumped against each other and made a gentle sound that suggested a rubber mallet on a wooden xylophone. And there was motion at ground level, too. Small blue tubes, like roots, periodically snaked between the trees, running with a whipcrack motion that might be quick and powerful enough to break a leg if you ran across one at the wrong time. Twice Turk saw paperlike objects fluttering overhead, occasionally touching or merging with the globes—varieties of the thing that had attacked Isaac back in Bustee. Mistaking him for one of their own, Turk thought; or maybe it wasn't a mistake.

Lise walked close behind him. He could hear her indrawn breath every time something rattled or fluttered in the dim and shifting light. He felt bad about that, about the fear she was enduring and whatever else she might have to endure before they were finished here. He turned and said, "I'm sorry I got you into this."

She wouldn't let him finish. "Do you really think you're somehow responsible for what happened?"

"For taking you on this half-assed trip west, maybe."

"I made that choice."

Which was true. But still, Turk thought. She's here because of me. The chorus of his biography appeared to
him as if conjured by the untrustworthy light: lost or purloined lovers, friends become enemies, friends damaged
or killed in bar fights or shipboard accidents. See my
bridges burning, he thought. See my trail of tears. He
didn't want that for Lise. He didn't want to drag her beyond the boundaries of the kind of life she might still
make for herself, a life in which kindness was not fleet-
ing and there was the possibility of something more
meaningful than nights sealed in the cockpit of an aircraft, months bunking below the deck of some stinking
freighter, years locked in the castle of his own head
while she waited for what he could not provide and grew
disappointed and finally bitter.

He would find her a way out of this jungle, he
thought, and then, if he could summon the requisite
courage or cruelty, he would find a way to leave her.

It is a communication, Avram Dvali thought.

He thought: There is no denying it. The Hypotheticals were all around him, a small but significant fraction
of the network that comprised their incomprehensibly
vast intelligence. All process, the dogmatic Martian
woman had said during one of their arguments, of no
more significance than the flowering of club moss or
periwinkles; put it together any way you liked, it was
only evolution, mindless as the sea. But she was wrong.
He felt it. He did not, could not, understand how these
organisms grew or what nourishment they derived from
the parched earth, but communication passed between,
of that he was sure; they had not grown randomly, but at
some precipitative signal.

He had been watching the canopy of the forest. The
clustered globes shifted color constantly, and it seemed

to him that each globe's color was affected by the changes in its immediate neighbors, perhaps according to some rule or set of rules, so that patterns traveled through the forest like flocks of intangible birds. This was communication in the sense that cells in the human brain communicated one with another and in concert produced the emergent phenomenon of mind. He was walking through the physical architecture, perhaps, of some great thought, a thought he could never comprehend. . . .

Though perhaps Isaac could. If Isaac was alive, and if he understood, finally, the nature of the gift Avram Dvali had given him.

CHAPTER TWENTY-NINE

It was warm in the ruined stockroom, and although most of the dust had settled out of the air—seemed to have been absorbed, somehow, into the rubble—no fresh air flowed into the enclosed space. Sooner or later, Sulean Moi thought, and most likely sooner, that would become a problem. And there was the body of Diane Dupree to think about. If she could tolerate such thoughts.

She crawled along the accessible perimeter of the room for the second time, feeling with her hands for anything hopeful—a draft or some promisingly loose heap of rubble. And for the second time found none.

She had begun to believe she might die in this awful place on this awful planet, haunted by the ghost of Esh. Haunted, that is to say, by the Hypotheticals.

In whom she did not believe, at least not in the sense Avram Dvali believed in them. The Hypotheticals were a network of self-replicating spaceborne machines. Some long-extinct civilization must once have seeded its local environment with these devices, or perhaps it had happened more than once, a multiple genesis over many millions of years. Either way, once variable self-replication was introduced into the medium of interplanetary and interstellar space the process of evolution was engaged—different from organic evolution in every detail, but not in principle. Like organic evolution, the process had generated strange and gaudy complexities. Even such apparently "engineered" devices as the Spin barrier that surrounded the Earth, or the Arches that linked planets separated by vast distances, were ultimately no more intrinsically intelligent than such biological constructions as a coral reef or a termite hill.

The periodicity of the ashfall and the truncated grotesqueries it generated were proof enough, she thought. What had been installed in Esh—and in Isaac—was nothing more than a tragic susceptibility to alien tropisms. Esh could not be a "communicant" because there was no one with whom to communicate.

Evolution did, demonstrably, produce minds, and she supposed it was possible that the long interstellar evolution of the Hypothetical machines had also produced minds—locally, temporarily. But such minds, if they existed, were the byproduct, not the process. They controlled nothing but themselves. They couldn't be "the Hypotheticals" as Dr. Dvali imagined them to be.

She remained unnerved, however, by the obvious fact that Isaac remembered Esh, who had died many years before Isaac was born. If Esh had become a memory in the networked ecology of the Hypotheticals, could such a memory possess volition? And who or what was the rememberer?

"Sulean—"

This was Mrs. Rebka, who wouldn't leave Isaac's side. Her voice came out of the darkness of their sealed tomb as if from an infinite distance. "Yes, what?"

"Do you hear that?"

Sulean hushed her own thoughts and listened.

An intermittent scraping. The *tack-tack-tack* of something solid tapping stone. Followed by more tentative scraping.

"Someone's trying to dig us out," Mrs. Rebka said. "It must be Avram and the others, they must know we're here!"

Tick-scratch-tick. Yes, maybe, Sulean thought. But then Isaac said, very suddenly and with startling clarity, "No, Mrs. Rebka. It isn't the other people who want in. It isn't people at all. It's *them.*"

Sulean turned toward the place from which Isaac's voice had come. She quelled her own fear and said, "Isaac, do you really know what's happening?"

"Yes." His tone was unexcited. "I can see them."

"The Hypotheticals?"

A pause. "You could call them that."

"Then explain it to me, please, Isaac. You're part of it now, aren't you? In a way Esh never was. Tell me what's happening."

For a moment there was only the *tick-scratch-tick* at the walls of the fallen building in which they were trapped.

Then Isaac began to speak.

CHAPTER THIRTY

Turk navigated by the fractured remnants of pavement and sidewalk through the alien forest that had lately been a settlement for oil riggers. He managed to find the parking lot of the workers' mall—white lines, cracked blacktop—and from there it was a short hike to the complex where they had left Diane Dupree, Sulean Moi, Mrs. Rebka, and Isaac.

Except it wasn't there anymore. He came upon rubble where the trees had grown more densely, further obscuring the dim light of what was, by now, afternoon. Here was an embankment of broken tile, wallboard, wood, sheet aluminum twisted into unlikely shapes. Beyond that, in the dimness, steel beams stood in skeletal rectangles. Some of these beams and pillars had been entwined by the rootlike extensions of the trees.

"We'll angle toward the south end of the mall," he said. Where the food store was or had been. "Might be something still standing there."

The haunted forest, Lise thought.

Boy, was it ever.

She found herself silently reciting a line from a story-book her father had read to her when she was small, book and story all forgotten except (in her father's melodramatic drawl) *Into the dark forest they stepped.* Into the dark forest they stepped. Into the dark forest of trees that harbored birds that resembled sheets of torn paper, the forest from which (another fragment of the same story) *they must escape,* but that was easier said than done. Because here there were wolves, or worse, and night was coming, and she didn't know the way out. She wanted to lunge up from under the covers and grab her father's hand. Wanted it more than anything.

But couldn't. She scolded herself, in her mother's voice this time: Don't be stupid, Elise. Straighten up. Fly right, girl.

She nearly flew right past a heap of plaster-specked metal, until Turk pointed it out: it was the car Mrs. Rebka had been driving when the two groups separated. She recognized the steel-mesh tires, on prominent display because a rod-like tree trunk had sprung up from the cracked pavement and tumbled the vehicle on its side. Useless now, the car, but any car would be useless until this forest shrank back into the ground, and that seemed unlikely to happen soon. If we leave here, Lise thought, we'll have to leave on foot. And that was a daunting prospect. The good news was that the car was empty: Isaac and the women weren't inside, hence might still be alive elsewhere.

"So we're near the food store," Turk said, and Dr. Dvali ran recklessly a few yards ahead, where the remains of the storefront were vaguely visible behind a picket of alien growths.

The quake hadn't spared this part of the mall, and if the others had taken shelter here they might be dead. This was so obvious it didn't need saying. Dr. Dvali wanted to start digging immediately—futile as that might be, the three of them versus a few tons of debris—but Turk said, "Let's circle around back first. The structure looks maybe a little more intact back that way."

Dvali stood slump-shouldered at the brink of the rubble field a moment longer, and for the first time Lise felt a degree of sympathy for him. All night, all morning, Lise had been imagining the women and Isaac huddled in some safe place; the group would be reunited, and then she and Turk could set out for some safe harbor even if the mad Fourths insisted on staying here in Freakland. That was her best-case scenario.

Now it looked like that might not happen. The story might end tragically. There might be no way to escape from the dark forest. Maybe, she thought, for Isaac and the women, the story was already over.

The rear of the mall seemed at first glance more intact than the front, but that was only because the concrete loading bays had been left undamaged by the quake. Structurally, everything was a mess. Lise felt heartsick, and Dr. Dvali seemed to be suppressing tears.

It was Turk who continued to pick his way along the border of the rubble field with grim determination, and it was Turk who finally turned and held up his palm in a stop-here gesture and said quietly, "Listen."

Lise stood still. She heard the usual flutterings of the forest, to which she had almost grown accustomed. The wind was up, and the luminous globes made their muted wooden music. But beneath that? Faintly?

A sound like scratching, a sound like digging.

Dvali said, "They're alive! They must be!"

"Let's not rush to judgment," Turk said. "Follow me and try to keep quiet."

Dvali was Fourth enough to suppress his surge of renewed optimism. The three of them walked within an arm's length of one another, Turk up front, following the sound. The digging-scratching sound grew more clearly audible with each step, and Lise's own optimism began to falter. There was something not right about that sound. The relentless gentle rhythm of it, somehow too patient to be completely human. . . .

Then Turk made his *halt* gesture again and beckoned them forward to look.

There was activity at one of the fractured loading bays. But as Lise had begun to suspect, it was Hypothetical activity. A dense hedge of the growths Dvali called "ocular roses" had grown here, their petaled eyes all focused on the debris. Around them the trees had expressed a thick and writhing mat of motile roots, some sharply pointed and some flattened into spatulate blades. It was this mass of roots that was doing the digging. Surreal, Lise thought giddily, especially since the debris included not just concrete and steel and plastic but crumpled cereal boxes, milk jugs, canned food. She watched an inky blue tendril wrap itself around an industrial-sized soup can, puckering the red and white paper label, lift it so the nearest eye-flower could examine it, then relay it to another tentacle that passed it on *seriatim* until it was deposited on a rubbish tip of previously cleared debris.

The process was so perversely methodical that she found herself wanting to laugh. Instead she stared, for what seemed like an immensely long time. If the ocular roses were aware of their presence they displayed no reaction. The patient digging went on and on. Scratching, probing, tapping, sifting . . .

She stifled a scream when Turk suddenly put his hand on her shoulder. "We ought to back off a ways," he whispered. Which struck her as an excellent idea.

Was the sun already setting? Lise had lost her watch somewhere along the trail or back in the riggers' dorm. She hated the idea of the coming night.

As soon as they felt free to speak (but still whispering, as if the ocular roses could overhear them, and for all she knew they could) Turk said to Dvali, "I'm sorry it wasn't the women we heard—"

But Dvali was still bright-eyed with hope. "Don't you see what this means? They must be alive under there— Isaac, at least, must be alive!"

Because it was Isaac the Hypotheticals wanted. These growths might not be sentient, singly or collectively, but they knew something of their own had been separated from them by rock and ruin.

They wanted Isaac. But what would they do with him when they found him?

"We can only watch," Dr. Dvali said. "Camp here and watch until the boy comes out alive."

Comes out to meet his fate, Lise thought.

CHAPTER THIRTY-ONE

In the darkness of the buried stockroom, Isaac struggled to cling to what was left of himself.

Beyond the debris that enclosed him he could see the luminous forest, a vast meadow of light, and at the center of it the unbearably beautiful structure that had erupted from the fractured sandstone and bedrock of the desert, a thing the memory of Jason Lawton wanted to call a "temporal Arch." Inert for ten thousand years in its hibernatory sleep, caverned in rock, it had called to him from the westernmost point of the compass, and now it had broken its bonds and shaken free of the earth, and grown immensely large and powerful, and if he could only pass through these walls he would go to it.

"Isaac—"

The Martian woman's voice came to him as if from far away. He tried to ignore it.

He could see the temporal Arch and he could see other things, too. He could see, unfortunately, the body of Diane Dupree. She was dead, but the not-entirely-human part of her, her Fourthness, was still faintly alive, struggling to repair her corpse, which of course it could not do. Her light guttered like a candle burned down to a puddle of wax and a final thread of wick. The part of Isaac that was Jason Lawton mourned for her.

These memories, the memories that belonged to Jason and Esh, had taken on an independent life in Isaac's mind, so much so that Isaac was afraid he might lose himself in them. *I remember,* he would think, but the memories were endless and only a fraction of them were his own. Even the word "I" had divided into double or triple meanings. *I lived on Mars. I lived on Earth. I live in Equatoria.* All these statements were true.

And he didn't want to suppress the contending memories completely, because they comforted him as much as they frightened him. Who would come with him into the vortex of the temporal Arch, if not Jason and Esh?

"Isaac, do you really know what's happening?"

Yes, he did, in part, at least.

"Then," and he registered that it was the voice of Sulean Moi, Esh's friend, Isaac's friend, "explain it to me, please."

These words had to come from Jason Lawton. He turned to Sulean, moved toward her, reached out from the darkness and took her hand as Esh or Isaac might have done, and spoke with Jason's voice:

"It's an embedded loop in the cycles and seasons of the . . . the Hypotheticals. . . ." *Seasons,* he felt the appropriateness of the word: seasons within epochal seasons, the ebb and flood of the galaxy's ocean of life . . . "In a . . . in what you might call a mature solar system, the elements of the Hypotheticals expand their mass, accumulate information, reproduce, until at some critical moment the oldest surviving specimens undergo a kind of sporulation . . . produce compact elisions of themselves that resemble clouds of dust or ash . . . and those clouds follow long elliptical orbits that intersect with planets where they gather. . . ."

"Have they gathered here?" Sulean asked.

Here, yes, he said or thought, on this rocky planet made habitable for the potential civilization to which it had ultimately been connected. . . .

"Do they know us, then?" Sulean Moi asked sharply.

Isaac was bewildered by the question, but the memory of Jason Lawton seemed to understand it. "The network processes information over light-years and centuries, but some biological civilizations survive long enough to be perceptible to it, yes, and civilizations are useful because they generate new machine life, to be absorbed and understood or, or—"

"Or devoured," Sulean Moi said.

"Or, in a sense, devoured. And civilizations generate something else that interests the network."

"What?"

"Ruins," the memory of Jason Lawton said. "They generate ruins."

Outside, beyond the walls of concrete and debris impenetrable to human vision, the ballet of memory proceeded at a quickening pace.

Memory, he told Sulean Moi, was what was happening here: ten thousand years of relentlessly gathered and shared knowledge was compressed into the spheres that made the canopy of the Hypothetical forest, information to be collated and carried forward, Isaac said, through the temporal Arch, which was opening its mouth to inhale all that knowledge: representations of the orbits and climates and evolution of local planets, of the millions of interlaced trajectories of icy cometary bodies from which the Hypothetical machines had drawn and would continue to draw their mass, of signals received from elsewhere in the galaxy and absorbed and re-emitted . . .

"Why *memory*?" Sulean Moi demanded. "To what end? Isaac—*what is it that remembers*?"

What remembered was the thing he couldn't see, though he saw much else. Not even Jason Lawton could answer the question Sulean Moi had posed. What was happening here was only a trivial event in the network, in the *mind* of—of—*oh, Diane, has it really grown out there among the stars, the thing you used to want so badly to believe in?*

"Isaac! Can you hear me?"

He fell back into the abyss of his own thoughts.

Because Isaac remembered Jason, it was also true that Jason remembered Isaac. Jason's adult understanding of the world had been overlaid on Isaac's raw experience, and that created a kind of double vision that was deeply discomforting.

It reflected his life as in a funhouse mirror. For instance Mrs. Rebka. She was someone close to him, someone he trusted. But when Jason inspected those same memories she became cold, distant, something much less than a real mother. To Isaac, she existed in a realm beyond judgment. To Jason, she was guilty of a profound moral recklessness.

Likewise his memories of Dr. Dvali, the aloof god who had defined Isaac's world, and whom Jason perceived as an obsessive monster.

Isaac desperately wanted not to hate these people. And even the part of him that was Jason Lawton retained some sympathy for Mrs. Rebka. She had loved Isaac, as much as she attempted to conceal it, and Isaac understood with some shame how difficult he had been to love. He had returned her studied indifference, and he hadn't been wise enough to recognize her pain and her perseverance.

He recognized it now. She hadn't spoken for more than an hour, and when Isaac went to her side and sat with her, when he looked at her with what he had begun to think of as his Hypothetical eyes, he knew why.

She had not been spared when the building collapsed during the earthquake. She was hurt—hurt inside, where it didn't show, but hurt so badly that her Fourthness was failing to repair the damage. She was bleeding internally. There was a coppery aura of blood around her. She whispered his name. Her voice was less loud than the sound of the Hypotheticals digging and scratching at the rubble—which had itself grown louder over the last few hours.

"I can take you with me," Isaac said.

Sulean Moi, overhearing, said, "What do you mean?"

But Isaac's mother only nodded.

Then there was a gust of quick cool air, and the darkness was dispelled by the light of the alien forest.

CHAPTER THIRTY-TWO

Lise said, "We need to get our bearings before the sun sets."

Turk gave her a puzzled look—he had just finished helping Dr. Dvali assemble a rough shelter under the lee of a concrete loading pier, close (but not too close) to the digging trees—then he interpreted her frowning glances at Dvali and said, "Yeah, you're right, we'll do that." He asked Dvali to gather up any intact canned food he could find among the excavated debris while he and Lise "scouted." Dvali gave him a suspicious glare—as a Fourth he probably recognized a half-truth when he heard one—but nodded tersely and waved them away.

So he walked with Lise back along the perimeter of the tumbled mall, steering wide of the dig, and as soon as they were out of earshot Turk said, "Get our bearings?"

She confessed that she had mainly wanted to get away from Dvali, if only briefly. "And I thought we could get above these trees and have a look around."

"How do you propose to do that?"

She showed him. At the south end of the mall there was a quadrangle of intact exterior walls where a steel fire escape was bolted in place. She had noticed it earlier in the day, she said. Turk surveyed it and decided it was sturdy enough to carry their weight, and yeah, maybe it was a good idea to look around while there was still some daylight left, if they were careful. So they climbed as far as the roof and stood on a steel mesh platform above the canopy of globes, in the simple light of the fading afternoon, and marveled at what they saw.

The view was similar to what Lise had seen this morning from the riggers' dorm, but it extended in every direction including the west—Isaac's direction, she thought dizzily—where something monstrous had grown out of the ground.

From this place above the canopy of the Dark Forest the ruins of human structures were easy to discern. The long line of the collapsed mall lay across the body of the forest like a train wreck. The building where they had sheltered last night projected from the trees like the prow of a grounded ship, and farther off she could see the silhouettes of drill rigs and cracking towers and storage. Something was burning in the oil fields: the wind scrawled a line of black smoke across the horizon. Hypothetical growths carpeted the desert in every direction, reflecting the light of the setting sun and radiating their own, a sea of dark jewels, she thought. She wondered how much mass these things must have extracted from the ash or the ground or the air in order to grow themselves, wondered if the whole inland basin of Equatoria had been hollowed out to build them. And in the west, against the glare of the sun—

"Hold on," Turk said as a brisk wind rattled the platform, but her grip on the railing was already painfully tight.

In the west, something immense had arisen. A kind of Arch.

Lise had sailed under the Arch of the Hypotheticals three times: twice as an adolescent, coming to Port Magellan with her parents (and leaving without her father), and once as an adult. That Arch, awe-inspiring as it was, had been too large to be perceived as a single thing: what you saw was the nearest leg, soaring beyond the atmosphere, or the part of it that continued to reflect sunlight in the hours after dark, a silvery blaze suspended over the sea.

What she saw now was less immense—she could see all of it at once, an inverted U against the sunset—but that only made its size more starkly obvious. It must have been twenty or fifty miles high, high enough that a haze of cloud paled its uppermost curve. But at the same time it seemed delicate, almost fragile: how did it sustain its own weight? More importantly, why was it here? What was it meant to *do*?

An even stronger gust of wind bounced the platform and carried Turk's matted hair into his eyes. She didn't like the expression on his face as he stared at the thing in the west. For the first time since she had known him he looked lost. Lost and a little scared.

"We shouldn't stay up here," he said. "This wind."

She agreed. The view was in an unearthly way beautiful, but it was also unendurable. It implied too much. She followed him down.

They rested at the foot of the stairs, back under the canopy of globes, like mice in a mushroom patch, she thought, protected from the wind. For a moment they didn't speak.

Then Turk reached into the left-hand pocket of his grimy jeans and brought out his compass, the same military-surplus compass in a battered brass case he had been carrying the day he first flew her into the mountains. He opened the case and looked at the gently swinging needle as if to confirm its alignment. Then he reached for Lise's hand and put the compass in her palm.

"What's this for?"

"I don't know if there's an edge to this fucking forest, but if there is you'll probably need a compass to find your way out."

"So? I'll just follow you. Keep it."

"I want you to have it."

"But—"

"Come on, Lise. All the time we've been together, what did I ever give you? I'd like to give you something. It would make me happy. Just take it."

Gratefully but uneasily, she closed her hand on the chilly brass case.

"I was thinking about Dvali," Lise said as they walked back to camp. She knew she shouldn't be saying this out loud, but the combined effect of exhaustion and the twilight glitter of the forest (not entirely dark, she had to admit) and Turk's peculiar gift had made her reckless. "About Dvali putting together his commune in the desert. Sulean Moi said there were other attempts to do the same thing, but they'd been stopped in time. Dvali must have known that, right?"

"I would guess so."

"But it seemed like he was pretty free with his information. He took a lot of people into his confidence. Including my father."

"Couldn't have been too reckless or they would have caught up with him."

"He changed his plans. That's what he told me. He was supposed to establish his compound out on the west coast, but he changed his mind after he left the university."

"He's not stupid, Lise."

"I don't think he's stupid. I think he's lying. He never intended to go to the west coast. The west coast plan was bullshit. It was *designed* to be bullshit."

"Maybe," Turk said. "Does it matter?"

"The story was supposed to derail anyone who came after him. But do you see what that means? Dvali knew Genomic Security was looking for him, and he must have known they would come after my father. Turk, he sat not a foot away from me and told me he knew my father was principled and loyal and wouldn't tell DGS what they wanted to know—except under extreme duress. Dvali could have warned him as soon as he heard DGS was in Port Magellan, if not before. But that's not what he wanted to do. My father disapproved of Dvali's project on moral grounds, so Dvali hung him out like a red flag."

"He couldn't have known your father would be killed."

"But he must have known it was a possibility, and he certainly would have expected him to be tortured. If it isn't murder it's the next best thing." Murder by indirection—the only kind of murder a Fourth could commit.

She didn't know what she could do with this thought, which had begun to burn like a brushfire in her mind. Could she face Dvali again? Should she tell him what she'd guessed or pretend innocence until they escaped this place? And what then? Was there any real justice for Fourths? She thought Diane Dupree might be able to answer that question, or Sulean Moi . . .

If they were still alive.

"Listen," Turk said.

All Lise could hear was the canopy of the Dark Forest rattling in the rising wind. She and Turk were back at the loading bays now, back where the creepy hedge of eyeball flowers had grown, but there wasn't even that maddening *scratch-tap* sound, because—

Her eyes widened.

"It stopped," Turk said.

The digging had stopped.

CHAPTER THIRTY-THREE

Avram Dvali was collecting canned food and worrying about the rising wind when the sound of digging abruptly ceased. He stood upright, chilled.

His first thought was: the boy is dead. The Hypothetical trees had stopped digging because the boy was dead. And for one long heartbeat it seemed not just an idea but a black-bordered truth. Then he thought: or they found him.

He dropped what he was holding and ran for the dig.

In his haste he almost blundered into the hedge of ocular roses. One of the tallest of them turned to inspect him, its eye as indifferent as a dark pearl. He ignored it.

He was startled by how much the digging trees had accomplished since the last time he'd looked. The spatulate roots were slow, but the sum of their groping and picking had exposed an intact wall and, beyond it, leading inside, an opening in the banked rubble.

He pushed past the ocular roses, pushed aside their fleshy stems, because somewhere in that cloistered darkness Isaac must still be alive, alive and in conversation with the forces Dvali had loved and feared ever since they embraced the Earth and stole it out of time: the Hypotheticals.

The roots of the Hypothetical trees had pulled back from the excavation they had made and lay in a motionless tangle at the entrance to the buried room. Dvali hesitated at the brink of that hole, which was just large enough to allow him to pass through, knowing it was unwise to go farther—the weight of the debris must be immense, tons of it balanced on the partially-intact ceiling with nothing to support it but a few joists and groaning timbers—and knowing at the same time that he couldn't stop himself.

The rising wind had begun to keen through the ruins with the urgency of a siren.

He took another step into the shadows and wrinkled his nose at the dismaying smell. Unmistakably, something had died here. His heart sank. "Isaac!" he called out. The dim ambient light showed him nothing until his eyes adjusted to it. Then certain shapes became apparent.

The Martian woman, Sulean Moi: was she dead? No. She looked up at him from the floor of this half-collapsed room with an expression of shock, her own eyes perhaps blinded by the sudden daylight. What a hell this imprisonment must have been, Dvali thought. She scrabbled on hands and knees toward the opening, and he wanted to help her, but his thoughts remained focused on Isaac. He wished he had a lamp, a flashlight, anything.

The wind howled like a wounded dog. A dust of plaster shook loose from the ceiling. Dvali pressed on into the stink and muck.

The next body he encountered belonged to Diane Dupree. The Fourth woman from the coast was dead, and as soon as he was sure of that he moved past her. The ceiling was low. He stooped as he walked. But in the deeper darkness he was able at last to see Isaac—thrillingly,

Isaac alive, Isaac kneeling over the prostrate form of Anna Rebka.

Isaac inched away as Dvali approached. The boy's eyes were luminous, the golden flecks in his irises prominently aglow. Even his skin seemed faintly alight. He looked inhuman—*was* inhuman, Dvali reminded himself.

Anna Rebka remained inert. He asked, "Is she dead?"

"No," Isaac said.

"**L**eave her!" Sulean Moi called from the fading daylight just beyond the entrance to the buried stockroom. "Isaac, leave her, come out, it isn't safe!"

But her throat was dry, and the command emerged as a feeble plea.

Dvali put his fingers on Anna's throat, feeling for a pulse but knowing as soon as he touched her that he wouldn't find one. Isaac was wrong, or was denying an obvious truth. "No, Isaac," he said gently. "She's dead."

"That's just her body," Isaac said.

"What do you mean?"

Haltingly, and to Dvali's astonishment, the boy began to explain.

This wind, Sulean Moi thought: it will kill us yet.

She saw Turk and Lise hurrying toward her through the accumulation of alien growths, a kind of forest—it was almost too much for her to register after hours of blindness in the buried stockroom. Overhead, a canopy of strangely glittering globes was attached to these . . . should she call them trees? And a sort of bramble of ocular flowers had grown nearby, and some of them had turned their mindless eyes in her direction.

The world was obscenely transformed.

And the wind: where had it come from? Its intensity increased almost by the second. It tugged at the ruins behind her, lofting kites of tattered drywall and tar paper high among the alien trees.

She turned her head back and called out, more audibly this time, "Isaac!"

It was the boy who mattered, not the foolish Avram Dvali.

"Isaac, come out!"

As the unstable debris shifted and groaned.

Dvali grasped immediately what the boy was telling him. It was little more than he had long imagined—Isaac had become a conduit to the Hypotheticals, but with this astonishing difference: Isaac had been able to acquire the memories of Anna Rebka before she died. She lived in him. As did the Martian child Esh.

He whispered, "Anna?"

As if he could summon her from the boy like a conjurer summoning a ghost. But the boy's eyes changed in some indefinable way, the corners of his lips turned down as if with distaste, and it was exactly the way Anna had been looking at him lately.

Then Dvali said a thing he had not anticipated saying, though the words were as logical and as inevitable as the last step on a long road:

"Take me with you," he said.

The boy stepped back from him, shaking his head.

"Take me with you, Isaac. Wherever you are, wherever you're going, take me with you."

Stressed timbers creaked as if the weight of the world was balanced on them. There was a sound like gunshots as the wood fractured.

"No," the boy said calmly, firmly.

And this was maddening. Maddening, because he was so close. So close! And because the voice that denied him sounded so much like Anna's voice.

CHAPTER THIRTY-FOUR

Sulean Moi was sprawled on the ground by the hedge of eyeball flowers. Lise swallowed her dread of the Hypothetical growths and pulled her a safer distance from the wind-torn debris field.

Turk leaned over the Martian woman and said, "Where are the others?"

For a moment Sulean seemed unable to answer. She opened her mouth, closed it. She was in shock, Lise thought. "Dead," the Martian woman finally managed. "Diane is dead. Anna Rebka . . ."

"What about Isaac?"

"Alive. Dvali is with him—inside, in *there*. Why won't they come out? It's not safe!"

Turk stood and surveyed the rubble and the small opening the digging trees had made.

Lise held his arm. Because he must not go in there, not into that teetering cavern: no.

He pulled away. She would remember that sensation of his forearm slipping out of her grasp. Like the best and worst memories, it would become indelible. It uld haunt her on long nights for the rest of her life.

But she couldn't stop him, and she couldn't bring herself to follow him.

It was dark in the buried stockroom. Turk almost tripped over the body of Diane Dupree before he registered Isaac and Dr. Dvali confronting one another against a wall of broken shelves and fissured cinderblocks. Dvali was grabbing for the boy and Isaac was retreating by steps, not wanting to be touched but not yet willing to run, and Turk could hear Dvali's low begging voice under the roar of this fucking wind that had come out of nowhere and seemed about ready to tip the continent off its hinges. He had seen enough weirdness today to last him a lifetime, but he registered one more eerie miracle: the boy's skin had gone milky white and was faintly luminous, his face a candle-glow around his golden eyes, his body a sort of jack-o'-lantern where his ribs showed through his torn and filthy shirt.

"Isaac," Turk said, and the boy turned to him. "It's okay. The door's open. You can go."

Isaac looked at him gratefully.

Then the wind made a sound like the horn of some monster ship leaving harbor, and all the ruin that had hung suspended above them began to fall.

Sulean Moi held Lise Adams in her arms as the building shifted and compacted. A wave of concrete dust and atomized plaster spilled over them and was carried off by the terrible wind. "Stay down," Sulean said. "You can't help them now."

Lise fought a little longer. Then all the strength spilled out of her, and Sulean held the girl against her shoulder, rocking her gently. There had been a terrible finality about the last collapse, Sulean thought. No one could have survived it.

Then she revised her opinion.

The ocular roses, bent by the wind, refocused their solemn attention.

"Look," Sulean said.

Patiently, the Hypothetical trees had begun once more to dig.

PART SIX

THE
ORDINANCE
OF TIME

CHAPTER THIRTY-FIVE

When it was over—when there was nothing left of the great glittering forest but a few palsied and rapidly decomposing stems, when the towering Arch had finished its work and turned to dust, when the desert basin of the Rub al-Khali had gone to sleep for another ten thousand years—Lise came back to Port Magellan.

The skies were fair and half a hundred ships lay at anchor in the harbor, though not as many as there used to be, or as there would be again, perhaps, when the oil industry had been reconstructed and the tourist trade revived.

She took a room in a hotel. Genomic Security seemed to have lost interest in her after Dvali's Fourths detonated their bioreactors at Kubelick's Grave, but her name might still be on someone's list. So she rented a room under an assumed name and thought about how she might begin to reassemble her life. And finally, a week after she had arrived—not by trawler, as she had once imagined, but on a bus with forty or fifty other refugees from the Rub al-Khali—she had gathered up her courage, what remained of it, and called Brian Gately.

When his exclamations of surprise and disbelief

subsided she agreed to meet him on neutral turf: Harley's, in the mild afternoon, at a table overlooking the hills where the white city tumbled down to the bay.

She showed up early and spent the hiatus considering what she wanted to say to him, but her mind refused to focus. A waiter brought ice water and bread to the table as if to distract her. The waiter's nametag said MAHMUD, and she asked Mahmud if Tyrell still worked at the restaurant—she remembered Tyrell from the night of the first ashfall, August 34th, when she had brought Turk here to look at the photograph of Sulean Moi. No: Tyrell had gone back to the States, Mahmud said. Many people had left Port Magellan after the strange things fell from the sky. Everything the same, Lise thought, yet, everything different. And as Mahmud left the table she saw Brian come through the door. He smiled tentatively when he spotted her. She nodded.

He came and sat at the table. Brian Gately, no longer of the Department of Genomic Security. That was one of the first things he had told her when she called. *I don't work for them anymore,* he said, as if establishing his bona fides, solemnly. *I quit.* He hadn't said why.

"You caught me just in time," he said. "Next week I'm out of the apartment. All I own right now is four packed bags and a ticket home."

"You're going back to the States?"

"No reason to stay. I'll tell you a secret, Lise. I hate this city. By extension, this entire planet."

Because he was no longer with DGS he couldn't help her. But neither could he hurt her. As a threat, he was more or less neutered. So the question was, would she tell him what had happened in the desert? Because he was going to ask. She was certain he would ask.

Hold on, Sulean Moi had told her and that was what Lise had done, even when it seemed like the entire world

was tilting under her. All around her the brightly fluo-
rescing globes shook loose from the Hypothetical trees
and were drawn toward the central vortex of the temporal Arch. The wind became a gale and the gale became a
hurricane, and she braced herself against a concrete pier,
too terrified even to scream. She was only vaguely aware
of Sulean Moi curled under the same ledge of stone not
far away.

The wind was unceasing, and she passed in and out of
consciousness, somehow remaining braced where she
was, coming to herself time and again as if awaking not
from but into a bad dream: and did the night pass? A
day, another night?

Eventually it did stop. The wind died to a breeze, the
world righted itself, and Sulean Moi was calling her
name: "Lise Adams! Are you hurt?"

There were a thousand ways to answer that question,
but she couldn't speak.

She must have slept at least some of the time. The impossible Arch in the west was gone, and most of the
Dark Forest with it. All that remained were broken
buildings, raw foundations, cracked and tumbled pavement, and the stumps of Hypothetical trees. Here was
the desert again, Lise thought. And the intolerable ache
of cramping muscles, and the infinitely deeper throb of
grief.

Days later she sat at the side of a barren road, hungry
and gaunt, in filthy clothing, next to Sulean Moi and not
far from a dozen other bone-weary men and women—
mostly men—who had weathered the crisis in abandoned buildings or the crevices of the ruined oil
facilities. They were waiting for a bus the rescue workers
had said would be along any hour now. The bus was supposed to take them to a recovery area on the northeast
coast, but Lise and Sulean planned to slip away before

that, maybe at Bustee, and make their own way over the mountains.

She turned to Sulean, who sat with her chin on the heels of her hands. "Are you thirsty?"

"Only tired," the Martian woman said, in that ancient voice that made Lise think of a badly-rosined bow abusing the E-string of a violin. "And I was thinking about Dr. Dvali."

Avram Dvali. Dead beyond redemption. "What about him?"

"He was wrong about so many things. But he may have been right about the Hypotheticals." The Martian woman's expression became even more mournful. "I believed there were no Hypotheticals in the sense of consciously acting agents—conscious entities. There was only the process. The needles of evolution, endlessly knitting."

Lise at this moment couldn't bring herself to care, but it mattered to Sulean, and Sulean had been kind to her, so she said, "Well, isn't that right? What happened here—you're saying it was *planned*?"

"Not planned. There was never any sort of Galactic Council that sat down and decided to put a temporal gateway in the middle of Equatoria. I expect it grew there over countless millions of years, the unpredicted outcome of whatever preceded it, like every other act of evolution."

"So Dvali was wrong."

"But only in the most literal sense." Isaac had explained this to her, she said, back in the ruined mall. "Millions of highly evolved self-reproducing machines collect and collate information about a volume of space. That information is periodically brought here to be compiled. The temporal Arch feeds it forward, ten thousand years into the future, and at the same time a similar body of ancient information is released into the present to be reabsorbed and to restore what has been lost to entropy.

That isn't memory in the passive sense. It's an act of remembering. And organisms remember in order to preserve or usefully alter their behavior."

"It's how the Hypothetical network remembers, okay, I get that, but—"

"But if the network remembers then it must have some kind of volition, at least a rudimentary sense of itself as separate from the rest of the natural world. In other words, taken as a whole, it's exactly what Dr. Dvali imagined it to be—a transcendent being so immense that even a detailed record of a human life is only an infinitesimal fraction of its smallest component part."

A detailed record of a human life. Like Esh's, for instance. Like . . .

"And that implies something else," Sulean Moi said. "Something perhaps even more dreadful. Consider Jason Lawton. Because he is remembered by the network of the Hypotheticals, he has achieved a sort of existence beyond death. Passive, perhaps, but still meaningful. And what will we make of *that,* Miss Adams, once the truth is out? Put it in the simplest terms: there is a god, and this god can enable immortality, and that immortality can be mediated by a drug: the drug that Jason Lawton took, the one that connected him to the Hypotheticals before it killed him."

Lise said, "But if it's deadly—"

"Physically quite deadly, but if one is *remembered,* if one passes from death directly into the mind of a very real god—"

"People will be tempted by it."

"More than tempted. They'll call it a Fifth Age. Mark my words. They'll call it a Fifth Age, not an adulthood beyond adulthood but a birth beyond death. They'll worship it, they'll fight over it, they'll create their Departments of Spiritual Security, and what that will make of us, in the long run, I dread to think."

The Martian woman closed her eyes as if against this intolerable vision of the future.

Lise was still trying to grasp what Sulean had said about the Hypotheticals; how if they were capable of re-membering they must be a thing with some sense of it-self, a sort of mind. A mind made out of countless millions of mindless parts, but wasn't that the definition of *any* mind? Her own, for instance?

The afternoon sun was merciless. Lise took a long drink from the bottled water the rescue workers had handed out and adjusted the brim of her hat, also a hand-out. She said, "If it has a memory, what else does it have? Does that mean it has compassion, say, or imagination?"

Sulean gave this a moment's thought. Then she smiled, which must have been painful, Lise thought, be-cause her ancient lips were cracked and in places bleed-ing. "I don't know. Maybe we have our own role to play. As a species, I mean. The intervention of the Hypothet-icals is making something unpredictable of us. Wouldn't you call that an act of imagination?"

So the network of the Hypotheticals remembered and maybe it even dreamed and factored humanity into its dreams. But did it feel grief? Did it wonder at the galax-ies beyond its own boundaries? Did it speak to them, and did they answer?

These were questions her father would have asked.

Her shadow lay before her like a dark twin. She squinted into the distance. That speck in the shadeless desert might be the approaching bus.

If it lived, she thought, did that mean it would it die? And did it know it would die?

And did it want to live forever?

Much of what Lise had seen first-hand—the alien for-est, the eruption and ultimate collapse of the temporal

Arch—had been captured on video by drone cameras and relayed back to Port Magellan. By now the images had been broadcast all over this world and into the more crowded one next door. Commentators had taken to calling it "a Hypothetical event of unknown significance." She told Brian she had been close to it when it happened and that she had been lucky to survive, but she refused to be drawn out on specifics. Not because she distrusted him but because the memory was too vividly present to put into words.

Brian seemed to accept that, but then he asked—with all the tact he could muster—what had happened to Turk Findley. And Lise closed her eyes and wondered what she could say.

All she could think of (and she couldn't speak of this) was the sound of his voice coming out of the wind and the night.

Out of the darkness lit by the glow of the fruit still clinging to the Hypothetical trees. The globes on their stalks shed a collective, ethereal starlight even as the wind howled around them and carried them off in increasing numbers. Their endlessly shifting colors played over the face of Sulean Moi, who had wrapped a tarpaulin around herself and crawled into the meager shelter of the concrete pier. In the morning, Lise promised herself, when the wind stopped (*if* it stopped), as soon as it was possible to stand upright, she would dig; she would dig where the Hypothetical trees were digging; she would dig out Turk and Isaac and even Dr. Dvali. But so much time had passed since the building had collapsed—hours—and the wind had grown steadily more fierce, bending the Hypothetical trees like penitents at prayer. Shrieking gusts came through the gaps in the concrete pier, and Lise could hear wallboard and sheet metal singing as it caught the air. The radiant globes rattled on their stiff limbs or broke loose and were carried upward. She saw or dreamed she saw them massing in the sky, a river of them above the now-naked branches of the Hypothetical trees, a flock, like luminous birds in migration, flowing into the temporal Arch.

"Lise," said a voice from behind her—loud enough to hear over the screeching of the wind, impossibly loud, but it was Turk's voice, and in her astonishment she sat up and tried to turn to face him. He was somewhere behind these concrete slabs, somehow enduring the gale-force wind. "Turk!"

"Don't look at me, Lise. It's better if you don't."

This frightened her so badly that she *couldn't* look. She imagined him hurt or horribly wounded. So she looked at the ground, but that was no better because she could tell by the shadows that there was a vivid light coming from the place where Turk must be standing— possibly from Turk himself. Which threatened to drive her into an even deeper chasm of terror; so she closed her eyes altogether. Closed them tight. And clenched her hands into fists. And let him speak.

"Lise?" Brian said. "Are you okay?"

"Yes," she said. There was a wineglass in front of her and Mahmud was filling it. Refilling it. She pushed it away. "Sorry."

Turk had said a few things.

Things that were private. Things she would carry with her to her grave. Words meant exclusively for her.

He had apologized in simple words for leaving her. He didn't have a choice, he said. There was only one door left to him.

When she asked where he was going, all he said was, "West."

"He went west," she told Brian.

And when she finally forced herself to raise her head and look, really look, what she had seen was not Turk but Isaac. Isaac was ragged, he was hurt, one of his arms was bent twice in the wrong direction, but he was shining like a full moon. His skin had become as luminous and shiftingly colorful as the memory globes, as if he had become one of them. And she supposed he had.

She understood this because Turk had explained it. Turk's body was back in the ruins, but his living memory was here, with this battered remnant of Isaac that had been excavated by the Hypothetical trees. And Esh was with him, also Jason Lawton, also Anna Rebka.

And Diane?

Diane, he said, had preferred to stay behind.

And, she had asked, Dr. Dvali?

No. Not Dr. Dvali.

Then the luminous shell of Isaac had given itself to the wind, and the wind had carried him west.

Brian was saying something about "your book."

"There was never any book."

"You learn anything about your father?"

"A few things."

"Because I did some investigation of my own. After you mentioned Tomas Ginn, I made some inquiries. Ginn is dead, Lise. He was killed in the course of a secret interrogation."

Lise said nothing.

"The same thing may have happened to your father."

"May have?"

"Well. No. *Did,* in fact."

"You have evidence of this?"

"A photograph. Not exactly evidence. It's not action-able. But that's the truth, Lise, if the truth is what you were looking for."

A photograph of her father—of his corpse, Brian seemed to be implying. She didn't want to see it. "I know what happened," she said.

"Do you?"

She knew what had happened to her blameless father, and she knew something even Brian didn't know: she knew what had killed him and she knew why. She had already sent a text message to her mother in California:

He didn't leave. He was taken away. I know this.

Her mother sent back: *Then you can come home.*

But that's where I am, Lise replied, and later, walking by the dockside in a morning fog, she realized it was true.

She had said goodbye to Sulean Moi at a rural bus stop on her way into the Port. Lise had asked the Martian woman whether she would be okay on her own, but of course she would be okay; she had lived for decades on her wits and the generosity of charitable Fourths. And she still had work to do, she said. Isaac had been her great failure. But there would be more battles. Whatever the Hypothetical network truly was, Sulean Moi still dis-approved of its commerce with human beings. "I don't want to be an element in some creature's vast transac-tions," she said. "Nor do I wish my species to be."

"So where will you go?" Lise had asked, and the Martian woman smiled and said, "Maybe I'll go west. What about you? Are *you* all right?"

No, of course she was not all right. Lise's memories of the Rub al-Khali would generate sweat-drenched dreams for months if not years to come. But she shrugged and said, "I'll survive," and must have been sincere, because the Martian woman had taken her hand and looked into her eyes and solemnly nodded.

"I wish it had worked out better for us," Brian said, which was his way of acknowledging that the marriage was well and truly finished. "I wish a lot of things had worked out better."

Which made it easier to be grateful for everything he'd done or tried to do on her behalf. Easier to see him as blameless.

Their lunch had gone long. It was already dusk. Down in the Port lights were starting to wink on, from the illuminated billboards along the Rue de Madagascar to the strings of multicolored diodes that glorified the souks and open markets. All that polyglot beauty, Lise thought, as if the city were a single organism, following its own diurnal rhythms and steeped in its own evolving imagination. She wondered if it would still be here in a thousand years—or ten thousand years, when Turk's ghost came walking out of the temporal Arch to begin another cycle.

Any real understanding of the nature of the Hypotheticals must take this into account. They were ancient when we first encountered them, and they are more ancient now.

The introduction to her father's book.

Brian took her hand a final time, then turned and walked away. Lise sat at the table a while longer. The cooling air from the patio was pleasant. The stars were coming out. Mahmud poured coffee from a silver carafe.

What we cannot remember, we must rediscover.

"I'm sorry—did you say something?"

"I said, it's getting dark."

Mahmud smiled. "It's these sunsets. Seems like they go on forever."